# The **Curse** of the
# **Dragon Medallion**
## Series

# Series and Books written by
# Lauretta Beaver

## Series #1: White Buffalo (New Beginnings)

Book #1: Passionate Alliance
Book #2: Raven & the Golden Eagle
Book #3: Revenge of the Silver Fox (Coming Soon)

## Series #2: The Curse of the Dragon Medallion

Book #1: Dream Dancer & the Celtic Witch
Book #2: Twin Destinies
Book #3: The Seeker & the Shadow Hunter

## Series #3: The Rise of the Ryuu Dynasty

Book #1: Shayla & Lashein's Quest (Coming Soon)

# The Seeker
## & the
# Shadow Hunter

Written by: **LAURETTA BEAVER**

ISBN

Paperback: 978-1-77354-371-0
ebook: 978-1-77354-372-7

Publication assistance by

PAGEMASTER
PUBLISHING
PageMasterPublishing.ca

I dedicate this book to **Patty Jenkins Carson**.
She has shown me what real strength is as she fights a
battle within herself, and still finds time for me...
Love you my best friend, forever!

As always, I wish to thank my husband, **Michel Pelletier**... I thank God every day for the love my Honey Bun shows me, even when sometimes he doesn't understand my need to write constantly.

To my two beautiful daughters, **Pamela Lynn Ryman and Jessica Alexandria Oper**, thank you.

Heartfelt thanks goes to **Eilene Pelletier, Mark Pelletier, & Bill Bremner** for accepting me into their family with open arms.

I would also like to thank **Page Master**, who distributes my books; plus, helps with my front and back covers.

To Aaron Klassen thanks for all your help in finding my new book distributers and assisting me in my self-publishing venture.

Heartfelt thanks go to **Pauline Lachance** for her help in editing and with the back synopsis.

# Illusions & Shadows

# The Prophecy

Many moons and suns shall pass before another comes to power. On the brightest night when the full moon unexpectedly vanishes, and the north star disappears... the White Buffalo shall conceive the seeds of destruction!

# DECEMBER 21<sup>st</sup>, 2020; 4:30pm

**In a remote, Mi'kmaq Indian village, straddling the border between New Brunswick and Quebec Canada...**

"Hee-hee-hoo... hee-hee-hoo... aaaah, phooo!"

Falling back to the pallet, the black haired young woman smiled in thanks when a cool cloth wiped the sweat off her soaked flushed face. Only the dark green unseeing eyes gave away the fact that she was not pure Mi'kmaq.

Flinging his coal black hair back impatiently, Chang was still not comfortable having a full head of hair hanging down in braids even after two years of being here; his Tianming Monk master would not approve... that he was sure of. Despite the dark brown eyes and dark coloured skin, there wasn't a drop of native blood in the mixed Oriental's bloodline.

The Tianming Monk threw the buckskin cloth back in the water before whispering encouragement to his wife lying on the fur bed panting as she struggled to give birth.

Today is the winter solstice, in the year 2020 or 21-12-20. Chang couldn't help but wonder if it was now the end days as the clock drew ever closer to sunset, which should happen around 4:44pm today; allowing the star of Bethlehem to be seen in the night sky.

According to historians, it's been eight hundred years since the Christmas star was visible to the naked eye. The time before that was in 7 BC, the year Jesus was born. The experts say that we won't see it again until the year of 2080.

Unable to help himself, Chang looked down grimly at his watch; he just couldn't help it, as White Buffalo lay heaving in excruciating pain. Again, the old Shaman instructed her to push one more time. Grimacing resignedly, the Guardian just knew that there would be more than one baby.

The fact that Chang's children were conceived at the beginning of a pandemic, and born the same day the star of Bethlehem would shine brightly... made the Tianming Monk shiver in dread as he prayed.

Shen is what Chang's Oriental people usually called God. Although his masters at the monastery preferred using, the Great Spirit of all living things.

The natives also used Great Spirit most often; they did have other names that they affectionately used occasionally in their own language.

Most nationalities preferred using God most of the time though. God was gender specific, making the spirit seem manly was important to many. Technically, the Great Spirit had no gender since a spirit was neither male nor female.

Shen had been silent for the last twenty years as the Guardians became less and less. His masters in Japan were dying out also; only three Tianming Monks remained... that included him. They were lucky if more than one student a year could be found now.

Chang finished his Tianming Monk training when he was only sixteen, packing up the young monk moved to Tokyo where he met a beautiful Chinese/Japanese Lady. Getting permission from his masters at the monastery, he married her after a whirlwind romance that lasted only two weeks.

Unfortunately, she died in 2018 giving birth to his second son. His first born was given to the Tianming masters to train the year before that, since he had the ability to become the next Guardian of the White Buffalo line after him. Ignoring his late wife's family who wished to keep his second born, Chang brought the boy with him on his search for his charge.

It had taken Chang close to a year, but finally the Tianming Monk found her in a remote Mi'kmaq Indian village straddling the border between New Brunswick and Quebec Canada. She was eighteen at the time... he was nineteen.

Something unexpected happened; they fell head over heels in love. Chang resisted for most of the first year knowing she would also die in childbirth, unsure if he wanted to experience that pain all over again. Praying, he begged for guidance from the Great Spirit seeking answers to his dilemma, but he received no help. His master in Japan had also been strangely silent on the subject.

Finally, the two lovers gave in to their passion unable to resist any longer. They were married on April 16, 2020 when they found out she was pregnant; now here the Guardian was watching his wife give birth to what could be the beginning to the end of the world.

Although, according to the prophecy the white buffalo hide was gone. Since the hide was laying part way under his wife right now with his carpet under her lower body as she gave birth… maybe he was wrong.

The Guardian was a direct descendant of Dao; his great, great grandmother was the one Edward Summerset, or Dream Dancer to the Cheyenne had healed with his powers after she was raped in Boston. She was quickly married off then sent back to her homeland when they found out she was pregnant from that encounter. She had a son, he married a Japanese/Vietnamese Lady… they had two daughters.

The youngest girl married a Chinese Samurai Lord that was competing in Japan; they had a son that married the daughter of a high ranking Japanese Lord. Chang was their second son, he was sent away to train with the Tianming Monks to become a Guardian.

Now, here Chang was wondering if because of him the end of days was now upon them as he waited anxiously for the birth of his children; he was still positive there was more than one, since the Tianming Monk could feel another heartbeat.

None of the prophecies foretold of a Guardian intermixing with the White Buffalo descendants… that is what scared him so badly. Had they done wrong in giving into their love, all he could do was wait anxiously and pray.

Frowning grimly, the Shaman watched his granddaughter lying there suffering, he knew what was coming. The old man had not wanted his son to marry into the White Buffalo line knowing the legends... he was afraid. His son's wife had died giving birth to his beautiful granddaughter, who was now lying there suffering. She was in full labour, but to give birth would cause her ultimate destruction. He had tried convincing her to abort the baby at first. She refused to listen though.

Reaching down, the Mi'kmaq spiritual healer supported the baby's head once it crowned then pulled gently to help her expel the infant. When the baby dropped into his hands, he sighed in relief... it was a girl.

About to cut the umbilical cord, the healer halted when his grandson-in-law told him to stop. Frowning in confusion unsure if it was an Oriental custom, he obeyed and passed the newborn to his sister; she was kneeling beside him waiting patiently to take the baby.

When Chang's first born arrived, he checked his watch in relief. It was still ten minutes until sunset. Sighing thankfully, he moved closer to admire his beautiful daughter in awe after making sure his wife was doing okay.

Chang frowned thoughtfully, unsure why a voice echoing through his skull had told him not to cut the cord to separate mother and daughter.

Shrugging perplexed, Chang examined his newborn anxiously before scowling at the full head of white hair. The mixed Oriental also noticed that she had a jet black patch of hair on the left side of her head just over her right brow... it was pure ebony.

The Tianming Monk couldn't help remembering the stories of Crystin, the mother of the first twins. When she had taken in the evil mist, her hair had turned completely white; did that mean his daughter was evil?

Putting his palm on her forehead, Chang searched... he could feel no evil. Exhaling in relief, the Guardian turned back to his wife grimly when she screamed in denial as another babies head appeared; damn, he had known there was another baby. Gnawing on the inside of his cheek resignedly, he scooted back over to put the cloth back on his wife's forehead before checking his watch quickly.

Thankfully, it was still six minutes to sunset. Leaning down Chang whispered encouragement and reassurances as White Buffalo heaved desperately.

Turning back to his granddaughter uneasily when she wailed forlornly in resignation, the Shaman was just in time to see another head crown. Again, the old Mi'kmaq spiritual healer reached down; like before, he gently pulled on the second babies head... now more scared than he cared to admit.

Catching the second baby, the Shaman sighed heavily relieved that it was another girl. He stared down at her in surprise; she had a full head of carrot red hair with an ebony patch of midnight black on her right, which is over her left brow.

The Shaman put her down before reaching for his rawhide cord to tie off the umbilical cord, but again he was told not to. Now convinced that it had something to do with his grandson-in-laws Oriental upbringing, he did not argue; he picked her up then handed the red haired baby to his wife when she knelt on his other side. He couldn't help grimacing in relief... no boy!

Unexpectedly, White Buffalo lifted of the bed slightly before screeching in painful shock as a gush of blood spewed out of her loins... soaking the Japanese carpet. She pushed feebly in desperation one last time as the light dimmed from her dark green unseeing eyes.

Chang quickly leaned forward to prop White Buffalo up against his chest; all he could do was whisper reassurance and his undying love to the second wife that he would lose in childbirth.

Mercifully, White Buffalo managed to push one more head out of her dying body as a third baby fell into her grandfathers shocked hands.

The Shaman had known she would die! They all died in childbirth, which is why he had not wanted his son to marry her mother. He thought back, but he could not recall any of the prophecies mentioning triplets being born to any of the White Buffalo line. He gazed down in shock at the ebony haired baby then shook himself out of his dazed state... he could feel no life in her.

Swiftly, the old Mi'kmaq yanked hard on the umbilical cord still attached to her dead mother needing the placenta to detach from the uterus; it would take too long for anything else. He watched grimly as the afterbirth was followed by more blood gushing out of his granddaughter.

The spiritual healer knowing time was of the essence had no time to be delicate. Neither could he detach the third baby from her sisters since the three shared the same placenta and the same embryo sack, making them identical except for the hair colour.

Chanting to the Great Spirit for help, the old man bent trying to breathe life into her. Sadly, nothing happened as both mother and daughter died together.

In anguish, Chang put his lifeless wife back on the bed; not having time now to mourn, he jumping up quickly needing to see to his daughters. Desperately, the Tianming Monk pulled the carpet out from under White Buffalo... drenched in her blood. Laying it on the ground, he checked his watch in relief. It was three minutes to sunset, but the Guardian was running out of time.

Chang was sure he only had until the star was visible in the night sky. Beckoning urgently to the Spiritual Healer, the determination was plain to hear in his voice. "Give her to me!"

Unhappily, the Shaman passed the tiny infant to the desperate father. She was smaller than her two sisters were... too small!

Having no choice, the two women had to scramble to their feet and follow the Oriental, since the babies were still attached by the placenta; surprisingly, with three umbilical cords that joined into one. Both quickly knelt beside the man they knew only as Spirit Runner.

The Shaman also a doctor had never seen such a sight before; he would document it and send it to his colleagues at the Halifax University. Maybe one of them could shed some light on the significance of them sharing one cord.

Chanting, Chang dropped to his knees on the rug before placed the still baby in the center... directly in the middle of her mother's blood. Urgently, the Guardian asked the Great Spirit to save his daughter. Seconds later an unfamiliar voice screamed in Chang's head. The Tianming Monk was unsure where it came from or even who it was. It did sound similar to the voice that had told him earlier not to cut the umbilical cord.

Nodding obediently, Chang took his oldest from his sister-in-law before gesturing hurriedly for the healer's wife to put his second daughter down on the carpet. The Guardian placed the oldest on the rug, now one was on each side of the tiny baby.

Noticing that the hair patterns did not match, Chang switched the babies around. He put the first born on the right side of the still youngest... his second daughter was put on the left.

The Tianming Monk grimaced hopefully when a glow pulsed in the black patches of hair on the two oldest girls followed by the umbilical cord throbbing. Unfortunately, nothing else seemed to be happening.

Chang put his two fingers in the middle of his daughter's chest and carefully he pushed firmly to compress her ribs; he did this thirty times. Bending over, he put his lips over her nose and mouth before pushing his breath inside her, so that her chest filled with life giving air. Once more, he gave her a breath then sitting back... he compressed her ribs again.

The man known to the Mi'kmaq as Spirit Runner again bent; he desperately held the air in his youngest daughter's lungs for a second then did another breath. Sadly, the Tianming Monk sat back... nothing!

Grimly, Chang checked his watch... 4:43 was the death of his third daughter. In grief, he looked up at the teepee dome. It was an unseasonably warm day for December so they had left it open when White Buffalo had went into labour early that morning; she had hoped the darkening sky would show them the star of Bethlehem.

**********

The boy spun around when he heard a giggle, she was hiding somewhere close. Hearing a loud 'snap' to his right he whirled on the ice searching, but she eluded him again. They had left their wigwams at four o'clock in order to go skating on the ice covered water... sunset was just under way.

Little Buck was born during the winter solstice on December 21, 2010 high in the Quebec mountains. His Cree people known as the Skinwalker tribe had kept themselves relatively isolated until about fifty years ago.

Every year, Little Buck and a few friends would sneak out to the creek then skate until dusk. He hadn't been so sure they would be able to go this year because of a small earthquake that had taken place a few days ago. Fortunately, only the waterfalls seemed affected by it.

Checking his watch quickly, Little Buck was relieved to see that it was only 4:25pm; they still had about ten minutes left. It was getting quite hard to see now though, as dusk approached. Unfortunately, he still couldn't seem to find anyone.

The moon was only at a quarter this year, there was supposed to be an extra star in the sky shining brighter than all the rest. Little Buck stared up intently looking for it.

The birthday boy caught a flash of movement briefly close to the waterfall; distracting him from the star of Bethlehem, which was just beginning to show itself in the pre-dusk.

Little Buck glided to the back of the frozen water; he paused listening for any more tell tail movement. Again, he saw a flicker behind the ice.

Squeezing behind the thick wall of frozen water, Little Buck could hear a crunching noise with several loud sounds of snapping shards of ice coming from under his skates. Was the ice giving away beneath him?

The birthday boy froze in fear, unsure if he should turn back. It took several long moments of silence before Little Buck sighed in relief; it was only the icicles laying where they had fallen after the severe shaking that were breaking beneath his skates... making all the noise. A few days ago, he would not have been able to get back here at all.

Frowning, Little Buck scratched his head. Nobody was here, but he was sure that he had seen movement. Biting his lower lip in concentration, he listened for the dreaded sounds of ice cracking; not hearing anything more from the frozen water, he shifted his weight cautiously... about to leave.

A sparkle of greenish light caught his attention when the birthday boy moved; it was coming from the ice. When any light hit at a particular angle an object trapped inside caused a glow to flicker every so often.

Little Buck forgetting his fear in his excitement, pulled out his ornamental hunting knife and chipped away at the frozen water... until something round dropped in his hand. Pulling it closer to his body, it all of a sudden stopped short of its goal as something long kept it attached to the ice.

Reaching over with his other hand, the birthday boy blindly felt along the length; by the feel of it, he figured it could be a chain of some sort. Finally freeing it completely, he felt it drop so he twisted it around his wrist to keep from losing it.

Carefully, Little Buck shuffled sideways out of danger. Once clear, he opened his hand and held up his treasure. As soon as he did, the star of Bethlehem broke free from the misty cloud that had covered it. Being so high up in the mountains the star seemed closer here, allowing its light to pierce the coming darkness as it shone brightly.

Green fire burst free from the center of the round piece he held, blinding the boy for several seconds; automatically his hand tightened around his treasure, even though he still had no idea what he held.

Without warning, Little Buck's watch alarm went off; letting him know it was time to head home for supper. Squeaking in fright, he back peddled in surprise then lost his balance.

The birthday boy fell hard on his backside before sprawling haphazardly on the frozen ice. The chain still wrapped around his wrist kept his mysterious object from being lost as he clutched it protectively.

Blinking several times in dread, Little Bucks eyesight finally returned or were they playing tricks on him. He stared up in shock; the moon was gone... with it every star seemed to have vanished too.

Little Buck squinting looked up trying to see something, but even the star of Bethlehem had disappeared. The night blanketed everything like a heavy shroud before a greenish mist lightened the sky a touch. Just as his watch alarm, howled a warning for a second time. Telling him that he needed to get home before his mother came looking for him.

Quickly, the boy shoved his treasure into his pocket then got up as his friends converged around him; they teased the birthday boy about his inability to find them this year.

**********

Chang staring up in awe was just in time to see the cloud hovering above move away allowing the star of Bethlehem's light to burst free at last.

It was only visible for a few seconds and seemed to touch the top of the tepee... blinding Chang completely; hiding the fact that all light around it disappeared before a greenish mist covered the night sky. The Guardian blinked several times letting his sight return to normal, he looked down sadly figuring there was no hope for his youngest daughter now.

About to pick her up to put her with her mother, the mixed Oriental felt a shiver of warning before the tiny babies ebony black hair began to glow. It pulsed in time with the other two black patches of hair on her sister's heads.

Still chanting, Chang watched in amazement as the black strip in the firstborn's hair started turning lighter. As her hair changed colours so too did the babies hair that was lying in the center as a thick strip started to turn white on the right side of her head, which would make it over her left brow.

The second triplet's red hair also turned colours before the ebony black patch over her brow turned red, while the rest of her hair turned ebony black.

Looking closer, Chang noticed the youngest now had a red strip of hair over her right brow with a white one on her left brow. Within minutes it was over, the glow vanished before the tiny infant took her first breath on her own as she gave a small cry of life. The Guardian exhaled in relief; quickly, he looked down at his watch. He frowned knowingly... it was exactly 4:44pm.

Reaching down, Chang picked up his two pound daughter. Without interrupting his chanting, he lifted her up towards the smoke hole at the top of the tepee. It was not until then that he became aware the moon and stars had disappeared... a greenish mist now blanketed the sky.

The Guardian inhaled in shock, the dragon medallion had been found. Instantly, another prophecy at the monastery flashed through his mind; he couldn't help reciting it out loud. "Beware the return of the Dragon medallion, for they are coming!"

Still holding his daughter up, Chang gave thanks to Shen the God of all living things for saving his baby girl. Suddenly the two patches, one white, the other red began to glow; immediately, the patches on the two older girls glowed too but only for a second hardly noticeable unless staring right at them. The Guardian brought his tiny daughter back down then cradled her lovingly before kissing her forehead.

Sitting up, the new father watched her slowly open her unfocussed deep green and black eyes... Chang knew instantly she was blind. The Tianming Monk inhaled in shock when he felt a dormant power waiting to be brought to life. He frowned deeply troubled; there had not been any babies with power since Dream Dancer's wife produced the first twins. He was certain now that she would be the next White Buffalo.

Putting the baby back down on his carpet between her sisters, Chang stared down grimly at the strange hair patterns on all three. For a quick second, all four colour strips glowed once more then settled.

Chang couldn't help contemplating the significance of the different patches of hair colour, besides helping bring the youngest to life. All three girls now had ebony black hair with the oldest having a white strip over her right eye that matched the youngest over her left brow. The second born had a red strip over her left eye, which matched the youngest strip on her right brow.

Scowling thoughtfully, Chang wondered who had found the Celtic Dragon Medallion and where were they located. He would have to go through Cecille's old journals to see if there was a description of the Indian village in Quebec.

Shaking off his thoughts, Chang looked over at the Shaman before beckoning him over. Pulling out his dragon dagger, he held it out to the spiritual healer. "Cut the umbilical cords and name your great granddaughters, please."

Awed by what had taken place and still quite baffled by the joining cords; the old Shaman knelt on the carpet then took the dagger with a nod of thanks. Chanting, he tied two rawhides around the cord of the first triplet... about a quarter of an inch apart.

One was close to the baby's stomach. It would fall of once the cord dried out. The other one was to keep the placenta from releasing any more fluid.

Closing his eyes; even though the Shaman did not expect to get a vision since he had not prepared properly. The spiritual healer put the dragon dagger between the rawhides then severed the thick cord, which surprisingly triggered a vision. He hadn't even needed to use his special plants or drink to get one. The old man was unaware that the rug he was on caused his vision.

The Shaman saw a black cougar cub with a white tip on its tail before his vision expanded. He saw her pounce on her prey as she growled fiercely.

When the cat looked up, the Shaman stared in fascination at the lightest green eyes he had ever seen. A thin black oval pupil went from just below the top of her iris then almost to the bottom of her eyelid. Golden rays flared out from there before a dark green ring surrounded the iris. Her eyes tilted up sharply reminding him of a large cat that he had seen recently.

Shaking off the image, her great grandfather spoke decisively. "Her name is Black Cougar, she will be fierce and courageous... a warrior!"

Nodding pleased, Chang heard another name echo in his mind unexpectedly. He was not surprised one bit this time to hear the same voice as before... he did add his last name though. "Alexandrina Maya Sumaiya Ryuu."

Chang frowned in surprise at the name, Alexandrina was biblical, Maya meant illusion, and Sumaiya could mean sacrifice... Ryuu was his last name it meant Dragon. He tried to shake of his misgivings at the unusual name.

His Oriental people prided themselves on choosing names with great significance to not only the newborn, but also to the family; there was always a hidden meaning to it. Wanting his second daughter named next, the Guardian gestured for the older man to go around him.

After moving around to the opposite side, the Shaman tied two rawhide leather strips that his sister brought him around the umbilical cord; when he sliced through it, another vision materialized in his mind.

Seeing a copper coloured wolf, the spiritual healer allowed the vision to expand. He saw the wolf standing in front of her den guarding her pups from a predator. Suddenly, the sun came out and its rays turned her coat a deep red.

The wolf stared intently at the Shaman, there was only a slight tilt to her eyes not very pronounced... unlike her older sisters. Her pupils were quite large with a glossy black look to them, that colour took up most of her iris; a deep yellowish green colour around the pupil made up a smidgen of her eye colour. "Her name will be Red Wolf; she will be a Guardian... a protector to her sisters!"

Smiling in pleasure at that name, Chang again heard that strange voice ring in his mind. His smile vanished when he added his last name to the end once more. "Magdalene Gilda Shambari Ryuu."

Magdalene was biblical, in the bible she was the one who cleaned the son of God's feet at the last supper. There was a lot of speculation that she was a disciple of Jesus; some even say they were a couple... it was never proven however. Gilda meant sacrifice, and Shambari means illusion. Ryuu was dragon, plus Chang's last name.

Taking a couple more strips from his wife, the Shaman scooted over when his grandson by marriage moved out of his way. He tied the last two rawhides to the final triplet's umbilical cord.

The spiritual healer couldn't help his wayward thoughts when he stared at the placenta sitting in front of him. He would make sure to take a picture with the three extensions that joined into one cord before it would be buried with the triplet's mother.

Shaking off his straying thoughts, the old Mi'kmaq frowned puzzled; he was partway through cutting the tough cord attached to the placenta and no vision was coming to him. Chanting harder, he tried to bring up another image as he sliced through the thick cord.

Without warning, halfway through severing the umbilical cord he saw a white buffalo charging at him. At first, all he could see was her intense deep green irises with a tiny speck of jet-black in the center for a pupil. With no ring around her iris, it made the colour quite a bit more vivid; her eyes only had a bit of a slant going downwards.

The animal was bearing down fast as she protected twins. Frowning in confusion, the Shaman watched the white buffalo shift into something very different; it was only for a split second, hardly noticeable.

Shuddering in fear, the Shaman watched it fly towards him... what was he seeing; before he could figure it out, the old man felt a deep pain in his chest just as she shifted back to her buffalo form then her horns slammed into him.

The Shaman barely got finished cutting the cord before the dagger dropped from his numb hand; he clawed at his chest as he fought for breath, trying to talk through the pain. He screamed out desperately as he was tumbling to the carpet. "White Buffalo... THE MOTHER!"

The old Mi'kmaq Spiritual Healer was dead from a heart attack just as the last word echoed eerily through the tepee; it was accompanied by a wail of shocked grief from the old man's wife and sister.

## Quebec, May 2023

A short dark raven haired youngster with slanted eyes and heavy grey baggy eye pouches, stopped instantly; he turned right before going down an old overgrown path searching, for what... he did not know! He was on his journey to find his adult name, but he had been wondering for three days now looking for the perfect place to set up his tepee with no luck.

Without thinking and not even realizing he was caressing it, Little Buck reached up to grasp the medallion hanging around his neck. Once he realized where his hand was, he let go of it immediately with a disconcerting snort.

Buck's mother had commented the night before he left that his habit of stroking the dragon several times a day was not healthy. He remembered the first time he had put it on, it felt so right as if it belonged there.

The morning after his tenth birthday, the Cree youngster had talked to every person in the village to see if anyone had lost it. Nobody seemed to know anything about the medallion with the cross and dragon on it, so he had put the chain around his neck... there it had stayed.

When it first touched the skin on his chest a tingling vibration ran through him then a quick moment of heat, but it was so fast he barely had time to react. The only indication that something happened was a shadowy mark in the center of his chest.

For the last three years, Little Buck had worn the medallion with nothing else unusual occurring... until the day of his thirteenth birthday. Normally, a ceremony to honor his coming of age would be performed; unfortunately, because his birthday was in December he had to wait until spring.

At sunset the year of his thirteenth birthday, the four friends had snuck away just after four as usual and met at the pond with skates in hand. Little Buck had felt out of sorts the whole day with periodic shivers of, he didn't know what...

**Little Buck looked up at the cloudy sky; most of the day had**

been quite dreary. Now it was getting darker by the minute, with no moon or stars visible. He wasn't worried that there would be no moon tonight for them to see by, they all knew this area like the back of their hands.

Chasing each other around, they tried to guess which kid they managed to catch in the deepening dusk before laughing hysterically when they were wrong; he managed to finally relax enjoying the fun.

When Little Bucks watch alarm went off at dusk, he stopped in shock when his eyes clouded over. Fearfully, he rubbed them with a moan of denial. Squinting, the boy looked around desperately! Several long agonizing minutes went by before he closed them, hoping to be wrong... he couldn't be blind.

Counting to ten, he reopened his black eyes. The Cree youngster stared around him in awe. Everything was brighter, much sharper looking... not as good as in daylight however. Now, he could see enough that he was able to identify all of his friends.

Little Buck did not understand it. A few minutes ago, they had just been dark shadows... indistinguishable in the darkening night.

Blinking in disbelief, Little Buck saw something rise up from the ground behind one of the girls. Floating towards her it attached itself to her, which formed some kind of bond; she did not seem to notice anything amiss. He continued to watch her as she skated towards him, but the shadow never left.

The Cree youngster went to her and gave her a big hug; he felt his medallion heat up instantly.

The shadow left her in a hurry, Little Buck turned away from his confused friend without commenting. Not wanting any of the others to notice the glow, he skated away... until it faded.

The boy saw a shadow occasionally after that day, but most stayed away from him. Little Buck still had no idea what they were; neither did he know if they were evil or good...

Shaking off thoughts of his birthday, Little Buck reached a small clearing with a creek running through it. He was only a few days away from a white border town that straddled Quebec and Ontario called Kipawa. He remembered his great grandfather telling him stories about his ancestor Shin, the Oriental that came with White Buffalo to help their people.

White Buffalo had saved Spirit Bear here from a vicious bear attack. He had pushed his twin away then took the swipe meant for Powaw. It was quite ironic that the younger twin would die soon afterwards when another grizzly bear attacked them.

The older twin married White Buffalo once she was recovered from a wound, a tooth from the silver tipped grizzly had imbedded deep inside her. Supposedly, it bit her before the younger brother came on the scene distracting the huge monster so it attacked him instead. Shin had shown up and killed the beast, but unfortunately not before it took off Powaw's head.

Little Buck's grandfather had a different view of things since he was sure it was impossible for the woman, no matter how powerful to survive being bitten by a grizzly.

When White Buffalo was five months pregnant she made a trip to New Brunswick with Shin... they never returned.

Spirit Bear heartbroken had gone crazy for a time, but then found solace in another... they had a daughter.

Shin's son, was also left behind with his mother. He ended up marrying the Medicine Man's daughter... they had a boy. He became a Shaman before marrying Spirit Bear's daughter. Buck's mother was born soon after, she ended up marrying the new Medicine Man's son; he was born soon after.

Many times, Little Buck had been told that he looked nothing like his people except for the brown eyes and dark skin. His eyes tilted down a lot with flabby pouches under his eyes. To top it off, he was the shortest of all the boys his age at only four feet.

Little Buck looked around again speculatively; he knew this was where he was meant to find his adult name. Quickly, he unpacked his dog then set up his tepee. He went fishing next and caught a couple nice sized trout. Starting a small fire outside, he ate before feeding his dog.

Afterwards, the boy prepared his drink and took it inside with him; he set it down close to the ring of stones where his main fire would be so it would keep warm, it was more palatable that way.

Putting his kindling in, Little Buck went out for a burning stick from his outside fire; slipping inside again, he started the central fire pit. Sitting back, he gave it time to be well established before he threw in the rocks.

Needing a few minutes to let the stones get red hot, the youngster left it while he put his special tobacco in his pipe. When he was done, the Cree/Oriental youngster poured water on the rocks allowing the steam to build up.

Unfortunately, Little Buck forgot where he left his drink and stepped on it. He swore angrily at himself; thankfully, after rummaging in his pack for several frustrating minutes, he found a small piece of root. Regrettably, the steam was thinning already. The Cree/Oriental youngster scowled in frustration when he noticed his pipe tobacco was almost out too.

In too much of a hurry to wait, Little Buck popped the root in his mouth then chewed it slowly before inhaling the rest of his pipe smoke. The root was too strong and he shuddered at the foul taste as the juice slithered down his throat.

Quickly spitting out the rest, Little Buck watched in fascination as it landed in the fire. Instantly, the flames flared upwards and a loud... 'Whoosh', burst from the firepit; smoke billowed upwards as soon as the root hit the steaming rocks. Unfortunately, it was already too late for him.

The tepee spun out of control causing Little Buck to groan fearfully. The boy was taken back in time; he saw the twin's fighting the old white bear. Next, he was shown White Buffalo's desperate race to save Spirit Bear before he saw the truth about the treachery and death of Powaw.

Time sped up again then Little Buck watched White Buffalo remove her medallion before giving it to Spirit Bear. He watched Shin give his wife the black bow plus a wallet, which the boy had received when he started this journey. The Cree/Oriental youngster saw White Buffalo's struggle to make it back for the birthing and finally her death in the remote Indian village. He was pulled back to Spirit Bear almost immediately; he watched his ancestor go behind the falls to hide the medallion.

Little Buck drifted for a bit; abruptly he was standing in front of one of those shadows. He saw it filtering around going from one person to another, even into a few animals... it didn't seem to be harming anyone. Suddenly, it halted near a person that was angry screaming at someone in fury; the rage inside the person drew the shadow, it entered her in glee and never came out again.

A knife was drawn then the other person was killed in her friends fit of rage. The boy watched himself tackle the woman before he pressed the medallion to her chest, the shadow immediately exited and flew off.

Spinning around, Little Buck sensed another shadow that was entering someone in their rage; he raced after him before pressing the medallion to his chest. Again, the shadow ran from him.

Turning in circles, Little Buck searched for more shadows; now he knew that Shadow Hunter would be his adult name.

Time came back around full circle to present day, Shadow Hunter saw himself enter the village then scratch at the Shaman's wigwam door. Immediately, he began his training as a spiritual healer in earnest.

Once more, the youngster was pulled further into the future; he saw an older Oriental man walk into his village, to take over his training. He would leave the Shaman's soon afterwards. His training would go beyond anything he could ever imagine, as he became the first ever Warrior/Shaman... hunter of the shadows.

Speeding through time again, Little Buck watched himself leave his village... he knew that he would never return.

# CHAPTER ONE

## July 16, 2029

'Moo, baa, grunt, neigh, stamp!'...

The loud sounds of animals milling around their pens in Calgary Alberta, could not completely drown out the low excited murmuring from thousands of people. It was a familiar thunderous sound at this time of year.

Except for the years 2020 and 2022 when the COVID nineteen pandemic almost destroyed the stampede... plus all other rodeo venues. Jamborees, festivals, K-Days in Edmonton, as well as horseracing were cancelled. Sporting events all over Canada and the rest of the world came to a grinding halt then went deathly silent, with nobody allowed in the stands.

The quiet at that time was more deafening than today and would never be forgotten as millions died from a virus that was called the corona. It had not seen the like since the early 1920's, exactly one hundred years before that when the Spanish flu killed fifty million people.

The crowd at the Calgary Stampede stood up in anticipation then waited expectantly. It did not seem to matter how many times they saw this trio perform, even seeing others do similar stunts did not have this effect. Always, complete silence descended as soon as the music began.

There was even an expectant hush from the Mother Earth.

The gusty wind that was playing havoc today with the tents and umbrellas all around the stampede, unexpectedly disappeared; not even a leaf dared to rustle in the trees. Abruptly, every animal went silent.

It seemed to the waiting people standing with breaths held in expectation that the moment played out in slow motion. Eagerly, they watched a galloping horse race around the arena at a steady even tread.

On top of the horse was two identical looking black haired teenage girls, one with a thick white strip over her left eye, the other had a red steak over her right brow... it was the only way to tell them apart.

The two girls were standing on the back of the stallion swaying gracefully to his galloping stride, not missing a beat. Neither showed the nervousness they felt as they contemplated the new routine with trepidation.

Waiting, they let the anticipation in the crowd grow for another minute. Suddenly, the one in front with the white streak standing on the horse's powerful neck and back gave a whistle of command.

The stallion turned on cue then bore down on another identical black haired girl. This one had a thick streak of white hair and one of red over each eye... she was walking slowly.

The crowd could hear the distinctive tap, tap of a cane. Gasps of concern were heard from the spectators; what could a blind girl be doing out there, shocked they stood up.

When she heard the whistle the one walking into the center of the ring dropped her stick; she turned in a complete circle, blindly she searched for the direction of the sound. Unexpectedly, she stopped and held up both hands.

The two teens on the back of the charging horse crouched; reaching down they each caught a hand.

In one graceful swoop, the one on the ground vaulted upward and squatted in the saddle. Wiggling her bare toes cautiously; the girl felt for the indents in the saddle that were put there to make sure she was in the right place and facing in the right direction. It didn't take her long to find them.

Satisfied, the smallest of the three stood up slowly between the other two kneeling girls. Keeping a hold of their hands for balance, she lifted a foot then put it on the shoulder of the one kneeling near the horse's withers. Carefully, she sprang up onto the shoulder of the one squatting on the stallion's rump.

She balanced there precariously for a moment, pausing she made sure she was stable before the girl with the vivid dark green eyes whistled a prearranged signal.

The two kneeling carefully stood up so that they were in a pyramid formation on the galloping stallion.

Once all three were stable, their interlocking hands released; the one on the top flung her hands high into the air in triumph. She threw her head back with a victorious war whoop. A laugh of pure joy floated out encompassing the spectators.

As if released from a spell, the crowds breathe held in too long... whooshed out; time speeded up once more at the thunderous clapping of awe.

After two full rotations of the arena the applause stilled, but nobody sat down; again the spectators caught their breaths waiting knowingly as the Earth once again stilled in anticipation... it too waited.

The teenager standing at the very top gave another loud whistle of command then held out her arms and counted the stallions hoof beats. All of a sudden, she sprang upwards before spinning gracefully in midair for two full rotations then dropped to the ground in a perfect stance. In victory, she lifted both arms above her head... howling ecstatically.

The crowd went wild when they realized she was standing in the exact spot facing the crowd that she had been in before being lifted up onto the horse.

A moment later, both her sisters dismounted in a half somersault; they landed one on each side of their much tinier sister. It was not until the three were standing close together that the spectators could actually see how small the girl in the middle was.

Time once again returned to normal as the three sisters bowed and the crowd sat in relief. Once done, the oldest with the white strip in her hair knelt before picking up the white distinctive walking cane that identified the user as completely blind. The smallest of the three had dropped in the center of the arena. It was the reason the spectators knew the girl had landed exactly where she had started.

The oldest of the three, affectionately called Alex; turned to her youngest sister with a murmur of approval before giving her the walking cane.

Born completely blind, the green eyed teenager known as Fai bowed to the awed crowd; they in turn gave her another standing ovation. Standing erect, she gave an unexpected shrill whistle calling to her stallion that was at the other end of the arena waiting.

The dark grey stud with a flowing white mane and tail reared with a screech of challenge; spinning, he raced to the center of the pen at full speed bearing down on the petite triplet.

The crowd once again hushed in anticipation.

Fai dropped her walking stick, this was a signal for the other two to step back to give her more room. The youngest triplet felt the ground vibrate beneath her feet; she carefully counted the stallion's strides.

Quickly, White Buffalo took two running steps then grabbed her horse's mane and the long white horn sticking up above the saddle; it was at least three inches in height. It was quite a bit thinner too, but taller than a standard one on a western saddle. It helped her vault up onto his back with no assistance.

The blind girl heard both her sisters whistle for their own horses; both were at the far end of the arena being held by their father, so they would not get in the way before it was time.

The Guardian instantly let the horses go before going back behind the gate out of the way. He watched with breath held, it did not seem to matter how often he saw his children do the stunts... they still made him nervous.

The petite youngest of the triplets with the two strips of colour in her hair hooked her foot into a rope designed to help her hang upside down on the left side of her horse. Once she heard her sisters galloping up beside her, Fai sat back up on her stallion; unhooking her foot, she jumped up and stood in her saddle. Wiggling her bare toes again to check which direction she was facing, satisfied she waited.

Alex riding up to her sister's stallion, put her foot in a strap that she would use to drop sideways out of the youngest triplets way. Watching Fai closely, she nudged her horse a bit closer making sure the distance between them was not too great; satisfied, she slipped out of the saddle then hung off the side of her horse.

Fai hearing a light whistle from her oldest sister that said she was ready for her, stepped across the empty space trustingly. Dropping into the empty saddle once safely across Fai hooked her foot in a strap on the opposite side; now she would be able to hang off the left side of her sister's horse.

Once Fai felt the gelding veer sideways away from her own stallion, the youngest triplet knew it was safe to drop out of the saddle. Both women waved their arms towards the clapping crowd.

After one full rotation around the arena, the blind green eyed teenager reached up and pulled herself back into the saddle. She reached down then hauled her sister up, until she was sitting behind her. The youngest got up then stood in the saddle once more, nobody noticed when she put her foot inside Alex's hand.

Fai listened intently to make sure that her sister's horses were close to each other and they were slightly ahead of her stallion. White Buffalo tapped her sister's head to give her warning, so Alex would help her vault higher into the air; she leaped up then did a half somersault.

The spectators watching gasped in shock as the tiny girl spun in midair. Several put hands up to their mouths horrified when it seemed the stallion wasn't going to get underneath her in time. If he didn't, there was no way the horse would be able to stop or get around her. They all knew he would likely trample the blind triplet to death.

The Guardian watching; jumped up onto the second metal rung in the gate getting ready to vault over it. His hand reached out beseechingly trying to catch his daughter. Unfortunately, all he could do was watch in horror as his worst nightmare was about to come true. Being a Tianming Monk, Chang was not supposed to have fears or weaknesses. Neither would his master approve of him showing such emotions.

Just as it seemed to the ones watching... spellbound; that a catastrophe was in the making. The stallion finding new strength, pinned back his ears in determination as he extended his long neck before surging forward.

Untucking herself from her spin, the youngest triplet landed feet first in the center of her horse's saddle, facing backwards. Doing the splits, Fai dropped unceremoniously into a sitting position; she pretended to feel around her stallion's rump blindly searching for her horses head.

All of a sudden, the stallion's tail swung up and several strands flew into her face... Fai flailed around trying to get rid of the hairs clinging to her.

In relief, Chang released his death grip then he dropped back onto the ground; the Guardian who also happened to be a mixed Oriental rubbed his face in relief. Sighing, he listened to the relieved laughter of the crowd at the stallion's antics as he teased his mistress.

Chang straightened before bracing against the gate again knowing they were not done yet... he shook his head in exasperation. His youngest was named White Buffalo by her great grandfather, who happened to be a Mi'kmaq spiritual healer. Unfortunately, he ended up dying from a heart attack minutes later.

The Tianming Monk had given her the name Fai Trinity Vienna, which means... beginnings, three fold or three in one, and chosen one; add that to his last name Ryuu meaning dragon, it was quite a unique name combination.

The mixed Oriental wondered; if it was the addition of the last name that made Fai like pushing that close to death situation too much at times... Chang couldn't help thinking.

The youngest triplet pretended to flail around comically, which was intended to give the crowd a bit of a respite. It also allowed them to get ready for the next stunt.

Fai listened closely until she heard her middle sister whistle that she was ready for her. The smallest of the three vaulted into a squatting position in her saddle before standing up; White Buffalo took a half step onto her stallion's rump.

Meanwhile the middle sister, affectionately called Maggie leaped up into a squatting position before turning to face her mare's tail then placed her hands on her horse's rump. Slowly, she did a handstand then turned herself so that her back would be towards her youngest sister.

Fai hearing a faint whistle took a hoping step over to Magdalene's mare. She landed in the center of the saddle then wiggled her toes checking her position before spinning to the left so that she was now facing forward.

Reaching behind her head, White Buffalo grabbed onto Maggie's ankles when she put them over her shoulders. The blind green-eyed teenager pulled down then tucked her sister's feet under her armpits, to get more leverage; she braced herself... waiting.

This was an awkward position for the youngest of the triplets, trying to keep them both steady on a galloping horse took years of practice. Still, occasionally the two would end up splayed out on the arenas dirt floor.

Feeling Fai's readiness, Maggie put her right arm onto the back of the raised saddle then pushed herself up. It lifted her just enough to allow her to clench her stomach muscles tightly. Carefully she pushed herself up, away from her mare. Straining, she managed to rise up enough to grasp her siblings head to balance herself; manoeuvering forward, the middle triplet was able to sit on her much smaller sisters shoulders.

Once in position, Magdalene let go of her sister's head then raised her arms ecstatically with a whoop of victory at having defied gravity.

They galloped like that for one full rotation of the arena before the one on top slowly leaned back once more; carefully, Maggie lifted both legs from her sister's shoulders... once Fai released her feet.

Now back in a handstand on her mares rump, Magdalene waited for White Buffalo to go then turned and put her right hand on the back of the raised saddle to rise higher. She opened her legs into a splits position before raising her left hand away from her horse to balance precariously with one hand. Suddenly, she twisted and pushed herself upwards then dropped into the saddle.

The youngest after whistling for her stallion counted to two before hopping across the empty space... again trusting her horse completely. Fai took a step to the right and stood on the top of his rump; she counted to ten then without warning she leaped off the back of her horse and did one full somersault.

Thankfully, Fai landed in a perfect stance with arms raised high above her head. The blind green eyed teenager heard her sister's drop beside her, so she lowered her arms; White Buffalo exhaled in relief, their new routine had went flawlessly.

Alex picked up the white cane then murmured congratulations to her two excited sisters before handing the walking stick to Fai.

The crowd went wild with whistles then thunderous clapping; the three girls bowed in appreciation at the standing ovation they received.

Fai, reaching out took her oldest sisters arm to be led out of the arena. She never had to guess which sister was where because the oldest triplet, Alexandrina or Black Cougar to the Mi'kmaq was always on her left side; since the white patches of hair in both of their hairs matched... it kept them connected.

Magdalene or Red Wolf to their native tribe was always on her right, since her red hair strip matched Fai's on that side.

The three girls each whistled their distinct calls for their horses; all three animals dutifully trotted up behind their mistresses... following obediently.

Once out of the arena a young Oriental clipped leads onto the horses before leading them away. No sooner were the animals gone then the three girls were surrounded by reporters; fans of every age tried to get close enough to touch. The sisters were bombarded by dozens of questions, all asked at once.

Fai hung back staying behind her oldest sister; she hated this part and did not like her picture taken at all, but she knew her sisters wouldn't let her disappear. Suddenly, White Buffalo stiffened when she sensed it... she inhaled deeply searching.

It was a he, a reporter Fai guessed by the click of a camera. Quickly, the youngest squeezed Alexandrina's arm three times in a prearranged signal then headed in his direction. Now, she had no problem being able to ignore the questions and click of the cameras since she had a mission.

Alexandrina followed her younger sister then put her hand around Fai's bicep when she stopped in front of a young blonde reporter; Black Cougar leaned down to listen to White Buffalo's suspicion. She looked over at Magdalene who had dutifully followed and nodded with a wink.

Instantly, Red Wolf put her right hand down onto a small dagger that protruded out of her belt; finally, she put her left hand around her youngest sister's right bicep.

Passing her walking cane to Alexandrina, Fai smiled sweetly at the reporter... she reached out her right hand to shake his. As he clasped it, White Buffalo made sure to cover his whole hand with her left one; she introduced her two sisters, trying to keep him occupied so she could keep his hand in hers.

The plump blonde reporter blushed at being signalled out by the beautiful sisters. Stammering, he tried asking questions, which helped to cover up Fai's light humming. Fortunately, he did not notice anything amiss in his excitement.

Continuing to hold his hand, Fai brought White Buffalo closer to the surface while her sisters answered the reporter. The two older triplets could feel a pulsating over their brows as the few strands of different coloured hair brightened just a bit.

The youngest of the triplets drew in the magic that the reporter had coursing through his veins; thankfully, he was unaware of it. She knew that all the young man would feel is a quick spark of electricity when they first touched then a warm tingling feeling from their joined hands.

The Mother Earth was slowly dying; as she did, her magic was being released in small quantities all around the world. Because her magic was a live entity, it could move from one person to another. Even into animals, until a host that could use it was found.

Take Houdini for instance; in 1891, he unknowingly became a host. He was the first person able to use the Earth's magic... he could escape anything.

It's how the first White Buffalo ended up in New Brunswick. Cecille had to go to Dalhousie in 1896 to give Harry Weisz who would ultimately become Houdini his spirit name. On her way back home, she ended up in a Mi'kmaq village that was straddling the boarder of Quebec and Ontario. There she had given birth to the next White Buffalo before dying.

The reporter was unable to use this magic, so the sisters were able to draw it out of him harmlessly; or it would eventually search for another host. It would keep going until a bondable human could be found.

It was the triplet's responsibility to find the Earth's magic then pull it into the youngest triplet. Why... they had no idea; only that the Mother Earth needed them to recover the magic that was escaping as she slowly died.

It was the human's fault that she was dying, since her essence was no longer able to move freely when needed. Every time they drained the oil pockets she depended on, they were stealing her life blood... causing her magic to be released. It was now too late to stop it; almost all the pockets of oil scattered around the world were gone, stolen by money hungry companies.

The only way to draw the magic into White Buffalo was if the three were together. Although, Fai had managed to draw in the magic on her own a few times. She could only hold it for a few days before it was released. Only drawing it into the three of them combined, with the help of the dagger could the magic be trapped inside the youngest triplet... unable to escape!

Unfortunately, Fai could not wear the dagger; for some reason it caused her to go into epileptic seizures with massive convulsions that could kill her. Why, nobody seemed to know.

Alexandrina wasn't able to carry it either since the dagger triggered her headaches, making them much more frequent and sever. Only Magdalene could safely wear it.

If the magic was being used by a willingly host, the triplets were able to draw it out without killing the person... only if the host was willing; most were not since they liked having magical powers, so the sisters had to wait for the host to die a natural death.

Their half-brother was in charge of booking shows at different times all around the world. He also had to monitor the ones that were bonded, so the sisters could rush there when the host died. If not they would have to follow the trail to the new host with the hope it was not being used.

Over the last fifty years, more people became bondable to the magic making it harder for them to get at. Magicians, witches, psychics, plus many other users of magic was now becoming the norm.

Unlike the old days they were accepted, even encouraged.

Most of the magic was harmless; it only enhanced a person's brain giving them a bit of power. They could pass down the ability to use magic to their offspring's, but not the magic itself. Only through bonding with the Earth magic could they become magical in their own right... yet anyway!

Unfortunately, there were a few the triplets had to hunt down then eliminate because they became a danger, their missus of the magic harmed others; that the sister's would not allow.

The last ten years a shift in the magic had them worried. It was becoming more sinister and quite a bit stronger, making it... unpredictable; it was able to forcibly bond with a host now, causing the person to change physically. Over time, they feared it could take over the host completely.

Fai and her sisters had to kill the forcibly bonded ones immediately before they could impregnate a human. Just in case their offspring's might inherit, the physical attributes of the shape change. The sisters were almost positive the actual magic was non-transferable... they hoped anyway!

When the tainted magic forces a human to bond with them the magic can't be taken away; only through death, can it be released safely.

The corpses would have to be cremated in these cases because when the magic was re-buried it poisoned the Mother Earth somehow. If burned, the magic could be drawn into White Buffalo then become harmless again.

Chang found an old journal before they left their Mi'kmaq tribe; wisely, he brought it with them. Once old enough to understand Fai had her half-brother read it to her. It was narrated by their ancestor Cecille, but written by her Tianming Monk Guardian Shin, while they were stranded in the Indian village; Cecille was the first of the White Buffalo line to have powers.

Inside, were the full names of the people she had given a spirit name too from the Mother Earth. There were a lot from Ontario, since she had lived there for years while training with the Ojibwa spiritual leaders. A good dozen when she travelled from Ontario into Quebec then another two dozen on her travels from Quebec to Dalhousie, NB.

Most of the names Cecille had given out though were at a kissing booth at the circus... there was a good hundred she figured. Almost all were sailors from around the world since several ships had docked while they were there.

Unfortunately, they had lost count and not all the names were recorded. Cecille's Guardian had written another few dozen names before her death.

When Fai investigated further, she found out that the magic was usable by the descendants in the book. The youngest triplet figured it was because Cecille passed a piece of herself to their ancestors. It gave them the ability to handle then be able to use magic, most of them anyway not all though.

Fai had decided that they needed help several years ago when they became too overwhelmed to do it on their own; the Guardian's son was put in charge of finding the offspring's that Cecille named in her diary.

Once Ronin found them, the three women went and talked to them. If they had the natural abilities needed, they enlisted them forming a coven of Seekers to help find the ones that were forcefully changed.

Just last year they had thankfully interrupted a man raping a woman; the magic in him had forcefully bonded which allowed him to change his body shape and become a wolf. The man was a shapeshifter. Fortunately, he could only change shape periodically for a brief time when he was in a deep rage.

Thankfully, they were not like the ones on TV; it had nothing to do with the moon! It had more to do with the darker emotions a human was capable of, like rage, fear, lust, or hate.

With the magic evolving though, who knows what would happen in the future. No one knew what would happen to the offspring's if they allowed them to breed, which seemed to be their objective.

There were also the ones that grew fangs. Thinking about them caused Fai to grimace in revulsion. She was just thankful; they were not like the vampires on TV either. They couldn't actually drink blood. But yes, their longer sharp eyeteeth could puncture the skin if they bit you hard enough. Fortunately, they could not suck out your blood. All they can do is lick at the two droplets that formed when the skin broke. Nor did drinking blood do anything for them.

They did not have longer life; neither could they turn others into vampires by biting them. They did have a bit more strength then a human, but it was not supernatural. They had a light yellowish to a greenish tinge; hardly noticeable unless they were in full dark... a bit of a glow could be seen at that time.

A few cases were reported of wings protruding; those ones had more of a pasty look to their skin with no glow at night. Unfortunately, neither the sun nor the moon had any effects on them either.

Again, keeping them from producing offspring's was the ultimate goal; because they had no idea what the magic would become if they were wrong and it was transferable to a viable human.

They definitely didn't want to find out the hard way that the offspring's could do what the TV said they could... the reality would be devastating.

Lucky for ordinary humans, the sisters were drawn to these abominations before they could reproduce. The coven having spread around the world, helped by capturing the ones they found and keeping them captive until the triplets could come and eliminate the threat.

It also seemed that the forcibly bonded hosts were drawn to Fai. For what reason, except to release the magic trapped in her they could only speculate.

Several times over the last three years, the abominations went out of their way to avoid the two older sisters before attacking the youngest. They all prayed that it was not because the forcibly bonded could draw in White Buffalo's magic and force it to bond with them once she was dead; the world would be doomed if that were to happen.

It made no sense to any of them why they did not kill the older girls so they could get to the younger one easier, but they didn't.

Because of this, one or both girls always stayed close to the youngest sister when they were together in public.

The Guardian or his son stayed with the blind green-eyed triplet when the other two girls were elsewhere; which seemed to be happening a lot more often now that they were older. The three girls wanted to live their own lives and who could blame them.

The only time Fai was able to draw out the bondable or forcibly bonded magic on her own; without the hosts permission, is before puberty... it is vulnerable then. Once puberty sets in only death can dispel the tainted magic.

Not often did the magic pick a child, unless they were able to use magic of considerable strength once older. The girls always monitored these special children knowing the magic would be drawn to them, so it would eventually try again.

It took Fai five minutes to finish with the reporter, once done she turned away. She only took two steps before halting suddenly; immediately, she turned right when she sensed the tainted one in that direction.

White Buffalo trying to be as inconspicuous as possible in such a large crowd of people, inhaled deeply... she followed the stench. It took her to a mother of three. The youngest was still an infant and the stink was coming from her. Thankfully, it wasn't coming from the mother; it reassured the green-eyed triplet that it was not a transfer from mother to daughter.

Fai suspected that a woman could pass the magic to its fetus quite easily; the transfer would be a direct one so much stronger. This would make the child extremely dangerous since the fetus was in their mother's womb for nine months... directly in contact with the tainted magic.

A man would have to pass on the taint through his sperm, which would weaken it substantially then into the woman first. It would make the infant less volatile since the mother would end up drawing in most of the magic. They had high hopes that it would reduce the effects of the tainted magic

Fai feeling the baby's aura even from this distance stopped in front of the mother and smiled sweetly trying to put her at ease. "I can smell baby powder... how old is she?"

The mother couldn't help smiling back. There was an innocent purity about the green-eyed sightless teenager with the two strips of colour in her hair; it helped to make one trust her immediately. Up close, she looked even tinier standing between her protective sisters... calming her instantly.

Looking down lovingly, the woman didn't even notice the girls slip when she gave away the babies gender... even though she was blind. Peeking at the three identical sisters, she answered shyly a little uncomfortable at being signaled out. "Her name is Carmen; she's six months old today."

Fai held her hands out invitingly. "Can I hold her for a few minutes... pleas; I just adore babies. My sisters do not want one of their own, but I can't wait to be a mother someday."

The mother frowned in surprise then stiffened protectively; an urge to run came over her suddenly, but the crowd of people would not allow her to move.

Touching the woman's arm in reassurance, Fai teased... trying to put her at ease. "I promise to give her right back. I just love babies and with this big crowd there's no way I can run off with her; we will sing her an old Mi'kmaq blessing."

The mother chuckled at her own foolishness then relaxed. She finally held out her baby, but there was still a visible reluctance... everyone laughed at her hesitation.

The baby scrunched up her face to scream in fear, but Fai pulled her close quickly. She whispered soothingly in the infant's ear as each of White Buffalo's sisters took a tiny hand in theirs. They needed the contact for this to work.

Maggie put her right hand over the dagger protruding from a pouch at her waist; it hid the glow as White Buffalo's lips touched the babies forehead then the three chanting drew out the tainted magic.

It only took a few minutes before Fai passed the cooing happy baby back to her anxious mother. She wavered in exhaustion, the taint always took away some of her strength and she would have to rest for an hour or so to regain it back.

The Guardian, watching from a distance pushed through the crowd instantly then picked up his youngest daughter. He turned towards their trailer.

Fai curled up in her father's arms trustingly and was sound asleep in minutes as the trapped magic inside her struggled to get free. It would take several hours before it would quit fighting the inevitable.

Alexandrina, the older triplet pulled out a notebook. "I will need your name, address, plus phone number... please; you will get a package of goodies in the mail for the three kids."

Magdalene murmured reassurance to the crowd of reporters before promising that their youngest sister would be out in a couple hours... patiently she waited for her older sister.

The baby would need to be watched from now on, she could be useful to them once grown depending on her abilities; unfortunately, it was too soon to tell what her magic would be. Red Wolf suspected it was something extraordinary or unusual since the taint couldn't wait to bond.

The Guardian's son from his previous marriage saw them coming from their campsite; he jumped up and opened the door of their camper unit to let them in. Closing it tightly, he positioning himself in front with his massive muscles bulging for all to see... he wouldn't allow anyone else to enter. After a few minutes, the crowd dispersed so he was able to finish seeing to the horses.

# CHAPTER TWO

## August 1, 2040

A shadow paused for a heartbeat at the mouth of an alley; Toronto, Ontario was infested with these dark dank creepy side streets. Listening, it waited with breath held ignoring the sounds of cars whizzing past the narrow alleyway.

The man could feel a presence; it was being consumed by a bloodthirsty rage. He wasn't sure why, but the grey shadows were always drawn to and could forcibly bond when someone's emotions were heightened by fear... or one of the other darker human emotions.

Being a stranger here, this monstrosity of a city had taken some getting use too. Fortunately, it had not taken him long to find his way around. It really wasn't the size of Toronto, which intimidated someone used to a Cree village; it was the people... ten million of them. Every year that number seemed to jump dramatically, it was bursting at the seams.

A car turning, allowed the headlights to briefly enter the dark side street; it was there one moment, gone the next. It did manage to highlight a man for a split second carrying a bow. At first glance, he looked like one of the Orientals in Chinatown... until one looked closer.

He slipped from shadow to shadow silently, unheard... barely seen. One with the shadows, he moved cautiously ahead trying to keep close to the building to hide his presence.

Grimacing at his wondering thoughts, he couldn't help remembering that he had just gotten back to Canada from France; it was supposed to be a holiday for him. Unfortunately, the whole ten days were spent trying to stop a wolf from breeding... a shapeshifter.

Regrettably, he ended up having to kill the wolf before burning it since the shadow had corrupted the human beyond recognition. It wasn't often he found one that he couldn't help, but lately there seemed to be a lot more of them.

Hearing a cry of fear, the man raced around the corner then stopped short in shock. A woman was lying on the ground; two huge cats, hackles raised were crouched staring intently at each other. He had never seen cats so big even at home, or known shapeshifter's to run together. Baffled, he watched the cream coloured cougar that was straddling the girl spring at the ebony black panther with a white tip on its tail.

Screams of challenge from both shapeshifter's filled the air, it drowned out all other sounds; before savagely, standing on their hind legs belligerently... they came together. Viciously, they tore into each other.

The man known in his Cree village as Shadow Hunter frowned in puzzlement. Well, they obviously were not together. Ignoring them, he opened the right side of his long intricately designed Japanese samurai cloak that fell to just above his knees. It had flowing elegant patterns pertaining to strength, endurance, protection, and invisible symbols; with four different types of dragons embroidered on it. Quickly, he hooked his bow back inside his smock by a strap designed to keep it in place.

Reaching behind his head, Shadow Hunter pulled out his sword then rushed towards the girl before straddling her protectively. He watched the cats attacking each other still quite dumbfounded. This was his first sightings of two shapeshifter's in the same area... never mind fighting each other.

The black was the smaller of the two cats; a flash of a cars lights reflecting off the hide showed telltale spots of a cougar, not a panther as he had first thought. The smaller black pinned the bigger golden red cougar to the ground and refused to let it up. Whining plaintively, it flickered before a red headed man took the cats place.

The black cougar with the white tip on its tail shimmered and a minute later, a woman appeared. She was quite striking with her coal black hair, a lighter patch of hair over her left brow gave her a unique appearance... impatiently she brushed it away. He couldn't see what colour her eyes were since it was too dark, but they had a bit of a glow to them that he found quite interesting. Although, he had keener eyesight at night than most it was still hard to distinguish. She wasn't that old... maybe nineteen.

Shadow Hunter frowned uneasily when she stood up in a police uniform; he could tell by her demeanour and the distinctive slant to eyes that she had Oriental blood... not full though. She hauled the red headed man to his feet before handcuffing him.

The woman turned towards the newcomer then smiled in thanks; she could tell by the black pouches and slant to his eyes that he was Oriental, mixed she figured. Alexandrina bowed with her two hands pressed together in respectful greeting. Calmly, she introduced herself. "I am Lieutenant Ryuu, the woman under you is no longer in danger... you may release her!"

Once the stranger moved back, Alexandrina walked over to help the young woman up. She leaned forward to whisper instructions in the girl's ear.

The young petite blonde nodded in agreement; turning, she quickly disappeared... her job as bait completed.

The Cree/Oriental native sheathed his sword with a frown. "I am called Hunter here, but my people at home call me Shadow Hunter! What are you?"

Alexandrina reached out to shake the man's hand; she needed him to forget what he saw. "I am Lieutenant Alexandrina Ryuu of the Royal Mounted Police... nice to meet you."

Taking her offered hand, Shadow Hunter felt an instant shock that travelled up his arm... making him tingle all over. He dropped her hand like a hotcake before reaching up to pull his shirt with his medallion away from his chest. It was burning his skin; finally, it settled. He massaged between his ribs in irritation for a couple minutes. When the sting went away, he rubbed his right palm grimly. "You still haven't told me what you are?"

Staring in shock, Alexandrina rubbed her fingers together trying to dispel the tingling. She eyed the handsome, but much shorter stranger in the long Oriental cloak; suddenly, she remembered seeing a sword. Alex ignored his question, with a frown of suspicion she gestured towards his smock. "Do you have a permit to carry that weapon?"

Shadow Hunter nodded and reached inside the left side of his cloak to pull out both permits, he handed them to her. While she was studying them, it gave him a chance to look at her more closely.

Alexandrina's coal black hair was pulled into a sever bun on the back of her head. He could tell the lighter strip of hair over her brow wasn't as long as the rest of her hair since it refused to be tamed.

Hunter smiled when she tried blowing the dozen or so strands out of her way... irritably. Her face was a bit long, with a stubborn chin. She was too slim, almost skinny with small up thrust breasts. He couldn't help noticing her nicely rounded buttocks, which showed off her long muscled legs. She was taller than he was, at five-foot-three inches.

A shiver of warning coursed down Shadow Hunter's spine before the colours on his cloak shifted in caution; there was something not quite right.

Looking up the Lieutenant handed him his papers, allowing their fingers to touch once more... he felt another shiver. This one was warm and tingly, leaning more towards a pull of sexual attraction. Unfortunately, the colour changing slightly in his cloak was a sure sign that something was definitely wrong; making him scowl in confusion.

Frowning irritably, Alexandrina sighed when she felt that shiver again. It had been quite some time since she had felt an attraction to a man; she studied him curiously. He certainly wasn't her usual type with his black puffy eye pouches. A shorter stature had never been a turn on for her either. His shoulder length black hair with the deep black eyes suited his square jaw, which helped to emphasize a cute indent right in the center. His nose was small; it flared out just a bit. His neck was thick. She could tell by the tight cloth that his arm muscles were quite extensive, Black Cougar loved muscles on a man; although, she had never wanted to date one with them.

Alexandrina shook off her wayward thoughts with a grimace before handing him his papers. "Your permit says you are from Quebec, so what are you doing in Toronto? You will need an Ontario permit if you are staying more than six months. What kind of bow do you have, I don't remember seeing it. Come to think of it, I do not see your sword now either... oh, there it is!"

A loud crackle of static sounded from the Lieutenants mic that was hanging from her RCMP uniformed shoulder; it had the two jumping in surprise.

A disembodied woman's voice broke the shocked silence that had fallen between them. "Alex, where are you! You are needed at the retreat immediately; I swear I just saw what looked like a vampire, unlike any I have ever seen before. Two are dead. Damn... it just disappeared again!"

Alexandrina looked down and grabbed at her mike in trepidation before pushing the button frantically. "Who is dead?"

Letting go of the button, Alexandrina waited; unfortunately, all she got back was static. She looked back at the man she was questioning, but he had vanished!

Turning in circles, the Lieutenant searched in vain. Finally shrugging, Alex ran over to the shapeshifter then gave a shrill whistle. Her white and black pinto mare trotted over.

Alex grabbed the man's arm before marching him down the alleyway. Switching the nob on her walkie-talkie to her police frequency, she reached back up to her shoulder before pushing the button down. "Stefan, I have a pickup for you in front of Moxie's on twelfth street. Hurry it up please; I have another emergency call that just came in!"

A squad car quickly screeched around the corner, a tall lanky German with a heavy accent jumped out. Last week marked their second year as partners; they worked well together... now.

At first, he had resented Alexandrina's need to ride her horse instead of being in the squad car with him; adding a rookie cop to their crew last year helped dispel that.

Andrew was from Jamaica originally, but his parents had moved here before he was born. He was quite dark with springy black curls... he didn't seem to have a serious bone in his body. It had been touchy between the two men at first, Alexandrina had to play peace maker for the first six months. Thankfully, it didn't take long for the two men to become fast friends.

Andrew jumped out; quickly, he opened the back door of the squad car. "Anything that you will need us for or should we head back to the station?"

After handing the man over, Alexandrina waved them on. "No, you can go... its personal; I will see you tomorrow. Charges are drunken disorderly, for now."

Stefan pulled the suspect to the car and pushed him down into the backseat. "Okay, let us know if you need us."

Alexandrina nodded then turned; quickly, she vaulted up onto her horse before turning north she raced up the street.

*****

Shadow Hunter followed at a distance on his motorcycle in stealth mode. He had no worries about losing her, since he had slipped a tracking device on the back of her uniform jacket. He was quite curious to find out more about this woman.

At first, Hunter had thought the uniform was a ploy to keep others from questioning her. The other two police detectives dispelled that assumption; it made him even more interested in finding out more about this mysterious shapeshifter.

The Lieutenant was quite different, Shadow Hunter could feel that she was able to shift her shape whenever she wanted; unlike the ones that seemed to be random or only when their emotions were heightened. That would make her much more dangerous; being a police officer did not mean that she was not evil.

After checking her out, he would have to decide if he needed to neutralize her. His medallion had not flushed any shadows out, so the magic must be hers. The fact that he was attracted to her had no bearing on what his decision would be... or so he tried to convince himself.

*****

Alexandrina raced headlong down the streets ignoring the furious pedestrians and honking car horns as she raced out of the city.

As soon as Alex reached the outskirts of Toronto, she galloped headlong towards a farm that was a good fifteen minutes out of the city. Her mind was spinning faster than she could keep up with unanswered questions. Had the coven that was hidden at the retreat finally been found, if so... by whom?

The Seekers were not a threat to anyone; they were a group of misfits that had a bit of magic in them with nowhere else to go. Most were hoping to become more powerful someday, these ones helped the sisters find tainted magic.

The farm was known as a spiritual retreat. It was a place you could find your inner self; meditation, communing with nature, learning to use the five senses, and finding spiritual guidance was encouraged there... it was a place of quiet study. Deep in the underground cellar was the Seeker's hidden chambers; this was the place of the real magic.

Once a year, a gathering brought magic users from across the globe to refresh their beliefs. There, they were encouraged to connect with others. More importantly, reconnecting with the three sisters was necessary. If they had any tainted magic users, they were brought before the Seeker's... to be purged.

A powwow for the native spiritual leaders was held at the same time, which helped to hide what was really going on. Orientals from all across Canada also came to show off their warrior skills;

they taught Buddhism, Tai Chi, plus many other inner meditation exercises. Dancing, swordsmanship, music, natural medicine, Shamanism, or communing with God... who was the Great Spirit of all living things, will be strongly encouraged at this time.

The yearly spiritual event was to start next week, by Sunday the place would be wall to wall trailers with hundreds of tepee's set up in every available space they could find. In addition, the three bunkhouses would be full to bursting.

The four story ranch house would have cots in every available space, exotic food from around the globe would be offered by every culture that came to this event.

Unfortunately, if the Seeker's had been unearthed the retreat would have to be cancelled... immediately. Already, it might be too late to stop it!

Alexandrina slowed uneasily as she rode up the lane, looking around grimly; there should have been horses racing around. It was deathly quiet... even Mother Earth was silent. Her horse trumpeted a call looking for her stable mates, but no answering cry was heard. Putting her hand down quickly, Alex quieted her mare.

*****

Shadow Hunter slowed; he stopped to read a sign that had, **'Spiritual Retreat',** in big bold letters then... **'All are welcome here!'** Was just below it, he frowned in surprise.

The Cree/Oriental Shaman had never been here before, but his agent had arranged for him to show off his skills next Friday at the place. That's why he was in Toronto to begin with. His big motorhome with the three horse compartments was to arrive at noon Sunday, his time slot was set for two in the afternoon next week.

Hunter had come straight here from France wanting to be early for some much needed meditation and quiet time. He turned to the right then put his bike on off road; the Cree/Oriental waited until it rose higher in the front making it easier to navigate the rougher terrain. Silently, the Shaman slipped into the trees lining the driveway. Instantly, he disappeared... becoming one with the shadows.

*****

Alexandrina slowed her horse when the lights of the ranch house came into view; three huge dogs raced over barking before quieting when they recognized the mare. Unexpectedly, the three animals suddenly veered away. Barking in excitement, they ran towards the trees. The oldest triplet was too anxious to find out what was happening at the house to pay them any mind.

Alex looked to the left when she heard a whinny of greeting to her mare. In relief, she saw two dozen horses milling about close to the barn. She scratched her head in puzzlement; feeding time was two hours ago... why were they still here!

Dismounting, Alex dropped her reins before taking a step towards the veranda. She halted when ten men, followed closely by fifteen young women ran out of the house then down the stairs and surrounded her. The fear was plain to hear in all their voices as they all tried to talk at once. Bombarding her with descriptions of what had happened; silently Black Cougar let them talk... waiting them out.

*****

Shadow Hunter halted at the edge of the trees before dismounting; he knelt then hummed reassuringly when three dogs ruffs bristled cautiously walked towards him. Humming soothingly, he put out both hands letting them come to him. He loved animals and had a special affinity with them, it was seldom he could not befriend one... wild or tame.

The three cream coloured farm dogs were immense; they were at least three feet at the withers before adding the huge neck plus the head to that. Even the smallest of the three reached almost to his ribs in height.

Shadow Hunter was sure it would take no effort at all for any one of them to rip him to shreds... if they so choose to; calmly, he continued to hum soothingly.

Sniffing the stranger's hands cautiously, the three licked them then tackled him trying to wash his face. It didn't take them long to loss interest in the newcomer though, as they raced off after a squirrel that thankfully caught their interest.

Rising with a low chuckle, Shadow Hunter pushed the invisibility button allowing his bike to disappear from view. Turning back, he watched the woman curiously; as she was surrounded by a bunch of young adults, most were in their twenties... he figured. Since her back was to him, he quickly joined the crowd to listen.

*****

The front porch door banged shut; instantly, quiet descended when an older man in his seventies followed closely by his wife walked to the stairs. The older woman was quite striking even with her dark hair mostly grey now. She was a bit plump giving her a typical grandmother look, but she had a commanding presence that was obvious.

The older woman stopped beside her much taller husband before holding up her hands for silence. You could tell immediately by her regal bearing that she was used to being obeyed. "Please, everyone! You must let Lieutenant Ryuu in to do her job; she cannot investigate the death of our friend out here. Only the five involved need to return to the house, the rest can stay outside... for now!"

Turning away, the owners of the ranch disappeared inside; Alexandrina followed with the ones needed trailing her.

Shadow Hunter stayed behind the last person; he made sure to keep in their shadow to hide his presence, silently he followed. Once inside, the Cree/Oriental Shaman stepped into the deeper shadows... disappearing once more.

*****

Alexandrina followed Tanya into the main living room, which was usually only used for entertaining outsiders. The owner and head of her Seeker's took a step to the side; it allowed the Lieutenant to see the woman slumped in a chair with eyes wide open... starring sightlessly. A shocked look of terror was plain to see on her white face.

Rushing over, Alex dropped down beside the woman but she didn't dare touch her. Sitting cross legged, she put both hands on top of her knees then touched her thumb and middle finger together; feeling herself ready, she raised both hands before examining the woman's aura.

The young woman was a Seeker, one of the youngest members and was able to use magic. One of the Mother Earth's shadows had found her recently; gladly, she bonded with it. The magic should still be here somewhere. The girl would need to be cremated for it to be released completely, since the host had been willing.

Alexandrina frowned searching frantically, but felt nothing; not even a residue of the shadow... or it's magic. Sitting back, Alex looked up at the head Seeker. "The other one is the same?"

Tanya shook her head in denial with a frown of concern. "No, luckily the other one isn't dead! The creature that did this finished with the one downstairs before disappearing."

Scowling grimly, Alexandrina got up before turning to the five; three were sitting on the couch waiting to be heard, with two standing. She pointed at the only male who was leaning against the arm of the sofa on her right. "Tomas, you are also bonded... willingly; did you see anything that might help?"

The young tall skinny Mexican stepped forward, he nodded before visibly shuddering in fear. "I was walking around the corner with Alice; what looked to me like one of the vampires was standing over Sue, it was holding her by the forehead. I saw the shadow being pulled out of her then it entered the vampire. That thing was completely naked plus it was hovering off the ground, I got the impression it could fly! It had the white pasty look of the newer vampires we have seen the last year or so but no fangs that I noticed. Its wing span was quite large compared to the ones I have seen in the past. Most of its feathers were missing, though.

The ones it did have were mostly white with only a few black feathers, once the magic was gone its wings seemed to grow by a couple feathers... two white ones darkened to black. The vampire thing was quite old looking, it seemed almost ancient."

The other four nodded having seen the same thing.

Alexandrina frowned perturbed before looking at the others speculatively. "Anyone see anything different?"

Three shook their heads negatively, but Alice piped up suddenly as she twirled a lock of red hair near her ear nervously. "It had red eyes and was definitely a female; it had thin black hair... come to think of it, its hair also seemed to grow just a bit!"

Turning, Alexandrina scowled before looking at the head Seeker... she gestured hopefully. "You have a burning pier waiting I hope; I don't want to take any chances that there is still enough magic to poison the Mother Earth!"

Inclining her head, Tanya gestured in reassurance. "Of course, it's all arranged."

The head of the Seeker's turned to the ones on the couch before waving for them to get up. "The stretcher is waiting; Dan will show you where it is. Please take her out the back, we will be along shortly."

Tanya beckoned to Alexandrina. "Come, the other one is still in the cell; we thought she was dead too, but wasn't. When we tried to bring her out, she attacked us so we left her there!"

Walking to the door that would take them further into the house, Tanya went through it. If you turned right, a long hallway ran the full length of the house with several meeting rooms on the left then led to the back entrance. If you turned left instead, a large vaulted room would lead you to the far end of the house.

Stairs going up to the bedrooms was there or if you kept going past the spiral staircase a door going down to the basement brought you to the end of the main floor.

Turning left the head Seeker pulled out a key that was kept on a necklace; in preparation, she pulled it over her head as they walked. She went to the door that leads to the basement, opening it they went down three steps to a landing.

There were two doors, the one on the right was never locked it led to the gym, game room, and there was an indoor pool with a Jacuzzi just to the left of it.

The other door was always locked; the head Seeker inserting the key then opened it before turning on a light. Starting down, she paused in surprise when the Lieutenant began to speak to the shadows.

Alexandrina paused on the top step before turning unexpectedly; she waved towards the door above them impatiently. "You might as well come with us Hunter, you are making me dizzy with your there one moment and gone the next routine. Since the hounds let you in, you can stay; they are specially trained to sniff out evil. If you wouldn't have disappeared in the alley earlier I would have invited you along; obviously, you are one of us!"

Perturbed at having his shield penetrated so easily; Shadow Hunter opened his cloak then walked into the light. He bowed respectfully. "I am sorry Lieutenant Ryuu, but I had to be sure of you."

Nodding in understanding, Alexandrina wasn't upset in the least. She had known since he had joined the five that he was there; Alex wasn't sure why she trusted him... she just did. Hunter had an innocence about him that was unusual in an adult male. Instinctively, she knew that he was aware of both his Po and Hun, making him pure in spirit.

Po was the Mother Earth's spirit, while Hun was the soul's spirit guide given by the Great Spirit... who was the God of all living things. The soul would return to Shen once the shell died; the Po would rejoin the Mother Earth briefly then would seek out another who was worthy to be guided. Shen and Po were names used mostly by the Tianming Monks and other Oriental religions throughout the Orient.

Shadow Hunter joining the two women was surprised when they

outdistanced the lights after fifteen steps down, but yet it stayed bright enough to see everyone ahead of him; looking around and then up, he smiled when he saw the sapphire of light following them... magic must have been used.

Frowning, Alexandrina shook off her thoughts of Shadow Hunter when they reached the bottom of the long stairwell that took them deep into Mother Earth. This is where the Seekers came to discuss business; here, they were able to get enough power from Mother Earth to help dispel the tainted magic when the triplets were around.

The archway ahead had big bold black letters around the entrance.

**'The first trinity will bring about the beginning that will lead to the end... or is it!'**

Every time Alex entered here, a different saying or maybe it was a warning illuminated the archway that led into a short hall; from there you could only go right or left.

Going through the entrance, Alexandrina turned to the right and Tania moved to the left... the two waited to see if Shadow Hunter would enter.

Frowning in surprise, the Cree/Oriental Shaman halted in shock at what he read over the arch in big black writing.

**'Welcome keeper of the dragon... the Alpha of the Omega has begun!'**

Shadow Hunter felt a shiver of uncertainty then his cloak shifted colours giving him a warning of, he didn't know what. This was only the second time since getting the cloak that the translucent colour shifted from its customary black, now it was a deep dark green... hardly noticeable; the first time was when he met Alexandrina, but what it meant he had no clue.

Looking down at his watch, Shadow Hunter grimaced knowingly... it was blank. The Cree/Oriental Shaman figured they were in a dead zone, being so far into the Mother Earth electronics would not work here. How they had managed to get this cavern so deep he would have to ask Alexandrina later.

Hunter could see the two women patiently waiting for him; he just knew though, that if he walked through that archway his life from this day forward would be tied to this place.

Staring at the Lieutenant intently, Shadow Hunter felt an attraction he had never felt before. Right on its heels, a shiver of warning again rippled through him; there was something dangerous about her. He grinned shrewdly at himself knowing that's what intrigued him so much.

With no more hesitation, Hunter stepped through the arch causing a tingle to run through his body. It wasn't an unpleasant feeling, now he could physically feel a hum of satisfaction from the Mother Earth beneath his feet.

Turning right, Tanya continued to lead them down a short hallway; the head Seeker took them into a room with three cages, only one was occupied by a sobbing middle aged woman.

Instantly, the woman jumped to her feet; she rushed to the door and grabbed the bars before shaking them violently. "Let me out of here... this instant! Who are you people, where am I? you have no right to keep me locked in this place!"

Alexandrina stepped closer before humming she lifted both hands then felt the woman's aura, but she could feel no taint in her at all. Finished, Alex smiled sweetly. "You were arrested for attacking your sister; you stabbed her twice with a butcher knife... don't you remember?"

The woman gasped outraged. "I would never do such a thing!"

Stepping back, Alexandrina rubbed her chin reflectively. "I don't feel any taint in her at all now. My theory is the thing that attacked here can draw out corrupted magic and not kill the host. Unfortunately, if the magic is bonded willingly when it is drawn out... it kills the host! Which is opposite to us, we have to kill the host when the magic is tainted; unless it is under adolescence age, only then do we have the ability to save the host."

Shadow Hunter stepped forward. "Give me a moment with her!"

Nodding, Alex watched puzzled as Hunter pulled out something that was hidden by his shirt; he stepped closer to the cage.

Bowing slightly, Shadow Hunter smiled disarmingly before reaching out to take the woman's hand. "I am called Hunter, what is your name?"

The woman scowled distrustfully for a long moment before relaxing and smiled back hesitantly... unable to help liking the man in front of her. "Sarah Lee Jamison, I live in the suburbs of Toronto. I am a nurse at the hospital downtown!"

Shadow Hunter nodded pleased that she trusted him enough to give him her information... it wasn't only dogs affected by his charisma. He sighed in relief when his medallion did not glow, neither did a shadow leave the woman; he stepped back then turned to the two waiting women.

Staring in shock, Alexandrina finally pointed at the medallion. "You have our Celtic dragon medallion... who are you?"

Frowning perplexed at first, Hunter finally grinned. "You are a descendant of White Buffalo; I am the great, great grandson of Shin and Spirit Bear... the last of the Skinwalkers. I'm a Shaman, trained by our Cree Spiritual leader. A Tianming Monk showed up in my village and trained me in the Oriental arts."

Alexandrina pinched the bridge of her nose feeling a headache coming on. "Spirit Bear had another child... that makes us related."

Shadow Hunter chuckled in acknowledgement. "Several times removed, but yes that's why I felt a connection when I first met you. Although, I didn't realize that was what it was at first. The medallion recognized you too; as soon as we touched it heated up and burnt me a bit, which has only happened once... when I first put it on."

Holding out her hand in demand, Alexandrina's tone of voice turned hard in command. "You will return it?"

Snorting in denial, Shadow Hunter emphatically shook his head. "Nope!"

Alexandrina crossed her arms angrily afraid she might reach for it regardless. "Why not, it is not yours!"

Shadow Hunter shrugged angrily. "Yes it is; it was given willingly to Spirit Bear. I am his direct descendant... plus, the last Cree Skinwalker!"

Throwing up her hands in exasperation, Alex couldn't help commenting sarcastically. "We are also descendants of Spirit Bear, so you are not the last; I even have the ability to shapeshift, which you don't seem to have!"

Folding his arms grimly, Shadow Hunter shook his head decisively. "No, your line is too strained there is barely any Cree left in you! As for you being able to change shape, I don't believe it is the same as what my people were able to do."

Harrumphing angrily at that logic, Alexandrina rubbed the back of her neck as the pain in her head increased. Finally, she dropped her hand in frustration. "Fine, I will contact my Guardian to see what is to be done about you! For now, the head Seeker will put you in one of the rooms upstairs."

Shadow Hunter grinned before putting his hands together, he bowed. "As you wish, but only until Sunday; my rig will be here by then, since I was invited to be one of your Friday demonstrators."

Tanya clapped her hands twice in satisfaction before smiling in delight. "Ah, you are the Cree/Oriental Shaman my husband booked two months ago?"

Nodding, Hunter grinned back. "Yes, I am your Friday night entertainer... trained by the best. Unfortunately, I was not meant to stay in my village as most do. So, I kept my Cree name instead of taking the Shaman's as my ancestors have done in the past; even though my training as a spiritual healer was completed."

'Bang... Bang!' "Will someone let me out of here?"

Alexandrina took the offered key from Tanya and unlocked the cell door. Taking the woman's hand, the Lieutenant helped her out. She kept Sarah's hand locked in her own in order to give instructions. "Come, your time was served at the retreat so no jail time will be needed. When you get home all you will remember is being in a jail cell for stabbing your sister before getting sent to a retreat for therapy and to serve out your parole; you were released early for good behaviour."

The four exited the cells then went up the stairs; Tanya locked the Seeker's door behind her and led them up into the vaulted room. She took them past the door leading into the living room that they had entered through earlier. She continued down the long hallway to the second door on the right, it took them directly to the kitchen... for a late supper.

The burning pier would have to wait for their guest to leave; the Seeker's husband had religious rights that allowed them to make certificates for deaths, births, and marriages... so everything was done legally.

Witnesses though were not encouraged since most corpses were cremated not buried; corrupted magic users were usually extremely grotesque to look at.

Sitting the woman down in a chair, Alexandrina walked off before turning her radio back on. "Stefan, can you come out to the retreat please; I need you pick up a lady named Sarah Jamison, she needs a ride home tonight. There will be no need to lock her up since nobody wants to press charges. It was a simple misunderstanding... it has been handled. I will also be taking my holidays early, so I will be staying at the retreat to help with guests who are starting to arrive a little earlier than we expected."

Alex heard the two men chuckling on the other end before Andrew's voice was heard. "Oh sure, leave us poor men to handle things on our own; by the way... thank you! I just made fifty bucks betting you would find a way to take an early holiday!"

Laughing in delight, Alexandrina pressed the button to tease. "Glad to help you out, see you in half an hour."

Waiting until she heard a mumble of agreement, Alex turned her radio off before going to the table to eat.

*****

Two hours later, Alexandrina was relieved to give the final wave of goodbye to Sarah and the two detectives as they drove off.

Once clear, preparations were quickly finalized; once everyone staying at the retreat was gathered, they stood around a pier. Locking hands, they began singing a gospel hymn. After a bit, the head Seeker took a torch that was waiting then lit the wood on fire.

Chanting in time with the others, Alexandrina the first Priestess of Mother Earth helped send the woman's spiritual guide or Po back to the Earth before the soul or Hun was released back to God... the Great Spirit.

When there was nothing left, but ashes; Alexandrina turned to Shadow Hunter before beckoning him to follow. "I will show you to your room, since it is across from mine."

Nodding, Hunter picked up the saddlebags he had grabbed earlier. Inside, he had a couple changes of clothes and toilet articles; he never left anything in his hotel room when in unfamiliar towns or cities, always unsure if he would make it back to the hotel.

Shadow Hunter followed Alexandrina up the backstairs to a deck that wrapped all the way around the house; a long overhanging roof kept the rain out.

When winter hit, a switch was turned so that Plexiglas windows could move down before connecting to the solid railing forming an enclosed deck. It allowed the year round inhabitants to gather in a heated sunroom so they could enjoy nature in relative comfort.

It could also be shut in when they needed extra beds, since the Covid hit in 2020 thirty cots was the maximum allowed. When the fair begins, this space would be used to house most of the apprentices accompanying the Seekers.

They entered the back entrance, a huge boot room with two big deep freezers full of food greeted them... almost everything was grown right here.

Shadow Hunter removed his moccasins, but picked them up to take them to his room; they were specially made for him so he would take no chances of losing them.

Alexandrina made no comment; after all, trust needed to be earned. With several dozen people around on any given day, she did not blame him for taking precautions.

Alex took him down a hallway with three doors on the right side, but only two on the left. She did not bother showing him inside the rooms, although she explained their purposes to the newcomer. "The doors on the right are private meditation or meeting rooms, they are sound proof. If you wish to use one Tanya is the one to see. The door on your left if you remember earlier, leads to the kitchen. Breakfast is served in the dining room from eight am to ten am, if a special diet is needed the kitchen is available for anyone to use after eleven am. The one further down of course goes into the sitting room; you were hiding in the shadows when we first went through it."

Shadow Hunter could hear the disapproval in Alex's voice; he chuckled but otherwise ignored her irritated tone.

Harrumphing at the chuckle, Alexandrina continued her explanation of the farmhouse layout without commenting on it. "There is an entertainment room in the basement, with a pool table plus a big screen TV. A gym is across from it, a small indoor pool is attached to the gym... it is heated. It also includes a sauna with a Jacuzzi tub for relaxation. In-between are shower stalls one for men and the other for women. The entrance to them is through the same door we took earlier to go down to the cells at the other end of the house. Once on the landing just turn right instead of going straight ahead, that door will take you down to the basement."

Pausing for a moment, Alexandrina went past the door they had went through earlier then walked back into the vaulted room before indicating the stairs; she continued her description of the house. "Upstairs on the first floor single rooms are available, there's ten in total. All come with a bathroom that includes a shower stall. Each has a wall unit inside the room that you pull out. A double bed will drop down. On the opposite side of the room is another pull down wall unit. This one has a desk with a laptop, TV, plus a telephone if you do not have a cell."

Alexandrina paused then decided to let Hunter know about the work out rooms further up, she knew he would want to use them. "Tomorrow, Dan can show you where the two training rooms are up on the second floor. There are also two small one bedroom apartments on the opposite side, suitable for a newly wedded couple or a single parent with a child who needs assistance. Above that is the third floor, there are two large apartments up there. One is occupied. The other is used for important dignitaries. Since you are only here until your unit arrives, just a room will suffice."

Shadow Hunter listened, but made no comment as he followed Alex through the doorway at the end of the hallway into the large circular room they had been in earlier; he had not had time to look around then, now he took his time not wanting to miss anything.

Several doors branched off with a stairwell that spiralled upwards in the center of the room; he could see the first floor quite clearly from here then more stairs that lead to the second floor training rooms and the small apartments above before more stairs leading to the third level greeted you.

It did not take them long to climb the ten steps that led to the first floor landing, which went completely around the entire upstairs. It was even big enough for two people to walk side by side comfortably without crowding each other. Short hallways showed doorways on each side, they went past three before turning right. The hallway seemed awful small with two of them in it; luckily, it was only two steps to the doors of the rooms.

Alexandrina handed him a door key, she jerked her hand back when a spark crackled between them. "This is for you; most of us do not lock our doors, but newcomers always do until trust is established. Enjoy your evening, Hunter!"

Bowing low without comment, Shadow Hunter turned before entering his room.

Spinning around, Alexandrina entered her own room; absently, she rubbed the hand that was still tingling from the contact with the Cree/Oriental Shaman. It was going to be extremely difficult dealing with that man if a shock happened every time they accidentally touched.

Sighing in aggravation, Alex walked straight into her bathroom and stripped. Turning on the hot water, she stepped into the steaming shower after releasing her raven black floor length hair; with a groan of relief, the pain in her head eased a bit. Black Cougar allowed the hot water to hit the back of her neck for a good ten minutes... it helped to soothe the ache somewhat. Washing quickly, she stepped out then wrapped her long hair in a towel before leaving the bathroom.

Finally, Alexandrina walked to her alcove; pushing a button, her desk with a large screen dropped down. She needed to talk to her sisters and father, unsure what to do about the medallion. The vampire hunting the Seekers was also a big concern. Biting her lip thoughtfully, Alex couldn't help thinking that maybe she was wrong... it might be after the Mother Earth's shadow magic instead?

Hitting the intercom on the phone pad, the flat screen TV lit up before an automated voice sounded. "How can I help you Alexandrina?"

Grimacing sadly at the image of her mother, Alex sighed. She had hated the first robotic image that came up on her screen when she first moved in here. Taking an old photograph of her mother, she loaded it so Black Cougar could pretend sometime. She had never met her mother... White Buffalo died giving birth to them. Her mother had been named after the first twins with power. "Cecille, can you do a four way call with Magdalene, Fai, Ronin, and my father please."

After two rings, Magdalene appeared on one half of her screen; the other half showed Fai sitting beside their brother, with dad in the background.

The disembodied voice of Cecille echoed once more. "Only two calls are needed Alexandrina!"

Nodding relieved to see that Fai was not alone, Alex gave a report of her day.

Having just seen the same creature for a brief moment, Magdalene sat forward intently. "I'm in Wales right now, I got a distressed call a few days ago from the Seeker's here... I was too late. Regrettably, only three are left out of a dozen. Unfortunately, I went straight to Snowdonia after hearing rumours that were quite disturbing or I might have saved one or two more. When I got there, the mist was gone completely; I was just in time to see the rock formation vanish entirely, all that's left is a broken black pillar. Whatever was hidden there is now free. It's not a vampire everyone is seeing but a demon that's loose. I think it is probably after the magic of the Mother Earth needing to fill its wings. Once it has enough of a wingspan, there will be no stopping it. Father be extra cautious, it might go after Fai if it becomes aware of her. With all the magic White Buffalo has trapped inside her it could complete its wings in minutes."

Scowling in surprise, Alexandrina gestured thoughtfully. "Corrupted magic has gone after Fai a few times, but they stay away from the two of us. Father, is there a reason we are avoided, but White Buffalo is sought out?"

Frowning perplexed, Chang shrugged bewildered. "Never really noticed, I will pull out my carpet tonight to seek answers. As for the medallion, this Hunter fellow is right; unless he gives it to you, it is his. Try to find out more about him, see if he knows why the medallion glows when tainted magic is about. Magdalene, you better hop on a plane and head home. Send the last of the Seeker's to the retreat, Alex can keep an eye on them. I will have Ronin check with the others that are elsewhere, most should be on their way to you already for the yearly retreat. I will send out a distress beacon and they should all start arriving tomorrow... instead of Sunday!"

Chang looked at his oldest daughter in concern as her forehead wrinkled in pain before she pinched the bridge of her nose. "You have another headache? Maggie, Fai; do either of you have any pain?"

Both shook their heads before answering as one. "No... father!"

Nodding relieved, Chang knew that if the other two did not have one too; it was from an old injury she got while saving a child. "Go to bed Black Cougar it is way later there then here, we can discuss this once I find out more."

Alexandrina nodded in agreement and goodnights were said. The oldest of the triplets, combed her long hair out before plaiting it in a loose braid. She pulled her bed down then crawled under her blankets; exhausted, she fell asleep quickly.

*****

Shadow Hunter put his ear piece in before lifting his arm and pushed a button on his watch; a small blue flickering holographic screen flickered on. A young woman appeared first then a man's head popped up over her shoulder. "Did you two get all that?"

There was a long moment of silence before the expected answer was received. "Yes, we are already on our way. I have looked in all the archives, so far we have no idea what creature that is. Trevor thought it might be a Grigori offspring at first. Their parents were the eighth choir made by the Great Spirit to be the watchers and teachers of humans. They were easily corrupted though, most took human wives creating giant children. Until a woman was mentioned, being that it is a female we are not sure now. Maybe it isn't an offspring, but a Grigori angel that hid becoming trapped between worlds. If it has scraggly wings, its main goal will be to restore them to their full glory. If it is true that they only grow when it steals magic, any user or relic infused with magic will be in jeopardy... like your medallion. We are only assuming right now trying to make educated guesses, but until we know more, stay vigilant. We are hoping to be there sometime tomorrow."

Loud static almost drowned out Hunter's assistant before her voice gained strength once more. "As for the woman there is not much known about her, I did find an article on a constable Alexandrina that got a medal for rescuing a child that nobody knew was in the building. They were just going through the door when a beam hit her in the head; she managed to get the child to safety before passing out. She was in a coma for three days and finally came out of it. Other than that I can find no birth certificate, siblings, parents or anything else on her... it's like she is a ghost!"

Tapping on his cheek reflectively, Shadow Hunter finally sighed before dropping his hand. "You do know who she is though, don't you? Will you tell her who you are, I would not want to blurt it out and have you breathing down my neck for it later!"

A snort of irritation sounded on the other end, a long silence followed before she came back with an angry indifferent shrug. "I'm not sure yet, my brother says he doesn't care one way or the other. Oh, whatever... it doesn't matter if she knows; we can talk about it later!"

A loud squeal in his ear had Shadow Hunter cursing. He pulled out his ear piece in a hurry before rubbing his abused ear. Of course, it mattered; by the sound of her voice, she was still holding a grudge. Oh well, when the two women finally meet face to face she could see for herself that the woman she feared was not a monster. All he could do was hope that his fierce little owl would finally find some peace afterwards. Heading into the bathroom, he had a quick shower then crawled exhausted into bed once he pulled it out.

# CHAPTER THREE

Magdalene got off the plane and walked down the long hallway following the other passengers to the baggage compartment. She had gotten several uneasy, shocked glances at the RCMP Master Corporal ERT special unit badge that she wore on a chain around her neck

It was mandatory, since she was carrying a gun in plain sight... plus other weapons that were hidden.

Inside Maggie's briefcase was her laptop, accompanied by pens and pencils; with several other articles not allowed on a plane. Not since the terrorist attacks in the USA on September 11, 2001 that is.

A long cylinder with a dragon protruding from the top, with Japanese writing on it kept Magdalene's Wakizashi sword hidden from others. It was usually worn on her back in a special harness that snapped the holder in place. If she grasped the dragon, a barely noticeable seam sprang open; instantly, a short sword intricately designed and made for her was released.

When Maggie needed a shield the cylinder was pulled off with it; a switch on the inside was pushed to activate a secret panel. Once triggered, it would shorten instantly then become a square before several dozen shards of titanium would spring out to surround it. Making it roundish... thankfully, it wasn't heavy though. On the front of the shield was their lost Celtic dragon medallion, it was carve into it.

Most of the passengers were gone by the time Magdalene got to the baggage area. Lost in thought, she had strolled along leisurely in no apparent hurry. It was probably the last plane tonight anyway since it was two am, there was hardly anybody about.

Within minutes of walking into the baggage area, Maggie had the room mapped out in her mind. She was specially trained by a division in the Royal Canadian Mounted Police or RCMP called

JTF2 or Joint Task Force 2. Red Wolf's training with her Oriental Guardian had been quite brutal, even though he was her father... so nothing was missed.

Magdalene was instantly aware that two janitors were cleaning near the furthest exit. Within seconds, she knew where the three main exits were located as well as both fire escapes.

Maggie saw a man sleeping on a bench probably waiting for the six am plane. Three giggling teenagers with their parents were the last of the passengers to gather suitcases before rushing past Red Wolf.

Finally, one broad shouldered six foot two man was the only one standing in front of the baggage trolley waiting. He gathered the last suitcase, turning around he waved his hand so that a single rose materialized. The blonde Adonis wasn't the typical Spaniard that was seen in most movies, but fair haired with light golden brown eyes. He bowed with a grin of pleasure. "A red rose, fitting for the most beautiful flower here."

Magdalene rolled her eyes in exasperation. Of course, they had to send him to pick her up. There were only two people in the bureau that knew who she was and what her missions entailed... he just happened to be one of them.

Being from one of the oldest Spanish families in Spain, Fredrick was quite wealthy; his parents had settled in Canada before he was two years old, so he had grown up in Calgary. Since his family owned the ranch to the north of her home, they had grown up together. She knew the only reason he changed from a homicide detective to the special RCMP task force, was because of her. They had tried a romantic fling once, but it had not worked out at all. He was too flighty, liking women too much... all women!

The final straw came when Fred bonded willingly with the magic against her wishes. Maggie was just glad their attempt at romance didn't wreck their long friendship.

Chuckling, Magdalene took the rose then used it to hit his deeply muscled chest before walking out of the terminal to an elevator that would take them to the parkade. "Thank you. Back from Madrid are you, when did you arrive in Calgary?"

Fredrick had a deep chuckle with a low baritone voice; he was too good looking for his own good. Not often, was he sent on undercover missions since he was too recognizable. Besides, they preferred having Fred as a spokesman for the bureau.

Fred pushed the required button then shrugged resignedly. "Two days ago, mother had one of her episodes of seeing things not there. I had to readmit her into the psychiatric hospital... Mom went too far this time though. She claims it was you, with wings and red eyes. You were attacking this poor old man; he was having a massive heart attack!"

Walking out of the elevator, Magdalene stopped instantly in shock before turning to look at her ex-partner in excitement when he halted beside her. "She saw that thing! Where was it? My sister had an incident with a shapeshifter with red eyes, black hair, it also had wings, and it was in Toronto. There was also one in Wales attacking the Seeker's; nobody mentioned a resemblance to us, now it's here..."

Beginning to walk towards the vehicles, Maggie's mussing's were interrupted when she flew five feet before landing with a surprised grunt of shock.

Reacting instinctively, Magdalene quickly flipped a switch on the case with the dragon prominent when she saw Fredrick on the ground with that thing on top of him; it was trying to draw out his magic. Instantly, her sword was released. She barely had a hold of it when she changed into a wolf without being aware she was switching forms, causing the sword to drop to the ground harmless.

The huge red wolf bounded over then grabbed the creature by its wings and tossed it across the parking lot; she stood over her stunned ex-partner protectively.

The female thing came flying back their way but stopped dead ten feet away; it pointed at Red Wolf then muttered something in a language that she did not understand... before vanishing.

At once, Magdalene's form transformed back; looking down at her right side, she frowned grimly. Red Wolf's little dagger was glowing a hot bright white, slowly the doves light dissipated and she knew the thing was gone for sure.

Feeling something tickle her lip, Magdalene reached up to scratch it. Surprisingly, a feather fell into her hand. She tucked it in her pants pocket before turning... quickly Maggie knelt. "Are you okay?"

Fredrick's mouth opened before closing a few times, as he struggled to think clearly; he let Maggie help him sit up, finally Fred managed to nod. His voice had quite a bit of strain to it so didn't seem quite as deep. "I think so! That's what my mother saw, she's right it does resemble you a bit. It looks ancient though, way older than you by the looks of all the deep lines on its face. The red eyes are also a dead giveaway that it is not really you... its hair was shorter too! After I drop you off I will have to go get my mother from the hospital, maybe she has never been crazy and does see things!"

Nodding thoughtfully, Magdalene turned back to Fred. "No! I will go with you it is too dangerous for you to go alone. Your mother could be a seer; we will take her to my place after we pick up the both of you some clothes. You will have to stay with me until my father arrives so I can keep an eye on both of you. If it tried for your magic once, I am sure it will try again!"

Magdalene helped him up, he wobbled a bit so she rushed over to gather her things before going back; pulling his arm over her shouldered Red Wolf manoeuvred him towards the passenger side. "I will drive!"

Fredrick nodded without argument; once in the car and strapped in, Fred fell asleep almost instantly beyond exhausted.

Loading all her stuff in the back seat, Magdalene finally got in. The first thing she did once the vehicle was running was to take her phone out of her pocket then pushed her code in. "Cecille, can you please connect to Bluetooth before calling my father! I need to see him so have the car put on self-drive, have it take us to the hospital it was at yesterday!"

Cecille's image appeared on the big Bluetooth screen on her dash before a disembodied voice was heard as the car backed up on its own. "Connected and driving to... Southern Alberta Forensic Psychiatry Centre; your father is on the line Magdalene!"

Chang's face instantly appeared in front of her. They were halfway to the hospital by the time Maggie finished explaining it all. "Why I changed to a wolf puzzles me, I had my sword in my hand?"

Scratching his head in bewilderment, Chang frowned troubled. "Your sister never mentioned a resemblance; the witnesses said it only had two dozen feathers, maybe there was more than one imprisoned there. If so, it could be some of the Grigori instead of the offspring's. There was mention of them being trapped on Earth in a valley, but I always thought they were male because they married human women before having children with them."

Sighing thoughtfully, Magdalene rubbed her right shoulder. She had hit it when that thing had sent her flying, so it was a bit sore. "The bible talks about the Gregory offspring's being giants which brings to mind the human side of them; what about the angel side. Sometimes when twins are born, one will look like the mother... the other could resemble the father. If he is black, they could have a white baby and a black one!"

Perking up at that, the Guardian nodded thoughtfully. "I see, what happened to the ones that looked like the angels not the humans. Wow... a scary thought if it is true. You are a direct descendant of Noah; the third son I believe is your ancestor. He was driven away for telling his brothers about their father's naked drunkenness. The third sons wife was not of pure descend, so let's assume she was part Grigori... possibly part Mother Earth's evolved race too. Some would have no wings so look more human than the giant offspring's. If the ones with wings were imprisoned just because they were children of the Grigori, once released they might want revenge. To get that they would need to be at full power. Stealing the Mother Earth's magic would allow them to stand against the Great Spirit once they are at full strength. If the three of you are descended from them, you will look like them not the other way around. Maybe that is why they are avoiding you; you are a part of them so they would not want to destroy their own kind. Especially, if it helps them keep a direct tie to the Earth!"

Sighing grimly, Maggie pulled into the parking lot at the hospital but Fredrick was still sleeping. "They can draw in the Mother's shadows, but so can White Buffalo... will they go after her next?"

Shrugging, Chang scowled grimly. "Not sure, right now your sister is in court trying to put a killer behind bars in Penticton BC; then we are heading to the condo in Vancouver for a meeting. Afterwards, we will be heading to the homestead. I think Alexandrina should stay at the retreat for now with the Shaman. I am still not sure what if anything, he might have to do with this. My thoughts on your involuntary shape change, is that your dagger triggered your transformation, which makes me think that those things can't steal magic if it is being used! You and Black Cougar have pure magic so are able to shapeshift anytime, unlike the bonded magic users. Fai has magic but it is dormant right now. Because she draws in all magic, there would never be a safe way for her to use it so she is its prison not a user. Why or for what purpose nobody seems to know, not even my Tianming Masters."

Magdalene frowned then gestured in farewell when Fredrick stirred beside her. "Okay, father let me know when you get close to the farm; I will send a car out to you. If you find out anything else, call me. Hugs and kisses to everyone... Love ya."

After pushing the disconnect button, Magdalene turned to Fredrick when he groaned in pain before opening his golden brown eyes. "I feel like someone took a club to me beating me black and blue, come to think of it that did happen once when your oldest sister decided she did not like me hanging around you so much."

Laughing, Maggie remembered that day as if it was yesterday. "She was just mad because you were not paying any attention to her; she had a big crush on you."

Fredrick sat up in interest. "She did... wow; I would have never guessed by the way she pummelled me all the time."

Chuckling again at the memory of her older sister's infuriated inability to get Fred to notice her. Magdalene finally shook off her amusement as she looked at her ex-partner. "How are you feeling now?"

Smiling reassuringly, Fredrick unbuckled his seat belt; he held his hand out before twirling it... a white dove appeared. He frowned disgruntled. "Well, I'm not quite up to par yet I think, since it was supposed to be a white rose."

Magdalene could not help chortling at his confused grimace; she opened her car door, letting the bird out. "Come on Fred, you can wow me later with your tricks. We're a little early so let's go across the street for breakfast, I'm starving."

Nodding, Fredrick felt a lot better when he no longer wobbled as he walked. He held open the door for Maggie before following her in.

*********************

The Cree/Oriental Shaman smiled at Alexandrina, they were kneeling facing each other in the training room. The walls were speckled with all sorts of old weapons that could be used, if one wished. Otherwise, the room was a sterile white allowing one to concentrate on their abilities... instead of the surroundings.

Shadow Hunter had gotten up at six am then went down to the exercise room, he found Black Cougar already there. The two spent an hour warming up before going to the pool to do laps.

Alexandrina had been right. The man had a muscled body most women would pant over; with a six pack that was tight enough one could probably bounce a quarter off it.

Alex invited Hunter to a training bout afterwards, now here they sat facing each other with his Oriental sword being admired. He had named it, Shadows Fury since it would cause a malicious Earth Shadow to burst into fragments.

Looking up, Alexandrina pointed at the Samurai sword curiously. "Where did you get the sword?"

Smiling, Shadow Hunter remembered back. It caused his eyes to mist over as he pictured his master with fondness. "A Tianming Samurai Monk walked into our village when I was seventeen. I had been training to be a Shaman for two years by that time. When I went searching for my adult name, I had seen the man in my vision so I was expecting him. He taught me to be a warrior before presenting me with this sword when my training was complete. The cloak I wear was also given to me at the same time. A Japanese master weaved into it a power that enhances my ability to disguise myself as a shadow, plus it helps break through barriers of illusion. When I put something against the fabric inside... like my bow, it will disappear. Unless you are trained to look with your inner eye, you would not be able to see it!"

Grimacing in understanding, Alexandrina remembered her surprise when she could not get him to forget who she was... now she knew why.

The pure black Algonquin bow sitting beside the sword caused a gasp of awe from Alex. A cross was carved into the black wood just above the grip, with one below it. The crosses had red flames curling around it forming into images of doves, one on either side... both were in flight. The grip was unique since it had a red cord wrapped around it giving your hand a better hold. The top and bottom both curved inward; making it easier to run through the trees, a branch would slide right over it.

Reaching out, Alexandrina touched the bow in awe. "There is a description with a sketch of this bow in Cecille's diary; I was quite young when I saw it. She had Shin write a journal for her before she died, since White Buffalo was blind with no knowledge of braille at that time. Unfortunately, writing or reading in braille didn't become wildly used in America until the late 1860s. The Tianming Monk must have added the bow later after she passed on."

Nodding, Shadow Hunter thought back trying to remember the exact description from Shin's journal entry. He knew Alexandrina would love hearing about the unique spiritualism associated with the bow. "Shin's journal said the incident was quite strange almost mystical in nature. It tells the story of an old native who found a log floating in the Petawawa River. Once the bark was removed the inside was an inky black, what kind of tree it was from baffled him... search as he might no other was ever found. The old Algonquin Bowyer had a dream of what the bow should look like, he knew once the vision played itself out that it was meant for great things. Years passed, not even one person was able to pull that string back. The old man had even forgotten about it until the day Shin walked into his wigwam. The Bowyer was shocked when the first arrow in thirty years was shot from the bow... it hit dead center. He took the bow away from the Oriental before giving it to the guide who was with the Tianming Monk; the big Irishman could not pull the string back even a smidgen. So the Algonquin Bowyer gave the bow to Shin as a gift from the Great Spirit, he refused all payment. Having a dream that night Shin called it Nightshade, the flaming destroyer of all things malevolent."

Putting her police baton down, Alexandrina gestured at it in explanation. "I have never been any good with a bow nor a sword, I prefer a staff."

Reaching down, Alex pushed a button on the side of the thick club causing both the top then bottom to spring open; out both ends, three layers of titanium steel flew out one after the other... forming a tier. It was quite long reaching from floor to her shoulder in height. If she pushed the button the other way only half would come out making it slightly smaller, which made it easier to use in tight quarters.

If more drastic measures were needed the oldest triplet would hold both titanium ends before pushing another button; the baton in the center would separate releasing two wicked blades, one on each end of the steel.

Shadow Hunter nodded impressed; he picked it up to test its weight since it was so long he figured it would be heavy, but it was light as a feather... too lightweight for him! He grabbed the other end figuring it would bend easily being so flimsy looking, again he was surprised by how ridged it was and unbendable.

Hearing a click, Hunter allowed the blades to go in and out testing them. Both were solid, wickedly sharp too he found out... the hard way. Quickly, he stuck his thumb in his mouth after nicking his finger on the blade with barely any pressure. The Cree/Oriental pulled his finger out before smirking; it was deviously brilliant, nobody would suspect anything by looking at the innocent police baton.

Handing it back after twisting it to tuck the blades away, Shadow Hunter got up with his bow in hand; he walked to the far wall and draped it on a hook out of the way. He walked back before picking up his sword, the Cree/Oriental Shaman expertly twirled it around getting himself ready. He watched in admiration as Alexandrina skillfully spun her staff; she twirled it with her left hand then laid it across the back of her neck... expertly, she caught it with her right hand.

The two combatants now warmed up came together, sparks flew when the two weapons met before a loud crash of thunder resonated of the walls; causing the hanging weapons to vibrate as the sound drowned out all else!

**********

The jurors braced themselves when they heard the tap, tap, tap of a cane. This trial had been going on for three days now, but finally the last witness to the murder of Sandra Lee was on the stand. He was the murderer's accomplice; a twenty-six year old, who allegedly only followed his seventeen year old girlfriends plan to humiliate her best friend. Unfortunately, she ended up killing Sandra in a fit of jealousy... or so he claimed.

The boyfriends testimony to his attorney earlier, explained how they ended up in the hills away from prying eyes since both girls were too young to drink. His girlfriend slipped something in Sandra's drink before they proceeded to rape her, but that was as far as it was supposed to go. While he was deep inside the victim, Stella produced a knife that he didn't know she had then proceeded to stab her friend three times.

The man sitting in the witness box winced when the cane hit the floor. The sound seemed to echo in his head, reminding him of the sound the knife made as it entered the young woman and blood flew everywhere... soaking him. Sandra's muscles contracted immediately, they clenched around his manhood so hard he had been held fast unable to get off her.

Stella had confessed to her boyfriend two days later that she saw it on TV, so she was curious to know if it would really happen that way. The girl had come prepared, using an axe she chopped the unfortunate Sandra up in order to release him. Even to this day, he still shuddered every time he thought of it!

The blind woman stopped in front of the witness box before banging her cane for emphasis. "You are trying to tell me, plus the jury here that you had no idea your girlfriend of seventeen had a knife stashed away without your knowledge?"

The man nodded his head emphatically then remembered that the opposing lawyer couldn't see it. "Yes, it was only supposed to be a little harmless fun against the perfect prissy Sandra Lee, which is what Stella told me..."

Fai let the man tell his story once again before scowling grimly once he was done. She knew this already and was aware of every detail, but it wasn't up to her to find him innocent or guilty that was for the jury to decide.

White Buffalo's job was to make sure the woman sitting with an uninterested smirk beside her attorney paid as high a price as possible for her crimes. She was the one the blind lawyer was really trying to convict... life in prison was not nearly good enough.

She brought her attention back as he finished his tale of horror.

The man put out a beseeching hand towards the jury knowing the woman would not see it. "I still have nightmares of being attached to that young woman. The last two years have been hell for me! I can't get close to any woman now without seeing that girl's look of horror or the sight of gleeful pleasure on Stella's face!"

Nodding, Fai turned slightly towards the judge. "I have no further questions your Honor."

Fai walked back then sat beside her assistant, which happened to be her half-brother and bodyguard when their father could not be with her. "How is the jury taking this?"

Ronin shrugged grimly; even though he knew she couldn't see it... it was done more out of habit. "I see lots of tears with a few grim fugitive looks towards the woman, who still has that gloating look I told you about earlier."

For another hour, the opposing lawyer tried to pin the blame on the boyfriend. Claiming his client was the innocent victim here; finally, it was over! The jury looking straight ahead solemnly walked out to deliberate.

Ronin leaned over before whispering hopefully. "It shouldn't take them long, your opening statement was brilliant... the closing one was even more so; I saw a lot of the jurors using tissue to wipe their eyes when you described the horror Sandra Lee endured!"

Sighing grimly, Fai shuddered in reaction. "That is because I know what the poor girl went through; Mother Earth was giving me images... I will have nightmares I'm sure for many days to come."

Patting his sister's hand consolingly, Ronin helped her rise when the bailiff told them to; allowing the judge to exited the courtroom. They went for lunch with their father who diligently waited for the pair. Normally they would fly home to wait, but Fai also figured it would not take the jury long. Chang sat across from his two children before telling them everything Magdalene said... plus the conclusions they had drawn.

Drumming her fingers lightly on the table, Fai listened intently to everything then stilled before leaning forward grimly. "I will talk to the Mother Earth tonight to confirm it, but I think Maggie is on the right track."

Nodding his agreement with that assessment, Ronin gestured thoughtfully. "As soon as we get back to the ranch I will try to find out more on the Grigori and their offspring's. I always assumed they were males, since that is how they are portrayed in the bible for the most part."

Shrugging, Fai gestured in confusion. "Maybe they hid themselves because of the evil of their brothers; I am pretty sure the children of the Grigori were not just males, there had to be some women too! It could be that the females were normal looking as children so ignored."

Quiet descended when their meal arrived. The three were just settling back with a drink when Fai's pager went off; she grinned then stood up. "See, told you they would not be long."

Once back in the court room, Fai couldn't help grinning in victory when the jurors found the girl guilty of first degree murder. She got life imprisonment with no chance of parole for twenty-five years. The man thankfully did not get off either; he was to serve fifteen years for accessory after the fact, rape, unlawful confinement... plus, a string of other offense's. White Buffalo was satisfied that justice had prevailed this time. She did not always win, but her percentages were climbing steadily compared to other lawyers her age.

Walking out of the courtroom in triumph, the two were greeted by the click of cameras and questions fired at them from a half dozen reporters.

Ronin, being Fai's press advocate stepped forward instantly. "Yes, we are quite satisfied by the verdict. Although, a longer prison sentence for the man would have suited us more, but fifteen years was better than no jail time. No, Fai Ryuu is still not sure what case she will take on next. Yes, we are heading back to

Vancouver for the meeting that will choose a new CSIS Chief. Of course, we were both saddened to learn of the death of our friend, James; he was one of the best Chiefs of the Canadian Security intelligence Service that we had the privilege to know, that is all for now... thank you!"

Pushing his way past the reporters, Chang kept the throng back while Ronin steered his sister out the door. Mercifully, they made a beeline for the escalade before thankfully climbed in. The driver turned; only when serving in court did they have a driver... it was just more convenient. "The jet is fueled and ready to go. Supper will be served on board since it is getting late!"

Fai nodded in relief. "Thanks John."

John turned back then pushed a button bringing down the glass privacy partition before driving into traffic... heading for the airport.

***************

Magdalene sighed in relief when she finally pulled into the driveway leading up to the ranch house. Mother and son had argued the whole way here.

Getting out of the driver's seat, Maggie walked to the back door to open it for Fredrick's mother. "Come Helen, I am sorry you are going to miss seeing your favorite horse jumping at Spruce Meadows, I think keeping your son safe should be your first priority though; it is only till my father gets here. We can all hope that by then the threat will have been contained so you can go back home. We both know he will not stay here without you if there is any possibility it will go after you instead."

Helen stared at the woman she had thought for sure her son would marry; unfortunately, it had never happened. She sighed in defeat before a nod of acquiesce followed. "You are right, of course!"

Turning resolutely, Helen marched towards the steps leading up to the veranda of the two story ranch house. It was small compared to her four story mansion three miles down the road, but she had always considered it cute when she visited; which was not as often since Magdalene had given back the engagement ring her son had given her a few years ago. The older woman could not blame the girl really... she was just glad they had stayed good friends. Still, she had hoped to have grandsons running around by now.

Rushing to catch up, the two quickly followed Helen; once at the door, Magdalene put her thumb on the small key pad protruding on the right side of the door way.

They all heard the lock open before Cecille's disembodied voice was heard. "Welcome home Magdalene, I see we have guests; I have already informed Abigail and Herbert so there's two guest rooms waiting. Supper will be ready in one hour. That should give everyone a chance to freshen up or change. If anyone needs anything else please do not hesitate to call out my name!"

Nodding, Magdalene waved at the hologram of her mother standing in front of the door. "Thank you Cecille, I am sure we can manage now."

Leading the way inside once her mother disappeared, Magdalene showed the two to their rooms; afterwards, she wearily trudged down the hallway to her own at the far end. Walking inside, Maggie grinned at her maid. "Can you ask Samantha to go see to Helen, she has always liked your daughter?"

Abigail nodded with a grin. "Already done, Cecille informed me Helen was here so I sent for her... she should be there by now. Your bath is ready; I put the blue summer dress on the bed for your dinner attire. I will go down now to help with supper if there is nothing else you need."

Magdalene waved her out. "A bath is all I want right now."

Abigail nodded then left.

Pulling her clothes off in unseemly haste, Magdalene crawled into her deep Jacuzzi tub; settling back, she turned on the jets with a sigh of pleasure. She was asleep in moments, beyond exhausted and still stiff from being thrown to the hard cement earlier.

*********************

Alexandrina stared in admiration. "That is your trailer; it looks more like a home on wheels... its huge!"

Shadow Hunter laughed mischievously. "Ah... but just wait; you have not seen the best part yet. Where is a good place to park it? It will need quite a bit of room to set up."

Before Alexandrina could say a word, Dan came around the corner having heard the sound of an engine. He stared thoughtfully at the huge motor home. Finally, he gestured for the driver to follow him.

Trotting to the far side of the barn, the older man waved for them to park beside it. It would be nestled in-between the horse barn and the big Quonset that held all the machinery to run the farm. Here it would be out of the way, but easily gotten too.

Walking over, Shadow Hunter stood beside Dan with a nod of thanks. "This will be perfect, lots of room for my rig to set up... plus, adequate room for my horses to graze."

Watching in amazement, Alexandrina saw the roof lift itself off the motor home. Once it opened, four sides rose up then added another story before the roof dropped back down sealing shut.

Next, the back moved out adding another ten feet to its length. It dropped down closer to the ground and a fence pulled away from the back; extending it another fifteen feet. A huge back door dropped down allowing three horses to walk out. Nonchalantly, they began eating grass.

Finally, two slides slid out; at the same time, stairs to the front of the small house dropped down. Alex couldn't see the back, but figured there would be more slide outs to add more rooms.

Seeing Alex's awed look, Shadow Hunter chuckled. "There are four bedrooms upstairs. The slide out just past the cab of the rig is a full computer room with a lab attached. The slide out closer to the back just before the horse stalls is a full kitchen and dining room then there's the living room between it, and the stairs going into the front entry. There is a slide out in the back; it becomes a deck with a Jacuzzi tub built in. You can also find near the back entrance a small laundry room, plus a bathroom. There is stairs there to reach the upper floor on the far side. You should be able to see the outline of my bike near the back, when I am not riding it... that is where it's stored. This is my home away from the ranch, it goes almost everywhere with me."

Impressed, Alexandrina gestured inquisitively towards the unit. "That must have cost you quite a pretty penny!"

Shrugging dismissively, Shadow Hunter paused for a moment. Finally, he nodded decisively; having nothing to hide, he answered honestly. "When I turned of age my bow was given to me, it included a journal with a package of papers. Inside, there was a bank account number. When I left home I went to Ontario first, I found an account worth just over two million in it. Where the money came from... nobody seems to know."

Figuring this would be a good time to discuss his assistants, Hunter gestured towards the cab of his unit. "While I was there I investigated a strange shapeshifter that seemed to be after two street kids. They tried to get help from a couple older bums that were in a rat infested alley; the two men, not understanding the language were trying to get rid of them. I had to kill the wolf in order to help the kids, so I took the two preteens in. Both are still with me today, they keep my rig up to date and running smoothly. I am sure you will meet them in the next few days, right now I imagine they just want to go to their rooms to sleep... it was a long drive for them."

Alexandrina nodded, not all that worried about it; they would bump into each other eventually... she was sure. "You will be moving into your rig tonight then?"

Shaking his head in disagreement, Shadow Hunter waved towards the ranch house. "Nope, I will stay in the main house for now. Once you need my room I will move, since I have an extra room you are more than welcomed to use it if your room is needed by others."

Inclining her head in thanks, Alex answered hurriedly when she heard the roar of another engine coming fast. "Thank you, I will keep that in mind."

Leaving quickly with a brief smile, Alexandrina went to meet the next vehicle as it rolled to a stop in front of the ranch house.

Dan trotted up beside Alex, so Shadow Hunter turned away needing to go look after his horses.

A private shuttle bus that came from the airport pulled in and two men followed by three women exited; Alexandrina rushed over to exchange hugs before she turned to the older of the three women, she was a Seeker stationed at their castle in Wales. "Gloria, nice to see you... Magdalene didn't come with you?"

Shaking her head, Gloria gestured in denial. "No, she got off in Calgary; the second Seeker said she will call you tonight."

Alexandrina sighed in disappointment then shrugged before her face saddened. "I am sorry to hear about the deaths at the castle. We lost one of our Seeker's here too."

Wilting in fear, Gloria wrung her hands in agitation. "It was the scariest thing I ever witnessed; unfortunately, we were all powerless to stop it. Only Magdalene's timely arrival saved the three of us!"

Grimacing in confusion, Alex reached over covering Gloria's agitated hands. "Yes, for some reason they seem to be afraid of us. Come, I will take you upstairs; Dan can take the men to the barracks to settle in. Supper is about to be put on the table, but we will wait for you to join us."

Not one of the three men was a Seeker; they were here only for the retreat. Food was served in the bunkhouse for the ones wishing to attend the fair; Dan would eat with them so they wouldn't feel left out.

The house was reserved for Seeker's, dignitaries, or religious leaders. Although, most liked to stay with their own people. If there were overflows, the deck would be utilized; they also had several pavilions that could be used if they were desperate.

It took another good two hours before everyone was gathered for supper... condolences were given to the new arrivals. Afterwards, a prayer was said for the slain Seeker's followed by supper being served; the cook had outdone himself again as everyone dug into the huge farm raised ham, scalloped potatoes, fresh vegetables, cucumbers in a heavy cream sauce then a deep dish apple pie was eaten for desert.

Not a word was spoken, and only the sounds of forks scrapping on plates could be heard.

*****

Shadow Hunter frowned; he could feel Alexandrina's sadness even from here as they slowly walked up to the rooms quietly. The Cree/Oriental Shaman waited until they were in the little hallway before surprising himself, he reached out to take Alexandrina's hand.

Hunter ignored the shock that he got and kept Black Cougar's hand in his; the Cree/Oriental Shaman reached up with his other hand to stroke her cheek. "Are you okay... that frown does not suit you one bit!"

A thrill shivered through Alex at the gentle tender touch, she felt the effects right down to her toes. She had never had such a fast reaction to any man before... it was a bit disconcerting. "Goodnight."

Allowing Alexandrina to pull away without comment, Hunter stared at her closing door with a bemused look; he rubbed his tingling fingers together before sighing in confusion.

Every time he touched her, not only did he get a burning need for more but the Cree/Oriental Shaman also ended up with a shiver of warning. Something was not right... he just could not figure out what it was. Shrugging, he knew it would come to light eventually. Turning, Hunter disappeared into his own room.

*****

Alexandrina leaned back against the closed door and stared across her bedroom sightlessly for a long moment; contemplating her mixed up feelings before a smile lit up her face. She liked him, unsure why... Black Cougar just could not seem to help it.

Pushing away from the door, Alex walked over then pushed the button on her alcove to allow her desk to drop down. "Cecille, can you get a hold of both of my sisters, and brother; of course, my father too... please."

Two panels opened on her laptop; she could tell by the images that her youngest sister and her half-brother were with their father on the private jet.

Magdalene was at home in her room with a book open in her lap.

Fai grinned at her oldest sister. "Feeling a little flushed, are we? Who's the new man... the Shaman?"

Magdalene laughed with Fai at her older sister's reddening cheekbones, when Alexandrina's blush deepened. "Yep, I was reading a steamy romance, but wasn't even at the good part yet when I felt this shiver of desire course down my spine... big sister is in love!"

Snickering with a knowing nod, Fai agreed with Maggie. "It has to be love, if it was just a fleeting shot of desire we would not have felt it too."

A loud harrumph sounded off to Fai's left as Chang cleared his throat noisily to get their attention. "You three are aware that there is others present... right!"

The older triplets cheeks reddened even more before Magdalene taking pity on Alexandrina changed the conversation to the things that were hunting magic users. "I was thinking a lot about Alex's victim that lived. If we could find all the hosts that are willingly bonded, they could be brought here to keep them safe; those things would have no choice but to draw out the forcibly bonded ones afterwards... freeing the hosts. It would help us out tremendously; they wouldn't have much choice if it needs magic that badly."

Chang shook his head with a grim sigh. "There's hundreds of thousands of people out there who have bonded with an Earth spirit, most are not aware that they have even done so. I am just glad those things take every scrap of magic away with them, since there has been quite a rash of deaths the last couple of weeks. Thankfully, Fai has not had any feelings of pain from Mother Earth. It will be a couple days yet before we can get to the farm, so everyone keep safe; try staying away from those things... please! At least, until we figure out what they want the magic for besides filling in their wings. Goodnight girls I love you both, talk to you tomorrow night."

More goodnights were exchanged before the screen went dark.

***************

Magdalene frowned in annoyance; she had forgotten about that feather again. Oh well, she would tell her dad tomorrow. Settling back, she fell asleep instantly but nightmares plagued her sleep.

# CHAPTER FOUR

Fai woke when she felt a touch on her shoulder. Inhaling, she knew immediately it was her father. Even though the Tianming Monk never wore deodorant or anything scented, his unique smell was quite distinctive. Every living thing had its own scent but humans like to mask theirs most of the time. "Are we home?"

Grunting in aggravation, Chang shook his head even though she wouldn't see it... it was done more out of habit. "No, we are not! Magdalene forgot to mention that she had a feather from that creature. We only landed long enough to grab fuel before doing a new flight plan; we took off immediately for Calgary. Red Wolf wants to meet us for brunch, so go freshen up before we disembark."

Standing up after unbuckling her seat belt, Fai turned right; she made sure to count ten steps before going left one step, which brought her to the entrance of the ladies room.

Turning to his youngest son, Chang gestured thoughtfully. "All the equipment needed is in the lab at the farm house, why don't you stay here with Magdalene and try to figure out what those things are; I can be Fai's assistant for now, she does not have anything scheduled that requires your immediate attention, anyway."

Nodding in agreement, Ronin walked over to his compartment before taking out his two duffle bags. One was quite long having his nun chucks, staff, and both Oriental daggers inside.

Ronin had designed the staff with a long elastic band inside it that would loosen on each end. When the silver tip on the last three inches were rotated counter clockwise; a hair line seam in the center barely noticeable by the naked eye would open up... he could fold it into two parts.

If Ron pushed a button that was in the center, the elastic would snap it back together; a sharp twist would make it a single piece once more. Otherwise, it would be too long for him to carry around in a duffle bag.

Fai's walking cane had given Ronin the idea, but he had not liked the flimsiness of it; getting an idea, he added threads so a simple twist would keep it tight when it was in one piece.

On occasions, when in tight places Ron could leave the two loose in order to use it as a long extended nun chucks. He had learned the hard way when first learning to use it, when split in two that the other end could come back with a wicked snap... hitting the wielder instead.

After several nasty bruises, Ronin preferred to leave it together; unless, he was surrounded by several assailants... it definitely came in handy at that time.

Both, Chang and his son had a private guard's license so they were able to carry weapons in plain sight.

Chang also had a small pistol, which was only for show... he never used it. The only time he could not have it, was in a courtroom; that's why he always sat in the hallway reception area waiting for his daughter and charge.

Once outside, they climbed into the waiting escalade. This one was a deep wine colour; the driver nodded acknowledgement before putting the partition up between them. Immediately, the vehicle took off.

*********************

'SMACK... THUMP!'

Alexandrina grinned in triumph as she dropped down on top of Shadow Hunter then straddled him; again, the two of them had met in the weight room first thing this morning.

Once done warming up, they went for a swim before they came here for another bout of training together. Panting in exertion, Alex gasped out. "Gotcha..."

Shadow Hunter grinned up at her in surrender. He waited until she relaxed then grabbed her by the waist before flipping them around, now he was the one on top. He stared intently down at the lightest green eyes Hunter had ever seen. A thin black vertical pupil went from just below the top of her iris then almost to the bottom of her eyelid. Golden rays flared out from there before a dark green ring surrounded the iris... reminding him of a cat. They had a sharp upward tilt.

Shaking off his straying thoughts, Hunter bent then gave her a kiss; before Alex could protest, he rolled away with a laugh. Lying on the floor beside her, the Cree/Oriental's comment came out breathlessly. "Maybe, but I just won."

Unable to help giving a knowing laugh at his smug tone, Alexandrina sat up; she bent over him before lightly touching her lips to Shadow Hunters. She rolled away quickly, hiding a fiery blush at her boldness. "Breakfast should be ready now... I am starved."

Smirking, Shadow Hunter got up. He was definitely glad he had initiated the first kiss; it broke the ice a bit between them. Keeping it playful helped Alex to stay relaxed at the mischievousness of it before she reciprocated.

Hunter was hoping for more of the same, but she was untouched as he was. He felt drawn to Black Cougar, which intrigued him... there was something unusual about her. The Cree/Oriental Shaman felt a resistance in himself too, where the reluctance was coming from he did not know or even why it was there.

Once downstairs they quietly entered the dining room, both immersed in their own thoughts.

*****************

Chang took the feather from Magdalene so he could study it more closely. He flipped it around looking for any kind of differences from a bird's plumage. "It's mainly black; to me it looks exactly like a raven's feather. If I had seen it on the ground that is what I would have thought it was. If you look closer though, there is a lot of silver along the edges and it is three times the size of a birds. You said it had more white feathers than black... with several layers?"

Nodding with a faraway look in her eyes, Magdalene brought up an image of the thing that had attacked them. "Yes, it had a ridge of thick muscles between its shoulder blades that ran up and around the shoulder then down its chest; its torso was twice the size of mine. The extra ridge ran down the back to just below the ribs. Bones were protruding from just below its shoulder possibly connected to the clavicle bone. An additional thick layer of muscle or membrane with extra tendons connected everything could be seen... with pinpricks all over it. They started about a finger wide on each side of the ridge. There were only two thin layers of feathers at the top of the wings with several scattered around the center of the membrane; one layer was around the bottom edge. I would say it might end up with at least four layers of feathers. It had breasts but no nipples... no hair on the vagina either. It had thin black hair about shoulder length. Fingers and toes looked normal, but the nails were a bit long. It shimmered as if not stable or anchored in this time. I think maybe its prison still has a hold on it somehow."

Rubbing his chin reflectively, Ronin inclined his head in acknowledgement. Using a napkin, he took it tentatively before studying the feather his father passed to him.

Thankfully, there did not seem to be any harm in touching it since Maggie had handled it several times. If Ron was in his lab, he would take more precautions. "That makes sense; it might need its full wings to break loose. I imagine, once it severs its bonds the creature will be completely in our time then it will probably have nipples and hair. Remember, I told you years ago that the shadows of magic did not seem rooted here. Not until they bond willingly to a host that is... maybe, that's why the person dies when the magic is drawn out. The ones that force a host to bond still are not fully bound to this reality so those things can draw it out without killing the host. Because humans of today are completely bound to this time but the forced magic isn't, when we draw it out the person dies since they are no longer completely in this aeon reality. I think what is happening is the barrier that holds back forbidden magic is dissipating, as it does more magic is available for humans to use. At one time, only the Great Spirit had available magic."

Pausing, Ron shrugged before gesturing decisively. "The Mother Earth would have to have magic too. That leads me to believe that magic users if not bonded willingly, will then be stuck in two different time realities. If my inkling is correct, aeon realities which are Earths true timelines are hidden in the heavens."

Passing the feather to his half-sister, Ronin continued pensively. "I also think we are looking at the shadows that are changing their hosts wrong. Take the ones we assume are vampires; if you look closer, their skin is a sickly green with small fangs. Their eyes are a burnt orange to a light brown in colour. I am guessing when the barrier disappears entirely... they will be orcs or goblins. Therefore, the ones with wings and no fangs could possibly be fairies. There are quite a few shapeshifters already. We haven't seen anything looking like elves yet or unicorns. Neither have centaurs, giants, or ogres surfaced."

Frowning in irritation, Ronin shrugged in apology then waved away his last statement. "No, sorry that is not quite right either; over the last hundred years humans have grown bigger, six to seven feet is now the average height. Close to eight feet in height is becoming more frequent over the last five years or so. Surprisingly, there were two cases in the last couple of years where over ten feet has been reached."

Rubbing his eyes tiredly, Chang gave an aggrieved sigh before looking over at his son resignedly. "Are you sure?"

Shrugging uncertainly, Ronin gestured unknowingly. "Well, not a hundred percent certain... but, pretty positive!"

Reaching over, Chang touched his youngest daughters hand to get her attention. "What do you think White Buffalo?"

Drumming her fingers lightly on the table, she thought about Ronin's theory; Fai finally nodded in agreement, as her fingers stilled. "I think he's right, at least for most of it. It is still a big question mark on the vampires and werewolves, they could have been a result of Lucifer, or his corrupted angels experimenting... we could end up with them also."

Grunting in frustrated acknowledgement, Chang rubbed his forehead in resignation. "I knew you were going to say that!"

Laughing at her father, Magdalene gestured teasingly. "Well, why did you ask then?"

Giving his second daughter a disgruntled look, Chang otherwise ignored her teasing. "Anyway, I don't think we need to worry about that right now. As long as the barrier remains, we have time. My main concern right now is what to do about these Nephilim, the children of the Grigori... if Ronin is correct? Maggie, did you get any sense of evil or malevolence from the one you attacked? You are the only one who has seen it up close, Alex got there after the fact! A couple of the young students that are in training saw it for a brief moment, but only from a distance."

Magdalene frowned thinking back. Finally, she shrugged indecisively. "No, not really... I switched shapes so fast I had no chance to study it; the only thing I could feel was a sense of uncertainty or maybe it was shock."

Frowning, Chang looked at his son to see what he thought.

Scratching his chin pensively, Ronin was just as baffled; finally, he dropped his hand with a shrug. "Not totally sure, but it could be because the girls were born with magic. They can use it without bonding to the Earth's shadow magic... unlike everyone else. All other users have to bond first. Even though they are born able to make use of it, they need the Earth's shadows to wield it with any success. Not the girls, they are magical in their own right."

Scowling in irritation, Fai interrupted heatedly there was a touch of jealousy in her voice that she couldn't quite hide. "Alex and Maggie have anyway! I do not have any; unless, you call trapping magic inside me... a magic ability. Shapeshifting would be so much cooler!"

Chang scowled in disapproval at his youngest daughter's resentful tone. He knew, to her it seemed she had been born with all the bad family traits but he could feel a dormant power still untapped deep inside her; what it was he couldn't say. He had a sneaky suspicion they did not really want to find out either.

Reaching over to pat his youngest daughters hand consolingly, Chang tried to give her some reassuring guidance. "Your time will come, White Buffalo... patience!"

Sighing, Fai nodded as her resentment melted away. This jealousy was not a good thing; it was something that White Buffalo had struggled with her whole life. It seemed to disappear for a time, but would crop up occasionally. Quite unexpectedly, like now.

Turning back to his son, Chang continued the conversation. "Does that mean the girls are not rooted here then?"

Ronin grimaced, remembering the first incident when the two older girls changed their shape. "Do you recall when the girls first transformed; they had both disappeared for a good ten minutes. We were in England at the time checking into the disappearance of the mist around the Celtic Druid circle... in Snowdonia. If I remember correctly, there is a passage in the first Cecille's journal about her being drawn to Snowdonia when an earthquake hit in the late eighteen hundreds. It caused the mist around the mountain of Snowdonia to begin disappearing, all except for a small area around a Stonehenge. The mist refused anyone entry into the Druid circle, except for a chosen few... that is until the day we arrived."

Paused Ron smiled up at the waitress when she set his tea in front of him; he put some honey in it before continuing as if he had not been interrupted. "We raced there when a report reached us that the mist had retreated up to the edge of the Stonehenge and the first row of stones was now visible. When we investigated, we still could not enter but the girls disappeared. We originally thought they had run off so they could trick us into looking for them. It was a good ten minutes that they were gone; they finally reappeared in their animal forms."

Chuckling, Ronin remembered the shocked look on his father's face as he refilled his tea. "Afterwards, the Celtic prison shook savagely before more of the mist disappeared. Right up to the third section of stones... only the inner circle was still unattainable. I suspect the Stonehenge was a prison or a gateway to one of the heavens. The bible refers to one of the heavens being filled with water, which was above God's throne."

Taking a sip of his tea, Ron tried to remember specifics of the bible before looking at his father and completing his theory. "Supposedly, there are six or seven heavens. If the girls went to one of them to change into animal form that could mean when shapeshifting their human essence is trapped there... until they change back again."

Siting forward indignantly, Fai gestured sharply. "I never went into the mist father, it rebuffed me! All I remember is a sense of loss; I could not even feel my sisters anymore. We were thirteen, Black Cougar and Red Wolf both had their coming of age ceremony the day before since they had started bleeding already. I was late in blooming... I did not become a woman until almost fourteen."

Turning to his middle daughter, Chang frowned thoughtfully. "I forgot all about that do you remember anything Maggie?"

Thinking, Magdalene chewed on her inner lip trying to remember that far back; a bit of a pressure between her eyes throbbed briefly then settled. "I remember that Alex thought it would be funny to hide from Fai among the rocks. She loved to tease the baby of the family, she always said it was good practice for our blind youngest sister to find people using her other senses. Black Cougar found us a crevice between the rocks that had no mist; she grabbed my arm then pulled me over to it."

Feeling a severe headache coming, Magdalene pinched the bridge of her nose hoping to forestall the inevitable. "As we crouched there, I looked over my shoulder uneasily. Suddenly, the mist came hurtling forward and surrounded us. I couldn't even shout a warning in time. We couldn't see a thing, I remember feeling trapped... disoriented. We wandered where it would let us go but if we tried to turn in a different direction, a solid wall stopped us. The thick grey fog didn't seem to have an end to it. Neither could we see if our next step was safe or if we were walking off a cliff, it was that dense."

Gasping in surprise, Magdalene moaned painfully then grabbed her head, but continued doggedly on. "All I can remember is falling to our knees after what seemed like an eternity of walking. I curled into a fetal position on the ground as pain ripped through my muscles before all my joints snapped out of place. I heard Alex screaming beside me. Unfortunately, there was nothing I could do to help either of us."

Stiffing a moan of pain, Magdalene finished her explanation in a hurry. "I was drifting in and out of unconsciousness with no concept of time passing. Finally, I heard a whisper of comfort followed immediately by a warm soothing hand placed on my forehead. It brought me back from wherever my subconscious had taken me. The grey wall of fog unexpectedly disappeared, with it the pain eased. When I opened my eyes, I knew instantly that I was an animal. Everything that had happened in the mist vanished once I realized I could change into a wolf. I still get these headaches occasionally, thankfully not as bad. I never saw who touched me or maybe I just don't want to remember. Until now, I had forgotten the pain of the first transformation. Luckily it doesn't hurt when I shift into my spirit animal now, but it is quite uncomfortable."

Reaching over, Fai took her sisters hand in concern feeling Magdalene's pain as her own then leaned over to whisper in her ear. "Let the pain go. Shh, it cannot hurt you anymore!"

A glow in both the red patches of hair on the girl's heads pulse just a smidgen; Magdalene's frown eased instantly as the pain disappeared. The faint light was a quick flicker, hardly noticeable... unless staring right at the patches.

Tapping his index finger on the arms of his chair in satisfaction, Chang couldn't help a sigh of relief; well, at least now he knew what the headaches were about in the two older triplets. He had taken them in for tests when the headaches refused to go away, but nothing showed in the scans. Whatever or whoever had touched the girls did not want them to remember... he decided it was best for now to leave it that way.

Getting up, Chang touched his youngest daughters shoulder in warning. "Come, Fai; we need to get back if we are to make your meeting tomorrow. Ronin will stay with Magdalene and work on the feather."

Quickly, goodbyes were said; afterwards, the escalade disappeared around the corner as the remaining two walked to Magdalene's jeep.

About to climb into her car, Maggie stiffened instantly before looking around. She could feel someone or something staring intently at her. Turning in a complete circle Red Wolf searched, but saw no one. She could feel her wolf rear up wanting to be released.

Ronin stared at his half-sister in surprise as she turned looking for something, he could feel Magdalene struggling with herself then he noticed the little dagger strapped to her thigh glowing. "Maggie, what's the matter... what is it?"

Spinning around, Magdalene stared at her half-brother intently concentrating on him as she pushed down the need to change. Suddenly, the feeling of danger disappeared as quickly as it had started. The middle triplet slumped against the door in relief before wiping the sweat off her forehead with her sleeve. She felt physically drained, as if she had ran a full mile.

Magdalene threw her keys to Ron as she walked around the car; she felt weak, exhausted by her inner struggle to stop the wolf from taking over. "Here, you drive... I will explain on the way."

Nodding perplexed, Ronin walked around to the driver's side; Magdalene never allowed anyone to drive her pride and joy.

Quickly, Ron headed to the homestead that they all called home... their safe haven. He couldn't help thinking that next week would be their seventeenth anniversary there.

********************

Alexandrina dismounted, she smiled in satisfaction over at Shadow Hunter. She had surprised the Cree/Oriental Shaman earlier by taking him out and showing him around the retreat. It was a beautiful sunny day, perfect for a ride.

It was a quarter section; fifty acres was in a hay mixture suitable for horses or visiting animals, with thirty acres in oats. The rest was ranch yard with a huge garden in the back that the Seekers in training looked after. There was sixty acres of fair grounds, pavilions, riding arenas, horse, cow, and bullpens... farrier barns with a large shop took up a good portion of land.

Rows of spectators seats were everywhere, most would seat twelve across and twelve up allowing a hundred and forty-four spectators in each section.

Booths for food were separate and scattered throughout the fairgrounds. They all had their own cooking nooks that included deep fryers, a stove, and a fridge with a large freezer; all that they needed to bring was food, even some of that was supplied.

A long building that had once been a lean too for horses had been modified. Now it was set up in sections with a wall between each to help give them a bit of privacy. Fifteen, ten by eight booths were available for all types of vendors who would show up to sell trinkets, perfumes, Avon, author's books, face painting, kid's tattoos, fresh veggies, or fruits.

Of course, some would bring their own tents and set up in designated areas depending on what they were selling.

There was a bakery with a butcher shop across from the vendor building, where a pig or a cow would be roasted for the festivities; fresh meat could be purchased from there as well.

An inspector would be showing up any day now to make sure all inspections were up to date. Two would show up on fair day to make sure everyone complied with the rules. All food vendors or anyone bringing homemade preserves had to be certified with registered safe food documents with home inspection reports done on a yearly basis.

Shadow Hunter was impressed. "You have quite a beautiful place here, how long have you been doing this?"

Grinning in pleasure at his obvious approval, Alexandrina gathered her reins as she started walking slowly towards the barn. "I had just turned sixteen when I arrived here to go to school. Seems I was too smart for my own good, so I ended up skipping a few grades. I came here to go to University; they have one of the best law schools in Toronto... law happens to be my passion. My father found an ad for renting rooms so we came here to check it out. At that time, it just had a riding arena with a few outbuildings; they were struggling financially since the advent of self-driving vehicles and short distant flying cars. With such advanced vehicle options, horse owners are getting quite rare. My father bought them out on the condition they stay here with me as my guardian while I was in school."

Looking around in satisfaction, Alexandrina gestured towards the fairgrounds before continuing. "The retreat was my idea it quickly flourished. Most of the money to continue running this place now is by donations and we get several government grants. We have many corporate sponsors too, like the Calgary Stampede committee, sporting goods stores, etc. Local businesses donate prizes; of course, we hit the bigger stores in Toronto as well. One of my younger...!"

Alexandrina's voice trailed off in surprise when the sound of an approaching helicopter drowned her out. Frowning, she looked up then saw the CSIS emblem on the side door.

Turning without waiting for her riding partner, Alexandrina sprinted to the barn pulling her horse along. Quickly, Black Cougar gave instructions to the stable boy before racing to the back of the ranch house with Shadow Hunter following closely.

Stopping, they waited for the four people disembarking to get to them; it gave Alexandrina a chance to study them curiously. There was one woman, two men, and one teenage girl around sixteen she judged.

The older man she recognized as the head of her special unit JTF2, which was an Emergency Response Team in Canada. He was wearing his official red RCMP uniform... Major General Anthony Terrif, she had several dealings with him in the past. He was one of the few who knew that she had magic and was a shapeshifter.

It took Alex several minutes to recognize the other man since it was not often she saw the Inspector General of CSIS, most stayed close to their computers watching for any terror attacks or cybercrimes.

Both females were British; Alexandrina frowned when she got a better look at the girl. She was a Princess, if she remembered correctly eighth in-line for the crown. Named after her paternal grandmother, she was the favourite of the people to ascend the throne.

After the longest reigning Queen in history had passed on, the royal line had gone into a downward spiral. Several deaths had occurred, some natural... others not, but never proven.

The woman looked around nervously, she held the girl by the upper arm. Nanny turned bodyguard, Alexandrina figured. She was dressed in a soft blue pantsuit; her brown hair was in a short pixie cut.

The Princess was in spandex leggings with a plain shirt trying to be inconspicuous. Her blonde hair was coiled in a bun. It was long almost to her waist, if Alex remembered correctly. The girl was just about to turn seventeen.

Scowling grimly, Alexandrina could feel trouble brewing; what could the head of CSIS, Inspector General Stevenson want.

Having the JTF2 Major General Anthony with him did not bode well for her piece of mind... that she knew for sure.

Saluting smartly, Alexandrina beckoned everyone to follow her not wanting to talk out here. Silently, she led everyone into the back entryway.

Of course, the head mistress of the coven was standing in the doorway with a door down the hallway opened waiting for them. Like usual she was one step ahead of Alex. "I put a small table with several chairs inside, tea will arrive shortly."

Getting a grateful nod of approval from Alexandrina, Tanya turned then disappeared.

Going inside, Alexandrina allowed everyone but Shadow Hunter to sit; she motioned silently for the Cree/Oriental Shaman to stand at the door to guard it.

Inclining his head in agreement, Shadow Hunter closed the door. Turning to face inside, he stood in front of it with a slightly open stance before crossing both arms.

Hunter was quite surprised she let him stay. Already, the Shaman could feel a bond forming between them. One of trust, friendship, and love; the three key ingredients needed for a long lasting relationship.

Looking down at his crossed arms, Shadow Hunter saw his watch blinking... quickly he switched it off. Black Cougar trusted him; there was no way he would jeopardise their budding relationship by recording this conversation.

Gesturing at the chairs in invitation, Alexandrina gave her unexpected guests reassurances. "This room is completely soundproof; nobody outside will hear what transpires here so feel free to speak openly. Major General and Inspector General it is such an honor and a complete surprise to see you both... especially together."

The girl pulled her arm away from the woman then gave a loud harrumph of anger before dropping into a chair sullenly. The Princess crossed her arms; obviously, not wishing to be here.

Hearing a knock, Shadow Hunter turned; he opened the door and took the tray with a nod of thanks before closing it tightly... refusing to let anyone in.

Waiting until everyone sat, except for Hunter... who returned to the door after depositing the tea tray; Alexandrina gave out refreshments before settling back with a cup of coffee. Alex having grown up part time in England was well versed in the intricacies of court.

The Inspector General of CSIS sat forward then gestured toward the door. "The man is trustworthy; I do not remember ever seeing him before Lieutenant Ryuu?"

Nodding decisively at the Inspector General, Alexandrina fibbed a bit; she hadn't asked him yet, but planned to do so in the next few days... Alex was sure he would accept. "Yes, he is in training at the moment so hasn't been sworn in, I can do so now if it's necessary?"

Major General Anthony interrupted and waved away the offer. "That will not be necessary Lieutenant Ryuu; your word is all that is needed! Inspector General Stevenson is just being overly cautious."

Stevenson frowned in aggravation at Anthony, but did not refute him as he leaned forward intently. "There has been a number of deaths recently, by nobody seems to know exactly what. The victim just sits staring into space with a shocked look as if seeing something they do not like. That is until the Princess's governess saw a woman with wings going after one of the palaces maids; she saw it draw out something through her mouth. Finished with the servant, it tried to go after the Princess but was stopped by the governess."

Looking at the woman in surprise, Alexandrina gestured knowingly. "You are a seer; do you have any other magic?"

Silvia Jones shook her head. "No, I can see things but have no other abilities. My charge can levitate plus move small objects with her mind."

Smiling, Black Cougar turned to the girl then put out her hand... hoping she would take it. "Hello Victoria, Maggie has mentioned you several times; I am Alexandrina, but you can call me Alex if you wish."

Frowning in surprise, Victoria reached out automatically to take the offered hand. "She has, I did not think she would remember me; you look like her and that thing who killed my maid. It did not have the white in its hair though."

Grimacing in relief, Alexandrina felt the girl's aura through their joined hands. "Well, I am glad to hear that there is something different about it. I will let the others know."

The girl had a bit of magic ability in her own right, which was highly unusual without bonding to the Earth's magic. Even so, without the bond it was negligible.

Magdalene had offered to help the girl but Victoria had refused, not wanting magic to be part of her life; her aspirations that long ago day ran to being Queen someday, Maggie had told her sister so they had let her be. Being that she had seven or eight others ahead of her vying for the throne it was unlikely she would ascend; maybe, the girl had changed her mind.

Pulling her hand away from the Princess, Alexandrina turned back to Inspector General Stevenson.

Black Cougars curiosity was beginning to get the best of her. "What can I do for you today? I am officially on holidays for another three weeks. I need to help the retreat get ready for its annual festival. My Guardian with the help of my half-brother is investigating other sightings of this creature. So far, it seems to be still trapped in-between; which means it is not visible to regular humans only to magic users. The goal so far seems to be stealing magic from humans who have bonded willingly or unwillingly. Unfortunately, some die from the shock but thankfully not all. We suspect they are from before the great flood, in Noah's time that makes them part Grigori and part human. The bible refers to them as Nephilim... so far all we have is theory to go on."

Inspector General Stevenson grimaced incredulously then gave Lieutenant Ryuu a shocked unbelievable look. "Are you telling me that the story in the bible is true? We can now expect to be haunted by giants that are half human and half angel... I find that pretty hard to believe!"

Shrugging negligently, Alexandrina sat back with a sigh of resignation. "Believe what you want, but we suspect that these things are not the giant sized Nephilim. They are the other ones... the female ones that take more after their angel forebears. They were imprisoned because of who their parents were, and for what their brothers were doing in Sodom and Gomorrah. They would not have been affected by the flood like the more human giants, so instead were imprisoned between worlds. The gateway was in the mists of Snowdonia, which has dissipated slowly over the years until only their prison was hidden. Now, there is no more mist. The stone hedge keeping them captive disappeared leaving only a black broken pillar in the center. The tower is still in Wales, but harmless now. The Nephilim's wings are still straggly, but every time it draws in magic, they fill out more. What will happen once they are full we do not know. Revenge would be my guess, whether against God or man... is speculation at this point."

Inspector General Stevenson looked over at Major General Anthony incredulously. "So, this is what your special units do! Are they all running around making up stories of long ago creatures... or just magical phenomenon's?"

Silvia Jones sat forward indignantly. "I will have you know that creature is real, whether you want to believe it or not! My charge will be staying here until we figure out what that thing is... I need to know why it is after her!"

Smiling at the angry nanny, Alexandrina reached over to pat her hand in appeasement. "You are welcome to stay here for as long as you want; I will have the apartment upstairs readied for you. I am sure both of you will love the festival we have every year. I will have my two assistants come and be on hand for additional bodyguards for the Princess, both men can see the Nephilim... since they have magic abilities."

Looking back at Inspector General Stevenson, Alexandrina shrugged with a frown at the stubborn CSIS General. "It does not matter to me if you believe; only a handful of people right now know the truth. Mother Earth is slowly dying, as she does more of her magic leaks out, once it's released it is available for humans to use. Once the Mother dies, the barrier between heaven and earth will evaporate... what awaits us after that is unknown. There are five more prisons scattered around the world, what they hold none of us wants to know. We have gathered as many magic users as possible over the years that can bond willingly, they all gather here yearly. This way when the unthinkable happens, these people will be able to help humans around the world; the Seekers will be humanities last hope."

Sighing regretfully, Alexandrina sat forward then gestured forlornly. "Unfortunately, many have died these last two weeks thanks to those things. We know there is two of them for sure, can you imagine what would happen if the other prisons opened or even what could come out of them! My hope is that having so many magic users in one spot might draw those things here. My half-brother will be coming here soon to help out, but the others are busy right now so can't be here until much later! We will do what we can to help."

Major General Anthony sighed uneasily. "Hopefully, I will not be alive by then to see it. I will send over Charles and Tyler to help you; they are both bonded so they should be able to see those things too. Your partners will be needed at the precinct."

Gesturing in concern towards the shocked Inspector General, Alexandrina saw his mouth quivering completely beyond words now. "Will he be okay or should he forget?"

Frowning in thought, Major General Anthony finally shook his head in resignation. "Unfortunately, it is time for the higher ups to be briefed; if the prisons are beginning to open it is only a matter of time until the rest appear. Let's hope they are not full of Giant Nephilim or rebellious Grigori... we might all be doomed if they are."

Shrugging resignedly, Alexandrina tried for a lighter tone but failed miserably. "What is meant to be will be there is nothing any of us can do to stop it. Ronin is trying to find a way to trap it, we need to try communicating with it; or failing that, a way to neutralize it would be best. Once it is fully in this world it might be easier or impossible, that's what we need to figure out before it's too late?"

Major General Anthony stood up... he put a hand on Stevenson's shoulder. "Come along, Inspector General; I will take you to my office where a full disclosure of my special units will be available. After, you can take everything to the Prime Minister of Canada then to the Chief of Staff."

Turning to the Princess once the two men left; Alexandrina smiled. Victoria did not know that they were related and she would never be told, which explained how she ended up with a touch of magic. Her great, great grandfather was the son of the first twins born so Alex was her great, great aunt.

Alex stood up before beckoning. "Come Princess, I will take you to your apartment upstairs then have your new bodyguards contacted. I know it is isolated here but by the weekend, this place will be bursting at the seams."

Trying to be as dramatic as possible, Alexandrina waved her arms expressively wanting the Princess to be as excited over the festival as she was. "There will be all sorts of amusement rides, fortune telling, flame throwers that do fire tricks, medieval jousting, sword fighting, horsemanship classes, and demonstrations. Vendors from all over the world will be here, magic will be everywhere; the very air will crackle with it. Every type of performer from all around the world will be here showing off their special talents... foreign food, costumes, plus exotic perfumes will be available for purchase."

Shadow Hunter opened the door then bowed as the three women exited. The Cree/Oriental Shaman fell into step behind them, listening with half an ear to Alexandrina's rambling commentary on the festival to come.

She had a half-brother; the Cree/Oriental Shaman was rather surprised by that, He would have to get his assistant to see if there is any information available on him.

Hunter still had a feeling something was not quite right about her... what it was he had no clue. At the same time, he felt drawn to her.

Alexandrina had explained to him what the grey shapes Hunter was seeing were. She also told him why sometimes he had to exercise one from its victim. Black Cougar was quite excited when told his Celtic dragon medallion repelled the shadows that forced magic users without killing the host.

Giving a huge sigh of aggravation, Shadow Hunter grimaced in irritation; they had not had any time at all to talk. It seemed that every time they had a moment to do so, someone or something interfered.

Hunter had noticed that the grey shapes were everywhere these days filtering from one person to another randomly. Usually, one or two were around the house somewhere until Alex walked into the room that is. Instantly, they would all disappear; not even one shadow of magic could be seen afterwards. Were they afraid of her or was the unease he kept feeling the same reason they avoided her.

Alexandrina had mentioned a Guardian a couple times now, where he was at the Cree/Oriental Shaman did not know. It was a bit confusing since his teacher had told him a Tianming Guardian always stayed with their charge. He had been here now for a week and not one sign of the Tianming Monk was evident. Could it be Black Cougars half-brother?

Shadow Hunters contemplation was interrupted when the three women entered the apartment; he waited silently in the hallway, needing a few minutes to try figuring out what was bothering him so much.

Alexandrina came out a few minutes later then they began descending to the main floor. Hunter turned to Alex inquisitively. "Your Guardian does not stay here with you?"

Looking over at Shadow Hunter, Alexandrina smiled. "No, he always stays with..."

"First Seeker...!"

Frowning in annoyance at the flushed youngster hurrying up the stairs, Alexandrina sighed in resignation. "What seems to be the problem, Shane?"

Shane stopped a few steps below before beckoning insistently. "The Algonquin Chiefs are here and right behind them is the carnival. The head Seeker wants to know where you wish to have them set up."

Grinning in delight, Alexandrina gave Shadow Hunter a playful nudge before answering the over excited boy. "Hunter, come on you can help me... we will talk later. Shane, I need to stop and make a quick call to my partners then we will be right out."

Nodding eagerly, Shane turned; he rushed back down followed closely by Alex and Hunter

Waiting in the entryway while Alexandrina made her call, Shadow Hunter could not help but wonder if something was being hidden that he was not meant to know. Patience, he could not help thinking... eventually everything would be revealed to him.

Putting the phone down, Alexandrina gestured impatiently in excitement. "Now it begins, come on!"

They rushed out to complete chaos.

**********

Fai grimaced then pushed a button on her cell phone. "Siri, what time is it?"

A disembodied voice answered immediately. "Four fifty pm."

Grimacing knowingly, Fai couldn't help but ask anyway. "Siri has headquarters called yet?"

The expected answer was received all too quickly. "No."

An exaggerated rattle of papers was loudly shuffled in the corner by Chang before a chuckle of amusement floated towards the aggravated youngest triplet. "Getting yourself all worked up Fai is not going to help any."

Sighing plaintively, Fai gestured sharply. "I know father, but this infernal waiting around unable to go anywhere except into the provincial building is starting to wear on my nerves. Why is it taking them so long to decide on a new CSIS Chief... it's been over a week now. I was hoping to go to the retreat this year for the magic festival, every year something seems to come up so I can't go."

Chang's voice held a note of caution and sympathy. "It will take as long as needed, patience Fai..."

Unexpectedly, Chang sprang to his feet in a hurry; in one smooth motion, he was pulling his dragon sword out of the scabbard while vaulting over his desk. The sword was never far from his hand even at home. He stood protectively in front of his youngest daughter and charge.

The hum of Chang's sword in warning was all that was needed to know something was not right. It wasn't until the Guardian held his sword that he saw a shimmer in the corner, one of those Nephilim or Grigori women materialized.

She had scraggly black thin hair; it was short with only five to ten white feathers. It could be the one Magdalene described since it had small breasts with no nipples or hair at the junction of its thighs. Its face was full of deep crevices... it was ancient looking. It had long nails, not quite claws but close. The Tianming Monk didn't see any resemblance to his daughters at all.

The creature stopped then put out a hand towards the sword.

Chang frowned grimly when his sword flickered for a moment in uncertainty. Suddenly, the soft white glow turned an angry red for a couple seconds before a humming vibrated through it... helping it turn back to its soft white glow.

The woman thing shrieked in frustration, the sword refused to relent... its magic was different.

Jumping up, Fai stepped around her father; she pointed at the abomination before shrieking in command... "BEGONE!"

Rearing back in shock, the one once known as Richell stared in rage at the girl who dared to confront her. It was not the sword that had drawn it here, but the girl. She had a power the Nephilim had not felt since she had been imprisoned centuries ago. Yet, it was incomplete and unused... why!

If she could get to that power, it would release the bonds holding her feathers captive allowing the creature to be whole again.

Drifting closer in excitement, she did not pay enough attention to how close she was to the man. The sword touched the hand she extended to try drawing out the untapped magic, instantly the blade turned blood red.

Shrieking in pained surprise, Richell turned then fled. The sword was rooted in all realms it could cause death to them; she would need help from the others... if they can be convinced.

The red colour of the sword dimmed first before the hum slowly disappeared; now Chang knew the creature was gone for sure.

Sighing in relief, the Guardian turned to look at his daughter. She had handled herself well. "It is gone, that thing did not look like you at all so it must not be the one Magdalene saw, which leads me to believe there's at least two... three, if Alex's was different. This one must not have found any magic users because it only had a few feathers and short scraggly black hair. Thankfully the sword hurt it, but whether or not it can kill it is another matter."

Sitting down hard in relief on the sofa, Fai rubbed her left hand... it was quite painful. "I felt its pain father."

Spinning around in dreaded shock, Chang watched his youngest daughter massage her left hand. His mind was racing trying to find a logical explanation. The alternative was too frightening to contemplate. That is not good at all; if she felt pain could she die if that thing was killed.

Reaching over, Chang took his youngest daughters hand to inspect it in trepidation. "Your sister never mentioned feeling pain when she tore the feather out."

Shrugging grimly, Fai let her father look at her hand. "Maybe it's because of the sword."

Frowning grimly, Chang inspected her hand. He could not see that being the problem, the sword was not tied to the white buffalo line; ah, but she was his daughter... could she be a Guardian? They would never know now because she could not be sent away to be tested.

Only one Guardian was ever born to any one man. Even with fifteen kids, his late great, great grandfather Dao only had one that could be trained as a Tianming Monk. Chang had never heard of two in one family or a female having the ability.

Could that be why White Buffalo's magic remained dormant, the mixed Oriental would have to pull out his carpet later to discuss it with his master. Right now, all the Guardian could do was hope they would have an answer for him.

Satisfied that there was no mark or any indication that it might be a problem, Chang pulled her up. "Come on, we will go out for dinner instead of ordering in tonight like we usually do."

Fai let her father help her up; they quickly changed before heading out the door.

**********

Ronin looked up briefly when his second half-sister walked into his lab. Usually, he locked the door when he did not want to be disturbed but knowing it was close to suppertime... he hadn't done so this time.

These three rooms were tucked away on the far left side of the basement; the only way in was through a steel door that was locked when Ron was not in residence.

Walking over, Magdalene grimaced. "Father just called... that thing went after Fai; father's sword injured it which shocked the creature enough that it disappeared. Unfortunately, he also found out that White Buffalo felt its pain when his sword hurt it. Thankfully, he does not think if it dies she will be affected since there were no marks or blood from a wound."

Jerking his head up in shock, Ronin gestured grimly. "That is not good news at all; did you feel pain when you attacked it?"

Shrugging, Magdalene shook her head. "No, but I had changed forms almost instantly."

Sighing resignedly, Ronin gestured at the feather. "I suspect it's because they are your ancestors, when I put it through a DNA test it was a perfect match to the three of you... seems you three come from their DNA. The only difference I could find is your ability to shapeshift; they do not have that kind of magic."

Waving her hand dismissively, Magdalene gestured to the door. "Put it away for now, supper is ready and our guests are waiting... finish your research tomorrow."

Nodding, Ronin carefully picked up the feather with tongs. He deposited it into an air tight container before sealing it; putting it in his safe, Ron took off his gloves before dutifully following his sister.

# CHAPTER FIVE

Shadow Hunter looked around in the twilight, he sighed tiredly beside Alexandrina. After a week of madness, finally tomorrow the gates would be open to the public. He was exhausted, he was sure Black Cougar was even more so. She had not shirked any of her duties; Alex seemed to be everywhere at once.

The only time they seemed to have a private moment was first thing in the morning when they trained, but by the end of it they had spent more time kissing... until others entered; talking was the furthest thing from their minds.

Tonight after supper though, Shadow Hunter was promised an entire evening alone with Alexandrina; his first priority was taking her to meet his assistants. Afterwards, they would spend the rest of the night talking... to get to know each other better. Perking up at that thought, he quickly followed Black Cougar inside to eat.

***************

Ronin sat back with a tired sigh before rubbing the bridge of his nose in frustration. Except for finding a link between those creatures and his half-sisters, he could not seem to find out anything else about them.

In the last week, Ronin had run every spec on every animal known to man; the feather did not match or even come close to any species alive today. This really didn't surprise him all that much, considering they were half angle.

Ron getting an idea, tried to cut off a piece of the feather. He had to get Magdalene's dagger to accomplish that feat, a regular knife would not work at all. First, he had set it on fire... it was not damaged at all. Next, he had poured acid on it but again nothing happened.

The bible did make a few references to the angles being human at one time. Some of the older religions though insisted angles were created so they were not from this Earth.

Adam and Eve were tempted by Satan, which means that angles came earlier than humans did. Everything pointed to life before; unfortunately, nothing living from that time existed except for some ruins.

Mostly because the Great Spirit had brought down meteors and the stars to defeat Lucifer, it would have incinerated every living thing on the planet. Massive tidal waves must have swamped Atlantis, causing it to sink into the ocean; keeping it relatively intact.

A few temples were destroyed outright leaving only shells, while others were protected keeping them relatively whole. Why was the Great Spirit so open about what took place with Adam, but so silent on what happened to the first inhabitants of the Earth?

The Tianming Monks were aware that good and evil must coexist with each other. Unfortunately, there was a constant battle between them because both wanted ultimate power.

Lucifer only had to tempt Eve with the apple of knowledge... once; then watch the humans infect themselves with sin. A nudge here, a whisper there, just pushed them a little closer to the edge. Even being imprisoned the arch angel was winning thanks to a human's fascination with sin and evil.

For many years now he had debated with himself on the possibly that there were more realities. Earths timeline's were called aeon realities by human scientists. His father's carpet could take you to the past or the future. That could be how it does it, who really knows for sure.

What about the seven heavens; could we have it all wrong, maybe they are alternate worlds instead of heavens. What if the soul had to travel through several of them before it was taken to the throne room of the Almighty to be judged.

Chuckling in disbelief, Ronin shrugged at his fancy before snorting aloud. "Not likely!"

However, that thought kept hounding him so he finally gave in allowing it to play out. It was an interesting concept if it was true.

The heaven closest to ours could hold magic; it was unravelling so the two worlds might someday become one. If magic, was in the first heaven... what was in the second? Would it also open someday? If so, how long would it take?

Getting an idea, Ronin pulled a blank piece of paper towards him then put seven lines one above the other, but made sure to leave a space to write in. At the bottom, he wrote Earth our reality is the age of technology.

Above our reality, Ron put magic in the first heaven with... 1st aeon reality in parenthesis plus Lucifer's reign.

Prison, Ronin put second before adding Grigori and offspring's of angels with a big question mark... to that he added hell in punctuation marks. He was not sure what aeon reality this would represent so he left it blank for now hoping something would come to him

The Great Spirit was in the third heaven with his angels that were loyal.

In the fourth heaven, Ronin started putting wavy lines for water then stopped. The Lord had filled the fourth heaven with water to keep Lucifer out of it... it was later used to flood the Earth, so all that water was probably gone.

About to put Satan imprisoned here, Ron paused; no, the Great Spirit had said they would all be imprisoned together. He added the arch angles name to the prison in the second heaven.

So, what could be in the last three heavens or reality? Maybe Eden was hidden in the fourth making this the 2nd aeon reality.

Jesus and those waiting for judgement day might be in the fifth heaven, Ronin added 3rd aeon reality and the birth then death of Gods son in parenthesis.

The sixth heaven had Ron in a bit of a quandary, what aeon reality could be here; unless, it was the rise then the fall of Gods and Goddesses like Zeus, Oceanus, Rhea, Phoebe... plus many more. This one would be before Lucifer he figured, but then again maybe this one was not a reality at all.

The souls yet to be born with the ones waiting for judgement might be in the seventh heaven, what reality if any this one was he had no idea so again he added a question mark.

The Great Spirit had said the prisoners would be held in the valleys of the Earth, so he put a pillar at the bottom of the page with the word Snowdonia then drew a line up to the prison that held Lucifer, and Grigori or their offspring's.

A shift in the magic had happened recently, could it be what was causing the weakening prisons? When magic unravels, it unlocks a prison.

Putting a round circle beside the pillar, Ronin wrote in it 'carpet' before drawing a line up to the seventh heaven. Since the carpet held the Guardian's spirits until judgement day, it only made sense that it would be a gateway to where the souls of the dead were kept with the ones waiting to be born.

Thinking about that for a long moment, Ronin finally shook his head; maybe he had that wrong again... magic could be in the seventh heaven. The souls of the dead and the ones to be born would probably be in the first heaven instead of the seventh because it was closer to the Earth. Allowing this one to be used the most out of all the heavens. It could be a three way key... the carpet since it would disappear before Armageddon could be the trigger to unlocking all three.

Inhaling in shock at a disturbing thought, Ron shivered then went back to the second heaven and put 'this aeon reality next'. Since the prisons are opening, Armageddon will follow soon afterwards... hell will then descend on us!

Ronin quickly wadded up the paper with a sigh of irritation at his disturbing thoughts, it was a highly unlikely scenario. Throwing the paper in the garbage he got up, supper must be ready by now... he left the room.

The paper hit the bottom of the trash can with a clutter, it rolled around for a second then settled without one mark or line evident anywhere on the crumpled page.

**\*\*\*\*\*\*\*\*\*\***

Fai's deep green sightless eyes didn't even blink as she held the phone to her ear with a frown of uncertain shock. "Can you please say that one more time, I am sure I did not hear you right? You want who as the new head of the agency..."

Sighing grimly when the expected answer was heard once more, Fai shook her head incredulously. "You do know that he has no prior training except in private investigation, with only two years of criminal psychology; he also has next to no RCMP protocol training... plus, only the basics on court procedures?"

An ironic twist to Fai's lip was the only indication she did not like the answers she was receiving. "I see; you want me to put my carrier as an attorney aside to become my brother's partner as head of the RCMP Special Unit. I don't understand why the bureau thinks we would be a perfect team. What if only my brother wishes to take this position and I do not?"

Sighing aggrieved, Fai rubbed the bridge of her nose when a headache suddenly materialized. "Alright then; you are not giving me much choice are you? How long do we have before we need to give the bureau an answer?"

There was another long pause as Fai listened before grimacing resignedly. "Yes sir, I will be leaving right away... I will pick up the papers on my way to the airport. Thank you sir, I will talk to my brother and you will have your answer before midnight of the twenty eighth. Goodbye!"

Muttering angrily under her breath, Fai dropped her phone on the counter then propped her arms up; she covered her face with both hands... rubbing it in frustration.

Chang brought over a plate of spaghetti with shrimp on top, done in a light wine and cheese sauce that he made especially for his youngest daughter knowing how much she loved it. Now, he was doubly glad that he had done so. "That was an interesting conversation... they want you both as head of the bureau?"

Dropping her arms, Fai's nose twitched in pleasure when it

caught the scent of her favourite dish; she nodded distractedly. "Yes, seems nobody could come to a decisive decision; half wanted Ronin... the other half wanted me. Several of my trials that were filmed got pulled. Since Ron was with me each time, they decided we worked so well together they want to keep us as partners. If one of us declines the job, neither of us will get the position."

Frowning in grim surprise, Chang turned thoughtfully as he dished up his own meal before sitting down on a stool beside his daughter. "They did not say why?"

Shaking her head, Fai swallowed her mouth full before answering. "No, there will be an information package I need to pick up, it is supposed to have all the information we will need to make a decision."

Taking a bite of his food, Chang silently contemplated this surprising development. There is something not quite right about all that; it was not like the bureau to pick the acting Chief younger than twenty-one or one that has never been an RCMP officer or a sheriff of long standing. He would have to study their reasoning's tomorrow once they were in the air and headed for Calgary to meet with Ronin. Quickly, the two finished eating... they went to their respective rooms to pack before sleeping.

********************

Alexandrina walked up the three stairs then took Hunter's hand when he extended it to help her up the last step. She did not need help of course, but his gentlemanly gesture thrilled her all the same.

Once inside, Alex stared around in amazement... it was huge; a fully functional kitchen was on the left, it had every amenity you could think of. The dining area was across from it, a huge dining table with enough room to sit at least eight to ten people, plus a built in china cabinet took up the rest of the space. Separating them was a huge island with an extra sink and more cupboard space. Three stools were placed on the dining room side so one could sit when alone or with only a couple visitors to eat informally at the island.

Taking her moccasins off; Alexandrina wiggled her bare toes in delight when they sank into the plush light red carpet leading into a huge living room with a four person couch... across from it was a love seat. To the left of that was a set of recliners. A huge TV went from ceiling to about midway down then under it was a glass shelf. All sorts of books, plus several different kinds of knickknacks were displayed on the first shelf. The bottom shelf was mostly dragon sculptures with lots of daggers mixed in.

Shadow Hunter chuckled when he saw her staring at his collection. "Trust you to find my passion so quickly; when I found the dragon medallion it sparked a love of the fairy tale creatures, they are so fierce and beautiful. The daggers are also a passion for me as is swords, but those I leave at my ranch. I really do prefer the bow most of the time though. I have a lot of different kinds that I have collected over the years. Someday, I would like to show them to you."

Gesturing across the room to a hallway going to the opposite side of the trailer, Shadow Hunter began a detailed description of his trailer unit. "To your left as you can see is the kitchen with the dining room. If you look a little further to the left you will see a door, which leads to a tack room then into the horse stalls. It also slides out a bit to give extra room to sleep close to the horses if a problem arises or they need to be watched."

Moving his arm around to the right, Hunter pointed ahead. "Now look straight ahead, that is our biggest slide out. It has a small laundry room with a washer and dryer plus a back door to the enclosed glass deck that has an eight man Jacuzzi... with a bar for entertaining. Stairs going to the upper rooms is over there, I will show it to you later. I have an extra bedroom upstairs if you would like to stay with us, so our rooms at the retreat can be used by others; you are more than welcomed to use it."

Nodding pleased by Hunter's offer, Alexandrina smiled in thanks.

"That would help out a lot; we still have a few that will need rooms. I will let my foster mother know."

Opening a door on his right, Shadow Hunter was glad Black Cougar did not take offense or think he was propositioning her. Not that he wouldn't be willing... he hid a guilty smirk at that observation. Shaking off his contemplation quickly, he went to his right then walked up three stairs before turning to offer his hand to Alexandrina. "Come, my assistants are this way."

Taking Hunter's hand again with a small-amused twist to her lip at the idea she needed help up a few stairs. Alex entered, but paused in the doorway. Her mouth dropped open in shock at the sight of the blinking lights; although, it was the bleeping noises of several huge TV screens that overpowered her senses the most... in what she could only describe as a computer lab.

Shadow Hunter had converted what was once the master bedroom between the living quarters and the truck cab, into a fully functional lab. Two monitors against the walls had computer data on one side then news stations from Canada, US, Russia, Spain, UK, Japan and China. With several other major countries so they could keep an eye on everything.

Gesturing around proudly at his working unit, Shadow Hunter explained to his stunned companion. "Since I do not get to go to my ranch often, I converted this into a computer room. These computers are all hooked into my main computers at home... you will find a description of every person, animal, or thing that I have saved; there is also detailed information on anything unusual that I have seen firsthand. I have three full time experts at home that I keep in constant contact with plus my two assistants in here."

A man got to his feet instantly then turned before a woman also stood up but much slower and obviously quite reluctant; they stared at the newcomer impassively... neither spoke.

Alexandrina's gaze went to the man first, he was tall at six foot three with dark auburn streaked hair accompanied by piercing dark green eyes; they were identical to her youngest sister's eyes.

Alex's eyes swung to the woman in shock with her black hair, and dusky red skin; she had medium green eyes like hers but without the gold streaks near the pupil. A smile of pleasure lit up her eyes as a thrill of recognition ran through her. "You both must be our long lost relatives from the late Earl of Summerset's Ojibwa children. Unfortunately, the journal that described Cecille's early journey was lost. A few attempts were made over the years to find the other half of our lost family. Unfortunately, there wasn't much for records pertaining to the natives kept way back then."

Turning to Hunter with a frown, Alexandrina's voice became a bit uncertain. "Did you know who they were?"

Nodding immediately not wanting to hide anything from her, Shadow Hunter explained quickly. "I found out quite by accident two years after I found them homeless and wandering the streets in the back alleys of Quebec. A wolf had drawn me to the city. One of my specialists at the ranch had reported it since it was acting quite strange. There were three sightings of this wolf. He knew it was the same animal every time because it only had half an ear on the right. The shapeshifter seemed to be searching for something. It had come across several eye witnesses that got close enough for pictures, but it never attacked them. Not even the females, which he found quite odd... so I went to investigate. On the second day of searching, I stumbled across these two being driven out of an alley by a pair of older men who had claimed it as their own. The two were about ten at the time. It was obvious they were petrified of something. Speaking in the language of the Ojibway, they tried to tell the men that they needed help."

Leaning back against the wall, Shadow Hunter gestured towards his two assistants. "Once I figured out it wasn't a family squabble, I stepped in to help the kids. Just as a wolf, the very one I was searching for tried to get at the two youngsters. I ended up having to kill it. Unfortunately, there was no indication or explanation on why it was obviously looking for these two. I kept them close after that. I put both through school after teaching them English. Neither knew why the wolf had been hunting them. The wolf in question I found out later was responsible for the death of their parents and that is why it was missing half its ear. Their father had bit it off while giving his twins time to run away."

Alexandrina frowned in surprise. "Twins... who was born first? What are your names?"

The woman stepped forward immediately; she had always been the more dominant one of the pair. "My name is Lily, my brother here is Buck. I was born five minutes before him... is there some significance in who is the oldest?"

Shrugging thoughtfully, Alexandrina gestured placatingly at the angry girl. "There is another prophecy that says twins will be born to Dream Dancer's line then they will be the ones to bring in Armageddon. As far as we know, the boy must be born first. Although, we are positive the Celtic descendants will be the ones to usher in the final twins. If others are aware of you being direct descendants of Earl Summerset's; getting rid of you both would negate the possibility it could be your Ojibwa line that produces the twins."

Reaching out, Alexandrina took Buck's hand first; she needed the physical contact to see if they had any magic or could bond with an Earth's spirit. Alex wasn't surprised when she felt his ability to use magic without bonding, like the Princess though it would become stronger if he did bond. Turning to the woman next, she reached out with a welcoming smile. "I am so glad to meet you both. I just wish it could have been sooner."

When Alexandrina touched Lily, a spark snapped between them. She felt the girl's anger instantly, but it was the ability to do magic without needing to bond at all that shocked her the most. Alex could feel that it was untapped and unused, which was probably caused by the girls rage. What the magic was Black Cougar could not say since it was dormant, so she ignored it for now. "My father will be so thrilled that we found you both, so will my...!"

A loud insistent banging was heard, which cut off Alexandrina's sentence... instantly. Looking up, she saw a frantic Dan obviously distressed out on the step.

Shadow Hunter raced to the door, with a concerned Alex following closely behind him.

Dan barely let the door open. "Come quick, that thing attacked our party... my wife was its target. The rest of us ganged up on it. Thankfully, it disappeared before it killed her but we do not think she will live much longer!"

Alexandrina grabbed her moccasins then pushed past Shadow Hunter without putting them on. She jumped to the ground in a panic, barefoot she sprinted towards the front deck as she cried out in panic. "Where is she?"

Pointing to the house in apprehension, Dan explained as they rushed towards the front steps. "We were in a large group riding to the far jousting field to inspect it; we did manage to get her back here, she is in her room now."

Without saying another word, Alexandrina picked up her pace as she ran the rest of the way to the house. Tanya had been a mother to her since she was sixteen; to lose her would be devastating.

Not just to the triplets but to everyone here too. Loosing Tanya as head of the coven would be a loss that they could ill afford. Especially, with those Nephilim killing all the Seekers and magic users they can find.

Taking the verandah stairs two at a time, Alexandrina rushed into the house. She went through the living room then into the vaulted room that held the stairs going up; she hurried behind them into a two-bedroom apartment that even had its own kitchen. Although, it was barely ever used since they preferred dinning with everyone else.

Going right, Alex rushed into the bedroom; she dropped down beside the king sized bed before taking the hand that was feebly raised to grasp her own. "Mother!"

Alexandrina gasped in shock when Tanya turned her head in her direction. The head Seeker's eyes were white and blank as she stared sightlessly at the daughter she had never had, but always wanted. She pressed a key into her hand. "I have prepared you as best I could, may God be with you child; you have made me so proud... I'm honoured to be your foster mother. Always look up when troubled, I will be watching you from above."

Feeling her husband take her other hand, Tanya turned to him. "I love you!"

With that last statement then one final breath, Tanya's eyes closed for the last time; gladly, she went to meet her saviour.

Shocked, Alexandrina stifled a sob... not yet she must prepare first. Getting up reluctantly, she reached over and put a consoling hand on her foster fathers shoulder as he sobbed forlornly. "I will go prepare the pier, take all the time you need to say your goodbyes. When I return, I'll bring two Seekers to prepare her for the funeral.

Not saying a word, Dan nodded jerkily then turned back to his wife; gently, he smoothed back her hair lovingly. They had been together for fifty years, what would he do without her?"

Turning away with another stifled sob, Alexandrina brushed past Hunter without a word; a stoic expression kept her grief hidden as she gathered several sobbing Seeker's to help her prepare.

Shadow Hunter stayed back, but he refused to leave her altogether knowing eventually she would need him.

*****

Hundreds stood together as the midnight hour came and went; finally, the last of the mourners put a special token or picture on the pier. Flowers, food, tools, articles of clothing, pictures with other special meaning items surrounded Tanya.

Shaman's, priests, with several other holy worshiper's danced or prayed near the pier.

Alexandrina and Dan each taking a torch did the honours, they walked to the funeral pier together to light it. Standing back, Alex watched as the flames slowly made their way up the tinder dry fuel soaked wood. With a loud, 'Whoosh'… her foster mother was consumed by the flames; she shuddered. Glad she had asked Hunter to make sure that the pier caught quickly. He had obliged, while she had went in to phone her father and the others to give them the sad news.

Unfortunately, none of them would be able to make it any time soon but they sent heartfelt condolences; Alex passed their sympathies on to Dan.

Within an hour it was done, Alexandrina threw her torch into the dying flames as one by one the mourners trouped past with murmured condolences. Refusing to leave, Alex stood still as she stared at the dying fire intently until the last of the mourners left.

Dan walked over once they were all gone then embraced Alex; he held his foster daughter tenderly as a sob finally escaped her lips. Heartbroken, Black Cougar allowed her grief to come out before wilting against him.

Giving the two a good twenty minutes to grieve together, Shadow Hunter walked over and put his hand on Dan's shoulder. "I will take her now."

Reaching out, Hunter swept a sobbing Alexandrina into his arms. Lovingly, he carried her into the house then up to her room. Laying Black Cougar on her bed, he quickly took all his weapons and put them beside the nightstand before crawling in beside her. The Cree/Oriental Shaman gathered her close allowing her to cry; stroking her back soothingly, he silently lent his support without a word needing to be said wanting her to let it all out.

Holding back emotions was not a good thing… anger, grief, hate, or fear could smolder for days or years then build a wall that some never recovered from. Kissing the top of Alexandrina's head, Shadow Hunter closed his eyes waiting silently.

***************

Magdalene sighed sadly as she turned off her cell phone, she had rudely been awakened earlier at her oldest sisters emotional upheaval; until now, she had no clue what it was about.

Alexandrina had loved Tanya dearly, as they all had. Regrettably, the two younger sisters had not been around the head of the Seekers for some time.

Getting up, Maggie went to the washroom to wash her tear streaked face before getting a drink then picked up her novel... she was wide awake now.

Magdalene's father and her youngest sister would be here sometime tomorrow night for a meeting. She would encourage her old partner to go back with them so she could head to Toronto. Red Wolf would take her mare; maybe enter the jousting competition, which had been postponed until next weekend.

On second thought, she would take Fredrick with her it would be company. Satisfied with that, Magdalene finished reading a chapter. Stifling a yawn, she laid back hoping to sleep the rest of the night.

It took Magdalene another hour to doze off, but a hot tingling sensation vibrated through her suddenly. Damn, so much for sleep.

Sighing in frustration, Maggie sat up and picked up her novel. Well, at least she was at the right part of her book it went perfectly with her sister's emotional roller coaster.

**********

Chang opened the passenger door for his youngest daughter before frowning at the flushed rosy cheeks in concern. "Are you feeling okay?"

Fai nodded jerkily. "Absolutely wonderful, just a little tired since it is six-thirty in the morning."

Ignoring her father's disbelieving snort, Fai got in quickly. She made sure to keep her head turned away from him then closed her eyes pretending to sleep. It was only a two hour drive, but they had decided to leave early wanting to have breakfast at their favourite restaurant before the Provincial building opened.

The meeting and gathering all the info Fai needed wouldn't take long she hoped. It would be another three hour ride to the private airport where their plane was kept. Once there, a flight plan had to be filed; only then could they leave for Calgary.

The youngest triplet was sure it was going to be a long day. Stifling a sigh, White Buffalo tried to sleep.

********************

Alexandrina cried on and off for the first two hours then emotionally drained she slept for a good hour. It was just after three am when the older triplet woke again. Feeling a bit better, Black Cougar smiled sleepily in contentment when she felt Shadow Hunter's deep breathing beside her that said he too had found sleep.

Propping herself up slightly, Alex stared down at him in contemplation; she could not figure out why she had fallen in love with him, he was not her type at all. He had a baby face with only a little stubble here and there, but he was quite good looking with his dark skin. His eyes had the puffy black pouches of his Asian ancestors. Still, they were not as pronounced as her brothers or father's. That could be what was attracting her, he reminded her a bit of her father.

Solving that mystery, Alexandrina smiled down in pleasure when Hunter's deep brown eyes with their black irises opened. He smiled tenderly up at her before raising a hand he buried it in her long flowing hair that had come loose from its customary bun.

Shadow Hunter drew Alexandrina's head down slowly, gently allowing her plenty of time to pull away if she wished. His deep brown eyes softened with love when she did not. Their lips finally met then nothing else mattered when sparks flared between them as passion drove them on. Fumbling between kissing and giggling they helped each other get rid of the few articles of clothing they still had on.

Rolling Alexandrina onto her back, Shadow Hunter kissed his way to her breasts. They were perky; about a handful... just perfect he couldn't help thinking. He lovingly molded them then kissed each one before taking one deep into his mouth, the

Cree/Oriental Shaman suckled gently. He did not linger long as an urgency he had never felt before threatened to release his seed too soon.

Feeling the same urgency, Alexandrina pulled Hunter's head back up for a deep kiss as he positioned himself between her thighs.

Alex pulled back with a giggle when Shadow Hunter cursed in frustration, unable to find the opening. She reached between them and gently moved his engorged manhood to the right area before removing her hand. The older triplet reached up then pulled the Cree/Oriental Shaman's head back down for another deep kiss as she wrapped her legs around his hips.

Unable to wait another minute, Shadow Hunter buried himself into Black Cougar in one powerful thrust.

Crying out in ecstasy... the momentary discomfort barely felt, Alexandrina tightened her long legs around him in encouragement. She arched her back, which allowed him to get an even deeper penetration.

Unable to hold back, Shadow Hunter groaned in disappointment as he ejaculated too soon.

Alexandrina clenched her vagina muscles several times when Hunter's manhood pulsed deep inside her. It triggered another deeper moan of satisfaction from Black Cougar as she climaxed hard for a second time at the feel of his manhood emptying itself.

Groaning in surprise, Shadow Hunter felt Alex's muscles clamp around him; to his utter amazement, another shudder of ecstasy ran through him and he felt a bit more liquid escape. Feeling weak for the first time in his life, Hunter dropped heavily on top of Alexandrina... unable to hold himself up any longer.

Running her fingernails up then down Shadow Hunters back, Alexandrina purred like a satisfied kitten. Having felt Hunter's manhood give another jerk, she suspected that it was rare for a man to have two climaxes. It was not impossible she had just learned, but uncommon she was sure.

Rolling off Alexandrina, Shadow Hunter still panting stared up at the ceiling for several moments. Finally, catching his breath he turned his head. With a mischievous grin that lit up his face, he couldn't help commenting. "That was way too fast; I think we need to do it again... practise makes perfect you know."

Alexandrina giggled girlishly and rolled over; she lingeringly kissed Hunter before lifting up slightly. "I agree whole heartedly."

With that statement, they proceeded to make love one more time but much slower now that the initial urgency was gone.

***************

Magdalene closed her book with a relieved sigh; her flushed feelings had disappeared an hour ago. Thankfully, she could no longer feel her oldest sister. She had been at a good place in her book though so hadn't wanted to quit reading yet. Finally, putting the book on her nightstand she turned off the light then went to sleep.

A dream snagged Magdalene instantly; it was so real she felt lost in it. A couple were making love with sparks or flames raging around them. At first, she thought it was one of her sisters... until the woman lifted her head. A red strip was the only colour in the black hair. When the two orgasmed, they became completely engulfed in the flames.

Immediately, the fire spread out until the entire Earth was ablaze. Greedily, it consumed everything in its path. People ran screaming for mercy but there was none.

Sitting up with a gasp of horror, Magdalene looked around franticly then fell back in relief when her familiar room came into focus. There had been some kind of beast in the flames, but it kept changing shape as it guarded what could have been an egg of some kind... making the beast unrecognizable.

Looking at the book she was reading that had demons with other unworldly animals, she shrugged with a light chuckle at her foolishness before laying back to sleep. No more dreams haunted her.

**\*\*\*\*\*\*\*\*\***

Fai had pretended to sleep, but it was the furthest thing from her mind as the hot flush continued to stain her cheeks. Her oldest sister's emotions were causing her to fidget uncomfortably. White Buffalo stifled a sigh of relief when the feeling started to dissipate.

The youngest triplet tried to doze off, but suddenly Fai's blank unseeing eyes sprang open in shock when a contraction deep inside vibrated through her.

A split second later, Maggie's cry of horror rang through Fai's skull. White Buffalo saw a man and a woman making love as flames consumed the Earth. When the woman looked up, she had two strips of colour in her hair... one red the other white.

Seeing a beast in the flames, Fai tried to see what it was but it kept changing shape faster than she could keep up. When it disappeared, she still had no clue what it could be. Unexpectedly, the smoke cleared; White Buffalo saw two eggs that the fire could not seem to reach or was it caressing them. Before she could figure it out, the vision disappeared. Try as she might to hold onto it... eventually, it vanished.

Frowning troubled, Fai put her hand down to stroked her belly thoughtfully before that feeling too disappeared. White Buffalo kept her head turned towards the window so her father could not see her expression.

Many times over the years, the triplets had felt or even experienced things the others had... especially, if it was a deep emotion. This went way beyond that, though; sighing, White Buffalo finally slipped into a deep sleep.

# CHAPTER SIX

Chang reached over and nudged Fai. "White Buffalo, we are here. Unfortunately, we will not be able to eat first since a big accident kept us immobile for an extra hour. I still can't believe you slept through that... are you sure you're okay?"

Turning to her father with a reassuring smile, Fai nodded decisively. "Of course I am, why wouldn't I be; guess I was just more tired than I thought."

Without comment, Chang opened his door before getting out. He went to the back and opened the hatch to pull the sword that was in its intricately designed case from the magnetic holder attached to the side panel, plus his other weapons. The Tianming Monk tucked the daggers back where they belonged then snapped the sheath back onto the harness attached to his back; finished, he shut the door. Walking around the escalade... he opened the passenger's door and helped his daughter out.

Unexpectedly, several reporters with light bulbs flashing converged on them; where they came from, Chang had no idea. He had not seen a single person when he had pulled up, not even when he was gathering weapons. Growling impatiently, the Guardian pushed people out of his way... guiding his daughter to the stairs.

Demanding questions about Fai's appointment as the new head of the RCMP special unit was thrown at her. Who had leaked that information to the press, White Buffalo couldn't help wondering silently.

Chang finally managed to get his daughter up the stairs to the front door. Security came out immediately, which kept the reporters at bay for a moment... long enough for them to slip into the building.

***************

Magdalene walked into the dining room, she smiled at her

brother. "Dad and Fai are on the way... they are stopping at the bureau first though; anything new on that feather yet?"

Ronin shook his head. "Nothing, it doesn't seem to have anything like it here on Earth. Neither does it appear to have any magical properties, unless being indestructible is considered magical. It would seem to be just a feather no more or less. The only two interesting information I have is that the genetics happen to be linked to your ancestors. I did find it fascinating though that only your little dagger with the dove can cut into it. I tried an axe, scissors, pruning shears, a razor, and several other cutting instruments; even my dragon daggers had no effect. I have tried using several burning acids, poisons, plus other toxins to find a weakness. Unfortunately, nothing alters it... not even fire!"

Fredrick walked in leading his mother, the two sat; quiet descended when the cooks help brought out breakfast.

Magdalene smiled over at her guests once the maid left; they were hungrily helping themselves to the scrambled eggs, bacon, hash browns, plus toast. "How was your evening, I hope you both slept well."

Grinning teasingly, Fredrick spread jam on his toast. "How can you not on those plushy mattresses."

Chuckling, Magdalene changed the subject. "How about a trip to Toronto; my sister needs some help at the retreat. The annual spiritual event has been postponed until next weekend because of the unexpected death of the head mistress. I am bringing a few horses and entering some of the competitions... company would be nice. If you would rather not, my youngest sister and father will be here tonight so you can go with them instead. Vancouver is beautiful at this time of year so if you prefer visiting the Island, that is okay too."

Fredrick looked at his mom in question.

Helen shrugged. "I prefer Vancouver; I will be able to stay with your Aunt Char... I haven't seen my sister in a couple years. You go ahead. I will go with Maggie's father."

Turning back to Magdalene, Fredrick nodded pleased that she had invited him along. "Yes, I would love to go; can we pick up Jane on our way?"

Magdalene rolled her eyes, but inclined her head resignedly; Fredrick's new girlfriend was your typical blonde bimbo, but at least it would keep him out of her hair. "Sure, if she can be ready by tomorrow around noon."

Fredrick quickly finished his breakfast then got up in excitement. "I will go call her right now!"

Magdalene nodded before getting up as well. "We will take the Volvo Toterhome with the pull out editions, it pulls the big trailer with the horse stalls in the back easier than a truck; I am not going to put food or water in it for the trip there, but we can do so on the way back since we will have way more time to camp. I will have Jim go over it so it's ready in the morning. After you are done talking to Jane head over to the barn, you can pick out the horses you want to ride; or, if you prefer we can make a quick stop at your place to get yours."

Waving farewell to her brother, Magdalene trotted out. She was really looking forward to some much needed relaxation at the retreat; she had taken an extended leave of absence from work. Surprisingly, the bureau had agreed to it without putting up much of an argument... she wondered what was up with that.

*********************

Alexandrina rolled out of bed unwillingly. Another bout of weeping then more lovemaking had made her night extremely short so she was still quite tired.

Regrettably, some decisions would have to be made today on the next head Seeker. She could not do it herself... Black Cougar's career was too important to her. Which reminded her, she would have to call head office in order to get a grieving leave of absence?

Shadow Hunter rose up onto his knee's before crawling over to Alex's side of the bed; he reached out and took her hands. "I love you... will you marry me?"

Staring down at Hunter flabbergasted at first; Alexandrina couldn't believe he would ask her that after only knowing her for two weeks. "Don't you think we should get to know each other a little more first?"

Shrugging negligently, Shadow Hunter lifted her two hands then kissed them before looking up seriously. "Nothing else matters but that I love you. The rest we will work around; besides, with that monster hunting the Seekers anything could happen to either one of us!"

Frowning thoughtfully, Alexandrina finally nodded as she stared down at him intently. "Okay, but I need to..."

'bang, bang!'

Sighing irritably, Alexandrina called out in exasperation. "Yes, what is it now?"

A muffled unrecognizable voice answered. "You are needed downstairs... immediately!"

Bending, Alexandrina kissed Hunter quickly. "We will discuss it later at lunch, but yes I will gladly marry you."

Nodding with a relieved smile, Shadow Hunter quickly dressed before they hurried out.

**********

Chang looked over at his youngest daughter resignedly before hiding a grimace when the airplane took a bit of a plunge, even though he knew she wouldn't see it. It was storming out; he could see forks of lightening everywhere. It was illuminating the black stormy clouds all around them.

One would think he would be used to planes by now as often as they seemed to be in one, but he hated them with a passion. Never would he admit that to any of his children, having a weakness was unheard of in a Guardian.

Turning back to the pages on his lap, Chang frowned thoughtfully as he remarked regrettably. "There seems to be no loop holes for one of you refusing, so either you both take the position or neither. I have a sneaky suspicion they will want your sisters too, twice now I have come across their names in references to the two of you. The one pushing for your appointment to the head of the JTF2 special units Emergency Response Team of the bureau was with Alexandrina recently. He took one of the British Princesses to her for protection that is why it had taken so long to get back to you. It seems he knows about those things hunting the Seekers, he is also aware of Alexandrina and Magdalene's special abilities almost right from the day they started."

Nodding, Fai looked towards her father before her finger stilled, not quite done reading yet. Of course, her copy was in braille. "Yes, your name too has been mentioned as an added bonus seeing as I never go anywhere without you. They plan on making you our official bodyguard... it comes with a nice salary."

Shrugging indifferently, Chang harrumph aggrieved. "You know I do not care about that! I could not find anything in here except for one reference to Alexandrina's warning of things to come. Major General Anthony already knows about the magic abominations. Although, his recommendation holds a lot of sway; I would have thought there should be other reason for their decision."

Laughing, Fai remembered back years ago to a show the triplets use to watch religiously as teenagers. "Do you remember that weekly TV show we watched all the time, it was with three women? A mysterious man helped them fight crime. I can't seem to remember what it was called?"

"Charlie's Angels."

Chang couldn't help laughing also when he remembered how the three girls would sit in a semi-circle around the TV then refuse to move as soon as he put the disk in. The only sound other than the show was Alex's voice describing for her youngest sister what the other two could see on the big screen. He always put one episode every week on for them.

Nodding in amusement, Fai gestured teasingly. "Yep, that's it;

we loved the remake of the 1996 crime drama just as much as the original. The only thing though is that we would have to call ourselves, Chang's Seekers and Sons."

They both laughed at that silly name. Chang sobered, he looked back down to read some more before sighing resignedly. "Here is another reference concerning all of us. Then it gives a detailed list of all accomplishments we have had in the last two years. A side note hints at the possibility of each sister being head of their own special forces unit tailored to each of your special abilities. They are also willing to give you jurisdiction in every province of Canada."

Frowning in unease, Fai gestured decisively. "I do not think it is a good idea father, I have a bad feeling about it!"

Looking over at his youngest daughter's uneasy expression, Chang couldn't help but try a bit of persuasion. "It would give us better access to their computers; plus, their lab is second to none!"

Inclining her head reflectively, Fai concurred. "That is very true; it's also a good point."

Shrugging, even though Chang knew she could not see it; he decided to leave it for now. "Let's hear what your brother has to say before you make a decision."

Nodding, Fai closed her folder and reclined back in her seat... extremely tired all of a sudden; dozing off, she drifted in a half sleep state.

Lying back as well, Chang was instantly asleep.

"Father!"

Waking quickly, Chang jumped up before hurrying to his carpet. He took it out of its cylinder then spread it out, turning the Tianming Monk rushed to Fai. Picking his youngest daughter up, he took her with him.

White Buffalo did not even twitch; Chang knew she was in the dream world already. Gently putting her down on the Japanese rug in front of him, the Guardian sat in the center of the carpet. He put both his thumb and middle finger together so they touched. He placed them upright on his knees lightly as he hummed rhythmically putting himself in a trance.

*********************

Alexandrina looked around grimly... she had gathered all the Seekers that were left; they no longer filled this room, which had once been packed full at this time of year.

Shadow Hunter stood at the door with arms folded waiting. He was quite impressive in his ceremonial Cree/Oriental buckskin that he artfully managed to combine two distinct cultures together into one.

The buckskins were a pure white, off a rare white Kermode Spirit Bear. He had went all the way to British Columbia, armed with only his bow; after receiving permission from the Elder Indian bands in the area, he had taken one bear for this purpose.

In thanks, Hunter had donated all the meat to the Indigenous inhabitants of the Princess Royal Island.

The bead work was spectacular, with almost every colour used. Going up the pant leg was an Oriental dragon, one on each side. The tail started at the bottom of the buckskin pants then weaved up and around the leg to just below the knee. The body and head took up the rest stopping just below the draped shirt that started about mid-thigh. White tassel's on the sides of his buckskin pants were only a few inches apart going from hip to ankle.

The shirt was tight, opened in the front showing off his hairless silky smooth deeply muscled chest. There were two small beaded dream catchers, one on each side around his nipple area. One had the image of a great owl; the other one had a buffalo in the center. Both sides of the shirt were slit open to about the waist so one could see the tassels clearly going down the legs.

Over top of his shirt, he had draped his Japanese cloak that also had several different kinds of dragons embroidered on it. Symbols of strength, endurance, protection, and invisibility were artfully placed around the four dragons. In every other available space were more Japanese Kanji symbols of illusion, fantasy, phantom, hallucination, and delusion. The cape went down to his knees in length; Shadow Hunter had it pushed back over his shoulders so the buckskins were prominent.

The colourful Japanese cloak went surprisingly well with the white buckskins; it gave Hunter a mysterious otherworldly appearance.

On the Cree/Oriental Shaman's head, he had a strip of white leather that had beaded diamond shapes on it with feathers from a hawk draping over his ears.

The sub-basement was colder than the rest of the house; the hanging lamps plus the mammoth sized hearth chiselled out of the far rock wall on the left side of the dais had been lit earlier... taking the chill out of the air.

Sitting up on a raised platform beside Alexandrina was three others, two men and one more woman; there were, three empty chairs that needed to be filled tonight. Right beside her was Dan, he would fill in for his wife until another was chosen; beside him sat Yvonne, second to the now deceased Trinity but she had refused the appointment of head Seeker and suggested a vote by all Seekers. On the other side of her was Jason who also agreed that a vote was best.

There were two reasons for this gathering; she smiled in excitement then felt her youngest sister, Fai, join her from the dream world. A few minutes later, Magdalene also materialized beside her. Knowing it was time, Alexandrina turned then nodded at Dan.

Obediently, Dan rose then regally descended the platform. He looked impressive at six feet two with his steal grey hair, which contrasted strikingly with his solid blood red flowing Seeker's robe; he was the only one allowed to wear that colour besides Fai.

When they first began the retreat the older man had went and gotten his license as head of their religious sect in order to perform marriages, death, or birth certificates so everything was done legally. He walked to the center of the room before halting in the first of the three joining circles then he beckoned Shadow Hunter to come to him.

Shadow Hunter eagerly walked forward to join Dan, having no hesitations. The Cree/Oriental Shaman had done a lot of talking at lunchtime to get her to agree to this, but it was the older man who eventually convinced her.

Dan had asked Alexandrina one simple question... "Do you love him?"

When she had answered yes, Alex's foster father nodded knowingly. "We will have the wedding tonight and pick a new head Seeker afterwards."

Now here Shadow Hunter was all dress up; he even made sure to pull out his Celtic dragon medallion so that it was hanging in plain sight, not very often did he let others see it.

Turning towards the dais eagerly, Hunter watched his wife to be rise. It was not until he entered the circles that his eyes caught sight of the two shadows flanking Alexandrina, he frowned in surprise. Having been trained by a Tianming Monk, Hunter was able to see with his inner eye. In addition, the cloak of illusion that he wore was triggered by the symbols of eternity he was standing in... chanting would be unnecessary now.

Humming, Alexandrina stood before nervously she smoothed down her white robe. It had silver embroidery for the three rings of eternity with a black cougar in the center of them prominently displayed in the front. Gold Japanese Kanji symbols embroidered all around the outside of the rings spoke of love, earth, air, fire... and peace. Finally, Celtic symbols of strength, courage, endurance, plus protection were scattered everywhere all done in silver. Red was the colour of the hood and so was the hem of the robe.

Alex was also wearing her foster mother's white wedding headdress that was a crown of diamonds; a small veil came down over her forehead but did not go over her eyes. It had a long train in the back that would spread out as she walked.

Magdalene's robe was gold, with black embroidered rings of eternity. A red wolf was prominent in the center. Her Japanese symbols spoke of strength, courage, endurance, plus protection all done in white. The Celtic ones for love, earth, air, fire... then peace, were done in silver; it was completely opposite to her older sisters. Her hood was also red, so was the bottom of her robe.

Fai's robe was a blood red. It contrasted beautifully with a black hood and hem. The three circles of eternity were embroidered in gold. A white buffalo graced the center. The Japanese symbols on this robe were silver. They also surrounded the rings of eternity, but there was many more. The same with the Celtic symbols done in white; although, there were twice as many as her sisters had. What significance if any the hoods had nobody knew? No other robes here had one, not even Dans.

Feeling the time was right; Alexandrina walked regally down the dais with her sister's flanking her. She made sure to halt inside the three connecting circles right where they joined.

Once in the center, the two shadows strengthened before each one stepped into Alexandrina causing the three to become one. Two more strips of colour appeared in her hair... the white was on the right, the red on the left; the third in the center had white at the top then changed to black, with blood red at the bottom.

Alexandrina felt a surge of power when her sisters joined her and they formed a whole. Only standing in the center of the three joining rings, could they become one. They had tried elsewhere, even at the Stonehenge they could not come together. Only here in the circle of eternity deep inside the Mother Earth could they become a whole.

Neither did it seem to matter which sister stood here. As long as one did the other two would feel a need to sleep, once they heeded the call the other two would enter the dream world then be brought here. Once together, the three could wield the Mother Earth's power without fear. Alone none of them could handle it, only together was it possible.

Smiling in relief, Alex saw her father materialize and join Dan.

Shadow Hunter watched his love in awe then shock as Alexandrina with midnight black hair left loose walked down the stairs. Her hair was so long that it trailed behind her with the long train draped over top. It actually looked like she was floating towards him as her robe, wedding train, and flowing hair rippled down one step at a time. Only the bare feet peeking out occasionally broke from typical wedding attire, he could not help grinning at that. She slowly walked towards him with the two shadow still following her.

Hunter felt a shiver of warning suddenly then a surprising need to flee as his cloak of illusion tried to warn him. Watching his love closely, he saw a quick look of disbelief; it only lasted for a brief second when she first entered the three rings. He could see her lips moving but he could not hear what she was saying, so she must be talking to the two shadows beside her.

Were the shadows the ones hunting the Seekers... was it all a lie. The three looked exactly alike and only by their height could one tell the difference between them. Maybe, he had been lured here so they could get his medallion.

A loving glow appeared on Alexandrina's face as she stepped into the three joining rings where they became one. Sparks exploded then the two shadows disappeared causing the cloak of illusion to settle, but his dragon medallion turned a blood red.

Suddenly, Shadow Hunter felt another's presence and saw an older man materialize. The Cree/Oriental Shaman could tell right away he was Asian then he noticed the sword, which caused him to feel an instant connection. Hunter had felt this only once before with his Tianming Monk Master and he relaxed calmed by the presence of another monk.

Looking back at his wife to be, Shadow Hunter saw an expression of loving awe on Alex's face. It made him forget all else when she stepped in front of him.

Chang stepped towards his first daughter before giving her a loving kiss on her cheek; thankful that the carpet he was on allowed him to solidify briefly as he took her hand to give her away.

Dreamily, Dan called out loudly. "Who gives these women to this man in holy matrimony?"

Extending Alexandrina's hand to Shadow Hunter, Chang called out his assent proudly... glad to be a part of his daughter's wedding even though he was physically still on a plane heading to Calgary. "I do."

Dan stepping to the side allowed Chang to move back so he could once again became a shadow, watching.

The Priest of the Seekers took both their entwined left hands in his before pulling out of his pocket a black and red intricately braided cord. He wrapped the cord around their wrists while chanting then once the love knot was formed loosely... the priest put his left hand over top of their joined hands.

Still with a dreamy unfocused look, Dan gave a speech that he had practiced earlier. "The Mother Earth, with the approval of the Great Spirit of all living things has blessed this union. Where once there were two, now they are one in mind body and spirit. Just like, the rings of eternity that you stand in let the love you feel for each other go beyond the physical. Even death cannot break apart this eternal bond of love you share. Love will never die if it is nurtured then allowed to grow with us as we live our hectic daily lives. I love you... should always be the first thing spoken in the mornings, plus the last thing whispered at night. Never take each other for granted or allow others to come between you. Let your love shine out to be a beckon for others to find, allowing them to share in your joy. Remember, love will always find a way!"

Pausing dramatically, Dan hearing a voice in his head couldn't help repeating what it was saying; instead, of his prepared speech. "Do you Shadow Hunter take these women, Alexandrina, Magdalene, and Fai Ryuu to be your lawful wives; to hold through any kind of sickness or health as long as you shall live?"

Shadow Hunter nodded jerkily with a bemused painful grimace that almost resembled a smile... his chest was burning. Only once before had he felt this deep pain; surprisingly, right in the exact spot it had burned him the first time he had put the medallion on. Unfortunately, it caused him to miss the first part of what was said then thankfully he heard the final question. Trying to stifle a groan of pain, he managed to gasp out hurriedly. "I do, forever!"

Dan turned to Alex next with a serene dreamy smile; unaware of exactly what he was saying as he repeated the words he heard still echoing in his head. "Do you Alexandrina Maya Sumaiya first of the three, Priestess of the Mother Earth. Magdalene Gilda Shambari second of the three, Priestess of the Mother Earth. Fai Trinity Vienna the prophecy of Trinity, High Priestess... chosen by Mother Earth; take Shadow Hunter a Cree/Oriental Shaman to be your lawful husband. To have and hold through sickness or in health as long as you all shall live?"

Alexandrina staring into Hunter's black intense loving expression nodded. Her ecstatic dreamy smile widened as a sudden thrill raced through her when she realized her sisters were still with her. "I do now and forever!"

Echoing twice more eerily through her skull, the three sisters each said I do before swearing forever. It wasn't until that moment Black Cougar realized Dan had named all three sisters. Alex felt a stunned silence from Maggie, Fai's shocked intake of breath was all she could manage as they too realized what just happened.

For the first time Alexandrina noticed the dragon medallion glowing red hot against Hunters chest, distracting her enough that she forgot all about her sisters. Black Cougar wondered why he did not seem phased by it; suddenly, he grimaced painfully just as Dan pulled the cord away from their joined hands then recited. "You may kiss the brides... with this kiss you will forever be united!"

Alexandrina still dazed and beyond thought kissed her new husband before stepping back, but her two sisters remained.

Solidifying again for a split second, Magdalene kissed Hunter then disappeared.

Fai received her kiss and she too vanished.

Shadow Hunter, unaware that Alexandrina had moved away felt two quick jolts from his medallion. Finally, the glow then pain dissipated once the shadows in front of him disappeared. Reaching up he touched his lips in shock; he was sure he had felt two soft flutters against his lips, but Alex was too far away for it to be her. What had just happened to him?

Dropping his hand to his chest, Hunter felt a stinging sensation where he touched. He dropped his hand when he saw the shadowy man beside Dan take a step towards him... the shadow once again solidified.

Chang reached out and put his palm on Shadow Hunters chest. His lips moved as if he was saying something then silently both the man and pain disappeared together.

Alexandrina stepped forward in concern then put her palm on Shadow Hunter's chest exactly where her fathers had been. "Are you hurt?"

Covering her hand, Shadow Hunter shook his head in reassurance. "No, it was just uncomfortable but it's okay now... who were those shadows?"

Smiling lovingly, Alexandrina explained. "My father who is also my Tianming Monk Guardian, and my..."

Hearing a thump behind her, Alex spun with a cry of disbelieving anguish to the fallen Dan then quickly knelt beside her foster father. "No, you can't go; I need you. Papa, please stay!"

Dan holding his chest in agony smiled up at the daughter he had always thought of her as. "You will all be fine now daughter of my heart. Tanya is waiting for me; I have fulfilled my destiny by joining the Priestesses of Mother Earth to the Cree/Oriental Shaman. We love you and leave you in good hands... in your room you will find the marriage certificate all filled out. It is signed by me then witnessed by Yvonne. All that is needed is everyone else's signature."

With that, Dan drew his last breath and gladly joined his wife.

Sobbing, Alexandrina dropped on top of Dan totally devastated by her second loss in only a few days.

**********

Fai sat up quickly when she heard a groan of pain then resignation from her father as he fell backwards on his carpet. Immediately, she got up on her knees before scooting over to him... in concern. "What happened?"

Sighing in regret, Chang reached up and stroked Fai's cheek tenderly before sitting up. "My time is short now; the Celtic dragon medallion had an old spell that was transferred to Shadow Hunter. The Celtic curse has been removed making the necklace harmless to the wearer now. As soon as we are done with Magdalene, we must return home so I can put my affairs in order. You will have to refuse the bureau's job offer then go to the retreat to be with your sisters, they will protect you from those things. Ronin will keep my sword and the carpet safe until my oldest son, who will now be your new Guardian... claims it."

With tears of disbelief dribbling down her cheeks, Fai threw herself at her father. "It can't be so, I need you dad!"

Chang kissed the top of her head tenderly; she was still so young. "You know that we cannot change the Great Spirits will. My time is near. I just hope we will be able to get everything done in time. We will pick Ronin up then he will stay with you until we can get you to the retreat. I love you White Buffalo, we all knew that I was not meant to stay with you forever. If I have fulfilled my destiny, I will happily join my father and ancestors."

Fai nodded forlornly before getting up as the plane prepared to descend.

***************

Magdalene jumped out of bed, the need for a nap earlier had come upon her quite suddenly. Excusing herself, she had gone to her room to heed the call. Now stumbling to her bathroom, she went to the sink before turning on the taps. Red Wolf splashed water on her face. Leaning against the sink once done, she stared at her image in shock.

This was not the first time the three had become one, but it seldom happened. It was usually only for a split second or two, hardly noticeable... until today. Maggie was still unsure exactly what had happened.

Only Alexandrina married the Cree/Oriental Shaman... right? The fact that Mother Earth had shocked them all with the news of the older triplet's pregnancy explained some of the reason for a hasty marriage. That exciting news had kept them all from realizing that Dan had named all three girls in the marriage ceremony. When Alex had kissed the groom, she had immediately backed away. Not understanding what was happening at first, the other two girls had no choice but to kiss the man too.

Grabbing her towel, Magdalene grimaced at the image in the mirror as it stared back at her in bemusement. She was now married to a man she had never even met before; wiping her face, she threw the towel into the hamper in disgust before marching out of the bathroom. Suddenly, Maggie stopped at a pounding at her door. "Yes... what is it?"

The muffled voice of her brother called out. "Father's airplane landed in the field so I had the car readied for us to go pick them up. Hurry up; they will be waiting for us!"

Magdalene grabbed a sundress waiting then quickly drew it on before rushing through the door and into the hallway.

**********

Fai hung up her cell phone, just as they were landed behind the ranch. Usually, they went to the little airport up the road but Chang did not want the hassle of fighting off reporters if they were spotted.

White Buffalo turned to her father. "Alexandrina did not take the news well. Seems they will be lighting Dan's pier tonight, he had a heart attack just after we left them. They still plan to go ahead with the festival next Friday though. A few did leave but said they would be back. Thankfully, they had done the ballets for picking a new head Seeker before the wedding. Unfortunately, no count was done yet... tomorrow she said."

Grunting dutifully, so that his daughter would know he was listening. The Guardian knew she couldn't see a nod but he really did not care who was picked as the next head Seeker. He did not want to hurt his daughters feelings though.

Chang could feel the curse slowly travelling through his body; he needed to slow it down fast. "Go out and see your sister, I need a few minutes alone... please!"

Frowning in concern, Fai finally nodded; she could hear the strain in her father's voice but knew he would not appreciate her questions. She grabbed her overnight bag then counted her steps before she exited the small plane by herself.

Going over to the carpet that he hadn't put away yet, Chang sat in the center. Humming, he quickly put himself in a trance. The Tianming Monks old master materialized instantly. "The poison is spreading fast my son and we need to quarantine it, I will help you. Your oldest son is on a mission in Africa looking for a sword hidden centuries ago. It is fabled to be from the old world so could possibly be infused with magic; it's a Japanese Keris sword that he will give to Fai... if they can find it. He needs more time as do you. I want you to go deep into a death trance, the carpet will guide you."

Lying full length on the intricately designed Japanese rug, Chang interlocked his fingers over his chest then raised his two index fingers. He put them together so they pointed upwards; both his thumbs were also pressed together, but they pointed towards his head.

Reducing his breathing, Chang slowly put every part of his body to sleep. Starting from his toes, he slowed the blood pumping through his veins. The Guardian pushed the poison from the bottom of his feet up to his groin and into his appendix.

Chang chose that organ since it was useless except for filtering the blood and if it needed to be removed, it would not kill him. Going through each vein, he pushed all the poison into it then sealed it tight. When it was time, it would burst and kill him almost instantly. Thankfully, not until the appointed day though.

After twenty-five long excruciating minutes, Chang was finally able to sit up. Humming, he contacted his master once more. "How long will it be before my son gets back from Africa?"

The Tianming Master shrugged. "We do not know for sure, he will be heading your way once he retrieves the sword... his training is complete."

Nodding pleased by that, Chang changed the subject. "Good; anything yet on those things hunting the Seekers?"

Shaking his head negatively, the Tianming Monk gestured impotently. "Nothing... Shen refuses to answer any of our prayers; it seems the Great Spirit of all living things has vanished without a trace!"

Sighing irritably, Chang shook his head grimly. "Which means we are on our own for now; I am sure the Great Spirit is out there somewhere watching over us. Have faith master, when the time is right our prayers will be answered once more. I must go, we will speak again soon."

Getting up, Chang rolled up his carpet then put it in the cylinder. It was specially made and could only be opened by one of his family; they had to have his DNA to trigger the lock. Snapping the lid shut, he put the strap over his shoulder then grabbed his bag on his way out before exiting the plane.

*****

Fai, using her white walking cane to make sure no obstacle was blocking her way; went over to her waiting sister and half-brother. After hellos and hugs were given, she stepped back with an aggrieved sigh. "Why is it that the only time we get to visit these days is when a catastrophe has happened... or is about to happen?"

Magdalene chuckled in agreement, but there was no real humour in it. "I know what you mean; it's too bad we could not stay children longer. How is father holding up?"

Shrugging, Fai gestured sadly. "Right now he is in quite a bit of pain, but hiding it well. He left his carpet out so I am sure that is where he wanted to go once I was gone. I hope that his Tianming Master will be able to help him hold on for a bit longer. Alexandrina did not take the news well when I told her about dad. Sadly, she was getting ready to send Dan to meet his wife in the afterlife."

Sighing forlornly, Magdalene scowled in aggravation. "Don't I know it, her emotional swings from ecstatic bride to grieving daughter is taking its toll on me... I'm not sure which emotion is coming next."

Turning to Ronin, Fai smiled lovingly. "How are you faring big brother? It does not look like we will be able to take the Emergency Response Team jobs for the JTF2 special forces... sorry about that, but they insist on having both or none."

The corner of Ronin's lip rose in a sardonic twist; he made sure his voice emphasized his dismissive tone. "I probably would not have taken it anyway, not unless you had insisted on it!"

Looking over Fai's shoulder, Ronin smiled sadly at his father when he joined them. He took the cylinder with the carpet inside unhappily before taking the dragon sword from Chang when he handed it to him. Thankfully, he had been the first to receive the news so had time to prepare himself for this.

Gesturing solemnly at his second son, Chang charged Ronin with the family's most sacred duty. "You will now take on the responsibility of guarding your sisters, the carpet of the Guardians, and the Dragon Sword until Dao arrives; which might not be for a while yet... seems he is in Africa looking for a relic. Please give these to him when he arrives, until then you have permission to use them if needed."

Bowing gravely, Ronin accepted the responsibility soberly before slipping into the harness that would hold the sword on his back. "I will not fail you father, you have prepared me well."

Smiling with pride, Chang put his hand on Ronin's shoulder while he was still bent over effectively keeping him from moving. "You have always made me proud and there is no doubt in my mind that you will be able to handle your three sisters!"

Both men grinned at two identical snorts from the girls. "Harrumph..."

Turning away from Ronin with a snicker of amusement, Chang turned to his second daughter. Sobering, he lovingly held out his arms to Magdalene.

With a small sob of anguish at the thought of losing her father so soon, Magdalene stepped into his embrace.

Tenderly, Chang kissed the top of her head fondly. "Shush now, we must make every moment we have together count. I am so proud of all of you and I will die knowing I have raised five strong, loving children; please, no more tears... I am content."

Nodding, Magdalene stepped back before wiping her cheeks. "Come, lunch should be ready by now; Fred will be with his mother at the house, they will both be hungry I am sure."

Everyone crawled into the dark blue escalade for the short trip to the ranch.

********************

Shadow Hunter watched his new wife in concern. Alexandrina had been a whirlwind of activity today. Hardly stopping, or slowing down right from the crack of dawn. She started with counting ballets then arranging for the new Seeker's to take their places.

Afterwards, Alex planned Dan's funeral and got the pyre ready. While she was on the phone making calls, the Cree/Oriental Shaman quickly slipped away for a washroom break.

When Shadow Hunter returned, his new wife was staring sightlessly at the far wall and tears were pouring down Alex's cheeks. As he rushed towards her, Hunter saw a stoic expression materialize before she got up.

What that was about; Alexandrina refused to discuss it now, a sharp... "Later!" Was all he received in explanation!

Several times throughout the day, he had stepped in Alex's way making her stop briefly; giving her a brief kiss of promise for later, he would smile at her lovingly. "I love you... I am here if you need me!"

Each time, Alexandrina would give her husband a grateful loving look then another quick kiss before going around him and continuing.

Shadow Hunter refused to leave his wife, helping where he could; staying back when he could not.

Quite a few people had walked over to give condolences then sadly informed them they had to leave right after Dan's funeral service. Most had promised to come back, three so far had cancelled their show outright; thankfully, none of them could use magic.

Most had known Dan would not last long without his wife. The two had been inseparable for years, but none had expected it quite so soon.

Shadow Hunter watched Alexandrina put the burning torch to the gasoline soaked wood underneath. With a loud crackling, 'Whoosh'... it caught instantly.

Hunter stayed close to her after the brief ceremony was over, while people gave condolences. He frowned in concern, when Alex just stood there unmoving. As soon as the last couple turned to leave, he stepped forward quickly just as she crumbled into his arms. Lifting his wife, he headed for the house without comment then took the stairs two at a time and hurried inside.

Not even bothering to take off his moccasins, Hunter quickly rushed down the long hallway to the stairs going up then went to the third floor; they had moved into the one bedroom apartment just before the wedding, he hoped that nobody would think to look for them there.

Tenderly, Shadow Hunter laid Alexandrina on their bed; he

stripped her before divesting himself of his clothes. He turned to the bed and smiled lovingly when he noticed Alex staring fixedly at him in shock. The Cree/Oriental Shaman frowned when she jumped out of bed then rushed to him in concern.

Looking down at what she was staring at, Shadow Hunter scowled perplexed... it deepened into shocked incredibility. His chest had still been burning earlier, but he had forgotten all about it after the Tianming Monk had touched him and took away most of the heat. In addition, his concern for his new wife had been his main priority since Dan had died.

Thoughtfully, Alexandrina traced the rings on Shadow Hunter's chest; the three circles of eternity were burnt into her new husband's torso. The two upper circles went from collarbone to just below his ribs... both entwined at his chest bone. The lower circle went from just above his chest bone then went almost to his belly button.

In the middle of the three joined rings was the image of the dragon on Shadow Hunter's medallion, but it was quite small. Unless, you were close it was hard to see it.

Looking up in suspicion, Alex gestured in demand. "Where is your medallion?"

Shadow Hunter awed pointed at the bedside table, he had put it there after putting Alex down so he could strip; he hadn't even looked at it, not since donning it just before the wedding.

Turning, Alexandrina grabbed the necklace and held it up. She knew before spinning around so Hunter could see that the dragon was gone. All that was left was the outer circle consisting of opened knots with the Celtic cross in the center.

Alex twisted the circle while holding the cross then a key fell into her hands. "This was hidden here in the early sixteen hundreds in case invaders took the coast of Wales; the women with all the children of the castle could hold up in that room for a long period of time. We no longer own this castle so the key is useless, but we kept it anyway. My father, who is a Tianming Monk and present at our wedding, took the curse that was concealed in the medallion into his own body."

Choking back a painful sob, Alexandrina continued stoically. "Nobody even realized it was cursed. When you stepped into the circle of eternity, it was released. For some reason, the dragon has now attached itself to you... why, I have no clue. My father's days are now numbered but he has refused to allow me to leave the retreat to go see him. My older half-brother will come soon to stay here with me until my new Guardian arrives, who also happens to be my father's oldest son. My two younger sisters will be coming too; Maggie is supposed to be leaving Calgary within the next two days."

Pulling Alexandrina close, Shadow Hunter hugged her consolingly feeling her pain. "I am so sorry love, if I had known I would not have let him touch me."

Stifling a sob, Alexandrina tried to sound resigned but failed miserably. "What is meant to be will always find a way, regardless of our wishes."

Taking Shadow Hunter's hand she turned sideways just a touch then put his hand on her belly. "I had surprising news revealed to me by the Mother Earth... I am pregnant!"

Opening his mouth to ask Alexandrina about her sisters, Shadow Hunter promptly forgot about them at the mention of a baby. "Are you sure?"

Nodding, Alexandrina pulled away. She reached over and cradled his cheek lovingly. "I will be right back."

With a bemused expression, Shadow Hunter watched his wife go into the bathroom. Hunter looked down. He lifted his hand to touch his chest... it no longer hurt.

What was the significance of the dragon attaching itself to him? He traced the tiny dragon in the center of his chest; it felt warm to the touch. Other than that, he could feel nothing else unusual.

Dropping his arm a crooked smile of incredibility surfaced... he was going to be a father. Shadow Hunter turned when he heard the bathroom door open. He gave Alexandrina a quick kiss before disappearing inside to get ready for bed.

Watching a bemused Shadow Hunter go into the bathroom, Alexandrina quickly crawled into bed. Thinking of Dan, tears began to fall as she cried out her heartache at the loss of two of the most important people in her life.

Walking out of the bathroom, Shadow Hunter went to the bed and crawled in. Cuddling his new wife close, he allowed her to cry as he held her gently. Questions about her family could wait until later.

Exhausted, it did not take either of them long to fall sleep.

# CHAPTER SEVEN

Magdalene reached over with a groggy mumble then hit her alarm. "Yeah, I am awake already!"

Yawning, Magdalene stretched before sighing in excitement but there was quite a bit of sadness too it as well. Her father, Ronin, and Fai had left last night. It had been a great week spent laughing, remembering their many antics as children then teenagers. She had a feeling that she would never see her father again so it had been a tearful goodbye.

Chang had taken Fred's mother with them to Vancouver; he would drop her off at her sisters. Maggie's father had warned the older woman that they probably would not be returning. Helen had informed them that she was a grown woman... finding her own way home would not be a problem.

The excitement was for this upcoming trip, the two were leaving right after breakfast. Jumping up, Magdalene headed into the shower. She had made sure that everything was ready to go, if all went well they should be at the retreat sometime tomorrow night. Fred would sleep while Maggie drove.

Occasionally, Fred's girlfriend would be able to drive but only on the open highway. It was an automatic with air, so she should have no problems. With three of them driving in relays, the thirty six hour trip should take under thirty... they did not plan on stopping except for food or fuel.

Finished with her shower, Magdalene brushed her teeth then got dressed. While she was dressing a thoughtful frown materialized, it added quite a bit of worry lines as she pondered the last two days spent with her family.

They had all went into Calgary for supper before combing the back allies looking for tainted magic users; surprisingly, they had found none. It had not been this quiet since the turn of the century. Now that she had more time to think, they had not seen a single

Earth Shadow either.

Finished, Maggie turned to the door; no use worrying about it right now, she would have to keep an eye open. Maybe, they had all went into hiding. The alternative was too frightening, if those creatures had already gathered all of them up and only the retreat had magic users left it did not bode well for any of them. Closing her bedroom door... she rushed downstairs.

**********

Ronin helped his youngest sister out of the car. Trying to be inconspicuous, he peaked over at his father getting out of the passenger seat. The poison was taking its toll already, he felt helpless to do anything to help his dad; Chang had aged ten years in the last week... his son sighed grimly.

Putting his sister's hand on his arm, they walked to the provincial building. Leaning over Ronin whispered. "Are you ready for this?"

Nodding with a perturbed sigh, Fai tapped her brother's arm calmly. "Yes, I hate to have to resign but things seem to be snowballing out of our control... there is no other way. Father is not doing well, the poison has advanced quickly even with the help of the carpet; his Tianming Master was not successful in stop the spread either. At this rate it won't be long!"

Squeezing his sister's hand in silent agreement, Ronin lead her to the stairs. Putting Fai's hand on the railing, he turned away to push a reporter out of their way with an impatient growl. "Later!"

They hurried up the stairs then disappeared inside.

********************

Alexandrina sat at the breakfast table, even after a whole week she still had issues going to the head of the table since she was now one of the owner of the retreat; Shadow Hunter sat on her left where Dan once sat.

It had been a quiet subdued training session this morning, Alexandrina appreciated her new husband's restraint on the hundred questions she knew he had. Tonight, Black Cougar had promised to answer them all.

The kitchen had out done themselves once again; there were scrambled eggs, bacon, sausages, pancakes or crapes, and toast with all the fixings.

After giving a brief blessing to the Great Spirit then Mother Earth, everyone dug in. Alex finished before reaching over and touching the princess's arm that was sitting on her left. "Magdalene is on her way here, she should arrive sometime tomorrow; they do not plan on stopping to sleep since there are three of them."

The princess showed her youth by clapping in glee. "Splendid, I just love..."

Her sentence was rudely interrupted when a boy of ten ran in; his face was white as a ghost. "That thing is attacking people... now there are two of them!"

Jumping up immediately, Alexandrina turned to the princess's nanny. "Get her upstairs then lock yourselves in... I will need Charles and Tyler with me!"

Racing out of the room without waiting for a reply, Alex was followed closely by Shadow Hunter, who grabbed his cloak that was by the door on the way out then hooked it around his neck as he ran.

The two bodyguards were next; the Seekers bunched together brought up the rear. They all raced towards the first group of tents at the fairgrounds.

Before the group even got close, they could hear frustrated shrieking from the creatures as they tried to get at the two women who were in the center of a group of lancers. A dozen men were keeping the two Seekers protected, refusing to allow those things to get closer.

Pulling out her Policeman's baton, Alexandrina pushed the button to extend both ends; quickly she triggered the two sharp blades so they would spring out of the tips.

Running beside his wife, Shadow Hunter opened the right side of his cloak. He grabbed his black bow. Shin having a dream on that long ago night just after he received the intricately detailed bow given to him by the Algonquin Boyer, in 1860; gave it the name Nightshade, the flaming destroyer of all things malevolent.

Hunter always had the bow strapped inside his cape. He pulled Nightshade out before letting go of the cloak. Next, he reached into the left side then pulled off two black arrows; they came away from the cloth easily, since they only had Velcro holding them there.

Unfortunately, only six arrows were ever made from the same black log as the bow... making them nearly indestructible. The Cree/Oriental Shaman knew that regular arrows would not work in this situation, so he ignored the small quiver beside the black arrows; it too was attached to his cloak.

One arrow Shadow Hunter put in his mouth, the other he notched then draw back the string. Not even pausing he let an arrow fly, while still at a dead run. It had taken him many years to learn to be able to fire a bow when racing full out... he was a crack shot.

Hunter, watched in satisfaction as the arrow drew ever closer to the first hoovering woman thing; Alexandrina had called them, Nephilim. Already he had the second arrow notched, ready to be released.

The Nephilim feeling a disturbance in the air, turned sharply and the arrow just grazed her upper left arm. She shrieked in pain before grabbing at her bleeding shoulder.

The group racing towards the creatures all stopped in perplexed shock when Alexandrina screamed too then clutched at her own arm. She stopped dead incredulously, Black Cougar stared at the mirror image looking back at her. Except for the wings plus the shorter hair which had grown to shoulder length... it looked exactly like her; the wings too had filled in substantially as it hunted magic users and Earth Shadows relentlessly.

It stared intently at Alexandrina, just as stunned then looked at Shadow Hunter with the string on his bow pulled tight... preparing to let another arrow loose. The only thing holding him back was his confusion over that scream from his wife, was it because of the arrow hitting that thing?

Clutching her shoulder dumbfounded, Alexandrina stared in amazement at those things. Bending slightly, she battled for control of her totem as the cougar struggled to be released when the Nephilim female glided towards them. Never had Alex ever had to physically push the beast down to stop it from getting out, always she was in control... until now!

The biggest Nephilim stopped a safe distance away feeling the woman's struggle to contain the beast within. She did not want her to turn, it could kill them since they were still quit vulnerable not having their full wings yet.

The animal, as well as the bow were both routed in the seven realms so death was a real possibility; there was no way back from the death realm... yet!

Clutching at the smaller Nephilim beside her, she used her other hand to point at the bow. "Too late, Ava, the Hunter has the bow and SHE is pregnant; although, not whole... what does that mean?"

Shrugging unknowingly, the smaller Nephilim growled in rage. "They are vulnerable right now, but so are we; the curse has been removed allowing the dragon to bond with the Hunter... why? What could have caused that to happen? It is impossible for him to be the dragon, something is not right. We will need her now!"

Grimacing in anger, not looking forward to that confrontation the two disappeared.

Scowling in confusion, Shadow Hunter eased the tension on the bow string as he turned to his wife in concern. "Are you okay... did you understand any of that?"

Inclining her head in reassurance, Alexandrina stood straighter then dropped her hand from her arm. The pain and the need to change form had disappeared with the winged Nephilims. "I am fine. I only caught a few words that seemed close to a language I know... its Hebrew. Unfortunately, it is an archaic version of the old language. I will talk to my father later; he might be able to shed some light on what they were saying. The arrow hurt me too, thankfully no wound surface so it is only the pain that is transferable. I hope that it means I will not die if it does. Although, I better prepare myself for a painful experience."

Frowning grimly, Shadow Hunter released the string on his bow then put his arrow away before hooking his bow inside his cloak; he turned to his wife uneasily. "Let's hope we do not have to find out the hard way. Did you notice that there have been very few shadows lately?"

Surprised, Alexandrina stiffened uneasily as she looked around. "No, I had not since they have always stayed away from me for some reason."

Nodding his head thoughtfully, Shadow Hunter didn't comment. He had noticed that and wondered why. Breaking away from the others the Cree/Oriental went to find his arrow, they were too precious to leave behind.

*****

Materializing inside their prison, which still had a firm hold on them... the two waited for her. They were not looking forward to it. Richell was the most evil of the three, terrifyingly crazy even for their piece of minds. It was not long before she showed up; none of them could be away for any length of time, but soon!

Scowling at the oldest of the three, Richell gestured angrily. "Zarina, what are you two doing here! Both of you should be out gathering your feathers."

Explaining quickly, Zarina told of their shock in finding the dragon bonded to the Hunter then their amazement that SHE was pregnant already.

Rubbing her upper lip thoughtfully, Richell listened closely until the older one finished. Using her long nail on her index finger, she began tapping on her lips reflectively for a long moment.

Finally, extending her finger... she point at Zarina. "Did you not tell me recently that you fought a SHE; before the woman turned into a wolf and pulled out one of your new feathers?"

Nodding in aggravation, Zarina pulled on her ear repeatedly. Even now, she could not get rid of that nervous habit. "Well yes! Come to think of it, it does not seem to be the one that we just saw; neither, was SHE... pregnant."

Gesturing at the missing piece of skin on her arm, Richell grimaced in anger remembering her confrontation with HER. "I also had a moment with one, as you can see it did not turn out well. SHE was with the Guardian, who happened to have the sword already. There must be three of them too; it's quite disconcerting that they look exactly like us. Is there some reason for that... it makes me wonder. One is pregnant, but the dragon bonded to the Hunter so the curse must have been removed somehow. Only the White Dragon would have the power to release it. I do not feel her in this age so the Celtic dragon must still be trapped."

Shaking her head in confusion, the Nephilim finally shrugged resignedly. "We might be wrong though? Maybe it's just a coincidence... could be that none of them are HER."

The middle Nephilim, called Ava by the others. Usually the gentlest, slowest in thought of the three; grabbed her two identical accomplices arms in excitement. "It doesn't matter we need to make sure the dragon is put back on the medallion so that the curse can be activated again. I just so happen to have the perfect plan to accomplish both in one shot!"

The other two listened in amazement, not expecting such deviousness from Ava. Suddenly... they disappeared. An evil cackle of satisfaction made even the prison shudder in reaction.

***************

Magdalene drummed her fingers impatiently on the restaurant table; next time she would insist on take out! One delay after another had stalled them. Fredrick's girlfriend was still in night clothes, it had taken another hour for her to be ready. She needed three stops for the bathroom all because Maggie had decided not to put water in the Volvo, now once again here they were waiting for that woman.

Fredrick sighed aggrieved knowing it had been a mistake to bring his pampered perfectly prissy girlfriend. She could be quiet efficient, although not very perceptive at times. She acted like a blonde scatterbrain when meeting new people, testing them. Jane's intelligence was almost at the genius level, but she hid it well. Maggie just did not know her well enough yet. "I will talk to her... I promise! Here she comes; go, I already paid the bill."

Nodding impatiently, Magdalene jumped up before storming out.

Stopping in front of the Volvo Toterhome, which Maggie had purchased a couple years ago, she couldn't help staring at it in approval. It caused countless heads to turn wherever she went, this was only its third trip out... it would also be its longest one so far.

It was quite a plush unit, which she had custom made to include two extra seats directly behind the front ones. Afterwards, she had them add a full partition with a small door to go inside the living quarters, needing privacy.

This rig had much better towing capabilities compared to a regular motorhome or a pickup with a fifth wheel. It had two pull outs so could sleep up to ten people in a pinch; plus, it had a full bathroom with a large Jet tub.

The colours were spectacular, inky black with maroon shot through it complimented the rearing dark steal grey coloured coat of Fai's stallion Grey; he was prominently displayed on the side with Maggie's tobiano black paint mare. The deep red brought out the full feathering around her hooves with the beautiful white mane and tail that turns black the last two inches. She looked so much like the Gypsy Vanner horse that Cecille had ridden so long ago.

On each door was the dragon medallion with white shooting flames around it with the caption, 'Triple Illusions' then under that 'All your trick riding needs.'

Walking past the Toterhome to the fifth wheel horse trailer,

Magdalene stepped up onto the running board to pat her horse knowing it would calm her irritation. The middle triplet was not use to being so impatient, especially when it came to friends.

Unfortunately, an urgent feeling just after waking up at four am this morning was nagging at Magdalene. Even now, the need to hurry was plaguing her; it seemed to be getting worse as the day wore on.

The black and white mare that the middle triplet named, Angel instantly stuck her head out with a whiff of air; she nuzzled her mistress's hand lovingly when Maggie walked over.

Sighing in delight, Magdalene relaxed instantly. Calm once more, she kissed her horse's nose in thanks; stroking the long black and white muzzle affectionately, Maggie smiled. "Soon my sweet, I know you hate travelling but it is only one more day... I hope. We definitely will not make it by suppertime tomorrow at this rate!"

Pulling her head back in, Angel went back to eating when her mistress left to check on the other horses. Fai had asked her sister to bring her horse along, Ronin hearing the request wanted his gelding brought too. Just in case he was able to make it, Magdalene included her fathers; if not, the mare would be retired to the retreat.

Fai's horse put his nose out then snuffled inquisitively. Feeling a need, she walked over to the steel dark grey stallion with its pure white mane and tail; he was an exact replica of his forefather that Shin had ended up riding against his will. He even had an unusual blue eye with a mismatched brown one. The intelligence he displayed was incredible, he even matched the playful get into trouble temperament his great, great grandfather had.

That is why Grey was always kept at the very back of a trailer. He was a regular Houdini when it comes to escaping from any stall, knot, or halter rope. Even barn stalls or locked trailer doors could not hold him for long, but with the other five horses in his way it effectively kept him contained... this time.

Magdalene laughed when Grey stuck out his long tongue trying to hook her heart shaped locket that she always wore around her neck. "You better just behave yourself!"

Grey snorted in rebuke when she left, but pulled his head in then went back to munching on hay. He hated being in the trailer; getting smart, they always hooked his halter on both sides so he could not turn his head to reach the buckles. It effectively kept him in place... for now.

Feeling the rig move, Magdalene knew her passengers were finally ready to go. Hurrying forward, she opened the driver's door and pulled herself up into the seat; she smiled in pleasure at the embellished door panel done in deep magenta with black swirling throughout. Inside was just as plush as outside with a black dashboard trimmed in a lighter magenta colour. The seats were cloth with white dragons on a black background again with the dark magenta embellishing everything.

Almost ready to put the truck in gear, Maggie felt a touch on her arm from Fredrick's girlfriend.

Smiling hesitantly in apology, Jane gestured in appeasement. "I'm sorry, I did not realize this was going to be a rushed trip; I thought it was supposed to be a holiday?"

Turning slightly, Magdalene put her hand over the one on her arm. "No, I am sorry for being so impatient; yes, it is a holiday of sorts but there is a need to get there in a hurry. Afterwards, you can take all the time you need to see things. I promise we will take at least a week to see the sights on our trip back home."

Nodding in relief, Jane was glad the air between them had lightened. "I will have a nap then I can drive for a while if you like since Fred assured me it is an automatic."

Sighing in relief that Jane understood, Magdalene pulled out of the parking lot and they were off once more. Unfortunately, for some reason her anxiety only worsened.

********************

Ronin shut the escalade door then turned to the reporters hounding them for answers on whether they had taken the appointment as head of the bureau or not.

Holding up his hands for quiet, Ron cleared his throat. "Due to our father's unexpected terminal illness we have had to sadly decline the position. We are both extremely grateful to have been chosen for such a prestigious opportunity; Fai Ryuu has also resigned her position at the law firm until further notice!"

Several questions were fired at him and Ronin shook his head negatively. "No, I have no idea who will now get the job, but I am confident they will decide soon... that is all for now."

Turning away before any more questions could be asked; Ronin went to the driver's side and got in. They had not used a chauffeur this time since they did not want anyone asking questions if their father didn't make the rest of the trip.

Within minutes, they were headed towards the realtors to put the condominium up for sale. It would be followed by a quick lunch. Their appointment at the lawyers would most likely take up the rest of the day. Ronin quickly peek in the rear-view mirror, he frowned in concern at the pasty white drawn look he received from his father... he sighed resignedly; if they get everything accomplished in time they would be extremely lucky.

Pulling impatiently out onto the freeway, Ronin got an angry honk from a truck that he unintentionally cut off; he ignored it. Looking up at the gathering storm clouds moving in fast from the East, his frown of concern deepened.

*****

Five hours later, Ronin sighed relieved as he pulled into traffic yet again. They had gotten all the important stuff done today and it was getting late. Looking quickly into the mirror, he noticed his father staring out the window. "Dad, would you like to stop in Chinatown for supper?"

Chang continued to stare out the window but nodded as he felt his destiny drawing closer once they turned towards their destination. He had one more important task to accomplish he knew; looking over, he reached out then touched his son's shoulder. "Here, we will eat at the Dirty Apron!"

Fai laughed in delight. "Good, I love their wonton soup."

Snorting in agreement, Ronin concurred. "Yes, it is good; although, I prefer their sushi."

Pulling into a side alley, Ronin went up the one way to the back of the restaurant. It was easier parking here, since there was no way to get to the front from the road they had entered on because of road construction. They would have to go all the way around with the escalade before doing a roundabout and driving the opposite way to get to the front... much better from here.

Once he was stopped, Ron looked up at the black sky in concern as rain began to fall in a heavy sheet. It had been threatening all day, just their luck it had to wait until now to start. He mumbled irritably when lightening flashed to the left then a crack of thunder sounded only minutes later.

Jumping out with a frown of irritation, Ronin helped his father out before rushing around to help his sister. He turned away from the vehicle in relief when he saw his father holding the sword... it was never left in the vehicle. They always made sure to have a security badge hooked to their belts proclaiming their legal right to wear weapons openly in public.

The three rushed around to a side door, but all of them froze at a scream of fear then the feeble cry of a baby further down the alley. Turning as one, they switched directions without even a hesitation.

Lightning lit up the sky for half a second allowing the two men to see six men grappling with a man and a woman. A squirming bundle was lying on the ground wrapped up in something; water was getting higher around it threatening to flow over the baby's protection.

Hearing an infant, Fai instantly started chanting letting out White Buffalo so she could see with her inner eye. Even while listening to her brother call out warnings of what he had seen in the brief flash of light. Disregarding Ron's caution, Fai headed straight for the bundle... ignoring all else.

Pulling out his two daggers, since his father still held the dragon sword. Ronin frowned in surprise. Chang was way ahead of them, his frail shuffling walk of earlier was gone.

The Guardian gave out a challenging scream trying to distract the men attacking the couple.

Shaking his head grimly, Ron got another quicker look at the scene as he raced after his father when a lightning bolt flared. Thankfully, the rain eased to a light drizzle; making visibility much better.

Ronin instantly knew that the six wearing identical robes with hoods were Ninja; the couple being attacked were also well versed in the arts. The two were effectively keeping the six at bay despite the fact that the woman was bent slightly in obvious pain then everything went pitch dark once again.

Just as the woman fell having lost way too much blood to stand any longer, Chang reached her and straddled the woman while keeping three of the ninja's from reaching her. His sword hummed in satisfaction as it cleaved through flesh as one of the assailants dropped to the ground dead.

Doing a roundhouse kick, the Guardian heard a satisfying, 'THWAK'... as he connected with one of the assailants head, knocking him out cold. He wanted at least one alive; to find out why highly trained Ninja's felt the need to attack a couple with a baby.

Originally in times long past Ninja's were trained as assassins but as time wore on, they diversified becoming bodyguards for higher. Still some adhered to the old ways... killing for money.

Reaching the three attacking the man, Ronin vaulted over top of the one then landed dead center of the three... taking over the fight.

The man exhausted, took the opportunity to fall back out of the way; he crawled over to his dying wife and gathered her close before looking towards the strange woman holding his baby. He frowned in determination, but turned away to look down at his wife as she clutched at his shirt desperately with a pained shake of her head. His frown deepened in angry disagreement. "It must be done!"

Giving another feeble plea the woman's eyes closed for the last time as her breathing stilled. "Please... don't!"

As soon as the woman died, the last man Chang was fighting jumped back then sheathed his weapon. He bent to pick up his unconscious comrade before they both disappeared.

The Tianming Monk frowned grimly in surprise, they did not seem to care that the man was still alive. It wasn't until that moment, he noticed the red sash on the attackers leaving; caulking his head inquisitively he looked towards the three Ronin was fighting and noticed they had white sashes.

It was all the distraction the man holding his wife needed; he jumped up then drove a knife his wife had hidden in her smock into his rescuer before turning he ran for the woman holding his baby.

Chang gave a grunt of shocked surprise when the man pulled the dagger out of his left side before running towards his daughter with the bloody knife held out threateningly.

The Guardian finding strength that he did not know he had charged after the man just as a lightning bolt hit Fai and the screaming baby.

Everyone froze in stunned disbelief before covering their eyes as the two disappeared in the bright white light.

*****************

Magdalene feeling her eyes droop for the second time sighed in resignation before pulling into a rest stop; she turned to Fredrick hopefully. "You can drive for a while, give me fifteen minutes to go to the washroom and settle into my bed. I will send your girlfriend out."

Nodding, Fredrick decided to go to the men's room as well. When he got back, Jane was settling into the passenger's seat. After he got comfortable, Fred leaned over to steal a quick kiss before easing the rig into traffic once more

Maggie had waited until after they negotiated Saskatchewan to pull over. Fred was definitely glad she had, driving through the boring province was quite challenging.

Thankfully, it should only take five hours to negotiate Manitoba; it was the shortest province out of all of them. Fred couldn't help thinking, if everything went well they should be in Ontario by midnight or thereabouts. They were making good time, despite the slow shaky start this morning.

Fred decided he would let Jane drive once they were about half way through the province, for a while anyway; before waking Magdalene up, so they could find a good place to eat. Turning the music a bit louder, he hummed as he drove.

*****

Settling into her plushy mattress in the large master bedroom of her Toterhome, Magdalene close her eyes; instantly, she was pulled into the dream world.

Looking around disoriented, Maggie cringed when thunder cracked right above her and rain drenched her. Seeing a flicker of movement, Red Wolf spun around in time to see her Guardian fighting three opponents trying to save a couple lying on the ground.

In grim disbelief, the middle triplet screamed out a warning to her father; it did her no good though. Maggie stood there watching helplessly as the man her dad was trying to save turned on him then stab him in the back.

Thankfully, Magdalene saw her father chase after his attacker when the man headed towards her baby sister with the dagger still dripping his blood.

Suddenly, everyone froze in disbelief.

Maggie cried out in shocked terror; her hand reached out beseechingly when a bolt of lightning came out of nowhere before striking Fai, as well as the baby she was holding

It gave Chang plenty of time to catch up to his stunned assailant.

Quickly, the Tianming Monk managed to dispatch the man even while keeping a hand over his eyes shielding them from the intense bright light.

Without warning, a pain exploded deep in Magdalene's chest; she screeched in stunned horror as her back arched. Red Wolf swayed before dropping to her knees... shocked. Maggie holding onto her left breast tried to stop the burning pain, but it refused to relent.

# CHAPTER EIGHT

Shadow Hunter frowned in surprise, he looked down at his watch speculatively; it was custom made so not only did it have the time, but when the button on the opposite side was pushed a mini holographic computer screen popped up. It also had calling capabilities so he had never carried a cell phone in his life. He had given Alexandrina one yesterday so he could now find her anywhere.

Who could be banging at their door so late, Hunter scowled when he checked his watch again. Well it was only seven, but because of the stormy black sky it seemed later to him. The Cree/Oriental Shaman could hear rain still drumming against the building; it had driven them inside earlier when lightning and thunder sounded in the far off distance.

Looking towards the bathroom, Shadow Hunter shrugged; his wife was occupied so he turned to the door. He had filled the tub earlier for Alexandrina and lovingly scrubbed her from head to toe before leaving her to soak for a while.

Just as Hunter opened the door, Alex walked out of the bathroom in a robe drying her beautiful midnight black hair. It caused the Cree/Oriental Shaman to turn back towards his wife bemusedly.

Distractedly, Hunter turned back to the open door then looked up... way up; at the eight-foot giant bodyguard of the princess's, he frowned in concern. "What can I do for you?"

Charles beckoned urgently. "The first Seeker must come immediately; the Princess wanted to go visit some of the tents looking for a Gypsy for a fortune telling. Our party was attacked by one of those things on our way there. It got to her personal guard and she is dead. Thankfully, it disappeared again. The Princess refused to leave her nanny, so sent me to get the Priestess instead."

Turning inquisitively, Shadow Hunter looked over at his wife in question.

Rushing to the wardrobe with a quick flick of her wrist, Alexandrina called out grimly. "Go, protect the Princess I will be there as quick as possible!"

Needing no second urging, Shadow Hunter shrugged into his swords harness before grabbing his cloak that was hanging beside it. Rushing out the door, he followed the huge guard closely. Draping the cloak around his shoulders quickly, he raced down the stairs.

Jumping down the last few stairs, Hunter switched on his watch as he ran towards the back door so that his assistants could record what was happening.

Racing out the front door, Hunter grimaced resignedly; it was still pouring out. Unfortunately, the thunder and lightning had gotten closer. He winced as a lightning bolt flared a couple miles away, in relief he counted to fifty before the thunder sounded. It was still a ways away yet, but moving fast it was getting uncomfortably closer.

Following the big man's flashlight ahead, the Cree/Oriental Shaman was thankful that he really did not need it since he still had exceptional night vision.

Hunter pulled out his sword when he saw a crowd of people ahead... just in case. It was pitch-black out with no moon, so only the guard's flashlight with the occasional lightning strike gave off any kind of light.

Instantly, everyone moved out of the guard's way so the two men could drop down beside the woman bodyguard.

Shadow Hunter grabbed the princess's arm angrily before pointing towards the house in demand. "Go to your apartment, there is nothing you can do for her now; hurry, the first Seeker is on the way... we must keep you safe."

Nodding reluctantly, the princess got up in a huff; flanked by her two guards, she raced off.

No sooner, were the three gone then the crowd surrounding Shadow Hunter scattered; the ones that couldn't dropped to their knees right where they were before covering their sensitive ears... several cried out in severe pain.

Two Nephilim, both looking exactly like Alexandrina materialized and surrounded Shadow Hunter; they both held swords awkwardly not after his magic... he had none.

Quickly, Shadow Hunter jumped to his feet and went to meet his destiny; sparks flew when three swords clanged together.

Unnoticed, the third Nephilim holding a red glowing spear materialized behind the Hunter then silently she waited for an opening. The spear must not only pierce the man in the center of his chest, but it must also penetrate the dragon that is prominent in the center of the three rings of eternity.

Drawing back her arm, Richell released the spear just as a cougar jumped between the man and the spear. At the same instant the spear entered the cougar's heart a bolt of lightning struck the huge cat... she fell to the ground dead.

The oldest Nephilim screamed in denial, but it was cut short as Zarina exploded then disappeared. The two others, in total shock vanished back to their prison.

Covering his eyes, Shadow Hunter wailing in disbelief tried to get to his wife; he could hardly see a thing in the blinding white light. The stench of burning hair singed his nostrils before her form changed back.

***************

A whisper of fear and uncertainty was plain to hear in the darkness of their prison. "What just happened? There is no way a mere spear, even with the curse of death attached to it, could cause the death of HER!"

Quivering anxiously the youngest shivered, Richell was not use to feeling afraid... she was now. The Nephilim waved her hand causing a ball of light to appear, she looked around expectantly, but they were now one less. "I don't know, I had him I'm sure of it.

Where the shape shifter came from I have no notion. Nor do I know why Zarina exploded; will we die too, if the other two do?"

Inhaling fearfully, Ava finally shrugged resignedly. "I have no idea, either."

Shrugging, Richell's back stiffened before she gestured sharply. "We must find another spear I could not get to the other one, in this age they are almost impossible to find. We must get the dragon back on the medallion; only the curse of death can trap it again. I will be back shortly, I am sure the lord of the dead will demand a huge price for another spear... you keep watch while I am gone!"

With that, Richell disappeared.

The Nephilim left behind could not help a squeak of fear not wanting to go anywhere close to the Hunter again, but obediently Ava left then blackness descended.

***************

Magdalene, feeling the pressure ease stood up straighter; she stared in amazement when her oldest sister floated past her before walking into the intense light surrounding Fai.

Watching in awe, Maggie saw the oldest of the triplets step into White Buffalo and the two became one causing the light to disappear as if it had never been.

A deep need hit Maggie suddenly, so she rushed forward to join her two sisters... for a split second the three became one; she felt the love of her sisters first then a thrill at an unexpected maternal feeling. Without warning, both vanished.

Bolting into a sitting position on her bed, Magdalene screamed out Alexandrina's name in denial. Tears streaked her face as she sobbed for her oldest sister in stunned disbelief and for the baby boy that would never be.

Maggie cried bitter tears of remorse for not having made it to the retreat in time; they still had a long way to go so probably wouldn't even make it for the burning of the funeral pyre. Lying back down on the bed, Red Wolf cried herself to sleep... heartbroken!

**********

Screaming his oldest daughter's name in shock after dispatching his murderer; Chang dropped onto his knees on the ground in anguish as he felt the death of his first born.

The Guardian had seen Alexandrina briefly in the bright white light from the bolt of lightning. Unfortunately, the light became too intense for him to see more. Mercifully, it winked out so he could see a glowing Fai in the darkness curled around a bundle.

Frowning in worry, Chang saw Magdalene for a split second; she also went to her youngest sister then disappeared. With blood pouring out of his back, Chang kept kneeling only by shear will alone. Thankfully, in relief he saw Maggie again as she left her sisters before vanishing.

The Tianming Monk finally allowed himself to drop onto the ground as he searched determinedly for the three heartbeats of his daughters; a grimace of resignation was all he could muster when all he could feel was two.

Unexpectedly, it was over and the last assailant fighting Ronin turned to flee in fear. Now that the intense light with the sizzling heat had dissipated, the older brother of the triplets raced to his dying father. Ron changed directions knowingly when his father instantly pointed at their vehicle.

Quickly, Ronin ran to the back of the escalade then pulled out the cylinder with the rolled up carpet before racing back; he was just in time to see Fai highlighted by the dwindling lightning still curled protectively around a now quiet baby, he couldn't help wondering silently if it was dead.

The lightening continued to flare further away, keeping the back alley bright enough for Ronin to see where he was going. It did not take him long to pull out the rug and spread it out on the ground. He helped his father into the center before going around to the front of the carpet then pulled it forward; now, it would cover up the pool of blood that was on the ground from his dying father... every drop was precious.

Chang reached out beseechingly towards his youngest daughter and ward when several minutes passed with no movement or sound coming from her or the baby Time seemed to stop for a long moment. The Tianming Monk sighed in relief when White Buffalo finally lifted her head up... she was alive at least.

The Guardian suddenly heard the baby yawn in the stillness of the alley; he couldn't help a relieved breath from escaping, glad the child had survived too. He inhaled incredulously when White Buffalo looked over at him just as the light faded once more making her vivid dark green eyes glow.

It reminded Chang of the first twins, Cecille had given her father quite a scare when he saw his daughter standing on the highest mast of the ship taking them to Quebec. She was drawing lightning into her tiny frame because Mother Earth had instructed her to do so in order to save everyone on board the ship. A freak storm was about to happen that would have killed everyone, including them.

Shaking off the memory knowing they did not have much time, Chang called out to his daughter. "Hurry Fai, come sit on the carpet... bring the baby with you."

Lightning flare again highlighting his son, so Chang gestured for Ronin to sit beside him so that now he was in the center of his two children. When Fai settled, she looked directly at him; Chang smiled relieved as he stared into those eyes then saw a flicker of black before the alley went dark again. He felt the dormant power in White Buffalo gain strength, but it was still unusable beyond her ability to wield it.

The Guardian watched the glow disappear from his youngest daughter's eyes and they turned back to green, a darker more intense green... he knew that two were now one.

Sadly, Fai stared down at her father; she knew that he was dying as she felt their bond fading. Still holding the baby protectively, her large bulky raincoat that she had donned when the rain began had kept him surrounded... safe from the lightening. White Buffalo reached out with her free hand then took her father's gravely. "I love you, father!"

Nodding knowingly, Chang released Fai's hand; he reached over before pulling at her coat insistently. "Let me see!"

Nodding, Fai let the bulky jacket fall open.

Chang looked at the baby intently. He was deformed a bit with huge ferret like brown eyes. His forehead was big, it hid part of his brow; there was no break in the eyebrows making them a single line... he did not have much of a chin either. The Guardian could see short arms with stubby legs, the child would be lucky to reach four feet.

Chanting, the Tianming Monk brought a blood stained finger dripping with his blood up then put a cross on the child's forehead. "He is meant for great things, one day he will save ONE!"

Feebly, Chang dropped onto his side having a hard time holding himself up. The carpet was the only thing keeping him alive now as it continued to draw in his blood, even the blood that had been on the ground under the carpet was gone.

Taking his daughters hand again, the Guardian gave it a gentle squeeze. He reached for his sons with the other one before addressing them both when Ronin took it. "Fai you must bring the carpet to life, I am too weak. Make sure to pull Maggie with us; hurry we must get to the retreat... Mother Earth is waiting! Ron will help you."

Settling the baby in the crook of her crossed legs, Fai was grateful that he fit perfectly being so small, lucky for them he had went right back to sleep.

Reaching past their father, the youngest triplet took her brothers hand with her free one. Chanting, the three went deep into meditation.

********************

Shadow Hunter cried out his wife's name in disbelief. Ignoring the sizzling sounds, plus the rank odour of flesh and hair burning he dropped on all fours before crawling to Alexandrina. It seemed to take forever for the light to disappear so he could see clearly again.

Gathering Black Cougar into his lap, Hunter wept bitterly. Heart wrenching noises continued to escape his lips involuntarily as he rocked his wife, willing her unfocused staring eyes to turn to him one last time. Finally, he reached up tenderly to close them.

Pulling out the spear, the Cree/Oriental Shaman threw it into the night not caring if he hit anything or not. There was no glow to the tip now; the curse could only be used once. "Alex how could you give up your life and sacrifice our unborn child, I'm not worthy of such devotion!"

Continuing to sob, Shadow Hunter ignored the itchy painful burning sensation in his chest that had worsened once he had braved the lightening to gather his wife in his arms. Standing, Hunter lifted his wife then turning he carried her to the house.

The crowd followed slowly... keeping a discreet distance; not a dry eye could be seen as they felt the emotional upheaval the Cree/Oriental Shaman was displaying.

Reaching the front steps, Shadow Hunter took the stairs two at a time before turning beseechingly when he reached the top. "Can someone please ready a burning pyre for my wife, once it is ready I will bring her out and a vigil will be held until tomorrow night. Anyone wishing to bring something meaningful to them for Alexandrina's pyre to help her on the journey to the Great Spirit is more than welcomed to add it."

A native woman dressed in an intricate Shaman's dress stepped forward. She held two bowls of something, and a soft deerskin cloth was draped over her arm. "I am Running Doe, a woman Shaman from the Mi'kmaq tribe where the Priestess was born; allow me to prepare her in our ways for the cremation. The Mother Earth has sent me special instructions that need to be followed for Black Cougar to reach the Great Spirit."

Eyeing the woman thoughtfully, Shadow Hunter finally nodded. He turned then the two slipped through the doors.

Waiting for them was the new head mistress of the Seeker's and her husband. She beckoned them to follow; the woman took them to the door leading to the basement before taking them down the three steps to the landing that led to two doors.

The one straight ahead went down to the Mother's caverns... the one on the left would take you to the basement entertainment rooms. The woman unlocked the door going to the Seekers chambers; it was the only door in this house kept locked at all times.

Carefully, Shadow Hunter had to negotiate the stairs down at an awkward angle so Alexandrina would not touch the walls, the narrow stairwell was only meant for one. It seemed to take forever as they slowly made their way down, but Hunter refused all help.

Finally, the Cree/Oriental Shaman was standing in front of the entry into the Mother's chambers... black bold writing illuminated the entrance.

**'Where once there were three now two remain, allowing the dragon to become caretaker of a seed'.**

Shaking his head in confusion, the Hunter ignored the writing; he walked through the door then turned left before going to the antechamber where his wedding vows were said and the head Seeker was chosen only a few days ago.

Once inside the room, Shadow Hunter blinked in shock. Every lantern was lit around the room, with candles on either side of him forming a walkway leading to the intricate web that was the center of Mother Earth's power; with more candles surrounding a stone alter that was in the center. It was only two feet of the ground, so kneeling would have to suffice.

Hundreds of robed Seeker's took up the entire room, except for the cleared path that led directly to the long slab of rocks. In the back of his mind was a disoriented question on how that had come to be there. It was a jumble of rocks hastily put together by the looks of the unsymmetrical platform, what was holding the rocks in place was a mystery.

Kneeling, the Cree/Oriental Shaman wept as he gently placed his wife on it. Careful not to scratch her delicate skin on the rough surface even though he knew she would never feel it... it mattered to him.

A young woman rushed in with Alexandrina's robe, the head mistress took it before walking over then knelt beside Shadow Hunter. "You must go up and purify yourself while Running Doe washes your wife in preparation; come back as soon as you are ready."

Clutching his wife's hand protectively, Shadow Hunter frowned not wanting to leave her here without him. He looked around at all the Seeker's surrounding them then scowled when he heard them humming; the Cree/Oriental Shaman had not noticed it until now.

Finally, in obvious reluctance Hunter kissed the top of Alexandrina's forehead before getting to his feet and disappeared out the door.

Nobody moved as they all waited for Alexandrina's husband to leave. Once he was gone, everyone in the room turned their backs... respectfully; it allowed the two women to strip the body so that they could wash her.

The low humming never ceased even when the two women preparing the body began chanting also. It was quite different in tone; obviously, in a language nobody understood. Sorrowfully, they prepared Alex for her journey to the happy hunting grounds of the Great Spirit.

The two women could feel that the Earth's Spirit or Po had already left the body; the two looked at each other in surprise. Usually, both the Po and Hun would remain until the burning of the body. The cremation would trigger the release of the Spirits from their host.

Shrugging perplexed, the Spiritual healer of the Mi'kmaq finished washing Alexandrina. The Hun was a person's soul and given by the Great Spirit. The Mi'kmaq tribes of New Brunswick called him, Kjiniskam, God of all living things. The Po was from the Mother

Earth, it was meant to guide and teach; unfortunately, most had quite listening.

Neither women had stopped chanting, but the humming did increase just a touch when they all felt a light vibration coming from the Mother Earth.

***************

Magdalene blew her nose than laid back down; she was beyond tired after crying for the last hour or so. Tucking the tissue under her pillow, the middle triplet drifted back to sleep. It seemed that she barely closed her eyes when she felt her youngest sister pull her into the dream world.

The middle triplet could feel her father slipping away and she whimpered in protest; Maggie felt her half-brother with them so knew they must be using the carpet... it was the only way to bring Ronin.

Swiftly, the four flew to the retreat then barely slowing they hurtled down the stairs before entering the antechamber of the Mother Earth. Here, Po was quite powerful and with the Seeker's all helping, she made sure the ones she needed arrived on time to do what must be done.

Sitting cross legged around Alexandrina the four shadows began chanting rhythmically; keeping time with the head Seeker as they waited, for what... none of them knew.

********************

Shadow Hunter threw his clothes into a heap to be burned later. Once he was inside his bathroom, the Cree/Oriental Shaman stepped into the shower to get rid of the blood and the scorched scent of flesh that still clung to his skin. Hunter was sure though that the stench would stay in his nostrils… forever.

Leaning against the shower stall wall, Shadow Hunter allowed the tears to flow unchecked. Finally, dropping his head he let the water run on the back of his neck.

Opening his eyes, Hunter looked down at his chest when the pain began to subside.

Blinked incredulously, Shadow Hunter shook his head... he must be seeing things. Hunter was positive the dragon had been smaller and both talons of the dragon were opened earlier; now it looked to him like the left one had closed. Shaking his head grimly at his foolishness, the Cree/Oriental Shaman shut his eyes again. He probably just didn't notice it earlier since he was too preoccupied with his new wife.

Scrubbing himself viciously, still unable to focus on anything for long except his wife's death, Shadow Hunter stepped out of the shower. He dried himself then left the bathroom to put on his Cree loincloth making sure his ornamental ceremonial dagger was at his waist. Putting on his moccasins next, he turned to pick up his medallion and put it around his neck.

Even without the dragon on it, the cross still held great significance for him... it nestled just below his white medicine bag. Now ready, Shadow Hunter left his room before racing down the stairs.

*****

Chanting, Running Doe finished painting the first Priestess of the Seekers face red. It represented the Earth; next, she painted her nipples the same colour. She had mixed bloodroot and raspberries to get a nice deep red colour. She painted around Alexandrina's belly button before the junction of her thighs.

Unexpectedly, the Mi'kmaq Priestess switched bowls. She pulled out a good handful of black paint then coloured the rest of Alexandrina's breasts in that colour. The bulge of her belly was next, but none was added to her thighs.

Running Doe was a bit confused; this colour pattern was used for rebirth. If someone had been raped, a healer would use this combination of colours then with the Shaman leading the victim they would go into a sweat lodge and performed a rebirth. This was done to take away the rape, making the woman complete once more. Only black paint should have been used right now... it represented the finality of death.

After the Mi'kmaq woman helped the head Seeker put Alexandrina's robe on, they became aware of the four visitors; neither acknowledged them, nor did they quit chanting.

Once the robe was on, the head Seeker cut a hole around the oldest triplets belly so that the black paint with the red around the bellybutton protruded. Unexpectedly, she moved down then cut a triangle out making sure the point was at the apex of Alexandrina's thighs. Giving an assistant the scissors and the two bowls, the women stood just as Shadow Hunter entered.

Going straight to his wife, the Cree/Oriental Shaman ignored all else. He dropped into a kneeling position before removing his dagger; he began chanting then wailed out his grief eerily, slicing into his flesh in a frenzy of anguish.

The two women standing over Alexandrina clasped hands before their chanting changed with the first slice of Shadow Hunter's knife and his blood flowed. Still neither recognized or understood what they were saying, but that did not stop them. They knelt one on each side of Alexandrina then placed their hands over the bulge on her belly.

Fai and Magdalene hurried over to place their hands over the entwined ones of the two women. A warm tingling feeling entered Running Doe's then the head Seekers hand's but just for a brief second before dying out.

The two women staggered back in shock, feeling compelled and still chanting. The four women turned to Shadow Hunter to lay their hands on him.

Shadow Hunter shuddered; already he had several deep gashes all over his body. It was the burning in his chest though that bothered him the most... since it had returned with a vengeance. When the two women touched him, the heat in his chest subsided to a more manageable level.

Blood was everywhere; it was not until then that he felt the presence of the others. When he looked up, they vanished. He frowned irritably wondering who they were and where they had gone. Hunter had not noticed them earlier being too preoccupied with his grieving.

The two women on either side of Shadow Hunter stood up. He watched in puzzlement as everyone in the room left... until only one remained.

The head Seeker put a consoling hand on Shadow Hunter's shoulder before pointing over at the door with the other one. "We will leave you now to finish your grieving alone. The Mother Earth has healed most of your deeper gashes, but there will be no more healing now. My suggestion to you would be to put the knife away and continue in a more moderate tone. When you are ready to go, Tod will be waiting by the cells to help you bring Alexandrina up. He has a long board to put her on; her pyre is waiting for the final goodbye."

Nodding, Shadow Hunter watched her leave then looked down at his blood soaked torso before sighing he sheathed his knife; knowing the Seeker was right. Sobbing softly, Hunter dropped his head onto Alexandrina's shoulder and wept quietly.

**********

Chang's hand dropped feebly from Fai's hand once they were back in BC on his carpet. This specially woven Japanese rug had been made centuries ago by the head monks in his monastery at the same time as Jesus rose from the dead.

It had been speculated by his late ancestor Dao that the newly risen son had helped in the weaving, giving it the power to transcend time; making it possible to visit the past or future. There were limitations though... need was the key. When it was a crises or a desperate need then one could go as far back or forward as required. If you wanted to check the football scores next month, you would not move even an inch. The carpet always seemed to know what was needed.

Fortunately, only his descendants could use the rug. The father of the triplets feeling Magdalene still with them whispered one last statement. "I love you all, take care of each other. Please make sure to give that message to your older brother, who will now be your new Guardian, when he arrives."

Chang's eyes glazed over and he saw no more, content now that his destiny was fulfilled. His symbol joined the hundred others on the carpet of the Guardians as he gave up his soul willingly.

Fai looked up with tears streaming down her cheeks when she felt Magdalene put her hand on her shoulder. White Buffalo shuddered as she whispered forlornly to her last sister. "I will bring him to the retreat."

Magdalene nodded then silently she disappeared.

Ronin got up before looking down at his half-sister with tears in his eyes. "I will go prepare the escalade."

Nodding mutely, Fai lifted the baby. She got to her knees before staring down uncertainly, not sure exactly what had happened to her. Inside, she was struggling to keep her identity as the much stronger and forceful Alexandrina tried to take her over. Inhaling deeply, White Buffalo forced her sister into the background.

Humming softly at first, it quickly changed to a loud chanting as White Buffalo blocked a part of her subconscious then shoved her shocked sister inside it... sealing it tight. She could still hear Alex and they could communicate if needed, but the older triplet could no longer take her over physically.

Sighing in relief, Fai opened her eyes just as a flash of lightning lit up the sky behind her returning brother. Shocked, she looked down at her dead father then realized she could see vaguely... there was no colour just a grey shape.

Ronin helped his sister up first; kneeling afterwards, he rolled his father with the sword up inside the carpet so it could continue to absorb the blood... leaving no trace behind.

The big Oriental passed the cylinder to his sister before standing up with only a slight grunt of effort. He hefted his dad into a better position and looked over at Fai. "Come White Buffalo, you can hold onto me. Do you want to eat first or go see Stephan at the morgue for a casket, I am sure he will allow us to store father until we can leave the city. We will have to drive to Toronto, there is no way we will be able to sneak dad on the plane. I would rather not answer questions on who stabbed him to death."

Stepping forward quickly, Fai took her brothers arm after switching the cylinder then the baby to her left side. The tub was quite long, with the infant added it was a bit awkward for her.

Fai decided not to mention the change in her sight. White Buffalo still could not see much, and it might be gone by morning. "I will eat later I'm not hungry right now. How soon before we can get away from BC; I need to get to Toronto as soon as possible... what should we do with the baby?"

Shrugging, Ronin walked to the back of the escalade. "Not sure about the baby, maybe we can take him to the retreat with us. As for leaving, three days is all I need... I think. I will rent a U-Haul tomorrow; we can load it with the stuff you wish to bring before we pick dad up."

Nodding, Fai settled in the front seat. Ronin took the sword out before wrapping a tarp around the rug... just in case. He walked around then got into the driver's side and they left the restaurant.

It only took them twenty minutes to reach the morgue. The big Oriental jumped out then raced to the back while Fai stayed with the baby. The infant was just starting to fuss when Ronin opened the door. "Stephan's wife will take care of the baby; they have been trying to adopt, but have been unsuccessful so far."

Sighing in relief, Fai had absolutely no experiences with babies and did not know what to do with him now that he was awake. She could see a vague shape behind her brother so White Buffalo held out her hand to the woman. "Thanks Susan, I appreciate it."

While holding the older woman's hand, Fai was able to read her aura; there were no angry black or hateful threads. Satisfied, she handed the now whimpering infant to his new mother.

Neither brother nor sister had any qualms about this couple at all. For years, they had helped quietly dispose of the bodies of deformed humans that could not handle the transfer of the

Mother's magic leaving them unrecognizable; the pair was quite discreet. Now that the bureau knew what they were facing, they were all hoping that hiding everything would not be needed anymore.

Ten minutes later Ronin got back in. "Stephan said he will have the papers ready for us when we want to go."

Nodding relieved, Fai sighed then sat back; she fell into a light sleep, exhausted beyond what most could handle.

Looking over at the youngest of the triplets, Ronin grimaced reflectively. His sister was different... he could feel and see it. He remembered reading a diary of the first twins; Cecille had an encounter with lightning on the ship that had taken them from England to Quebec, Canada. In the diary, she had confessed to feeling strange afterwards. Not only could she now feel bad weather coming, but also if there was any malevolence associated with the storm.

If there was lightning clouds, Cecille had to take shelter since it seemed the bolts would seek her out. The temporary Guardian would have to watch Fai closely. One lightning escapade was more than enough for his peace of mind.

Thinking of his older brother reflectively, Ronin couldn't help grinning eagerly... it would be nice to see him again. His older brother was named after their ancestors, Dao Shin Kane Ryuu. He couldn't help but hope that the new Guardian would be arriving soon, their father's death would have begun a compulsion in him to find White Buffalo; she would now be his responsibility.

The Oriental pulled into the driveway and hit the switch to open the garage door before pulling in. After the overhead door closed, he quickly got out then went around so he could open the passenger door.

Except for a brief mumble of protest, Fai never woke up; Ronin gathered her slight form effortlessly, he went up the three steps before shouldering open the door between the garage and the house.

Not even pausing to take off his shoes, he carried his baby sister up to her room. Tenderly, the hulking Oriental removed White Buffalo's shoes then her coat.

Ron pulled a blanket over her before leaving to go get the rug. While he was at it, the younger brother emptied the escalade of his father's things.

Sighing tiredly, Ronin finally trudged down to the basement. His alarm had went off on his watch at the same time as the lightning had struck Fai, but he had no time since to check out what was causing it. Although, he had a sneaky suspicion that he knew what the problem was.

Going past his room, Ron headed for the office then entered before pushing in the code that silenced the vibrating watch. Walking to the safe the Oriental punched in another code, which opened the door.

Frowning grimly, Ronin took out the empty glass box... the feather was gone! These rooms were not as well protected as the ones at the farm; still even a professional thief would have quite a hard time getting in here.

Turning, Ronin walked to the opposite wall to turn on his computer; he typed in his logo before bringing up the cameras... they were hidden of course. Not even a hair moved in the three level duplex, what seemed even stranger yet was that the camera in the safe was the only thing disturbed as he watched the feather vanish without a trace.

Scratching his head baffled, the big Oriental stared at all the cameras again... nothing moved. The safe had not been opened so how could it disappear like that.

Could it have something to do with Alexandrina's death? Until they reached the retreat and Ron questioned everyone, it would have to remain a mystery for now.

Sighing tiredly, Ronin reset all the alarms then left the room. Once his brother showed up it would be a good time for him to retire; maybe go back to the Orient to find himself a wife.

Feeling a brief second of contentment, he knew his father approved. All he had to do now was keep his sisters and himself alive until Dao showed up. He knew that was not going to be easy with those things attacking everyone.

Shrugging resignedly, Ronin quickly showered then crawled into bed. Sleep was a long time coming though as he tossed and turned with nightmares of death stalking them all.

# CHAPTER NINE

Magdalene frowned grimly; she checked her watch as they pulled into the retreat two days too late. It was three in the morning.

Pulling up to the Quonset, Maggie parked her rig on the far side since the area beside the barn was taken. She turned to Fred when he woke and sat up groggily. "Go sleep in the back, we can unload everything later. I don't want to wake everyone so I will sleep in Alex's room tonight."

Yawning tiredly, Fredrick obediently left the truck to join his girlfriend in the sleeping quarters at the front of the horse stalls. All he received was an irritated sleepy mumble from Jane when he crawled in beside her before he too slept.

Turning around, Magdalene went into the small bunk to pull out a suitcase she had waiting then climbed down from the truck. Rushing towards the farm house, she veered going around to the back where she knew her sister's pier had been lit.

It was gone and only a pile of ashes remained, but the smell still lingered... making Magdalene grimace. Sighing in regret for not having made it on time, she knew that it would haunt her for the rest of her life.

Turning away, Red Wolf went towards the back stairs. A warning growl halted her instantly... Maggie had forgotten all about the dogs.

Giving a sharp distinct whistle, three dogs came bounding out to greet her. Kneeling, the middle triplet let them accost her with a fond chuckle before patting each one in turn. Finally able to get up, Red Wolf went to the back entrance then pulled out her keys and quickly entered.

Taking off her shoes, Magdalene silently hurried down the hallway then up the stairs to the second floor before slipping like a ghost into her sister's private room.

Alex had left the bed down so Maggie put her suitcase on it. She opened the case to pull out her robe before stripping. Going to the bathroom first, the middle triplet quickly had a shower and put her robe over her naked body.

Afterwards, Magdalene walked to the desk; pushing in her code, she waited for the unit to set up before running her fingers under the desktop. She heard a satisfying click as an extra compartment opened. Red Wolf took the marriage certificate out then signed it beside her sister's name and right underneath Shadow Hunters signature.

Once done, the middle triplet put it back inside and closed the compartment; Fai would have to sign it once she arrived from B.C.

Feeling compelled, Magdalene left the bedroom; she rushed to the landing then descended the stairs. Her ankle length raven hair with its one strip of red trailed behind her, it seemed to float down each step in quick succession

Once at the bottom, Maggie turned right. She opened the door that led to the basement before hurrying down the three steps and unlocked the Seekers door.

The Mother was calling her, she must heed the summons; figuring nobody would be about at this late hour, she did not bother locking it again.

Maggie ran barefoot down the stairs then paused on the bottom step knowingly to read the black lettering. It was never the same twice and was usually a warning or a message only the one about to enter should be able to understand.

**'Some sacrifices bring about the beginning... others are the end of ones journey!'**

Frowning in confusion at that cryptic statement, Magdalene chuckled dryly at herself; well maybe not every message was understood. Shaking off her bewilderment, the middle triplet walked through the entrance before turning left. Going to the double doors, she only pulled one of them open then entered the Mother's vaulted chamber.

The first thing Magdalene saw when she entered was the raised stone slab right in the center of the three entwining rings. It seemed much bigger than when she was here in the dream world... now it was covered in dry blood.

Maggie couldn't help giving a forlorn cry of sorrow; she rushed over and dropped down beside it. Red Wolf wept in mourning for her oldest sister as she fell across the stone regretfully wishing she had made it in time.

It wasn't long until the middle triplet fell into a light sleep draped on the stone as the Mother Earth crooned soothingly to her.

*****

Shadow Hunter bolted upward in shock as he felt the spear pierce his chest. The dream had started innocently enough as he made passionate love to his wife, it had quickly turned weird after that.

Getting up restlessly, Hunter decided to go for a swim; a few laps in the pool should help him sleep. Knowing nobody else would be up at such an early hour, he donned just his loincloth. He didn't even bother putting on footwear.

As an afterthought, the Cree/Oriental Shaman pulled a towel off the rack before draping it over his shoulders; just to be on the safe side... he couldn't help thinking.

Once on the landing where the two doors were, Shadow Hunter turned to the one on the right that would take him to the basement. He paused at a creaking of a door hinge; he looked towards the one that led to the Mother Earth's caverns where the Seeker's had their rituals.

Hunter frowned in surprise, that door was always kept locked. Wondering who could be wondering around at this ungodly hour, the Cree/Oriental Shaman switched directions before hurrying down the cellar stairs.

Somebody could have just forgotten to lock it; shrugging resignedly, Shadow Hunter decided it would be prudent to check first not wanting to lock someone in by mistake.

Walking off the last step, the Cree/Oriental Shaman automatically looked above the doorway for the black lettering; curious to see if something different would appear.

**'Another willing sacrifice is necessary to secure the seeds of destruction!'**

Having no clue what that could mean Shadow Hunter ignored it. He went through the doorway and turned right to check the prison cells; nobody was there so he retraced his steps before going past the doorway leading up.

Hunter kept walking until he got to the door leading to the vaulted Seeker's chamber where Mother Earth was strongest. He frowned in surprise when he saw that one door was open slightly.

Entering the room, Hunter did a quick cursory glance making sure to keep his gaze away from the three rings where the slab of stone had been just two days ago. It was where he had said a final goodbye to his beautiful wife of only a week.

Frowning, Shadow Hunter grimaced in confusion; it was hard for him to fathom that he had only known Alexandrina for less than a month... it seemed like forever!

Shaking off his wondering thoughts, Shadow Hunter turned when he did not see anything; the Cree/Oriental Shaman froze in shock as inadvertently his gaze fell on the slab of stone that had not been there yesterday... his wife was still lying there.

Giving his head an incredulous shake before closing his eyes, Shadow Hunter pinched the bridge of his nose. He chanted silently... 'You're seeing thing; Alex is dead and was burned on a pier early this morning... this is a dream!'

Dropping his hand, Shadow Hunter looked again then slowly in a daze not even realizing his towel had fallen in a heap... he walked towards his wife. Hunter could not help holding his breath praying she would not vanish and this was not really a dream.

Reaching the rock platform the Cree/Oriental Shaman knelt carefully, afraid she would vanish at any moment; he stared down at her longingly.

About to reach out, Hunter paused when suddenly the woman opened her vivid bright green eyes, with the largest pupil Hunter had ever seen. They had a glossy black look to them and the colour took up most of her iris. A deep yellowish green colour around the pupil made up a smidgen of her eye colour. The Cree/Oriental Shaman, sucking in a shocked breath... it wasn't his wife!

**********

Grumbling irritably at the insistent pounding on his door, Ronin checked his watch in anger; it was midnight and he had not slept well at all, he growled impatiently. "I'm coming already!"

Throwing the front door open angrily, the swear word Ronin was about to hurtle at the unfortunate person behind the door was hastily swallowed.

Ron stared in stunned shock at the red robbed Samurai standing there. The man was a foot shorter than he was and slight; neither could the mixed Oriental see any features because of the hood hiding the face, but he knew.

Bowing immediately with both hands pressed together formally, Ronin could not help the pleasure and relief that entered his voice. "Brother!"

Pulling his hood off, Dao bowed back hurriedly. "Quickly Ronin, we must get Fai on the carpet... I have no time to explain now."

Turning without hesitation, Ronin beckoned then led his brother through the hallway before going down the backstairs to his room.

Rushing to his bookshelf, Ron pulled out a special book causing a section in the wall to lift; it revealed a cubbyhole with both the cylinder that held the carpet, as well as, the sword that he had stashed inside before going to bed. The section in the wall was not high but quite long, the younger brother reached in taking out both items.

Ronin led Dao out of his room then into the library. He went to the recliner in the center of the room. After putting the cylinder down, the mixed Oriental pull on the rug that was under the chair.

The colourful carpet with the chair on top moved exposing three rings in the middle of the floor.

Giving his older brother the sword of truth that would now be his, Ronin picked up the cylinder and opened it. He flipped it over so the carpet of the Guardians would slid out before lifting the container up, away from the treasure inside that it kept hidden.

Once the rug was unrolled, it was put over the three rings of eternity; Ronin turned to Dao. "I am not sure if Fai is awake, that lightning strike took a lot out of her."

Dao raised his hand to forestall his younger brother's explanation. "I already know everything; if you have to carry her... do so. She must be put on the carpet quickly. I will prepare myself while you are gone!"

Ronin rushed out immediately, without further comment; he took the stairs two at a time then hit the landing running. As fast as he could he went to the back stairwell and vaulted up them before running to the third bedroom on the right. Banging on the door first, Ron called out in a rush... breathless. "Fai, I am coming in I sure hope you are descent."

Opening the door, Ronin cautiously peeked around it; his sister was still sleeping. With two long strides he got to the bed, hesitantly he reached out to shake White Buffalo's shoulder. Unfortunately, all he got was an irritated mumble... her eyes remained closed.

Shrugging, the hulking Oriental pulled back her covers to lift her up. He frowned in surprise; well she must have been up at least once during the night. Fai had put on her Seeker's robe so she must have had a nightmare that is the only time she ever wore that robe to bed.

When Ron had teased her about it years ago, she had shrugged. "It's the only way I can sleep when nightmares refuse to stop."

Shaking off his thoughts, Ronin retraced his steps then ran into the library. Dao was already kneeling and humming softly, so the younger brother tenderly laid Fai on the carpet in the center.

Ron sat across from his older brother when Dao gestured for him to do so. Closing his eyes, the big Oriental put himself in a trance; patiently he hummed, waiting for what... he had no idea.

Suddenly, with a lurch they were on the move; they traveled through space quickly before a sickening whirl of motion stopped the three traveller's dead.

It took Ronin a few minutes to realize that they had materialized once more in the Seeker's vaulted chambers on the outskirts of Toronto.

Looking towards the raised daze, Ron was just in time to see a spear hurtled through the air towards them.

********************

Feeling an intense stare, Magdalene opened her bright green eyes; there was just a hint of a deeper green right in the center. Unless you were extremely close, it was hard to see the different colour.

Looking intently at the man Maggie had just signed the rest of her life over too; she reached up to pull his head down, refusing to let him talk or pull away.

After a few intense moments of heated passion, Shadow Hunter reared up in shock then tried to wake himself up. This must be a dream... his wife was dead.

Staring down intently at the woman he was about to enter; unsure even how they had ended up with no barrier between them, Hunter tried to clear his thoughts.

Having none of that, Magdalene pulled Shadow Hunter's head down for another steamy kiss before wrapping her legs around him in demand.

Unable to resist anymore, not even sure himself why he was fighting it; Shadow Hunter entered her in an urgent frenzy. Hearing her sharp uncomfortable intake of breath, he now knew for a certainty that this was not his wife.

Not being able to stop now, Hunter ground his hips into hers in ecstasy. Unwillingly, his manhood exploded deep inside her; he groaned in disappointment, it was too quick. Expecting Alex to disappear now that he had found fulfilment, he frowned in confusion when the dream continued.

To his amazement, the Cree/Oriental Shaman's manhood emptied a second time, which had not happened since their first encounter... the day before they married.

Dropping on top of her in exhaustion, Shadow Hunter instantly became aware of two shocking occurrences... no, make that three; the woman beneath him still did not disappear. Again, a deep burning feeling in his chest was making him extremely uncomfortable. Three, the Cree/Oriental Shaman could feel a vibration coming from the stone alter. It reminded Hunter of the sounds that a cat or woman would make when everything went her way.

Magdalene lay quietly not daring to move and break the spell that they seemed to be under; the Mother Earth was giving her images of two sperm breaking away from the others before traveling up rapidly. She knew the instant one entered the membrane of her egg, causing a smile of excited pleasure to light up her face.

A split second later, Maggie inhaled in shock as the dagger still strapped to her thigh flared in waring. Quickly, without thought she flipped them so Shadow Hunter was now beneath her as she instinctively protected him. Still joined together, Red Wolf began shifting into her spirit animal... unwillingly.

Shadow Hunter screamed in painful shock when the pain in his chest flared out of control... burning him unmercifully. His pained cry was cut short when his head hit the rock platform; the Cree/Oriental Shaman knew no more as blackness descended.

**********

Fai groggily blinked in shock, unsure how she ended up standing here. The last thing she remembered was putting her robe on hoping to halt the nightmares she couldn't seem to stop from happening before crawling back into bed.

Looking around in bemusement, Fai had no clue where she was... at first. She sucked in a shocked breath when she became aware that a spear was coming straight towards her. Unable to move, White Buffalo followed its path in fascination. When it got closer, suddenly it arched downward.

It was not until then that Fai saw her naked sister lying on top of the Cree/Oriental Shaman. Whimpering in denial, White Buffalo lifted her hand up beseechingly. Unfortunately, she was powerless to stop what was taking place.

The youngest triplet screamed out Magdalene's name in warning, but it was seconds too late as Fai felt the spear tip puncture Red Wolf. Instantly, White Buffalo grabbed her own chest in excruciating agony.

Staring past the spear as it came rushing towards them trying to find the threat; Ronin inhaled in shock as the one that threw the weapon put out an imploring hand when the spear entered the wrong victim. Shuddering, he frowned in shock when not one, but three screams shattered the silence before one of the creature seemed to explode.

Dao had kept a firm hand on his younger brother keeping him from moving or interfering; knowing Ronin would try to stop this if he could... what is meant to be will always find a way!

*****

Screeching in fear and uncertainty, the last Nephilim returned to her prison in horrendous agony then dropped to her knees. This time Ava had felt the pain of Zarina, unlike the death of the older Nephilim. It ripped through her system uncontrolled for several long minutes as she rocked herself keening; finally, it was over.

Ava sighed in relief... now what was she going to do. By herself, she would be as helpless as a newborn since she still had limited abilities and feathers.

Standing up the Nephilim looked around her prison forlornly. "I am alone; we should have never gone after the dragon... oh how stupid we were."

"Oh, shut up so you can hear me!"

Ava spun around searching the prison in agitation, the quiver of fear in her voice was hard to miss. "Who's there... show yourself?"

"We can't show ourselves we are now part of you."

"Ava can't be that stupid, can she Richell."

"I do not believe so Zarina, I think she is just clueless."

Ava sat down hard, even more scared now then she had ever been when alive and facing lifelong imprisonment. Keening she rocked herself, unsure what to do now. Suddenly, she stopped when her whole body began twitching before the much stronger Richell took over the body then shut the much weaker Ava behind a wall.

Zarina chuckled in delight. "Oh, that is so considerably better. We must kill the dragon before it becomes too strong for us. Trying to put it back on the medallion now will accomplish nothing... it is too late for that; the only way out of this predicament, is to kill the Shaman and hope the dragon on his chest dies too.

Richell's smile was more of a grimace as Ava finding new strength pushed back trying to retake her body, but it only lasted a few minutes.

Screaming in rage, the youngest Nephilim fled further into the background. Satisfied that Ava was gone, the older Nephilim waved and the three now sharing one body... disappeared.

*****

Alexandrina finding herself released from the prison Fai had shut her into, stepped away from her youngest sister. A man looking exactly like her father, only younger grabbed her and White Buffalo by the hands; he pulled them over to the rock so they were next to Magdalene. Not having time to be gentle, he yanked them down before putting their palms flat on their middle sisters back as her nerves continued to twitch.

Dao keeping his hands over the two girls chanted fast and furiously feeling time slipping away. In satisfaction, he felt

Magdalene's Po release from her body; once completely free, he released Alexandrina then pointed at Maggie's spectral form.

Standing, Alexandrina walked to her middle sister. She opened her arms and they embraced... slowly the two became one.

The three watching could see the two girls fusing together, as four arms became three then two before two bodies merged into one... followed by the legs.

Staring in stunned disbelief, Fai rose with the man when he pulled her up insistently. Shaking her head in shocked disbelief, the youngest triplet felt an insistent pull towards her sisters; it was so strong White Buffalo could not resist it for long.

Hurrying to the center of the joining rings of eternity, Fai gathered her sister's towards her. Suddenly they were entering her body. It was nothing like her experience with Alex inside the lightening; this time there was more pain than she had ever felt in her entire life, it was excruciating as the three joined until they were all one.

Throwing her head back, White Buffalo screeched eerily. Unexpectedly, a white light rose up from the three entwined circles on the floor and surrounded the triplets.

Fai's pain eased, but only slightly as she felt all her bones moving; next her skin began stretching to accommodate her knew growth. Finally, an extra layer of cartridge formed and another menisci or articular disks with several more ligaments developing in each of her main joints.

Unable to help grinning in satisfaction, the youngest triplet realized she now had the ability to shift into her spirit form

White Buffalo's full powers though were still trapped, but she now had a piece of the puzzle as to why three had to become one. Although, what the outcome would be or even how such a thing was possible Fai had no clue.

Another colour strip began entwining Fai's black hair; her eyes still a dark green were now flecked with black, and gold swirling flecks of colour that changed constantly... hardly noticeable.

Floating above the ground, Fai moved to the entwined couple still on the rock platform before entering Magdalene's body; she felt a brief moment of ecstasy when the fertilized egg disappeared now safely hidden away as the glow from the rings of eternity encompassed the Cree/Oriental Shaman.

Leaving her sister's body, Fai again found herself back in the circle of eternity then one more time she was surrounded by a white light for a brief second before she disappeared... with both men

**********

Fai opened her eyes before blinking; she squinted not yet used to the light as she looked up at her two concerned brothers as they waited for her to come around.

White Buffalo moistened her lips and cautiously moved each limb, but only slightly. They felt so heavy, almost as if she had gained fifty pounds in one day.

The youngest triplets mind was racing faster than she could keep up; all these years there was a vague sense of always feeling incomplete. Now Fai felt... whole, complete.

White Buffalo frowned suddenly, no something was still not quite right, what was missing she had no idea.

Opening her eyes just a bit more, Fai smiled before forcing her arm up so she could touch Ronin's face. She could not keep it there long and it fell heavily after only a minute. "I can see you now; you are just as handsome as I knew you would be."

Blushing in surprise, Ronin chuckled in disbelief. "Well, obviously you have never seen another man before so I will ask your opinion next month."

Gesturing at their older brother, Ronin made introductions. "Fai, meet Dao, he will now be your Guardian."

Looking intently at her oldest half-brother, Fai studied him. He was short like their father with big saggy eye pouches. The slant of his eyes pointed down a lot more than Ronin's showing the stronger Japanese side. He was extremely thin and had a baldhead that went from the forehead to the top of his crown then there was a thick bun; there was no hair on either side or underneath of it because he plucked out everything around it.

Fai would learn later that the hair in the bun reached to his waist. White Buffalo knew instinctively that he look exactly like their father.

Smiling knowingly, Fai tapped her chest for emphasis. "Yes, I can feel the bond it's quite strong."

Dao nodded in agreement. "It is; how do you feel, can you get up?"

Shaking her head, Fai sighed grimly. "Extremely weak and thirsty, I think trying to stand right now is not a good idea."

Immediately, Ronin scooped his baby sister up into his huge beefy arms then stood up. The difference between the two men was astounding, especially considering they had the same parents. He was twice his older brother's height and weight.

If Ron had stayed in Japan, he would have become a great Sumo wrestler. It had been his mother's hope since it was her family's legacy.

The only thing that had kept him here all these years is his great love for the little package he was holding right now. He loved Fai beyond anyone; even the other two girls as much as they looked so similar had paled compared to her, he would die for her... without batting one eyelash.

Even though Ronin knew that Dao was bonded to Fai so could find her anywhere, he was distracted enough by his concern for his sister that he explained anyway. "There is a bottle of water in the fridge, can you bring it upstairs. White Buffalo's bedroom is at the end of the hall on the right."

Without waiting for his brother's response, Ronin strolled purposely out of the room. He climbed the stairs then exited the basement, which was near the back entry. He walked through the laundry room into the front foyer and took the stairs to the upper rooms

It wasn't long before he gently laid Fai on her bed, on top of her white buffalo hide; tenderly he drew the covers up... tucked her in.

Pulling out her left arm, Fai tenderly cupped Ronin's face before he could pull away... she smiled sadly. "I release you. You are now free to go home to become a great Sumo wrestler, as you always wanted. Our older brother will now be my Guardian so you must find your special someone and father many children; for you will produce the next Guardian. Go my brother. Remember a special place in my heart is reserved for you. My gratitude will forever be yours for all the sacrifices you endured on my behalf."

Ronin stood up in surprise then stared down at his baby sister intently. "Are you sure, White Buffalo?"

Nodding, Fai waved dismissively. "Yes, you big oaf... now skedaddle. Oh, don't forget to take the little plane with you it is yours; I will no longer need it. Father left you a sizable inheritance wanting to make sure you were well taken care of for all your years of sacrifices. A package with all the information you need is in my study on the desk, go with my blessings."

A grin lit up Ronin's face and he bent to press his lips to her forehead, giving her a fond kiss before standing up once more. He bowed deeply then pressed his hands to his forehead. "I will come to say goodbye before I go; always know that I will forever love you little sister, it has always been a pleasure guarding you above all the others."

With that, Ronin brushed past his older brother before disappearing to pack his things. He had not realized that his sister knew about his desire to become a wrestler; Ron couldn't help feeling a sense of relief, he was quite eager now to begin a new chapter in his life. He didn't really have any friends here since his sister's had always taken up all his time; except for Fai, nobody would miss him.

Dao watched his younger brother leave with a sigh of regret; he had hoped to have some time with him. Oh well, he would go see him after he left Fai.

Walking further into the room the young Guardian stopped near the bed, he smiled down tenderly at his younger sister before passing her the water. "How are you feeling now, White Buffalo? You gave us quite a scare."

Shrugging, Fai propped herself up a bit then gratefully drank deeply before handing the bottle back and settling under the covers. "Not bad, a little confused though; I want to mourn for my sister's, but technically they are not dead... they just became part of me. What about the babies, are they dead? If not, where did they go?"

Gesturing in reassurance, Dao sighed trying to find the right way to tell her so she would understand. "No they are not dead, the dragon is guarding them. How or why it is so, I cannot tell you a hundred percent. Even my master in Japan could not give me an explanation; sleep now... later we will talk."

Putting his hand on Fai's forehead, Dao hummed soothingly then watched in satisfaction as her eyes slowly closed... obediently she slept. Turning, the Guardian went to his brother's room.

Standing in the doorway, Dao watched Ronin piling things in his suitcase with two cardboard boxes on the opposite side being filled as well. Not waiting for an invitation, he entered the room before walking to the end of the bed... he sat. "Fai mentioned a plane; do you know how to fly it or will you need a pilot?"

Looking up with a smile of reassurance for a moment, Ronin went back to packing. "Yes I know how to fly it, it's just a Cessna TTX... it seats six. Father sold the bigger one; he said you would not need it. Remember to pick him up when you leave town there would be way too questions if you tried getting him on a plane."

Nodding in agreement, Dao gestured inquisitively. "The jungle kind of swallowed me up so I lost track of things here. My last communication with dad was after Fai won that trial, can you fill me in?"

About to begin, Ronin remembered that his brother had arrived with nothing. Frowning thoughtfully now distracted, he could not keep the curiosity from entering his voice. "Where is your luggage and how did you get here?"

Chuckling, Dao gestured in reassurance. "My things are at the airport, they arrived two days before me. One of our new recruits gave me a snake serum that completely paralyzed me then slowed my heart until it only beat enough to keep me alive. Afterwards, he stuffed me in his suitcase. When they scanned his luggage he told them I was a large Samurai doll that he was taking to his children, he even had an authentic sales receipt. With no heartbeat or heat sensor warning them, he slipped me right past security. Once in the parkade, he opened the suitcase then gave me the antidote."

Grimacing in amazement, Ronin was unable to keep a touch of amusement out of his voice. He opened the drawer beside his bed before pulling out their father's wallet. "Since you are a splitting image of dad, you can probably pass for him. Lift your eye pouches a bit; add black charcoal to tilt your eyes a little more. Oh, don't forget to add a few age wrinkles so nobody will know the difference. I will have one of our security team members go and get your bags. He will also take your fingerprints then switch father's to yours."

Ronin tossed the wallet to his brother then got up before walking towards the door to his room. "Come, I will order a pizza... you must be starved."

Cocking his head curiously, Dao followed his brother with a puzzled frown. "What's a pizza?"

Hooting in delight, Ronin slapped the Tianming Monk playfully on the right shoulder. Forgetting how much smaller Dao was; Ron almost knocked the Guardian down the stairs. "Do I ever have a treat for you big brother. Now hurry up, I am starving too. I will explain everything that happened here once our food is on the way."

*********************

"I can't get him to wake up, we have tried everything."

"I found a lump the size of a goose egg on his head, other than that I can find nothing else wrong with him."

"Her father is going to be furious... two are now dead. I would not want to be in his shoes, Hunter will be lucky to keep that thick noggin of his once Chang gets here!"

"Oh, quit your blubbering you two... get him upstairs. James and Karen will help you; his assistant is there already waiting for him. Hopefully, he will wake in the morning."

Shadow Hunter listened to the four people, the first one was definitely male... the second person was female. Possibly, the same one who had bathed Alexandrina then got her ready for burial.

The third one had a nasal voice making it hard to distinguish if it was male or female; he did not recognize the voice at all.

The last voice was definitely the new head Seeker. Hunter wanted desperately to open his eyes, but they were glued shut; neither could he move. What happened, did he fall down the stairs going into the basement.

The last thing he remembered was reaching for the door to the subbasement where the Seeker's gathered, after that... nothing.

"Head Seeker said it looks like the same spear that killed the first; she has no idea how either of them got down there. Neither does she know when the Priestess arrived; she must have had a key."

"Are you at the top yet, he's heavy."

"Yes, but I have to wait for the others to get out of the way. Dave brought the other board, they will load her and take her to the burning pyre... it will be lit at dawn; her brother called, we are not to wait since the rest of her family cannot be here for at least a week so we are to go ahead with the cremation."

Shadow Hunter tried again to open his eyes... whose cremation; what happened, why couldn't he remember? Hearing a curse just as the stretcher he was on tilted precariously then hit something. Pain exploded in his head... he heard no more.

# CHAPTER TEN

Dao sat up in excitement. "He called her... what?"

Ronin frowned thoughtfully, thinking back. "He called her 'Fai Trinity Vienna... the prophecy of Trinity; High Priestess, the chosen of Mother Earth'."

Scratching his head in bafflement, Dao scowled when he looked back at his brother before dropping his hand. "There has been a lot of arguing over the last thousand years on the use of the name Trinity in the bible. Some figure it is because God refers to not only himself but also the son of God, plus the Holy Spirit or sometimes referred to as the Word; put the three of them together it forms a triangle of three or a trinity."

Drumming his fingers lightly on the table, the young Tianming Monk frowned as his mind raced trying to piece together the puzzle. "There are three main parts to the bible the Old Testament, New Testament, and finally Revelations. There are six heavens or realities. God's throne room is in the third so that means there are three heavens above. If you add the Earth as the seventh, that makes three below. There are three Nephilim and they look exactly like the triplets."

Dao gestured towards himself with a thoughtful frown. "I do not believe myself that the triangle is the right symbol, even though it is in the bible; mostly, because of the fact that according to revelations the triangle with a six in each corner is the mark of the antichrist. The Celtic or witches of old use a long oval shape that entwines called the Triquetra, it is a pagan symbol used in Wicca and Neopagan rituals. So it would not be used either."

Shrugging, Dao nodded decisively figuring his musings were on the right track. "I think the three perfectly round circles that we saw at the retreat in the basement are better suited to the Almighty as it is for Mother Earth. In the Great Spirit's case, one circle is the father, the next is the son, then the final would be the Holy Ghost or Word... the center of course is God. The one for Mother Earth I assume would be Earth in the center, air, water, and fire. These perfect circles are for life continuation or eternity, they keep rotating so life keeps revolving; what once was will be again. We had magic then there was the rebirth, and finally we have technology that is our reality now. If magic unravels, what should be two Aeon realities will merge into one instead. If they become one age, it could change the fabric of time and magic would then be the reality once more."

Pausing, Dao took a drink of the sparkling fizzy strange tasting pop that his brother called Pepsi before continuing; he remembered finding an ancient book in his master's library that he secretly took to his room. "There is an old prophecy at the monastery that says, 'Three will be born, but only one should exist. The power of the trinity can only be made complete after the creatures of old are no more. The Hunter will absorb the dragon seeds keeping them safe. Fire will be their legacy bringing about the rebirth of the Mother Earth. The key will open the gates to bring about a new reality merging old and new... into one'."

Picking up another piece of pizza even though he was full, Dao took a bite. He couldn't help giving an ecstatic groan of pleasure at the exotic taste hitting his taste buds.

Afterwards, Dao waved it in the air for emphasis. "When I was in Africa searching for the lost sword I saw another prophecy, but some of it was missing. Nobody seems to know who had written it or even when it was etched into the cave wall. One of my older guides interpreted it for me. 'When the sword of Kris, once known as Trinities Crystal, is found it must be bonded to be able to destroy the demons of old to bring about the power trapped within'. Two lines were scribbled out or had faded beyond recognition, the next part read. 'Holy Spirit reborn in the trinity'... more missing words then, 'Emmanuel, house of David' with more faded words we could not make out before 'his sister will complete the trinity and birth the twins then one of them will bring about the destruction of the Earth.' The rest was also missing."

Ronin shook his head grimly. "Wow that could be interpreted in any number of ways. Could the two prophecies go together? 'Three are born, but only one should exist'; that could describe the triples. Three were born, now only one lives, since the other two girls are dead. You found the Kris sword and plan to give it to Fai. Let's hope, it will destroy the Nephilim. We both know she has a power untapped right now, so maybe that will release it."

Ron opened his two hands then closed them for emphasis. "The dragon medallion has merged with Shadow Hunter. To me it looks like the talons are now holding something. Let's hope it is the unborn babies of the two older triplets. We all know the Mother Earth is dying; every year seems to bring another catastrophe of some kind. Twins will be born that will destroy then help bring the Mother back to life. How I am at a loss, but I think it will have something to do with fire."

Sighing in confusion, Ronin shrugged unknowingly. "The power is still dormant in Fai, maybe it has something to do with the Holy Spirit being reborn in the trinity. Opening the gates could be the carpet since it might be a gateway. Another prophecy says it is supposed to disappear with the white buffalo hide though."

Rubbing his chin reflectively, Ron's thoughts turned to God's son. "Emmanuel is another name for Jesus; he describes himself a few times in the bible as being from the house of David."

Taking a salt and pepper chicken wing, Ronin took a bite before continuing. "Who they are referring to being the sister of trinity I can't imagine; unless it's Tianming Monks sister, since she is your half-sister and you found the Kris sword. To me it looks like she could be the trinity, even her name has Trinity in it. I remember father saying that when she was named by her grandfather, he happened to be the Shaman of the Mi'kmaq tribe where she was born at the time. The old man called her the mother just before he died, so maybe she will birth the twins. I'm unsure how that is possible with the dragon now on Hunter's chest. I still think that the talons could possibly be holding two babies from different mothers. I can't imagine what else could be added to that prophecy."

Dao stared at his brother dumbfounded then finally shook his head in disagreement. "I think that your reasoning could be pretty close, but not altogether accurate; especially, the sister part... I do not think it has anything to do with the Tianming Monks and without having the rest of the prophecy it is only guess work at this point."

Ronin got up with a snicker before throwing the bone from the wing into the garbage box. "Yep, I agree; the two prophecies probably do not even go together. It gives you something to think about though. Maybe another prophecy will crop up to shed more light on the missing words. It's five am. I will leave you now so I can finish packing. Your things should be arriving shortly you can have dads room. I will go get a U-Haul then help load it with everything that goes to the retreat before I leave."

Standing up, Dao bowed before leaving his brother with a thoughtful frown. He headed back to the room that had the carpet still waiting for him to take control of it. Picking up the sword of peace, the Tianming Monk turned it and stepped onto the carpet. He pressed the tip into the center of the rug then knelt. "Father!"

Instantly, Chang appeared. He smiled lovingly before reaching out to put his left hand on his sons head. Time quickly went back; he saw his father's life unfold until the very end. It seemed to Dao to take forever but in reality, only fifteen minutes had passed. Now, he was back on the carpet in the den. "I will protect her with my life father... rest in peace now!"

Chang nodded knowingly, he put his hands over his sons on the sword... a jolt shook Dao. "This sword and carpet is now yours; you must protect her for she is vulnerable, if the Trinity is destroyed all will be lost so the rebirth of Mother Earth will never occur. It will destroy all hope for the merge and humans continuation. Once the rings of eternity are broken there can be no return, all life will cease to exist."

Nodding, Dao bowed his head. "I will die protecting her... this I swear to you!"

Dao looked up when he felt his father's final approval before he vanished now able to rest knowing he had left his daughter in capable hands.

Taking the tip out of the rug, Dao sat then put the sword across his knees before going deep into meditation. He opened his eyes and smiled at his Tianming Master now sitting across from him. "I have arrived safely; the sword plus the rug have both accepted me. The Kris sword is on its way here, but my last sister is weak. It seems that they were the Trinity... now they are one."

Gesturing knowingly the master nodded. "As we suspected; once the sword arrives put her on the carpet with it, she must put the point in the center then accept the bond. If she refuses it the magic will die and the sword will be useless... you must prepare her well."

Getting up once his master disappeared, Dao rolled the carpet up. He put it into the cylinder before hefting it onto his shoulder; kneeling he picked up his sword. Getting to his feet, the young Tianming Monk trotted upstairs. He went to the front then up to the bedrooms. Stopping between Fai's room and his fathers he paused, closing his eyes the oldest of Chang's children checked for any disturbances... he felt none.

Turning right, the Guardian entered his dad's room. He went to the bed, seeing the holster that would hold the sword on his back the older brother slipped into it then sheathed his new sword.

Looking at the headboard of the huge four poster bed the Oriental ran his fingers beneath it knowingly; he heard a satisfying click as part of the front dropped open. The cylinder fit perfectly inside, satisfied he closed it. Turning, the mixed Oriental left in excitement when he heard the doorbell ring.

Dao raced down the stairs, but Ronin beat him there and opened the door.

Taking the long box that was handed to him, Ronin turned to give it to his brother before turning back he accepted two suitcases. "Thanks Frank, its only seven am so come back in two hours... don't forget to bring Stanley; the U-Haul should be here by then, we will need your help loading it."

Saluting, Frank turned before disappearing.

Nodding towards the first step of the stairs going to the upper rooms, Dao turned and headed towards the back to go into the basement in excitement. "Just leave the suitcases there; I will take them up later. Can you grab a crowbar before meeting me in the den?"

Dropping the cases obediently, Ronin quickly ran into the garage to grab the required item before racing after his brother... eager to see what all the fuss was. Once kneeling beside Dao, it did not take him long to open the crate.

Digging inside, Dao pulled out a long Styrofoam padding then using his knife he cut around the seams before pulling open the top.

Inhaling in pleasure, Ronin stared down at the fancy jewelled scabbard. It had white doves throughout and different types of cherry blossoms entwined around them with a cross in the center. He frowned before jumping up, without an explanation he raced to his room then opened his little hideaway; reaching inside, he pulled out the old journal.

Trotting back into the den, Ronin knelt and opened the book carefully... several pages were missing. He ignored them as he continued to flip to the second last page where a drawing of the Celtic medallion was sketched. Just as he thought, turning the book around the younger brother pointed at the cross. "It looks exactly like this one."

Nodding in agreement, Dao grinned in excitement before pointing at the other page. "What is that?"

Looking down at the opposite page, Ronin outlined the dagger's circle in explanation. "It is the dagger that Magdalene always wore; it has a dove in the center of a golden open ring right at the top of the pommel. When it takes in evil, the dove turns black then breaks loose before rising to heaven. Within seconds a new white dove takes its place."

Smiling mischievously, Dao flipped the sword around. On the other side was an exact replica of the dagger with more doves and cherry blossoms all around it.

Ronin sucked in a stunned breath. He had such an awed look on his face that Dao had to laugh. "The doves are mother of pearl; the flowers are done with tiny gems in a variety of colours. The cross, and the dagger are done in gold; the black background is in a material none of us could figure out. You can see the scabbard has a slight wave on the edges, giving it a fancy unique look. It's very light, it goes from fingertip to elbow in length... it's definitely a woman's blade."

Flipping the Kris sword around, Dao showed his brother the pommel. It was quite wide where the blade met the hilt, but then it tapered down quickly and the grip became quite slim. It was done in gold with intricately connected Celtic knots. At the very end was a dove perched with just a hint of the wings about to open or close. Unlike the dagger, there was no ring around this bird; its claws were all that was holding it in place.

Ronin wondered if that dove also changed colours when evil was drawn in before it rose upward towards the heavens. Since the webbing around each knot was open, you could see right through them so the weight was negligible; only the dove had any substance to it.

Frowning, Ronin shook his head in amazement. "Magdalene's dagger must be connected to this sword making it way older than any of us suspected. It's the same with the dragon daggers I carry they are connected to the sword that you just received from father. Although, I am the one who used them most of the time. That reminds me, I will bring you the two daggers later they must stay with the sword."

Seeing Dao's nod of approval, Ron continued as he stared at the sword in admiration and curiosity. "That grip is too small for my hand... what does the blade look like?"

Shrugging unknowingly, Dao gestured in frustration. "Don't know nobody can take the scabbard off."

Looking up in surprise, Ronin scowled perplexed. "Magic protected... maybe?"

Nodding in agreement, Dao put the sword back in the box. "Yep, that is my guess; only the one meant to wield it can remove it."

Ronin gestured inquisitively. "How did you manage to get it out of Africa?"

Grimacing in caution, Dao shook his head. "You really do not want to know; my Tianming Masters can be very persuasive when they want something!"

Chuckling, Ronin shrugged dismissively; he jumped up before gesturing around for emphasis. "Let's get this place ready to go there are no beds going, no big furniture either; unless it is an heirloom, since the retreat has all this stuff already. Come on, I have to go get the U-Haul soon."

The two men shirt sleeves rolled up... got to work.

*********************

Jumping up hurriedly, Lily pulled the covers down and watched grimly as they brought Shadow Hunter in on a stretcher. She had wanted him in the trailer, but the head Seeker had refused outright. Hunter was caked in blood, so he needed to be washed first. Secondly, the doctor needed room to maneuver around; the trailer unit was just too small, the assistant was told. Unfortunately, they were all good points she had to admit... grudgingly

Coming in right behind the stretcher was Running Doe of the Mi'kmaq; she carried a distinctive black bag that caught Lily off guard. "No don't put him on the bed yet, take him into the bathroom. Put him in the tub... board and all. I will wash him in there so he doesn't get blood everywhere."

Lily frowned at the petite, black haired native. "Who are you;

what tribe are you from?"

Smiling gently, Running Doe gestured in reassurance then put her bag down by the bed. "I am a Priestess from NB, the same Mi'kmaq tribe that Alexandrina was born at. I go by Doctor Smitt I'm a licensed physician. Our people decided after the big pandemic in the year 2020 that shut down all Canadian boarders and kept most people in their homes for three years that all tribes in NB should have one licensed doctor on the reserve... just in case."

Relieved that she was a practicing physician, even though Lily was also native; she still preferred an educated doctor to a Shaman. She watched the woman hurry to the bathroom. Getting impatient, she walked to the doorway before moving aside to let the four out that had carried Shadow Hunter in. The assistant entered, wanting answers. "Do you know what happened?"

Taking down the shower head sprayer, Running Doe ran the water before checking until it was the right temperature. Thankfully, there were no clothes to wrestle with, since the Cree/Oriental Shaman was gloriously naked. Except for the loincloth, the doctor had quickly moved it back into place once the second Seeker was lifted off him.

With her back to the woman, Running Doe gnawed on her lower lip indecisively. Unsure, if she should tell the younger woman the truth. Although, none of them really knew what that was anyway. "I am sorry; all I know is that we found him unconscious under the second Priestess who was dead. A spear exactly like the one used on Alexandrina was also used to kill her."

Running Doe got up when she was done before grabbing a towel to pat Shadow Hunter dry. Satisfied, she got up then called to the ones waiting in the bedroom. "Okay, you can put him in his bed now... please."

Backing away, Lily went back to the bed and watched anxiously as the four deposited her injured employer before leaving the room with the litter. Several questions were ringing through her mind, ones that she knew the woman couldn't or wouldn't answer. She waited impatiently wanting to get a better look at Shadow Hunter; from what she could see, which wasn't much since the doctor always seemed to be in her way... no more blood was visible. "Why is he still unconscious?"

Shrugging distractedly, Running Doe pulled out her tools then ignored the girl. She put a stethoscope around her neck before putting a blood pressure cuff on Shadow Hunter to check his vitals. Satisfied they were good, she pulled open each eye and shone a light in them, but they were fine... quite responsive in fact.

Running her hands over each limb, she checked for breaks, bruising, or injuries of any kind. Thankfully, she found none. Turning the Shaman onto his side, she checked his back. There was a few scrapes from the rough stone alter, but they were just superficial with minimal bleeding. Looking up with a frown, she gestured impatiently. "Hold him up for me so I can check the back of his head."

Carefully, Running Doe checked his skull; she expertly probed for any signs of trauma. Except for the one lump, that she had found earlier nothing else seemed to be wrong with him.

Sighing in frustration, Running Doe waved the girl off then settled him back onto the mattress before covering him. "There is a lump on the back of his head, but I don't see nor feel any other injuries. Without an MRI, I cannot determine if his skull has been fractured. He definitely has a concussion though. If he does not wake up within the next two hours, I will give him an IV. If he wakes before that have someone get me immediately."

Grimacing resignedly, Lily nodded and watched the doctor leave. She pulled up a chair before sitting down hard in a huff. Well it did not look like she was going to get any answers until Shadow Hunter woke. Reaching over, she shook the Cree/Oriental Shaman's shoulder impatiently. "Hunter, wake up will ya!"

Getting no response, Lily sighed in frustration. She stared down at the man she had been in love with since he had rescued them.

The older twin would never tell him that knowing he did not feel the same for her.

Lily pulled the blanket down to see for herself that he wasn't hurt. Her eyes hungrily dropped to his muscled torso then they widened in shock at the sight of the dragon burnt into his chest. She had barely seen him since arriving at this cursed place. Reaching out she tentatively touched it, but it felt old as if he had it for years. She knew though that it was not there a month ago.

A knock on the door had Lily jumping to her feet... almost guiltily. She quickly covered Shadow Hunter before walking over she opened the door to a boy of about sixteen.

The boy held a tray filled with food. "The head Seeker sent me to feed the Shaman and she added some food for you too."

Nodding, Lily stepped back and let him in. "I'm not hungry right now; I will come back in a bit."

Lily rushed out needing to find her brother.

***************

After eight long hours the two brothers exhausted, but satisfied that the refrigerated U-Haul had everything; including their deceased father in his casket. They had hid him under everything else so nobody would see him, not wanting any questions about the knife wound that had caused his death. He needed to be cremated at the retreat. His ashes would be collected so his two daughters could be buried with him.

Trudging tiredly into the kitchen to make supper, Ronin chuckled as he looked around at the bare cupboards. "I will call for KFC for supper, another treat for your pallet big brother. Go up and see if Fai feels good enough to join us, she has been sleeping a long time."

Nodding, Dao took the stairs two at a time before knocking on his little sister's door. When there was no answer he opened it a crack to peek around the door, but she was still sleeping. About to close it, he heard a moan of fear coming from inside.

Immediately, Dao pushed the door further open before going to the bed then put his hand on White Buffalo's forehead. He frowned at the heat he could feel coming from her skin.

Chanting, the Tianming Monk brought their bond to the surface and crooning he managed to calm her raging body. Stepping back, the Guardian frowned in concern... she's fighting it. He had better pull out his carpet after he talked to Ronin, maybe if they put her on it that would help.

Turning away, Dao rushed back downstairs... Ronin was just getting off the phone. "Fai has a nasty fever; I managed to calm her somewhat, but she is fighting herself. Should we take her to the hospital or bring the carpet to life?"

Looking at his concerned brother, Ronin shook his head. "No, we have a pool in the backyard that will cool her off; if she doesn't come around after being in the water for twenty minutes, we will put her on the carpet. The hospital would be the last place I would want to take her."

Nodding in agreement, Dao went up to his room then pulled out the carpet while his brother waited for their food.

*****

Ronin knocked on Fai's door, but received no answer so he walked in and went to the bed. Lightly he shook her shoulder, but all she did was moan before turning her head away. Pulling back the covers the big Oriental sighed in relief, she must have gotten up then changed into her pyjamas after he had put her back in her room; thankfully, it would make it easier to manage her in the pool.

Ron had slipped on a pair of shorts that he always wore swimming and a robe. Picking her up, Ronin grimaced in concern; White Buffalo was not boiling, but quiet warm to the touch. Negotiating the stairs, he headed for the back entry, where Dao was waiting.

Sighing grimly, Dao touched her forehead with a tsk of worry. "She is not as hot, but still has quite a high fever."

Opening the back door, they went onto the veranda then down the three stairs to a small pool that Chang had built so he could do laps every morning. Their father had always said that water was the best medicine, a great way to relieve the worst stresses of life; now, Ronin was hoping it would help Fai. When she was in school, White Buffalo had won many swimming competitions. It was her second love, only horses and trick riding could best it.

Placing Fai in a lounging chair, Ronin took off his robe then jumped in the pool and held out his arms. "Give her to me please, Dao."

Picking her up, the older brother did as he was told. Afterwards, he took off his own robe before jumping in the pool.

Keeping a supportive hand under Fai's head, Ronin allowed her to float; while Dao cupped water in his hands before letting it slowly dribbled over his sister's body.

After ten long anxious minutes, Fai finally opened her eyes; she smiled up at her two concerned brothers. "I can see you!"

Chuckling, Ronin nodded. "We can see you too, I am glad that you are finally awake... how are you feeling?"

Frowning in surprise, Fai wiggled her fingers in the water. "Why am I in the pool; I feel strange, hot, thirsty... weak."

Sighing, Ronin grimaced uneasily. "You have slept the whole day away. Your body was burning up. Seems it does not like the change you underwent and is trying to reject it. The pool has cooled you down some; the two of us are hoping it will help revive you."

As soon as Fai mentioned thirsty, Dao moved over to the pools edge; there he had piled towels, bottled water for the three of them... plus their robes.

Moving Fai closer to the pools edge; Ronin propped himself against the side of the pool then put an arm under his sisters torso to hold her up so Dao could tip the water bottle up to her lips.

Gulping down a good three quarters of the bottle, Fai turned her head away when she had enough. Feeling her brother ease his hold White Buffalo moved fingers toes, ankles, and wrists. She lifted each arm then her legs taking inventory, needing to make sure all her limbs were working properly.

Closing her eyes, the surviving triplet began humming before going deep inside looking for any problems that could be causing her body to rebel. "Ronin you can let me go now."

Gingerly, Ron allowed Fai to float away but he made sure to stay close in case he had to grab her.

Crossing her legs, Fai sat on the bottom of the pool. It was not deep here so only part of her was submerged, the water reached just below her collarbone. Continuing to hum she searched; White Buffalo frowning, finally looked up at her brothers. "I need to change form, but my body is fighting it."

Scratching his temple thoughtfully, Ronin sighed grimly. "I see the problem, your sisters changed at the Stonehenge in England and they had help by something that blocked their memories. Magdalene said Stonehenge had disappeared so going there won't help you now; what about the carpet, would it do you any good?"

Shrugging, Fai grimaced unsure. "I don't know... it might. The water is helping me, I am not sure it's a good idea to leave it right now; can the rug be put in the water?"

Chuckling, Dao headed to the pools edge. "I don't see why not, water shouldn't harm it... only one way to find out."

Getting out, Dao hurried inside. Seeing the crate sitting beside the carpet, he reached in then brought that out too. Maybe she could bond with the sword at the same time. Sitting on the edge of the pool, the Guardian put the sword down before opening the cylinder; pulling out the rug, he jumped into the pool. Wading over to the two waiting, the mixed Oriental paused Inquisitively. "Do you want to stay in the shallows or go deeper so you can stand?"

Gesturing, Fai pointed down. "Here is good, I can keep my head above water; over there I might become too weak and possibly drown."

Nodding the two men spread the rug out between them then Ronin began pushing his end down into the water. He kept going until it touched the bottom. He put his foot on the edge to keep it in place, while Dao fought with his end. Finally, he too managed to put his feet on the edge and hold it down.

Using her arms to maneuver forward, Fai drifted over then settled in the center of the rug; both men sat on the edges of the carpet to keep it in place.

Ronin towered above his two siblings; the water only came up to his nipples, where the other two were up to their collarbones.

Humming, Dao brought the carpet to life. Instantly, they rushed back through time until Fai was stepping into a deep mist. She could hear two mischievous giggles before her father's voice drowned them out as he called for Magdalene and Alexandrina insistently. Immediately, White Buffalo knew she was in England at the Stonehenge. They had gone to investigate the mist disappearing around the strange formation of rocks; the deep gray mist had hid the Stonehenge for centuries... few could enter here.

Hearing both her sister's screaming, Fai quickly followed the desperate sounds. As she rushed forward, a lighter shade of gray ahead appeared; once in it, she could feel a difference. Unexpectedly, an even darker shade drew closer. Again, it felt different making her shiver apprehensively.

Several more changes in the fog happened before she saw both her sisters lying on the ground. The youngest triplet ran over, she knelt between them then put a hand on each of their foreheads. Crooning soothingly, she took in their pain; staggering to her feet, she left the two. White Buffalo wandered aimlessly as the pain continued to eat at her, until she dropped to her knees unable to keep going.

Back in the present, Fai felt her bones shifting before her skin ripped as she slowly transformed. It was the second most painful experience of her life, only her sisters merging with her exceeded it... she screamed.

The youngest triplets cry was cut short when a white dove landed at the edge of the pool. White Buffalo stared intently at the beautiful bird causing her to relax her rigid form; instantly, she felt an easing of her pain. Unexpectedly, her transformation was complete.

Standing in the shallows of the pool the buffalo watched the dove open its beautiful pure white wings before flying away. Concentrating, the white buffalo shimmered; a few minutes later a black cougar with a white tip on its tail replaced it. Feeling compelled, Fai concentrated once more letting a red wolf take the cougars place. Howling in triumph the wolf disappeared, the surviving triplet was back sitting on the carpet. Lifting her face to the sun, she gave thanks to the Holy Spirit for the help in changing shapes.

Having jumped up out of the way, Ronin stood there staring in shock; he could hardly believe his eyes. "You can take the form of all three?"

Nodding, Fai smiled in wonder. "Yes, remember when Magdalene was saying someone had touched them in the mist before their pain eased. It was me, I helped them; in doing so, I am now able to shift into their spirit forms. Did you see the white dove?"

Smiling, Dao nodded; he too had stood up before moving away to accommodate the huge form of the buffalo. "Yes, it was quite beautiful."

Shaking her head in amazement, Fai gestured incredulously. "It helped me somehow then I got this weird impression that I knew it or should know it; it was the strangest feeling I ever had. I am okay now, but I want to do a couple laps around the pool before I come in to eat."

Dao held up his hand quickly to stop his sister from rising. "Wait there Fai, I have something for you and you must be on the rug to accept it."

Frowning in puzzlement, Fai watched Dao rush to the edge of the pool. Her eyes widened in wonder when it fell on the beautiful scabbard with its white doves done in mother of pearl; the cherry blossoms, plus the cross were done in beautiful gemstones. When her brother turned it to show her the dagger that Magdalene wore at her waist, White Buffalo could not help reaching for it reverently. "It's gorgeous."

Pulling the sword out of Fai's reach, Dao flipped it around before holding out the pommel with the white dove protruding. "This sword was made at the time Lucifer was caretaker of the Earth. The Great Spirit brought meteors down to defeat then imprisoned the archangel. Unfortunately, it caused an ice age to happen and almost all life was destroyed."

Looking at his sister intently, Dao gestured in caution. "Fai, this sword was made by an ancient civilization nobody has ever heard of. I suspect that a meteor rock from the battle was used in the forging before the ice age began. They hid it away afterwards, knowing that someday it would be needed. It has an old magic to it that nobody alive today can wield... except you. If you accept this blade, it will bond to you so no others can use it. When you pull the blade from the scabbard, you must thrust the point down hard into the center of the carpet. Both hands must stay on the pommel, no matter what happens you have to be willing to allow it to bond. How it will do so; I do not know."

Chewing her lower lip, Fai hesitated as she stared at the beautiful sword in fascination; there was a wide gold piece for a cross-guard, a quillon block was in the center of the guard. The gold extended arms of the quillon tapered down on either side of the blade before curling up just past the ricasso, which was close to the hilt.

This part was usually left unsharpened, so the wielder could put a finger on it for added leverage. This is also, where the swordsmiths puts their mark. Fai could see a gem imbedded, green the youngest triplet knew. Celtic Symbols with knots twined together formed a slim round grip that one could see through, yet they were small enough even a pinky finger could not slip through.

At the very end was a flat fan like half round golden flat piece with a small mother of pearl dove perched on it. It looked to her like the doves wings were just starting to unfold in order to rise from its perch. White Buffalo's hand reached out, but paused as she thought of the dove that had just helped her.

Feeling compelled, Fai grasped the hilt before pulling out a wavy black blade that tapered slowly down to a lethal point. The slight wave on either side of the blade gave it a unique look. A vibration tingled through her hand; quickly, White Buffalo pulled the sword closer before grasping it with both hands.

Opening her crossed legs wider, the final triplet drove the sword downwards with all her might into the center of the carpet right between her legs. Holding on tightly to the hilt the vibration intensified, she felt a sting on her right hand but refused to move.

Suddenly it was done; Fai pulled the sword out of the carpet then lifted it. She stared in shocked surprise. The blade was now a dark deep green with black, gold, and hazel specs flickering throughout. It now had a crystal look and shone brightly when the sun hit it.

Looking up dumfounded, Fai couldn't help stating the obvious. "The blade changed?"

Nodding in wonder, Dao smiled. "Trinities Crystal was once the name of the sword, now I know why... the blade reflects the wielder; it has taken on the colour of your eyes."

Taking the scabbard from Dao, Fai shook her head in amazement then sheathed the sword before looking at her left palm. She frowned in surprise. The three entwining rings of eternity were now burnt into her palm. Giving the sword to Dao, White Buffalo stood up so she could dive into the deep end... she disappeared.

Both men turned away to give Fai some privacy, they pulled up the rug before taking it to the edge of the pool and laid it out to dry in the sun. Getting out, Dao put the crystal sword on top of Fai's robe. Afterwards, they each took a towel to dry themselves.

The two men donned their robes then Dao bent to lift the rug up.

He turned to Ronin with a chuckle. "The carpet is dry already; not sure why I am surprised by that considering it absorbs blood, but I am."

Chuckling in agreement, Ronin opened the cylinder while Dao rolled up the carpet and put it inside before waving for his brother to take the rug inside while he waited for Fai.

Swimming back to the shallow end, Fai moved cautiously to the edge then bracing her arms, she lifted herself up onto the lip of the pool. She knelt there for a couple minutes testing her strength; but the weakness, fever, and unbalanced feeling were gone.

Standing, White Buffalo looked at Dao speculatively; springing into a fighting stance, she attacked her Guardian.

For twenty minutes, the two spared back and forth until finally, Fai stepped away before sitting on the lounge chair in exhaustion. "Thank you, I needed that. After I eat, I will pack my room up... I want to leave soon."

Smiling, Dao bowed formally. "Always at your service; come you must eat, we can discuss leaving after."

Nodding, Fai put on her robe before grabbing her new sword then they disappeared inside.

# CHAPTER ELEVEN

Fai stared out the window reflectively; it was getting hard to see now with the rain beating on the window, which allowed an early dusk to take place. She had made this trip by car or in their plane many times over the years, but this was the first time she could actually see anything.

Ronin had arranged for Frank to drive them since neither Fai nor Dao could drive. The burly bodyguard knowing they were in a hurry brought his brother Stanley with him as a second driver; between the two men driving in relays, they were already in Ontario. It wouldn't be long before they reached their destination, an impressive feat considering they had only been driving for two and a half days. They would have been at the retreat already if it was not for Fai's penchant of halting them every time she saw something that picked her interest... wanting to investigate.

Sighing forlornly, Fai brought up an image of her last goodbye to her best friend, brother, and constant companion since her sisters had left home wanting their own lives; she would miss Ronin something terrible she knew. Add that on top of her father dying plus both her sister's recent deaths it left a big hole in her weary heart. Ron had promised to call her as often as he could, but she knew once he found his special someone she would then take second place.

Wincing, Fai frowned grimly when a fork of lightening flared to the left of them; it was getting uncomfortably closer. She thankfully could not feel any malevolence in the black and purple clouds hovering above them, it was just a regular summer storm. Unfortunately, lightning would be drawn to her now no matter what kind of storm it was.

The same thing had happened to Fai's ancestor Cecille after she had drawn into herself a lightning filled sky that would have killed everyone on the ship. The unfortunate Cecille had lamented in her journal that the lightning seemed to be constantly seeking her out afterwards. Whenever the sky darkened a bit, she would have to find a hiding place... almost as if being hunted. She was hit twice that they knew of by freak lightning bolts.

Dao, feeling Fai's sadness through their bond, reached over then took his half-sister's hand before squeezing it in reassurance. "I promise you are not alone..."

Snapping his mouth shut on the rest of his sentence; Dao pulled Fai into his arms, away from the door and window when unexpectedly the hairs on the back of his neck stood straight up before his fingertips tingled.

'BANG!'...

A loud explosive sound inside the escalade had them all covering their ears in painful shock as the back end of the Buick lifted then fire shot out the back. The only thing keeping the vehicle from flipping was the heavy load of the U-Haul unit behind them.

Smoke filled the front of the vehicle immediately and all the airbag's deployed. The horn howled for several minutes before dead silence ensued as the motor quit; thankfully, the big SUV came to a halt on its own.

Fai pulled away from Dao; frantically, she hit at the partition that was always in place when others were driving. "Frank, Stanley... can you hear me!"

Getting no reply, Fai sat back in shock when smoke began filtering in from the seam of the glass. The two in the back tried to open their doors, but they were sealed shut.

Dao turned after undoing his seat belt then kicked desperately at the window, this always worked in movies; unfortunately, it didn't in real life... they were trapped!

**********

Lily mumbling irritably under her breath jumped up to begin pacing again. The one guarding the door ignored her, quite use to these random ranting's after two and a half days of it. His friend was on the other side of the door, periodically they would switch just so they could relieve some of the boredom.

The head Seeker had implemented the guards for two reasons; one was to keep Lily or her brother from spiriting Shadow Hunter away. The two had gotten the Cree/Oriental Shaman half way out of the house before they were caught red handed.

Their lame excuse was... 'This place is cursed so we are taking Hunter far away from here!'

Chris had been with the head Seeker at the time so the burly seven-foot guard had marched over; with hardly any effort, he hoisted Shadow Hunter into his arms and took him back up to his apartment.

The Cree/Oriental Shaman was now hooked up to a heart monitor that took his vitals before sending the information to a computer in the doctor's room; this way if he became distressed, she would know immediately.

An IV had been inserted to make sure Hunter stayed hydrated; he wouldn't like the catheter the doctor put in either, but she didn't want his bladder or kidneys to be stressed in any fashion.

The second and most important reason for the continued use of bodyguards now that Shadow Hunter could not be moved; was because of that thing hanging around.

A concerned head Seeker had sent all non-magical persons home. She also decided to cancel the faire for this year. Only the second time since starting the retreat had a complete cancellation ever happened.

Afterwards, Yvonne proceeded to move all magic users into the main house and it was bursting at the seams. Cots had even been set up in the house basement, as well as the Seeker's vaulted room. They were using the prison room too; every spare inch was filled with sleeping pallets.

Guards roamed the hallways trying to keep the peace as inevitably arguments cropped up with so many bunched together under one roof.

Walks outside were permitted, but only in groups of ten; for each group at least three guards were needed. Everyone carried a weapon... even if it was just a stick.

Excited whispers had been heard since early this morning; the High Priestess of Mother Earth was on her way. She was the last of the three, the one most had never seen before. It was rumoured that she was blind, but nobody seemed to know for sure.

'Eeeek!'

Everybody in the house froze; some even covered sensitive ears. Periodically one of those creatures would show up, nobody knew where the other two were... it seemed to be searching for something. It would stalk around the grounds, sometimes for twenty minutes other times it could be an hour. Once frustrated enough it would scream then disappear for a while before coming back several hours later. Whether it was the same one or one of the others, nobody wanted to get close enough to see.

Twice now, the Nephilim had gotten into the house; it was quickly driven out again. They all wondered how long before it refused to leave or it came back with the others.

None of them could kill it and only the bow that Shadow Hunter had used seemed to affect it. Neither could anyone pull the drawstring back on the bow in order to use it to defend the house; they had all tried.

Lily standing at the window stared out distractedly, she winced as a fork of lightening flared outside; the bright flash of light allowed her to catch a quick glance of that thing just as it vanished, causing her to shiver in disgust. Thunder crashed a second later, followed closely by a downpour as the rain came down in a solid sheet obscuring the view of Hunter's trailer.

Hearing a loud bleep of the heart monitor behind her, just as the bedroom door flew open; the older Ojibwa twin spun around when Shadow Hunter bolted up with a cry of denial. "Nooo!"

The head Seeker and Running Doe came running into the bedroom; they were both halfway to the bed when they all heard a cry of fearful denial from Shadow Hunter.

The doctor checking her patience vitals on the computer in her room was just in time to see a flurry of activity on the screen. Running Doe calling out a warning to the head Seeker raced out of her room, they made it just as her patient bolted upwards.

Running Doe was donning gloves before they even reached the bed. The two women split up; they each took a different side of the bed.

Doctor Smitt put her hands on the Cree/Oriental Shaman's shoulders hoping to keep him from getting up. "Easy now, Hunter; calm yourself, I need to check you out. Do you have any pain anywhere?"

Shadow Hunter frowned in confusion. "A headache, lightheaded, I also feel a bit dizzy... what happened to me? I remember going down to the basement to go to the pool, I reached for the door then nothing afterwards."

Rubbing his eyes wearily, Hunter suddenly dropped his arm. "I could hear a lot of voices mumbling around me. Some I could understand... most I could not. Did I fall down the stairs, what's with all this stuff?"

Running Doe and the head Seeker looked at each other in concern before managing to ease Shadow Hunter back onto the bed.

The Seeker tried to distract him so the doctor could check him over one last time; patting his shoulder she managed a semblance of a smile, unfortunately it ended up being more of a grimace. "Were you having a nightmare, I could not help hearing your outcry?"

Scowling when both women ignored his questions, Shadow Hunter finally shrugged. "I saw my wife being hit by another lightning bolt, only this time she was in a black vehicle driving down the highway. It was the strangest dream, since I have only seen my wife on horseback. The big SUV was instantly engulfed in flames! I have been having some pretty weird dreams lately, like making love in the strangest places... even in the Seeker's chambers."

Lily standing by the window with her arms folded in anger at being ignored saw the look of shock the two women exchanged then stepped forward immediately. "What do you know; I can tell there is something?"

The Seeker looked at Running Doe, but she just shrugged leaving it up to her to decide if she should tell them. "Ladies, please turn around so I can take the catheter out."

Shadow Hunter couldn't help a squeak of surprise at the thought of having a hose attached to him. "Catheter; how long have I been in here...?"

"Ouch...!"

Shadow Hunters exclamation was cut short and he couldn't help yelping in surprised pain when the long tube was extracted, not having expected her to just yank it out without any warning.

The doctor pulled a steal tray over that had all the equipment she needed on it then placed the Catheter with the urine bag on the bottom shelf in a chamber pot to be disposed of later. Taking her light, she pulled back each of his eyelids checking both eyes; thankfully, they were both clear... quite responsive in fact. "Do you feel nauseated or are you still dizzy?"

Shaking his head, Shadow Hunter answered grimly. "Not any more, just hungry, and thirsty!"

Running Doe nodded satisfied, she pulled a bandage apart then began taking out his IV.

Eyeing both women angrily, Hunter finally turned to the doctor. "How long have I been here?"

Lily stepped forward tired of being ignored. "It has been a week, Hunter; they brought you in here full of blood, but none of it was yours. You had a large lump on the back of your head."

The Seeker stepped between Lily and Shadow Hunter with a scowl of warning. "Please go get Hunter a pitcher of water. If you ask the cook she will heat up the chicken soup she made earlier, maybe have her add some Jell-O or pudding if she has any. We will discuss what happened after he eats; he needs to get some of strength back first.

Giving a loud snort of anger, Lily marched past the Seeker then left.

Going back around the bed, the head Seeker patted Shadow Hunter's arm consolingly. "I know you have many questions right now and we will answer them, but we are hoping it will come back to you before then. We know very little at this point, only you have all the answers."

Turning, the Seeker gestured for the guard to come over. "I need to make a phone call before I can confirm my suspicions on Hunter's nightmare. I need you to help him up and get him walking around, make sure he does not fall or reinjure his head. I will be back as soon as I can."

Without waiting for an answer from any of them, the Seeker spun around before racing out,

Shadow Hunter grumbled irritably under his breath then let Running Doe help him sit up.

The guard walked around the bed, he stood at the ready in case the Cree/Oriental Shaman needed a hand. Wisely, he did not try to help knowing Hunter would need to do this on his own and would resent his interference.

Running Doe went to the closet before grabbing a robe then rushed over to help him in to it. Except for a loin cloth, Shadow Hunter was still gloriously naked... not that she minded all that much. Turning away to hide a guilty grin the doctor stood back, but stayed close in case her patient needed help.

Just getting back to the bed, Hunter's supper arrived; they set up the portable table for him. Watching him eat with gusto the doctor nodded satisfied. He seemed no worse for wear and sighed thankfully

**********

Having no luck with kicking at the window, Dao hastily put his feet back down. He reached out then push a few buttons on a keypad that was on the back of the front seat, a panel popped open and the Guardian sighed in relief... the little safe had not been affected by the lightning.

Hearing Fai coughing beside him, Dao quickly pulled out one of the daggers that were sealed inside when they were travelling. The Oriental reversed it before banging insistently on the window, it took three well placed blows to get the glass to crack; he turned again to beat on the glass with his boots.

Finally, the window shattered and fresh air quickly filled the back seat. Kneeling on the seat, Dao carefully removed all the glass then hoisted himself out the window. He looked up; it was still drizzling a bit, but the main storm with all the lightning clouds had moved off. Thankfully, allowing the sky to lighten considerably.

Reaching in, Dao pulled out a coughing Fai.

Two cars were stopped, a man and a woman from each raced over. The man carried a hammer and the woman had a crow bar.

Dao smiled in thanks then took the hammer; he knocked on the driver window first to give the men in front a warning. "I am going to break the window, cover your eyes if you can."

Not hearing a sound, Dao used the hammer; he hit close to the left corner, hoping to put a big enough hole so that the smoke would clear while they worked on prying the door open. Two hits with the hammer and it went through, allowing the smoke to billow out as the man continued prying with the bar until finally the door was wedged open.

While the man and woman helped get the unconscious driver out and administered CPR, Dao and Fai raced around and pried open the passenger's side. As soon as Stanley was on the ground, the Guardian began CPR.

Sitting down hard on the ground in bemusement, Fai ran her still tingling fingers through her hair in frustration. Hearing sirens in the distance just as Stanley groaned painfully then a bellow from Frank, White Buffalo jumped up and raced around the escalade before dropping down beside her guard. "We are all fine Frank, but my beast is dead!"

Frank frowned puzzled for a moment then couldn't help chuckling as he raised a hand and cupped his employer's cheek tenderly. "You can buy another one Fai."

Moving back, Fai allowed one of the paramedics to bring oxygen to the distressed guard. Thankfully, she saw the other medic going to Stanley. A few minutes later, both men were taken to the ambulance for further assessment. White Buffalo was glad to see both men hobbling towards the emergency vehicle without assistance.

Turning to the man and woman who had helped them, Fai smiled sweetly. "Thank you both so much for your help, we would have never gotten our friends out in time without the both of you."

The woman grinned crookedly, she was blonde and plump with a few teeth missing so had a bit of a lisp. She accepted the crowbar back when the Oriental came around the black SUV and held it out to her. "Thank you... I am just glad the lot of you are okay; I thought for sure everyone in the vehicle was a goner when I saw the lightning hit and flames blow out the back. I called 911 immediately."

The red haired tall skinny man standing beside the woman nodded in agreement, he had a distinctive Scottish accent. "We did too, lucky that you had the trailer or I'm sure you would have flipped er and rolled into the ditch. Your vehicle was engulfed in flames for at least two minutes."

Frank and Stanley both exited the ambulance then hobbled over, unaffected physically; a bit of oxygen into their distressed lungs was all that was needed before the paramedics released them.

The two men shook their rescuers hands in gratitude.

Stanley turned to Fai. "The ambulance driver called for a tow truck, it should be here shortly."

Nodding in relief, Fai bid their rescuers goodbye before going to the escalade to empty everything out of it... it was not long before the others followed her

*****

After three long hours, Fai climbed wearily into the back of the new Cadillac... thankful to have that done. This one was a burnt orange and pretty fancy compared to the old beast. Unfortunately, it was the only one they had... it cost her, a pretty penny too.

Inspecting the trailer closely, Dao was happy to report that the refrigeration was still working and nothing seemed damaged.

Fai grimaced in relief, they definitely did not want their father to start stinking now. She was hoping to make it to the retreat by morning. They had a quick bite to eat while they waited for insurance and registration papers. The final triplet was glad Vancouver was behind them three hours or they would have been stuck in this little town overnight on the outskirts of Toronto, so close yet so far away from their destination.

Dao got in then held the cell phone out to his charge. "It is the head Seeker."

Smiling in thanks, Fai took the phone then listened for a moment before a surprised look of confusion crossed her face. "How do you know about that? He did... that's strange! Yes, we are all fine."

Fai mouthed inquisitively then held her hand over the mouth piece. "How long do you reckon?"

Stanley now in the driver's seat had to wait for his automatic gas pedal, seat, and steering wheel to adjust before adding the address to the navigation system. The bodyguard waited as it calculated. "Five hours it says; barring any more unforeseen stops that should be about right."

Frank just getting in, heard his brother's comment; chuckling he couldn't help teasing. "I would not count on that, with our little miss running things, there is no telling what will happen next!"

Harrumphing in annoyance at the two bantering men in front, Fai uncovered the phone and gave the head Seeker the info she wanted. Listening once more to the one on the other end of the phone, she nodded even though White Buffalo knew she could not see it. "Yes, I find that quite interesting; I will see what my Guardian has to say about it. I will leave it up to you; it is fine with me if you want to tell Hunter. Okay I will discuss it with Dao... see you soon."

Handing the phone back to her half-brother, Fai explained to the confused Dao about Shadow Hunter's week long coma and his sudden nightmare of them being struck by lightning which woke him up. "The Seeker was not a hundred percent sure the dream was about us; she wanted to tell him, but needed to confirm her suspicions and make sure we were alright first."

Frowning in thought, Dao drummed his fingers on the door arm rest. Finally, he turned and looked at Fai. "The medallion on his chest could be what is keeping him connected to you. Without you the birth cannot happen."

Grimacing knowingly, Fai nodded then shrugged resignedly... resenting that fact. The higher powers were always manipulating her family and none of them seemed to have a choice in the matter.

Shaking off her resentment knowing it would do her no good dwelling on it; Fai gestured thoughtfully before giving him the rest of the information she had received. "The head Seeker is quite concerned and confused by the Nephilim's actions lately. Only one shows up now and it wonders the grounds searching for something. When it does not find what it is looking for, it screeches angrily then disappears. It has tried a couple times to get in the house, but they have guards posted everywhere and they have managed to drive it out each time. Yvonne is not sure how long they can keep it out of the house though"

Rubbing his chin reflectively, Dao remembered the conversation he had with Ronin; they had discussed his younger brother's suspicion that the Nephilim were connected to the triplets.

After the carpet had accepted him, the Tianming monk was shown the death of Alexandrina. Deliberating on the unexpected death of the first triplet, the two men figured it was not Alex the creatures were after but the Shaman.

Turning to Fai finally, Dao gestured ominously. "I was shown both deaths just after the rug accepted me. It seemed quite strange to me that the Nephilim were attacking Shadow Hunter. Your sister was not anywhere nearby when the attack began. When the spear was thrown, I saw a look of shock and denial on the face of the creature who threw it. When we were taken to the Mother Earth's chamber when the second spear was cast, again a look of fear and horror flashed when Magdalene flipped and the spear entered her instead of its target. Both Nephilim exploded at the same instant your sister's died. I am now positive it was meant for the Shaman; since he was unconscious, it could not find him. Now that he is awake it will know the minute it returns to the retreat."

Sitting forward urgently, Fai put her hand on Stanley's shoulder. "Push the speed limit as much as possible without getting pulled over for speeding... please!"

Nodding, Stephan pushed the pedal down until it was ten km over then set the cruise; most cops would not bother you at that speed.

Turning back to Dao, Fai gestured pleadingly. "Call the head Seeker and warn her."

Nodding, the Guardian pulled out his phone.

**********

Restlessly, Shadow Hunter got up in irritation... maybe a swim would help clear his mind. Turning towards his bathroom to take a quick shower first, he halted in surprise when both his assistants barged in uninvited.

Frowning, the Cree/Oriental Shaman looked down at his watch. It was quarter to ten. They were an hour and a half late for the meeting he had asked for while having supper. "Too late now Lily, we can meet in the morning at ten; I will have a meditation room readied for us. I am...!"

Lily interrupted her employer quickly. "We have to get out of here Hunter... this place is cursed."

Seeing a look of disbelief and amusement flash across his employers face, Buck put his hand on his sister's arm to halt her tirade. He knew this was not the way to get Shadow Hunter to see reason. "I'm sorry sir. My sister is a bit over dramatic at times. We just learned from the head Seeker that those things hunting magic users are after you; now that you are awake, it will be able to sense you and will try again. For some reason while you were unconscious, it could not feel you and that is why it disappears... it's looking elsewhere. We fear it is only a matter of time until it shows up here again."

Looking from one twin to the other in bewildered incredibility, Shadow Hunter shook his head in amazement. "I can't believe you two, how many years have we been hunting creatures like these and some even worse. Just because I am now the hunted does not change anything. This place was my wife's legacy and I will not allow that thing to destroy it now that I am the owner!"

Lily rushed in quickly. "But that's the thing Hunter you are not..."

'BANG, BANG!'

Scowling in frustration at the interruption, the Cree/Oriental Shaman looked at the door. "Come in."

The head Seeker walked in with two burly guards flanking her; Shadow Hunter had banished them from his room earlier.

Gesturing angrily at the twins, she berated them both. "I told you to wait and I would explain things to him myself now that I have confirmation..."

Turning, Lily pulled away from her brother angrily then interrupted the head Seeker heatedly. "No, we are all leaving immediately; he does not need any more of your half-truths and lies, this place is cursed!"

Buck grabbed his sister's arm again, trying to make her stop before she said something that she would regret later; he had known for many years that she was infatuated with the

Cree/Oriental Shaman. Unfortunately, it was no use trying to get Lily to halt. The two women hackles raised continued to argue heatedly.

'CRACK!'

Silence fell instantly as the five looked in shock at the bathroom door; it was still quivering from being slammed shut.

Shadow Hunter leaned back against the door then pinched the bridge of his nose painfully. His headache was now pounding out of control and he needed blessed silence. Turning, Hunter hung up his robe and swimming trunks then stripped and climbed into the shower.

Leaning against the shower wall, the Cree/Oriental Shaman allowed the water to run on the back of his neck; sighing in relief the pain finally eased, he looked down at his chest and noticed that the dragon had grown again and the second claw was now open slightly and holding something.

If those creatures were after him, could it be because of the medallion on his chest? The burning question on Hunter's mind right now is; what if anything could the dragon be holding in its claws. Having no idea at all, he shrugged before turning his thoughts in a different direction.

Since Shadow Hunter could not seem to get the medallion off his chest then a plan to capture those things or kill them was needed. He would have to be the bait of course, but thinking right now just made his head throb again. A few laps in the pool and then an hour of quiet meditation was what the Cree/Oriental Shaman needed right now, the rest would have to wait.

Finishing his shower quickly, Shadow Hunter dried himself then donned his trunks and put on his robe. He caressed the silky material and smiled when the cloak of illusion brought up an image of his old Tianming Master. Hunter hadn't realized that he grabbed his Oriental cloak by mistake. Shrugging dismissively, he decided to leave it on as he walked out of his bathroom.

As soon as the door opened, the five people waiting for Shadow

Hunter got up from where they had settled.

Seeing Lily opening her mouth to begin again, Hunter held up his hand for silence. "I do not wish to talk right now; I am going for a swim to clear my head than an hour of quiet meditation before I will discuss anything."

The head Seeker stepped forward with a nod. "I will have all the guards stay back and silent, but they will be spaced around the pool... that creature can show up here anytime. The Mother Earth wishes for you to go to her cavern for your meditation and again I will make sure the guards stay back. Afterwards, we will have a meeting and everyone can have their say."

Lily scowled then harrumphed in angry agreement.

Ignoring his fuming assistant, Shadow Hunter went to an alcove and pulled out his sword and scabbard just in case. He did not put it on his back, but carried it as he silently walked out of his apartment.

There was half a dozen men waiting for them and they surrounded the group of six, silently they followed.

Once at the bottom of the stairs on the main floor, Hunter turned right and went to the big door that led to the basement. He walked down the three steps to the landing before hanging another right; he reached out for the door handle then paused once it was in his hand.

Shadow Hunter looked towards the other door for a brief moment as a quick flash a memory tickled the back of his mind. Suddenly it was gone. The Cree/Oriental frowned grimly before turning the door handle in his hand. Quickly, he went down the ten steps with everyone following behind him.

As soon as Hunter was off the stairs, he looked to the left when he overheard the TV going in the entertainment room then a crack was heard of a cue hitting two balls together. Ignoring the noise, the Cree/Oriental Shaman turned right and walked through the exercise room. Several people were about, using the equipment... that too he ignored.

Shadow Hunter walked towards the back where an arched alcove could be seen. Once through it, he entered a vaulted room with an indoor pool. Alex had told him the water came from an artesian underground spring that had never dried up, not since she had been here anyway.

On the far side was two curtained off rooms, one had a five person Jacuzzi, and the other had an eight person sauna. In between them was two shower stalls, but he already had a shower so he ignored them.

The head Seeker gathered the guards around her; quickly she gave each man instructions to stay back but vigilant.

Shadow Hunter took off his robe and put everything on a bench before running to the edge of the pool, he dove in. He ignored everything and everyone around him needing the quiet as plans on how to catch the Nephilim plagued him.

# CHAPTER TWELVE

After everyone was arranged to the head Seeker's satisfaction, she pointed at Lily and Buck then crooked a finger for them to follow her, expecting no refusals. "We will wait for him in the Seeker's chamber, he will not be able to clear his mind with you two scowling at him. I have a large folding table being set up as we speak and chairs will be available for the meeting. I had his wives Seeker's robes and their spirit animal hides draped on the little alter for Hunter to sit on while meditating, the Mother Earth commanded it."

Lily shrugged not caring about all that then changed the subject to one that interested her more. "Who is the woman coming that everybody is talking about? I'm a bit suspicious because as soon as we get close they clam up and refuse to discuss it?"

The Head Seeker frowned and looked over at Hunter's assistant in disapproval. "We will wait for Shadow Hunter to join us; I will not be repeating myself twice."

Lily followed the Seeker back through the training room and up the stairs in a huff. The two had never been in here before since they had refused to go to Hunter's wedding. The older twin's feelings towards her boss and the volatile angry hurt feelings towards the other half of her lost family had not allowed her to approve of their hasty marriage; after all, they had only known each other for two weeks.

The younger twin had followed her lead... not wanting to provoke his sister.

When they walked across the landing, Lily frowned in surprise when the head Seeker produced a key and unlocked the other door. It was made out of solid mahogany wood with stainless steel and iron accents placed around it to give a solid castle style type of door meant for repelling a siege; the door was solid enough even a battering ram would be hard pressed to dent it.

Using all her strength, the Seeker pulled the heavy door open and it creaked in protest. What was so important behind that door? The other one had not been locked and was made out of a lighter stainless steel.

A switch was pushed and several lights going down lit up. After descending to twenty steps all light vanished before a ball of light appeared above them and followed the group down another thirty stairs.

An archway greeted them when they stepped off the last step; over the top were bold black words that read…

**'The greatest human emotion is love, without it the world would be doomed!'**

Pausing, Lily was unsure if she wanted to step through that doorway; she had a feeling that if she did nothing would ever be the same again.

Getting impatient and having no qualms, Buck walked around his sister and through the arch; he felt a tingle run through his body, but other than that he felt nothing sinister… only a sense of peace.

Looking over at the head Seeker as she stood to the side watching his sister intently, Buck opened his mouth to call out reassurance. The younger twin snapped it shut when the older woman held up her hand to silence him.

Shaking her head, the head Seeker frowned in warning. "It must be her decision to step through that doorway; she must relinquish the anger that has been eating at her all these years for her to be able to move on. If she does, one day she will become one of the most powerful Seeker's we have seen and will only be second to the Priestess of Mother Earth herself.

Frowning in surprise at that, Buck wondered if he should have been so hasty to go through that door. He had seen nothing sinister about the entry and the saying around the door had not triggered any alarms either…

**'The shield must always stand fast and protect the innocent!'**

What was so offensive about those words that would cause his sister to not want to enter here... did he miss something?

Lily stared at the black lettering and frowned. She had been angry for so long it was hard to remember when it had started. Her Ojibwa/Cheyenne father had shown her an old journal of Cecille's half-sister, Black Rose. It was penned in the year of 1908; she was only thirteen years old at the time.

Black Rose and several others ended up being spirited away from their people by a Catholic Priest. He took them to a residential school that educated Native child. It wasn't just Indian children though. Several different nationalities were kept there; Irish, Russians, African Americans, and Scottish youngsters even quite a few white children that were from poverty-stricken homes.

Lily had been so influenced by that diary...

**Rose tried telling the Priest that she was the daughter of Earl Summerset from England, nobody believed her of course. Every day, she was given a lashing on her bare back by the nuns trying to make her confess that she was lying. They even made her change her name to Mary-Lou and her Ojibwa name was never to be spoken again.**

**Black Rose steadfastly refused to give in no matter how badly they hurt her, until her birthday.**

**'I turned sixteen today and still I refuse to answer to Mary-Lou, but the beatings are getting worse. I was shocked when the Priest showed up today and halted the nuns whipping, it was the first time he had ever done that.'**

**Father Joseph handed me a paper with a satisfied flip of his hand. "I decided to end this nonsense once and for all; last month I sent a letter to Lord Summerset and this is what his reply was."**

**Grabbing the paper eagerly, Black Rose scanned it quickly then frowned and had to go back to reread it in disbelief.**

**'Dear Sir, there is only one legitimate child that was born to the late Earl Summerset and no others have ever been**

**recorded. If there is another it would have been born a bastard and has no claim to England... do with her as you will!"**

**Black Roses heart dropped and the letter slipped out of her trembling hand then settled under the bed and was forgotten by the Priest as he left satisfied by the heathens shocked look; it was not long before she began answering to Mary-Lou and her heart now broken, hardened...**

Shaking off the memories, Lily sighed; she had kept that diary and read it often, Black Rose had filled the pages with the horror of her life. The only thing that had made it bearable was her budding love for the Shaman's son who had also been taken.

Black Rose was seventeen when the two Ojibwa youngsters managed to run away from the school. After years of being away, and having their beliefs stripped from them the two found their tribe but were shunned. Heartbroken once more, they found shelter in an old shack on the outskirts of town and they survived the best way they could.

The first time Lily had read the journal a folded piece of paper fell out, written on the back was the date 1908 and one sentence... 'my heart is dead!' she opened it and scanned the terse letter of rejection and the young impressionable ten year old felt Black Roses pain as her own.

Lilies father's obsession with finding their missing heritage brought them to ruin and put them on the streets. More letters of rejection now filled the diary, all with her father's handwriting. He had sent them not only to the Summerset family but also to the Queen herself. Most had been unopened, with a return to sender; the ones that were opened had nasty notes added then sent back.

The rage and disappointment Lily's father showed openly had rubbed off on his daughter and her anger climbed daily as hunger and fear plagued their lives.

The death of her parents by that shapeshifter would never leave Lily's memory; and still to this day, she had nightmares of being stalked by that wolf.

The timely arrival of Shadow Hunter had saved the twins, but it was too late to halt the anger and resentment festering in the older twin's heart. As time progressed, her feelings eased and an infatuation for the Cree/Oriental Shaman had taken the place of her fear and hunger.

Closing her eyes, Lily remembered the meeting with Alexandrina; when they had touched, she had felt a tingle of recognition and a genuine joy from the other woman at meeting the twins. The sincerity and truthfulness of her trying to find their lost Ojibwa family was glaringly obvious.

Looking up towards the caverns ceiling, Lily's lip twisted in a sardonic grimace. "Well father, I think we were looking in the wrong direction. It is too bad I found her too late, but at least we did meet briefly."

Lily felt the resentment melt away and the years of hate began to dissipate. Resolutely she took the step that had her walking into the antechamber. A feeling of inner peace rushed through her and she inhaled in relief; she was free. After all these years, she could now live her own life... instead of her fathers.

The twins followed the head Seeker silently into a vaulted cavern and Lily's jaw dropped in awe; the huge room held hundreds of robed Seeker's. This was the first time she had seen so many in a robe, usually only the head Seeker wore her robe constantly.

Blinking, the older twin noticed the majority of the robes were white; some with gold scrollwork, others with silver... a few had a bit of green added here and there. A dark green coloured robe could be seen periodically. It was so dark a green that when light hit it, it looked black. Those ones also had silver, gold, or white scroll work embroidered on them.

The head Seeker was the only one though that had the green coloured robe with all three colours entwining embroidered on it.

Having seen several movies over the years of robed witches, Priests, and Satan worshiper's Lily noticed immediately that none of the robes here had a head covering or collar. The sleeves were not long either, nor did they bell out and touch the ground. These sleeves were almost none existing only going to just below the shoulders.

The white robes were ankle length, but the green ones brushed the floor. They did have a braided rope around their waist, all in various colours; most were the same as their scrollwork. Although, some had a dark green rope which was contrary to their embroidery.

The fabric did not look heavy or cumbersome either, it had a bit of a shimmer to it; being that it was translucent, one could almost see through the material. It reminded Lily of the rayon and polyester smock that she wore when wearing her halter top or bikini top... light and airy... she definitely approved of that.

A pathway opened immediately and Lily walked forward in a daze, she felt a bit lightheaded and she seemed to be in a different world... ethereal.

The three entwining circles with the rock alter in the center pulsed, reminding Lily of a heart beat; periodically, a two second hesitation would happen but then steady and the rhythmic pulsing would continue.

The head Seeker stepped into the first circle then turned to the twins not allowing either to join her just yet. She reached out and took Lily's left hand into hers. "Can you feel the Mother calling? She is beseeching you to join her. To do so, you must accept the magic within you. You are the ancestor of one of the most powerful Shaman's ever born; in you, his power resides. Unfortunately, until you release all your darker emotions it will remain blocked, unusable by you; only one of pure heart can enter the first of the three rings to accept the Mother Earth's power!"

The light chanting from the Seeker's intensified and Lily closed her eyes then felt a light pulsing from the Earth on her feet even through her moccasins. One more time, she relived her younger years and opened up her heart to purge the last of her hate and fear; it allowed the Mother's voice to become stronger. She took the step needed into the first ring, accepting the Mother Earth... heart and soul!

Giving Lily's hand a squeeze of relief, the head Seeker turned to the youngest twin then reached out her right hand and took Buck's right one in hers. "In your veins runs the Ojibwa and Cheyenne warriors, you come from a long line of Chief's and war Chief's... you must step away from your sister and become who you were meant to be! Accept the Great Spirit and your Ojibwa/Cheyenne blood then discard all white man's impurities. In doing so you will become the mightiest warrior able to withstand the unthinkable and see beyond. As you step into the first of the three circles of eternity you must speak your new name."

Looking over at his sister in surprise at that, Buck scowled thoughtfully then turned back towards the Seeker. The younger twin had not realized how often he allowed his sister to take control

Thinking back a sardonic grin flashed for a brief moment; he closed his eyes remembering. Only once could he remember going against her that was just after Hunter had found them. She had wanted to leave in the middle of the night. He planted his feet and refused to budge. The older twin had left him there and disappeared.

For three days, Buck fretted stifling the urge to go find her. This was the longest time they had ever been apart in their entire lives. Struggling with his need to find his older sibling, the young Ojibwa/Cheyenne youngster refused to move knowing this was where they belonged. If he gave in now they would be running for the rest of their lives and she would keep him under her thumb... forever.

It was close to midnight, his sister had been gone now for four days...

**Buck paced the trailer, mumbling constantly to himself refusing to relent. "No, I will not give in!"**

**Getting more worried by the moment and needing to get out, he left to go see the horses to get his mind off his twin sister. Standing there, he smiled when the horse Shadow Hunter had given to him walked over for a pet. He had named the pure black gelding, Midnight.**

**Relaxing for the first time in four days a feeling of peaceful calm settled over him. Suddenly, he looked up at a piercing call and saw a hawk silhouetted by a full moon against the deep night...**

Buck shook off the memory before taking the step needed into the first of the three rings. "Beshk is my new Ojibwa name... it means, Nighthawk."

Nodding with an approving inclination of her head, the Seeker reached over with her left hand then took Lily's right one again. Bringing the two closer, Yvonne joined their hands together. "The Great Spirit approves of your choice, now you will both band together and become a shield for the innocent. Together, you will be the strongest defence against the coming storm... each powerful in your own right, but invincible as one unit. The Almighty and the Mother Earth will work through the both of you to help us in our darkest time of need."

The Seeker let go of the twin's hands then turned, she took three large steps; stopping on the other side of the second ring before the junction of the joining rings, Yvonne turned towards brother and sister.

Reaching out; again, the head Seeker took Lily's left hand into hers. "The magic is strong in you! Can you feel it coursing through your body? Unlike others, you do not need to merge with an Earth's Shadow to use it. You must accept who you are to become all you are meant to be. Search deep inside yourself... as you step into the second ring of Eternity you must speak your new name!"

Frown in surprise, at that revelation; Lily shook her head in denial, she had magic! When did that happen? Closing her eyes, the oldest twin looked within but felt nothing.

About to give up, a childhood memory long forgotten flared to life. Lily looked to be about five year old at that time. She could see herself squatting beneath an old oak tree in the backyard before they had become homeless...

**Lily stared at the baby chick that was squawking painfully; it had broken its leg when it fell out of the nest in the upper branches. With tears streaming down her gaunt cheeks, she sat cross legged before picking it up. Her brother had gone inside already to tell their mother.**

**Crooning, Lily held the chick close to her while more tears of compassion coursed down her cheeks. Hearing a hoot above her, she looked up at the red owl starring down at its injured chick.**

**An image of a man she did not know flickered briefly in her mind before Lily's hands heated; healing the chick's leg just as the red owl screeched once again...**

The memory faded before the Seeker's image flickered then the man she had just seen as a child smiled at her. "I give you the name Ma'e'mestaa'e, Cheyenne for Red Owl. Red is the people's most spiritual colour it will help in your journey through the dream world. For you will become the next most powerful dream walker in our history. The owl is associated with life and death so represents our most sacred Medicine Man and Shaman. Beware; a life given or taken without consulting with the Great Spirit can alter the future... with disastrous consequences. Only Heammawihio, the Great Spirit of all living things can take life or give it."

The image blurred and the Seeker was once again herself.

Lily could now feel her magic pulsing within her. Taking the step needed to enter the second circle of life; the older twin spoke decisively knowing that her people must be represented here. "My name is miskoo'oog; it is Ojibwa for Red Owl."

The Seeker nodded pleased, the owl suited the volatile girl; one minute she seemed soft and sweet and the next her claws came out and she could scratch your eyes out. Yvonne had heard herself speaking, but the older woman had not understood any of the words she was saying.

Shrugging dismissively, the Seeker let go of the older twin then turned to the younger brother; again, she took his right hand. "You also have the ability to use magic, but you must bond with the Mother Earth's shadow first. If you do accept, you will gain the ability to see through your power animals eyes. All warrior skills will be enhanced, and you will gain the ability to see beyond. A Shield Totem name must be uttered as you step into the second circle. When you do a shadow will rise up, you will become one so that the Great Spirit can interact through the Mother's spirit in order to guide you."

Nighthawk frowned thoughtfully; they had grown up on stories of the Ojibwa. Unfortunately, only once could he remember going to the reservation. Their father had gone inside and the twins had been told to stay outside. He was only seven at the time, inquisitively he had wondered over to stare in fascination at the tall totem pole that stood eleven feet tall. At the very top was a huge bird with wings outstretched and it seemed to be staring intently at him...

**A chuckle to his right, had Buck spinning in that direction; he had been so intent on the pole he had not noticed the old man sitting cross-legged pocking holes in a hide. A round hoop with several skins attached already was sitting on his knees.**

**Getting curious, the young Buck walked over and squatted. "What are you making?"**

**The old man gave a toothless grin. "I am making a war shield, to be effective against arrows and spears it must have three or four hides pulled tight; if it is meant to stop a bullet, at least six to eight hides are needed. Each hide must be stretched as tight as possible. Rawhide is poked through these holes then tied tightly to the round wooden hoop. Any**

kind of dyed rawhide can be used to wrap the wooden hoop to make it more decorative. On the last hide, an image of your tribe's totem should be painted on. Feathers and beads that have meaning to you can be added later."

Buck frowned inquisitively. "How do you know what your totem animal is?"

The old man gave a half shrug. "Usually a Shaman has a vision for the one seeking a totem."

Pointing at the boy in satisfaction, the wrinkled old man chortled. "I had a vision just last night, I walked many miles to sit in front of this totem; as I sat here working on a medicine shield, thunder and lightning came to me than spoke!"

The old man finished the shield and presented it to Buck for his approval; it had eight hides that were stretched to the limits, in the center was a thunderbird with lightning bolts surrounding it.

While the boy was admired the shield in awe, the old man got up before disappearing mysteriously...

The twins helped search the village with their father wanting to return the shield, but the old man was never found.

The youngest twin still had that shield; it was proudly displayed over his bed. He had added feathers and other special items to it over the years.

Nighthawk took a step; proudly he spoke his totem's name. "Binesi, it is Ojibwa for thunderbird."

When he stepped into the second ring of eternity, he felt a shiver as a shadow entered him. Instantly, he felt invigorated, alive, and powerful; looking around in awe, he could see shadows everywhere. Most were attached to a host, but a few were floating around aimlessly.

When the Mother Earth's pulse hesitated for that extra second, another shadow arose from the center of the three joined rings.

The Seeker nodded pleased by that then took Red Owl's hand to join both sister and brother together in her own. "The Thunderbird will now shield and teach you both the ways of the spirits, the great bird will bring the power of lightning to the ones sheltered by it; may the giant Thunderbird, show you both the way."

Letting go of the twins, the Seeker took three large steps then halted in the last ring. She turned to the look at both brother and sister. Reaching out she took Red Owl's left hand. "The third and last circle of eternity is your future. The Mother Earth is calling you to her service. She is a demanding Mother, if you accept you will wear the dark red robe of our new spiritual leader that was once held by Dan. You will also become our sacred Medicine Woman."

Gasps of shock were heard throughout the room. Their religious order was only a front so deaths and marriages could be recorded legally to the government and they were not bothered. To add sacred Medicine Woman to that was unprecedented. Especially, without a vote by all Seekers like Dan had been. At the very least, it should have been deliberated by the seven Seekers that compromised the elders. By the shocked looks on their faces, none of them had known what was coming. Not only would Red Owl be the first woman to hold that office, but she would also be the youngest.

The head Seeker ignored the shocked crowd. Yvonne gestured to an apprenticing gold Seeker to bring a robe that was waiting over to them. "Once you put this robe on and take the step into the final ring of eternity; the Mother can speak to you directly. She will give you a task that you must help her with... only you will know what it is. If you accept that task you must step into the center where the three rings of eternity join together."

Red Owl turned with a frown and looked at the robe the girl was holding out to her. It was a deep red with gold, white, and silver embroidered animals; a white buffalo, silver wolf, and a black cougar plus the golden dragon medallion that Shadow Hunter wore. Oriental scrollwork was interwoven all over the material. A white sash was the cord that would hold it closed.

It was the only red robe in the room; Red Owl could not help but wonder what the Japanese letters strewn throughout the cloak meant. She inhaled in shock when the girl turned the cloak around and a red owl with wings outstretched was prominent on the back. How had they known she would name herself Red Owl, it was a question she would have to ask later.

Shaking off her straying thoughts, Red Owl reached out tentatively before stroking the cloak thoughtfully... did she really want this?

Looking over at her younger twin, Red Owl frowned. She couldn't help remembering their one and only separation period; she had stormed out after Buck refused to leave Shadow Hunter. Lily had not trusted the Cree/Oriental, but her brother had. She had not gone far at first, staying just out of sight watching and waiting for her brother to give in.

The second day; angry with her twin, cold and hungry she went into town...

**Sitting at a street corner with a plastic cup, Lily begged passer's by for a coin so she could get some food. They didn't understand her of course; after sitting there for most of the day all she had gotten was three dollars... dejectedly she took the change out. Maybe it was enough for a sandwich at the convenience store down the street.**

**Rising, Lily turned before barrelling straight into a man walking up the street. Stiffening in shock, she backed away hurriedly ready to make a run for it.**

**Holding up his hands the man smiled disarmingly. "Don't run... are you hungry; would you like something to eat?"**

**Lily backed up two more steps; she did not understand a thing he was saying.**

**The man took a step forward. "Do you comprehend what I am saying?"**

**When the girl just backed away further and looked confused, he put his hand up to his mouth then pointed across the street at a little restaurant. "Food, do you want**

something to eat?"

Stopping instantly in hope, Lily nodded emphatically. All of a sudden, two men grabbed her from behind then pulled her back into an alley. The one that had distracted her followed quickly. "She is a pretty little thing, I think Gustav will like her, I want a taste first."

Struggling for all she was worth, Lily stomped hard on the smaller guys foot; hoping to shock him into letting his grip lessen enough for her to escape... no such luck.

Seeing a couple silhouetted for a moment at the mouth of the alley, the older twin desperately called out for help. Instantly, it was cut short when the man hit her hard enough to make her head real before he stuffed a dirty rag into her mouth. Groaning in disbelief, she saw the two hurry past not wanting to get involved.

The two burly men lifted her effortlessly up by her arms so she could not touch the ground and they marched her down the dingy alleyway.

Moaning, Lily shook her head to clear it then began struggling in earnest as they took her further away from any possible rescue from passersby.

Unprepared, Lily grunted in pained surprise when they threw her hard onto the ground causing her to hit her head on the cement. Dazed, she felt her head split open and blood splattered everywhere on the ground.

"Idiots, Gustav is going to be furious! Be more careful; now hold her still for me!"

Unable to focus, Lily could feel a burning coming from the pit of her stomach and her head felt like it was going to explode. She heard her clothes ripping as if from a long way off before a heavy body fell on top of her.

Screeching in fearful confusion, Lily's body arched up; she could hear the three men curse then three identical screams of terror filled the alleyway. Incoherently, she saw the men holding their heads before backing away from her.

Blinking in disbelief, Lily saw a blur of motion and a sword flashed as three bodies dropped dead on the ground. Seeing Shadow Hunter drop to his knees before grabbing his head painfully the older twin realized that she was still screaming... unable to stop the burning. She felt it encompass her whole body.

Lily felt a shaking beneath her then the ground heaved under her as green vines began wrapping around her until she was cocooned completely. Hearing a far off crooning then a pressure in her head as her injury healed itself, she finally was able to relax before the burning subsided.

The screeching dwindled to a soft sob before Lily opened eyes that were now black and the irises had a red tinge to them; an image of the man that she had seen in her childhood appeared before her. He had auburn hair, high cheekbones, and the dusky skin of a half-breed.

Smiling lovingly, he reached out and touched Lily lightly on the forehead with his left hand. "Shh... you are not ready yet. Sleep, you will not remember any of this until the appointed day that the Mother Earth calls you to her service. Remember, taking a life or giving it is forbidden unless the Great Spirit is consulted first. Be cautious, the ability to heal is a responsibility that should never be taken lightly; it's a solitary ability and must not be revealed to anyone. You have the strength of my sister Raven running through your veins, may she guide you on a journey that will not be easy."

Lifting his hand away, Dream Dancer kissed his great, great, granddaughter before disappearing; as he did so Lily's black eyes returned to a soft dark brown.

Watching from a distance, Red Owl saw Shadow Hunter hide the bodies while she was still cocooned. Once done, he turned then disappeared. She saw the vines unravel and die before she woke confused; getting up finally, she went back

**to her brother with no recollection of the Cree/Oriental saving her for a second time...**

Red Owl couldn't help marvelling at the realization that her long deceased ancestor, Dream Dancer, had appeared to her three times now. Shaking off the memory, the older twin eyed the beautiful cloak. She looked up at the young girl holding the robe expectantly.

Ivy smiled innocently in reassurance; she could feel Red Owl's hesitation. Leaning forward she whispered hopefully. "We need you... please!"

Lifting her hand, Red Owl cupped the girl's cheek tenderly... a shiver of fear coursed down her spine before she saw a child cowering in a corner holding up her hand to try stopping her mother from hitting her again.

Pulling back in shock, Red Owl stared at the beautiful pixie face; she noticed a small scar on the right side of her lip that had never healed properly after her mother almost beat her to death.

Nodding decisively, Red Owl turned and allowed the girl to help her on with the cloak. As soon as the robe was in place, she took the step into the final ring of Eternity.

As soon as she entered a vision of Shadow Hunter, lying on the ground with blood pouring out of his chest flashed in her mind. Red Owl dropped to her knees in shock and anger when she saw Alexandrina standing over him with a glowing sword dripping blood... wait that wasn't Hunter's wife!"

Nighthawk took a step towards his sister when he heard her cry out in denial. He halted when the head Seeker stepped forward and blocked him.

Yvonne lifted a cautionary hand to stop the younger twin; Nighthawk must not interfere. "You have to let her accept or reject the Mother's request, you cannot save her now. She will need your strength soon enough to help her through ordeals that she is fated to have. Remember, interfering too quickly can bring catastrophe for you both. It will be your job to help others weaker than you are.

It won't always be your sister who needs your protection!"

The younger twin saw Red Owl nod, she rose with a stoic expression on her face before taking a step into the three joining rings... accepting the Mother's request. He knew by the look his sister had that whatever she needed to do would be done. He had seen that look one too many times over the years, even if she had to step on others to achieve her goals; she would without blinking an eye.

Nighthawk had covered up for Red Owl's heartless determination more times than he could count. He blamed that on his crazy father who taught her to shut her emotions off when needed. It was as if she became another person and he shuddered in dread at that look.

The head Seeker took a step to the side then swept her arm towards his sister in invitation. "Nighthawk, your call to serve the Great Spirit awaits; before you enter you must also accept a task set for you."

Beckoning a girl forward, she brought towards them a long cloak over her arm. Once close enough, she allowed the head Seeker to take it. Yvonne opened the dark green cloak that looked black when not in the light.

A hood could be drawn up to cover Nighthawk's head and would drop low on his forehead. A dark green gem gave it enough weight it would hold it in place. The diamond shaped gem hung below the edge of the hood so it would settle between his eyes with the point at the bridge of his nose.

A draw string could be tied around his neck to keep it in place; or he could put both arms through two slits if he wished to use it like a coat instead, leaving his arms free to use a weapon. On the left side was a red owl outlined in gold, on the right was a hawk done in silver scrollwork.

The head Seeker turned the cloak, on the back was a thunderbird done in white with bolts of lightning all around it done in silver and gold embroidery. Turning the robe back around,

Yvonne opened the right side so he could see the two weapons hanging inside.

Frowning curiously, Nighthawk reached for the long black round baton then pulled it out. Pushing the button in the center a click had both ends extending, allowing it to become a staff. Smiling in pleasure, he spun it in circles; the staff made a satisfying whirling noise, the weight was perfect for him. Halting it, he held the staff up inspected it closely; it was perfectly balanced. He saw a thumb indent so pushed on it... immediately two blades extended out. "Wow, it's beautiful! Where did you get this?"

The head Seeker watched him closely, curious to see Nighthawks reaction. "It belonged to Alexandrina; there is also a dagger on the opposite side that goes with it. If you accept the Great Spirits request, they are both yours.

Nighthawk reset the baton and put it back before pulling out the little dagger. He eyed the dove suspended in the center then took a finger and inserted it all around the bird, but nothing stopped his finger from going completely around the loop. Taking his hand away, he scratched his head in bewilderment. What held the dove suspended inside the circle? The blade was slim and tapered down to a wicked point; it reminded him more of a letter opener then a dagger. Feeling the blade, he instantly stuck his finger in his mouth as a drop of blood marred the blade. Giving a grunt of approval the youngest twin put the dagger back.

Turning, Blackhawk allowed the Seeker to put the cloak over his shoulders. It was a perfect fit, falling to just below his knees in length. The younger twin could feel the gem on the hood keeping it flattened against his back; other than that, there was barely any weight to the cloak. He tied the closure around his neck then put his arms threw the holes. Moving his arms around experimentally he was pleased to note that it did not hamper his movements at all. It even seemed to cling in all the right places as it flowed around him.

The Seeker waited for Nighthawk to turn back to her then she took his right hand in hers. "Only you will know what is expected of you. Remember, innocence takes all forms and shapes. It will be your responsibility to keep your sister on the straight and narrow, plus others safe from the terrors of the world. knowing when you are needed will come from within; always listen to your gut reaction and your heart, they will never steer you wrong."

Stepping to the left out of Nighthawks way, the head Seeker stood there watching him closely.

Nighthawk frowned then remembered back; it was just after moving to Shadow Hunters ranch on the outskirts of Quebec. School was hell the first few months as they learned to speak English and French. Being almost six feet already and husky the other kids his age did not bother him much, but his much smaller sister was an easy target when he was not around. Lily was beginning to blossom now as her gaunt cheeks filled in and her strength returned thanks to Shadow Hunters care. The twin's began training with Hunter, both learning how to defend themselves.

Every day the same three girls would find a way to get his sister alone then tease her, they would call her names and push her around a bit; once in a while they would get over zealous and Lily would end up with a bruise or two.

The young Buck watched his sister in confused silence, why was she allowing those girls to bully her. He could feel her angry hurt feelings but she refused to tell Shadow Hunter or the principle about it. She had made her twin promise not to tell anyone either...

**The last week of school, Buck felt a change come over his sister that worried him. He saw a grim look of determination replace the hurt angry feeling that he had felt from her since the beginning of the school year. He had only seen that look once; it was just before their parents died, while she made a solemn vow to their father to look out for him.**

**Putting his books in his locker, glad he was done for the year; Buck all of a sudden, felt a swift feeling of satisfaction**

course through him. Slamming his locker door closed, he raced down the hallway and out the back door heading as fast as he could towards the playground.

A ring of kids were surrounding two girls sitting on the ground shocked as they held bleeding heads; but it was the one lying on the ground with his sister on top of her beating her senseless that concerned him.

Pushing through the crowd, Buck grabbed his sister's arm as it was falling one more time. It took all of his considerable strength to hold it; when she looked at him in fury, he winced at the blank black rage infused look she gave him. "Lily, two wrongs do not make a right, you are killing the girl... look at what you have done!"

Lily blinked and her black eyes went back to their soft dark brown; when she looked down at the broken girl under her, the older twin jumped up before backing away in horror at what she had done.

Buck stood up then looked around at all the kids staring in shock. "Let this be a lesson to everyone; when you push someone beyond thinking they are bound to snap sooner or later... now begone, all of you!"

Turning, Buck pointed at the other two bullies then beckoned. "Not you two come here and sit beside your friend. Lily, come sit beside me."

Cleaning up the girl's face still lying on the ground dazed, Buck was relieved to see it was not as bad as he had at first thought. She had a small cut under her right eye that had bled a lot, but would not need stitches.

For two hours, the younger twin talked and cajoled the four girls; by the time Buck was done they all shook hands. While none of them became friends, a silent truce was given and the teasing never happened again...

Smiling at the memory, Nighthawk was quite proud of his ability to help others see past there baser instincts. He knew though that his sister was quite capable of killing someone when she allowed her rage to control her. Thankfully, it did not happen often, he just hoped that she had outgrown it by now.

Shaking off the memory, the Ojibwa/Cheyenne warrior stepped into the final ring of Eternity. Instantly, a vision snared him; Shadow Hunter was lying on the ground dead. Blackhawk was behind him with the little dagger clutched in his hand dripping blood.

Alexandrina stood above Nighthawk with a glowing sword before he heard his sister scream out a warning as she charged towards the woman.

Frowning in confusion, Nighthawk could not make any sense of the scene then a dove blocked his vision and words formed in his mind; nodding in agreement, the younger twin stepped into the three joined rings of Eternity next to his sister and silence descended.

The head Seeker stepped forward before throwing her arms out dramatically as she addressed the stunned silent cavern. "I give to you Red Owl, our new spiritual healer; and for the first time ever our very own Medicine Woman. She will keep the Mother Earth strong until the appointed day... may she serve us well. To her right is Nighthawk who is now our Paladin, a warrior and protector of the innocent. It will be his responsibility to recruit then train others to begin preparing for the evil that is already here and the ones yet to come, may he serve the Great Spirit faithfully."

Red Owl and Nighthawk looked at each other in shock. Neither had expected that little revelation.

Waving to the two still standing inside the rings, the head Seeker gestured for them to follow her. "Come, I will introduce you to the others."

The twins nodded and dutifully followed.

# CHAPTER THIRTEEN

Fai woke with a start at the touch of her Guardians hand on her shoulder. She had managed to sleep a bit, but her dreams of mythical creatures kept waking her. Only to fall back asleep with nightmares of brutal wars that had plagued the Earth once an angel with wings arrived; which White Buffalo figured must be Lucifer... he was caretaker of the Earth for a time.

Shocked, Fai watched a huge multicolored flame steak from the sky then solidified into a roaring inferno. It was followed seconds later by a red and white flame... much smaller than the first. She had a sense that they were connected in some way; the two appeared in front of Satan and his minions.

The ground shook as huge craters formed, some rose up becoming mountains before fissures cracked breaking up the land. Causing the Earth to be transformed forever as magic was used in the most brutal way. People ran screaming begging for mercy, but there was none as cities crumbled or they were swallowed up.

Hundreds of stars crashed into the Earth; it changed the land for millions of years. Ultimately, it would cause an ice age to grip the planet for thousands of years.

Screaming in rage, the arch angel and his minions were captured then imprisoned but not before humans and creatures of magic lay dead or dying everywhere. A great many of them just disappeared; several cities that were still standing vanished with them... becoming legends.

Fai felt and heard a crackle rippling across the land before the white and red flame split into two parts... the red began to grow. As it did, the multicolored flame dwindled becoming smaller. White Buffalo could see a vague human form inside enlarging as the red flame grew; it looked like a man's form, but she knew it wasn't.

There were no words spoken only a sense of them communicating in some way that transcended Fai's ability to understand. Suddenly, she felt the acquiescence of the red flame. Once the responsibility was accepted, it changed its shape before a roar of victory reverberated across the land; even the Mother Earth would bow down.

The white flame began expanding next and another shape grew inside... was it female? Before the youngest triplet could figure it out another form took its place.

The multi-coloured flame now just a handful, rose into the air in satisfaction before streaking upwards. Fai knew deep down that it had left this world.

The red flame disappeared after a few minutes of communicating with the white flame. Again, White Buffalo had a sense that the red flame could be... **'I AM'** maybe or were they both since they had just been one a moment ago; could they now be, twins?

The white flame began drawing in every spec of magic and as it did so, a vague human image inside changed form; Fai watching was sure a great white dragon took its place.

The white light expanding got so bright that the youngest triplet had to put her left hand up to protect her eyes as it engulfed the Earth. Unexpectedly, White Buffalo felt a sting on her open palm that was shading her eyes.

The dream vanished as a roar of triumph rang through Fai's skull, just as her half-brother woke her. White Buffalo shook off the images that seemed so real, almost as if she had been there.

Fai yawned before stretching stiffly; she shook her left hand at a stinging sensation. White Buffalo looked and saw an odd shaped white oval burn dead center of the three rings of eternity that the sword had branded into her palm. It was there only for a split second then it was gone.

The youngest triplet frowned in confusion as she closed and opened her hand, but nothing was there. Without pain evident at all now... it could only have been a dream.

Fai couldn't help remembering Magdalene's penchant for reading fantasy books that were filled with strange creatures, magic, with good and evil beings. The youngest twin harrumphed in amusement, maybe her sisters memories were seeping through… confusing her subconscious recollections.

Would White Buffalo get some of Alexandrina's flashbacks too, it would be interesting to see what her oldest sibling's fondest memory had been.

Shrugging dismissively, Fai looked at the front clock; it was eleven, they had made better time than they thought they would.

Sitting up in interest, the final triplet watched the headlights shine up a long winding road. A fence was on the left and trees lined the opposite side. Fai had been here a few times, but this would be the first time seeing it.

Entering a clearing, Fai smiled in pleasure at the four story building revealed by the high powered headlights. She knew that when this place was first built in the early 1800s, it was an orphanage. That's why the main floor and the first floor had several single bedrooms with just a washroom.

At that time, it had been called a boudoir; it was used to keep the young girls dresses hanging so they didn't wrinkle. They even had a chamber pot with a small tub partitioned off in the corner.

The boys had only one large room, their chamber pot was kept under the bed; a wooden wardrobe was used for their clothing. Once every two weeks it was mandatory for them to go into the basement to use the bathing room that had several tubes in a row. Only if a prospective parent was arriving were they pushed into bathing sooner.

The small apartment under the stairs in the back had been for the Priest, the two small apartments on the second floor had been for the councillors. The training room had been a meeting room at that time for perspective parents to meet children that were handpicked for them by the Priest that was in residence.

The large apartment on the top floor had been for the owners of the ranch. Now it was reserved for the Ryuu family and when not in residence, it was used for dignitaries or important visitors.

When Daniel Green bought this place in 1930's they renovated it and put in running water. Dan inherited it then married Tanya and it went through another change before the Ryuu family became partners in what would become a retreat for magic users.

Turning to Dao, Fai grabbed his arm. "I need to run up to my sisters room on the first floor, can you bring my suitcase please... I will need my robe. The head Seeker said they will be in the Seeker's caverns and we need to head down there as soon as possible."

Getting a nod from Dao in agreement, Fai turned and put her hand on Stephan's shoulder. "Can you and your brother take my father out of the trailer and put his casket where the platform is in the back. The head Seeker promised the burning pier would be ready then come into the house, a room is waiting for you both."

Satisfied when she got an acquiescent nod from the two men in the front, Fai jumped out of the vehicle after getting her sword that was draped over the front seat with the new harness that would keep her short sword attached to her back. White Buffalo raced up the front stairs then inside.

Once in the entry, Fai closed her eyes then remembered back; opening them, she trotted through the visitors sitting room to the back left corner then pulled open a door that led into the vaulted room that had the stairs going upwards straight ahead, with the head Seekers apartment behind it. If you turned right, a hallway took you to the back entrance and the three meditation rooms were down there.

If Fai turned left from here instead, she would be greeted by a huge door that would take you down to the basement or to the Seekers vaulted cavern.

Going straight, White Buffalo headed up the spiral stairs to the first floor then trotted to Alexandrina's room; entering, Fai went to the wall unit and dropped down the computer table before putting her sword on top.

Running her fingers under the table knowingly, the last of the triplets quickly found the latch; she popped it open then took out the marriage certificate. Grabbing a pen, Fai added her name and signature then pushed the paper under her sword distractedly.

*****

Dao walked to the front steps then heard a growl; he should have known there would be dogs. He put the suitcases down before pulling the cylinder from his shoulder then looked to his left. Three massive hounds with fur bristling carefully walked towards him. The Tianming Monk disliked dogs and they hated him.

Touching a puckered scar on his right forearm, Dao couldn't help remembering when he was ten; two dogs attacked him after getting loose from a kennel. The Guardian barely survived the attack... both dogs did not!

Dao looked up in relief at a whistle from the deck.

"Friend Bailey, Max, and Freddy go lay down somewhere... damn dogs; I told the head Seeker they should be tied up with all the coming and goings of strangers lately!"

Nodding in agreement, Dao picked up his cylinder then swung it back over his shoulder before picking up the two suitcases; he mounted the stairs. "Thank you, dogs do not like me... but cats adore me."

The tall husky seven foot guard bowed deeply with hands pressed together, he chuckled. "I am the opposite cats hate me, but dogs love me. Name's... Chris; the head Seeker asked me to meet you. The Mother has requested your presence in the Seeker's chambers. Yvonne, who is our new head Seeker, will explain when you get there."

Once Dao put the suitcases down, he bowed back.

Chris took one of the cases. "We will leave these by the stairs going to the bedrooms; my brother is helping your drivers with Chang's casket. I was very sorry to hear of his passing... he trained me years ago."

Dao inclining his head accepting the condolences before the guard turned away leading him into the house. Dao frowned confused, unsure why they could not wait for him to freshen up or for Fai to join them.

Having strict instructions from the head Seeker, Chris hurried the smaller Oriental to the back then put the suitcase by the stairwell before turning left towards the basement stairs. His brother was waiting at the door with Fai's white buffalo hide over his arm. Silently with just a nod, the older and larger guard took it; he draped it over his arm.

Quickly, Chris took the Guardian down three steps before pulling open the heavy door; he led Dao down the stairs to the Mother's cavern deep underground. Once the guard stepped off the stairs and walked through the archway, he paused to wait... familiar with this reaction by newcomers.

Stopping dead, Dao read the black bold words framing the top of the entrance.

**'What was hidden must be found before the Guardian can lead the way!'**

Shaking his head confused, Dao walked through the archway and the two men turned left. Chris still leading pushed the huge vaulted doors open then stepped back and let the Oriental through first before closing the door, he turned to follow him.

Within seconds, Dao had the room mapped out; he knew hundreds were gathered around the walls with gold, white, silver, or green robes and all had their backs turned as they hummed soothingly.

A dais at the very back held a table with several chairs around it. A huge hearth was lit in the far left corner, keeping the dampness at bay.

In the center was a rock platform that he had seen in his vision, with the three rings of Eternity around it; behind it stood two women and one man.

Looking at the alter in the center of the rings again in surprise; Dao noticed as he walked forward that it was three times the size as it had been.

The platform was taller, as well, than when they used the carpet to come here only a few days ago. The Guardian stopped at the edge of the rings and waited as the head Seeker came forward.

Smiling in thanks, Yvonne took the white buffalo robe from Chris before he spun around then left the chambers. The Seeker in turn went to the rock platform and put it over top of the red wolf hide with the black cougar robe peeking out from under it.

Yvonne turned back to Dao then pressing her hands together; the older woman bowed respectfully. "It is a pleasure to finally meet the Guardian and older brother of our beloved High Priestess of Mother Earth."

Nodding in acknowledgement, Dao bowed back before pulling the cylinder off his shoulder. "It is nice to meet the new head Seeker, but should my charge not be here too?"

Shaking her head, the Seeker gestured behind her. "The Mother wishes you to put the carpet on her alter and sit in meditation as she gives you instructions."

Lifting an eyebrow high in surprise, Dao finally nodded then pressed a thumb to the top of the cylinder before taking the lid off. Flipping the canister over, he let the rug slide out. The older brother of Fai gave the empty container to the head Seeker then walked to the platform. Still quite confused, the Guardians dealt with the Great Spirit; seldom did they have anything to do with Mother Earth, but it had happened occasionally.

Looking at the three hides, Dao shrugged then unrolled the carpet over top of them. He eyed the two youngsters standing on the other side of the large platform then ignored them as he jumped up into the center of his carpet.

Gracefully, the Oriental sat then crossed his legs; he put his hands upwards on his knees before touching middle finger and thumbs together. Humming, the Guardian closed his eyes putting himself into a trance.

Instantly, Dao felt time moving or was it him; unsure at this moment, he let himself drift. Searching for what, he had no idea.

Frowning, the Oriental remembered the writing on the door...
'What was hidden must be found'.

Ah, so that's it. What was he looking for and who had hidden it?

Suddenly, Dao halted in front of two great pillars and he walked through. There were six towering grey stone rocks spread out in a circular pattern; all were about fifteen feet high. If you included the stone archway, that would make seven stones. They all had different carved patterns going up about halfway, which were about seven feet before a deep engraved line separated the next section.

Directly above the line was a single elemental symbol a foot high before a deep indent partitioned off the next section. Each stone had a different element. Stone one had an air symbol. Stone two, had the fire element. Stone three, had a water symbol. On the fourth stone, there was the Earth element.

Surprisingly stone five had an aether or quintessence symbol, which was a spiritual element; because there was no physical attribute to it, five circles entwined were used. This one was often forgotten by religious leaders as one of the five elements.

It reminded Dao of the three rings of eternity that were used by the Mother Earth in the Seeker's chambers.

The sixth stone had the sun/moon symbol, which brought to mind light and darkness.

Past the elemental symbols just above another indented line, a picture was drawn for the last six feet of each pillar. It was an engraved picture of Jesus or it could be **I AM** encircled by the angels; they were helping him fight an enormous dragon or serpent of some kind. Why each pillar had the same image at the top when the bottom seven feet of each stone was completely different, the Guardian couldn't figure out.

There were so many symbols that almost every available space on the bottom of each pillar was covered. There were markings associated with healing, and some regarding sacrifices; why they would have protection as well as warning symbols on the same pillar was a mystery. It was identical to the healing and sacrifice stone, both were opposite to each other on the same stone pillar.

Dao looked up at two other pillars with the same images at the top engraved on them then spun around knowingly. He was now facing a black pillar in the center. Loud cracks of thunder reverberate off the stones; the Guardian covered his ears instantly as his head rang.

Out flew the three cackling Nephilim as the first prison opened and the great Stonehenge disappeared, leaving just a broken pillar behind. The Guardian was in Wales at the mysterious Snowdonia, as the first of three prisons opened; which had happened several weeks ago. If Ronin had guessed correctly, once they all opened the first heaven would merge with our reality. It would allow magic, in all its glory back into this world or Aeon reality.

Looking up, Dao saw a hole appear in the sky high above him but quickly it closed. He frowned in concern when a spec of black remained; it was hardly noticeable, unless you had a telescope. The Guardian wasn't even sure it would be then either. One could hope that it was only visible to those with the ability to see beyond.

With a lurch, Dao was on the move once again. This time though, it was only a few minutes. Looking around in interest, the Guardian figured he was in another stone circle... this one was much larger; by the relatively rolling ground and emerald green grass, he figured it might be in Ireland.

Counting quickly, Dao got to sixty-four stones, but there was a lot of rock debris in the center so could possibly be up to eighty or more at one time.

Seeing a flicker out of the corner of his eye, the Tianming Monk humming brought his ability to see beyond to the surface. A black pillar materialized instantly, the Guardian was extremely relieved to see that it was still in one piece.

What was even more interesting is the fact that all the stones in Wales with the exact carvings on them were now surrounding him here, but would only visible if one could see beyond... why?

Would the Stonehenge from Snowdonia move again once this black tower opened up? Or could it be that was what was once in the center of these stones.

Looking up, Dao saw a ray of light going upwards into the sky. Suddenly, it flickered and a minor quake trembled beneath him before the light steadied and the ground quieted. How long it would hold, the Guardian had no clue. They would have to find this place quickly... even now it might be too late.

On the move again but this time for only a heartbeat, Dao stared around in confusion. There was a lot more stones to this large circle and the one in the center was brown not black; in the distance, he could see mountains with fog obscuring the tops. The land here was rolling with hardly any trees.

Chanting the Guardian turned quickly, the rock in the center changed to black. Seeing the ray rising towards the sky he sighed in relief... it was holding steady.

Back in motion once more, Dao frowned in thought. The three prisons were quite close to each other. Wales, Ireland, and Scotland he figured; the prisons should be easy to find now that he had a sense of where they were.

The Guardian was taken to several Stonehenge's and Megaliths, but there was nothing interesting even when chanting. Dao had a feeling that they were looking for a specific one, where it was even the carpet did not know.

They went from burning desert to freezing cold temperatures; he could tell every time they stopped, he was in another country. It seemed like hours since Dao had begun this journey, but he knew time here was only seconds in the Mother's cavern.

Dozens of Stonehenge's came and went; suddenly, they halted in a huge round four layered Megalith with a stone alter in the center. The platform was similar to the one he was sitting on now. Where he was at, the Guardian had no clue. He felt a shiver of uncertainty course down his spine.

Chanting Dao looked around carefully, but there was no black pillars here... so it was not a prison. Walking to stone alter, he put his hand on top and a flash of green crossed his vision.

Feeling compelled, Dao jumped up then sat; he crossed his legs then put his thumb and middle finger together in meditation before chanting

Instantly, the Tianming Monk felt a whirling motion then both alters that he was sitting on converged and became one. As it did so, a lush green land opened in front of him. Tree's towered high, Dao felt magic beneath his feet; this place was untouched by man, pure and mythical.

The Guardian inhaled in shock, Eden... he had found the lost garden. Shocked, Dao now had proof that his rug was directly connected to the garden of Eden. Of course, his masters in Japan had suspected all along.

Now that it was found and in our reality, whoever sat on the Mother's alter in the rings of Eternity would be brought here in the physical form. Dao stopped chanting then stepped off the platform, instantly he was in the Seeker's cavern.

The head Seeker stepped forward quickly, the relief on her face was quite apparent. "You completely disappeared for ten minutes!"

Inclining his head knowingly, the Tianming Monk looked around; thankfully, nobody had moved. All the Seekers were facing the wall and he could still hear them humming.

Dao looked over at the two standing on the other side of the rock alter; the Guardian assessed them quickly. Finally, pointing at the man, he beckoned him forward. "You are a warrior... can you see beyond?"

Bowing, the younger twin nodded affirmative. "I am called, Nighthawk. I am an Ojibwa/Cheyenne warrior for the Great Spirit, my shield totem is the thunderbird. The Mother Earth has given me the charge of protecting the innocent; in agreeing, she has bestowed on me the ability to see beyond."

Nodding impressed, Dao gestured towards the platform. "You

will guard this alter with your life; unless given instructions from the Great Spirit or Mother Earth nobody is to go anywhere near it!"

Frowning at a discerning thought, the Guardian continued in warning. "Detain anything that tries to come out, too!"

Scowling in surprise at that, Nighthawk saluted smartly. He could see green periodically through the shimmer of reality, he pulled out his baton then extended it before walking closer; he turned to keep watch.

Satisfied, Dao looked at the head Seeker. "I must go prepare myself; do you have sage here?"

Inclining her head, the Seeker called to one of her apprentices. "Chasity, go into the cell storage room and bring a bundle of sage... please."

Grunting in satisfaction, Dao nodded gratefully. "Good, I will gather a branch; the rest you can throw into your fire when you feel the time is right. I need to prepare myself and talk to my master in Japan."

Without saying another word, Dao turned and rushed out. He only stopped briefly to pull off a dried stem of sage. He rushed back to the archway then took the stairs two at a time.

Dao looked at his watch; it was only twenty-five minutes after eleven. Even though it seemed like hours, a messily twenty minutes had gone by since he arrived here. Rushing out the door then across the landing and up the three stairs, he walked through the door into the main house.

*****

Shadow Hunter walked out of the basement door; he was just in time to see the door going into the house close. Shrugging uninterested, he walked to the intricate heavy wood and steal door going down; the Cree/Oriental Shaman ignored the dozen men following him.

Walking down the stairs in no rush, Hunter glanced down at his watch once he stepped off the last step. It was eleven thirty, later then he usually stayed up but he had a burning urge to meditate at the Mother's alter for some obscure reason.

Looking up, Shadow Hunter hesitated in confusion at the black lettering around the door frame. It was completely different from the last time he had stood here; then he had not known he would fall in love with the black haired beauty he continued to think of as Black Cougar... it had suited her much better than Alexandrina.

Shaking off his straying thoughts, Hunter reread the words on the door.

**'The three now one, must absorb the seeds of destruction. To do so, the ultimate price must be paid. A dragon will be sacrificed to allow the MOTHER to conceive the seeds, which will bring about the fulfilment of the Trinity prophecy.'**

Scratching his head perplexed; Shadow Hunter finally walked forward... what Trinity prophecy? Shrugging confused, he felt that peaceful tingle vibrate through him and he promptly forgot everything else.

Turning left, the Cree/Oriental Shaman went to the Seeker's chambers. His guards followed him but Hunter continued to ignore them as they shut the doors behind him.

Hearing a light humming, Shadow Hunter saw robed Seeker's standing in the shadows. Feeling a pull, he walked towards the platform that he was sure was now quite a bit larger.

Even stranger yet, was his two apprentices. Lily standing behind the rock alter looked different. The red robe she was wearing gave her black hair and dark dusty skin a glow that made her plain brown eyes darker; a red in her pupil must be reflecting off the cloak.

The older twin had a determined seriously sad look that did not match her slightly hunched shoulders as if she really did not want to be here or maybe she wanted to run. Hunter had seen that look many times in the past, just not directed at him... well not since after he saved Lily the second time that is.

It was Buck that Shadow Hunter noticed the most change in; his stance was determined, strong, and he no longer had strings attached to his sister. What had happened there he wondered? For years, he had trained the younger twin but had despaired of him ever becoming a true warrior like his ancestors because his attachment to his sister made him weak. Now that the strings were severed, he could see the strength of warriors in his countenance that he had known was there but could not bring out of him.

The cloak Buck was wearing was a match to the one the Cree/Oriental Shaman had, he wondered where it had come from. The staff he knew instantly was Alexandrina's and Hunter scowled at that... nobody had consulted him!

The head Seeker stepped forward then put a comforting hand on Nighthawk's shoulder in sympathy. "You must let him meditate here, the Mother is calling him!"

Nighthawk's shoulders slumped in protest; he hesitated before nodding then moved aside with a scowl of uncertainty. Turning towards his sister, the younger twin could not help looking towards Red Owl. He noticed the same reluctance in her now too.

Shadow Hunter looked at the twins then shrugged, maybe he had just imagined the two had changed; they looked like themselves now. Ignoring them, the Cree/Oriental Shaman climbed up on the dais then crossed his legs. He touched his thumb and third finger together then humming Hunter put himself in a trance.

The head Seeker waved to her apprentice and the bundle of sage was thrown into the fire.

Inhaling deeply, Shadow Hunter smiled at the scent of sage filling his nostrils... it reminding him of home. Still humming, the Cree/Oriental Shaman disappeared.

*****

Hearing a noise behind her, Fai spun and smiled in relief when Dao entered with her suitcase. "The head Seeker said for you to take the room across the hall from me, the Princess is still up in our apartment so we will use these rooms for now."

Distractedly, Dao put her suitcase by the bed then turned to leave. "Yes I know. I need to jump in the shower and meditate in preparation before I go down to the Seeker's chambers."

Inclining her head, Fai gestured towards the floor. "I will meet you down there then."

Turning to the bed once Dao left, Fai smiled sadly at her sister's suitcase that was still on the bed. She lifted the gold robe that was on top then brought it up to her nose before inhaling deeply; her middle sister had loved to wear Channel #5 perfume and it still clung to the material.

Sighing forlornly, Fai draped the robe on the edge of the bed then took the suitcase off and put it on the floor before pushing it under the bed. She would go through it another day... right now there was no time.

Picking up her suitcase, Fai put it on the bed before opening it. Pulling out her red robe, White Buffalo draped it on the bed beside her sisters.

Fai felt a shiver; looking towards the desk, she saw the marriage certificate fall from the table onto the floor. She frowned grimly. White Buffalo was sure that she had shoved it under her sword. There was no way that it was close enough to the edge to fall off the table. Walking over in trepidation, the final triplet picked it up before scanning it.

Scratching her head in bewilderment, Fai put the paper back in the drawer angrily then slammed it shut. Now only one name and signature was on the marriage certificate... it read Fai Alexandrina Magdalene Ryuu.

Turning, White Buffalo marched to the bed then grabbed her robe before going to her bathroom; she slammed the door decisively. She was being manipulated again! The youngest triplet knew shutting the door so hard would not have any affect except to make her feel better. She chuckled humorously at her foolishness then turned on the shower before releasing her ankle length midnight black hair, with the two distinct colour patterns entwining the black... one red the other white.

Looking closer at the mirror grimly, Fai reached up and touched a few strands in the center of her scalp that were beginning to turn colours. Again, the colour pattern was red and white but they were entwining each other. It would not be long before the colours took over the black giving her three strips of colour.

Shrugging irritably, Fai went inside and closed the shower door with a resounding... 'Thump.'

*****

Dao, rubbing his wet hair walked out of the bathroom gloriously naked; his biceps rippled at the vigorous rubbing and his stomach muscles contracted, showing six distinct lines of bulging muscles... most would drool over. Walking gracefully to the bed, he grabbed his flowing Japanese robe and donned it.

Opening his suitcase the Guardian pulled out two incense burners then took his sage branch and put some in each before lighting it. Inhaling in pleasure the Tianming Monk waved his hand in front of the smoke and drew it towards him.

Going to the bed, Dao sat crossed legged on it; humming, he lit a pipe he had waiting before inhaling deeply on it. Since the Guardian had started using the carpet, he did not need to use his harsh drugs to go into the spirit world. The Tianming Monk knew that right now he had no choice. With his carpet still draped on the stone dais in the Seeker's chambers.

Frowning grimly, Dao shook his head in disbelief as an image expanded for a split second then disappeared. Opening his eyes the Guardian looked up imploringly, he could not help his cry of disbelief. "Why must it be... we are not ready yet?"

Sighing forlornly, Dao got up to change. What must be, will be... whether they were ready or not!

*****

Leaving her bedroom, Fai with hair flowing loose behind her and barefoot raced to the stairs then descended quickly. All she took with her was the sword she had dubbed... Crystal.

Turning right, Fai went to the basement door then through it; she went down to the main huge old fashioned wooden door and heaved it open before hurrying down.

Fai paused in surprise at the bottom of the stairs when she saw the bold writing around the entrance to the caverns.

**'The Trinity prophecy will not be fulfilled until the Nephilim are no more; a dragon must be sacrificed to enable the seeds to be absorbed by the MOTHER!'**

Shrugging in confusion, Fai walked through the opening then smiled ecstatically at the shiver of warmth she felt upon entering the vaulted caverns. Turning left, the Priestess of Mother Earth smiled in greeting at the guards standing at the door; hurrying forward one of them opened it for her then stepped to the side.

Walking forward slowly, Fai could not help feeling awed and thrilled at the same time. She had seen these chambers with her spiritual eyes many times over the years when bringing out her white buffalo totem. Seeing it for the first time with her own eyes though, and in colour gave an ethereal aspect to it.

Inhaling deeply, the Priestess of Mother Earth smiled at the scent of sage perfuming the air. It was a familiar scent from her childhood; growing up in a Mi'kmaq village in New Brunswick it always seemed to be in the air.

The head Seeker walked forward then knelt. "Priestess... I am so sorry about your two sisters passing; the fact that they both died here grieves us deeply!"

Reaching down, Fai took the older woman's hands and helped her up. "Please do not kneel in my presence, I am just a woman no more or less; thank you for the condolences it means a lot, but I assure you both my sisters would have not wanted to die anywhere else but here."

The head Seeker, not quite all the way to her feet groaned then grabbed her head painfully before dropping to her knees once more; cries of fear echoed through the cavers, everyone around her clutched their heads in pain.

"EEEEK!"

The Priestess of Mother Earth forced herself to get up after falling to her knees in painful surprise; Fai holding her head watched the Nephilim float towards the platform. She could see it arguing with itself as it pointed at the rock alter in shock, obviously awed by what it saw.

"No, it can't be so Ava... where did it come from? Eden has been lost since before we were imprisoned."

Seeing the creature of old holding a glowing spear, Fai shook off the pain in her head then raced around the head Seeker to the front of the platform; unsheathing her sword as she ran.

Jumping up onto the platform, White Buffalo thrust her glowing sword into the Nephilim before it could reach the entrance to Eden. The High Priestess screamed eerily as pain ripped through her own chest.

Nighthawk seeing his opportunity lunged to his feet with the dove dagger clutched in his hand. Grabbing the handle with both hands, he lifted them above his head before jumping up onto the dais and coming down with all his might.

Being so close to the edge of the rock alter, Nighthawk's unsteadily footing caused the Ojibwa/Cheyenne warrior's momentum to shift. His aim a bit awkward now, allowed the dagger to enter the neck crease of the Nephilim; thankfully, severing not only its jugular vein but also its carotid artery.

Nighthawk determinedly held onto the dagger with all his strength; as it glowed, the younger twin watched the dove turn black in seconds with not a spec of white to be seen anywhere.

Red Owl, vaulted onto the rock alter then grabbed the Priestess of Mother Earth by the left shoulder; chanting, she brought her power to the surface trying to keep Fai from dying with the creature.

Still screeching in shock and pain, Fai watched her sword turn black; greedily, it pulled in every speck of magic that the creature had stolen from the Mother Earth and others around the world.

Vaguely through the pain, the Priestess of Mother Earth saw a man rise up with Magdalene's dove dagger; he stabbed the Nephilim... cutting deep into its neck. She saw the dove on the dagger turned black almost instantly. Knowingly, White Buffalo looked at the dove on the end of her own sword... it too was turning colours.

Fai's sword began humming, desperately she grasped her sword with her other hand as magic surged into her from the sword. As the magic transferred, White Buffalo's sword began turning back to its deep green crystal colour before both doves turned white once more.

A tingling on Fai's left shoulder almost had her lashing out; quickly, she stopped when the soothing touch eased the pain in her chest as the transfer of magic from the sword into herself became more bearable.

Arching, White Buffalo's feet left the ground and she opened all her senses letting it happen. Once she did, the transfer increased; a white glow from the three rings of eternity encompassed the Priestess of Mother Earth, adding more intensity to the transmission.

Unexpectedly, the dagger and sword both hummed at the same instant causing the Nephilim to burst before disappearing as three bodies dropped to the ground... out cold.

Blackhawk and Red Owl both on the very edge of the platform fell off the dais. Thankfully, the Healer fell on top of her brother cushioning her fall.

Unfortunately, the High Priestess of Mother Earth falling backwards off the platform hit her temple on the corner of the dais; it left a splash of blood behind that quickly disappeared.

*****

Pulling the heavy door open desperately, Dao raced down the stairs as fast as he could. He was holding onto his left chest as a burning swept through it; telling him his charge was in extreme distress.

No sooner, did the Guardian reach the bottom of the steps

leading into the Mother's caverns then he stumbled and dropped to his knees with a shocked gasp of pain.

Looking up, Dao saw a black message flare across the entrance to the caverns.

**'The Trinity prophecy has now been fulfilled! Let the seeds of destruction be absorbed as the death of the dragon draws ever closer!'**

Shaking off the pain, Dao vaulted back to his feet; hurriedly, he stumbled through the entrance. The pain eased and a calming tingle vibrated through him, he turned left immediately before racing to the doors.

The two guards instantly opened it for Dao.

Nodding without comment, the Tianming Monk ran towards the platform. The Guardian was just in time to see the woman who had stood behind the dais earlier roll off the young warrior and lift his head into her lap.

Ignoring everything else, Dao quickly scooped up his half-sister and charge. He took a step towards the platform then paused at a call from the Seeker.

Grabbing the sword that was lying on the floor in front of her, Yvonne yelled out quickly. "Wait, Dao!"

The head Seeker rushed forward with the now inconspicuous sword and laid it on top of Fai. "Go!"

Nodding in thanks, Dao seeing the scabbard on the ground ignored it then jumped up on the platform without a word; chanting, they disappeared.

# CHAPTER FOURTEEN

Feeling compelled, Shadow Hunter opened his eyes then inhaled in shock; he looked around at the lush garden surrounding him. Jumping to his feet in panic, he turned in circles looking for the Seeker's chamber that had completely disappeared. Hearing the scream of a large cat, the Cree/Oriental Shaman ran blindly ahead looking for a way out.

Finally, exhausted Hunter dropped to his knees panting in dread; until his palms touched the Earth, a calming peace rippled through him immediately. Awed by the feeling of purity beneath his hands, the Cree/Oriental Shaman sat back on his heels then looked around him for the first time.

The trees were huge and towered so high he could not see the sky. Flowers of every description were everywhere and beads of moisture in the air kept them hydrated. The air here was pure; not a smell of human or pollution had ever touched this place.

A black cougar walked out of the trees and the first thing Shadow Hunter noticed was the white tip on its tail. The memory of meeting his wife in the alley in her shapeshifting form surfaced; he inhaled in shock as he stared deep into her eyes and knew that it was Alexandrina. He put out a beseeching hand willing her to come to him as tears streaked his cheek. "Please... my love."

The huge cat turned away; she stopped in front of the thick trees and looked back at her mate expectantly.

Feeling a need, Shadow Hunter arose then obediently followed.

*****

Stepping through a mist then into the lush untouched garden of Eden, Dao carried Fai effortlessly. Hearing a noise to his right, he was not surprised when a red wolf walked towards them... behind it was a white buffalo.

Ignoring them, the Guardian feeling a compulsion walked ahead purposely; a pathway seemed to open before him. He was thankful it did, Dao would have cleared a path if he had too but marring such beauty would have pained him.

It seemed to the Tianming Monk that he walked forever, but he knew it was only moments in his time. Hearing a trickle of water, he turned left then followed the sound to a small brook. Looking to his right at a loud roaring sound, the Guardian saw a waterfall with all sorts of different coloured rainbows sparkling around it in the far off distance.

Dao, seeing a blanket of thick emerald green moss beside the water he walked purposely to it then set his charge on top. He knew instinctively, it was deep enough to cushion her whole body. The Guardian scooped up a handful of water and let it trickle out of his fingers over the small cut on her forehead.

Watching in satisfaction, Dao saw the blood disappeared before the cut on her temple began to heal itself. The Guardian leaned down to kiss his half-sister on the cheek before getting up and leaving her there.

The animals that had followed them were nowhere in sight now; he could feel them watching him though. Silently, the Tianming Monk made his way back to the entrance and disappeared back into the Seeker's cavern.

*****

Frowning painfully, Red Owl watched the Oriental scoop up the woman lying unconscious then vault onto the rock alter before vanishing. The woman was a splitting image to both Alexandrina and the Nephilim... it was uncanny. The head Seeker had warned her, but until she had actually saw her; the older twin had not fully comprehended.

Red Owl stroked her brother's hair soothingly. He had hit the back of his head against the ground hard when he cushioned her fall. Their part in this was not over, yet; she winced, praying her twin would not wake up until it was too late. She could try healing him, but...

Nighthawk groaned in pain then stirred, dashing his sister's desperate prayers for a reprieve. Looking up at Red Owl, the younger twin smiled hopefully with a crooked grin. "Is it over... is that thing gone?"

Nodding with a sad smile, Red Owl's voice held a definitive sound of satisfaction. "Yes, the three of us defeated it and now the Nephilim are no more."

Sitting up, Nighthawk groaned then rubbed the back of his head painfully as his head pounded.

Getting to her knees, Red Owl reached up and cupped her brother's head. Chanting, she tried her first healing on Nighthawk's headache.

Grinning in thanks, Nighthawk rose before searching the floor; he picked up the little dagger and examined it. There was no indication whatsoever that anything untold had happened to the dove, but he was sure it had turned black. The snow white dove still hung suspended, not a speck of any other colour was anywhere to be seen.

Shrugging, Blackhawk opened his cloak then put it back in its holder. Seeing his new baton, the Ojibwa/Cheyenne warrior knelt then clicked the button to have both ends retract before putting it in his cloak.

Noticing the spear lying beside the platform, Nighthawk walked over then picked it up and studied it intently for a few minutes. Liking the feel of it, the younger twin decided to keep it.

Looking around again, Nighthawk searched for the woman then turned to his sister in trepidation. "Is the woman dead... where did she go?"

Shaking her head in denial, Red Owl pointed at the rock podium. "No, her Guardian came then carried her to the platform and they disappeared."

Just as Red Owl finished talking, Dao stepped off the rock dais; he pointed at Nighthawk then crooked his finger. "Come, I can only take one of you at a time."

Nighthawk nodded knowingly then looked down at his sister and extended his hand to help her up; smiling lovingly, he kissed her cheek once she was standing. "I will always love you... no matter what happens!"

Smiling sadly, Red Owl nodded then watched the two men disappear. Feeling a hole in the pit of her stomach and an ache in her heart the older twin knew that this is what it would feel like for the rest of her life if her brother never came back.

Looking up imploringly, Red Owl caught back a little sob. "I don't know if I can do this!"

Feeling compelled, Red Owl looked at the dais then stepped forward reluctantly as Dao appeared then beckoned for her to follow. Straightening her spine in resolution, the healer took his hand and they vanished.

*****

Fai wandered through the dream world. She had been here a lot in the past, usually to meet her sisters. This time was different since they were part of her now. It didn't feel quite right this time; White Buffalo wasn't sure what the difference was.

The dream Fai had in the Escalade of magical cities that had once graced this world then the brutal war that destroyed the Earth kept flickering through her thoughts. Not noticing, White Buffalo stepped into a shimmer that was directly in front of her.

Halting in shock, Fai looked around; all she could see was ice, it covered everything and no life was evident at first. Suddenly, the ground beneath her feet trembled as huge animals roamed a world that was gripped by an ice age. Groups of strange looking humans hunched over and covered in hair wandered trying to survive as they evolved, most lived in caves or underground.

Time passed, suddenly a meteor that was dislodged thousands of years ago by the fight for the Earth that ended up leaving it paralyzed; finally entered Earth's atmosphere. It incinerated every living thing on the planet. Now there was no light where she was at, or warmth. Oddly there was no cold either, there was just... nothing!

Unexpectedly, a red flame appeared in the distance; Fai watched curiously, as it moved closer. Inside the fire was a vague human form that she had seen in a previous dream. White Buffalo sensed a feeling of determination radiating from it.

The final triplet held her breath in wonder as the Mother Earth was once again brought to life; Fai felt privileged to watch the Spirit in the flame work its magic. Awestruck, the High Priestess of Mother Earth watched the seven days unfold as life once again stirred on the barren planet.

Eden flourished under the Great Spirit's gentle guidance, so too did Adam and Eve. Feeling an angry urgency unexpectedly, she saw the spirit in the flame vanish.

Powerless to stop what was taking place, Fai watched Eve being tricked into eating the fruit of knowledge then she gave the apple to Adam. By the time the Great Spirit appeared, it was too late; furious at the betrayal, Eden was hidden away.

Furious the spirit in the flame disappeared, leaving Adam and Eve to fend for themselves in a newly awakened Mother Earth... or was it?

Frowning in thoughtful surprise, White Buffalo remembered that the garden was in between heaven and Earth so time was barley moving here.

The Earth on the other hand had aged a few thousand years since it was brought back to life and now Fai could feel others. Like the ones evolving when there was nothing but ice, could they be the result of the white flame that she had not seen since it split from the red one in her last dream.

Shaking her head, the High Priestess was positive the Mother Earth had encouraged the evolution; bringing into being another type of human. How she knew that, the youngest triplet could not say... she just did.

Where was the white spirit hiding? Fai wondered if the flame could be the Mother Earth, no she was sure it wasn't. White Buffalo had seen a vague human form inside; it had felt more feminine before a dragon had replaced it.

The twin flames Fai felt were caretakers; red for Earth and re-creation, father of the Israelites. The multicolored flame in the first dream had given most of itself to the red flame, and Jesus the son would ultimately come from the spirit in the red flame.

Could the Holy Spirit be the white flame, which would ultimately form the Trinity? White, Fai knew was for magic; it was also the colour of the dove, which represented the Holy Ghost.

Could Fai's younger brother, Ronin be right? Are the heavens actually Aeon realities better known as Earth's historical timeline. The Aeon realities would house, Luciferian age, the prehistoric age, as well as the mythical or magical age. The one she lived in now would be considered the technological age.

God of course was in the 3rd heaven that is why Lucifer wanted the 4th so he could be above the Creator, which did not go over well. Eden the High Priestess was sure had been put there once all the water was released to flood the Earth.

Of course, there is also the prison realm that had the entire watcher Angels and their giant offspring's. Was the spirit in the white flame caretaker of the heavens or Earth's Aeon realities? What would happen if the realities merged, would the red and white flames become one again?

Being distracted with her thoughts, Fai was not paying much attention to her surroundings until suddenly... a wail of anguish made her shiver. She watched a furious Great Spirit imprison his Grigori watchers with the devils henchmen in one of the heavens. The few female Nephilim were also imprisoned then the heavens opened up and a flood ravaged the Earth again destroying every living creature, except what was on the ark.

Next, Fai saw Sodom & Gomorrah's demise before time moved on again. White Buffalo watched in surprise as the spirit in the white flame was dispatched to impregnate Mary; inside the flame was a spec of red. As the Holy Spirit stood over Mary, the red ball with a smidgen of white in the center entered the mother of Jesus.

The youngest triplet scratched her head in confusion... why was she being shown all this; unfortunately, the High Priestess was unable to turn away. Next, she watched the birth of the Messiah before his life payed out quickly.

Observing the last supper, Fai perked up in shock as wine was given out freely and most lay in drunken stupors. She watched Mary Magdalene, a follower of Jesus... some say she was actually one of his apostles; take the Messiah by the hand and led him out before helping him to his bed then laid down with him.

Surprisingly, a coo of satisfaction from a white dove landing on the window had White Buffalo staring in fascination as a bit of a glow filled the small bungalow. Had the Holy Spirit orchestrated another birth... to what end? The youngest triplet watched the death of Jesus; she made sure to pay close attention to Magdalene when the messiah's disciple was kneeling below his feet as he hung from the cross. Fai saw a bit of a bump beneath the shawl the woman was using to hide it.

After Jesus's resurrection then rise to the heavens, Magdalene too vanished across the big sea to Wales; there she gave birth to a boy and a girl... twins.

Fai continued to watch knowing deep down she was seeing her own family history unfold. It did not stop until she was standing in the birthing room of Dream Dancer as his son then his daughter Cecille was born. The youngest triplet felt the power radiating from the baby girl then nodded in approval when her father's Guardian took in the evil mist; freeing the little one from its dark clutches. When she opened her blind eyes, the one watching knew that every girl would be born without sight until the three became one.

Suddenly, with a blink she was back from the dream world. Even though it seemed like years since she had been ensnared by it; in reality only a few minutes had elapsed. Slowly, White Buffalo opened her eyes as she felt the man she was destined to love forever gather her close.

*****

Shadow Hunter followed the cat curiously; a shimmer reflected around the black cougar and for a split second, it disappeared. Inhaling in confusion, Hunter saw the cat solidified once more and he frowned troubled. Of course, the animal was not real. His wife was dead this could only be a shadow of her totem. Where it was leading him, the Cree/Oriental Shaman had no clue.

Occasionally the cat would look back to make sure he was still following; Shadow Hunter could feel time moving differently here. Was it hours or days that they walked, he could not tell for sure... they just kept going.

Unexpectedly a clearing opened in front of them, Hunter could hear water rippling. It was the first real sound other than his breathing and footsteps that he had heard in all the time he had been walking. No branches or leaves rustled, there was not even a breeze... one could lose themselves here.

Shaking off his wondering thoughts, Shadow Hunter saw two more animals ahead... a red wolf and a white buffalo. On the ground between them was his wife; crying out in shock, ignoring the animals he rushed forward then fell to his knees. The Cree/Oriental Shaman gathered her into his arms and rocked Alexandrina gently.

The buffalo turned before disappearing into the surrounding trees; the other two shimmered then vanished.

Fai opened her dark green eyes, she had a tiny speck of jet-black in the center for a pupil; flecks of gold, black, and light green floated throughout her irises... giving them a unique look. White Buffalo regarded her new husband, intently.

The High Priestess smiled in pleasure at the feelings of love that Alexandrina had for this man. Instantly, it gripped her too before passion flared deep inside her. The youngest triplet now knew exactly what was expected of her; gladly, she embraced her destiny. It wasn't long until all other thoughts flew out of her mind when a hunger for Shadow Hunter's touch gripped her.

Unable to believe his luck, Shadow Hunter lay beside his wife then gathered her against him; tenderly he kissed her. When she responded and did not disappear, he became more aggressive as he pulled her hard against his engorged manhood. Her blood red robe was no barrier to his roaming hands and quickly it fell open.

Fai groaned against Shadow Hunters lips; running her hands over his deeply muscled chest, she racked her fingernails downwards. Reaching his loincloth, White Buffalo quickly made short work of his covering. Suddenly, he was gloriously naked.

Unable to wait a moment longer, Shadow Hunter reared up then positioned himself at his wife's core. Suddenly, another memory flared to life; it halted Hunter's entry instantly. Watching the events from above, he saw a woman under him that looked exactly like Alexandrina but it had not been her...

**Hunter stared in shock, as love softened the bright vivid-green eyes; she had large black pupils that took up most of her iris with a hint of a dark green surrounding the pupil.**

**The Cree/Oriental Shaman climaxed hard, unable to help himself. The lady under him, join him in an orgasm and his seed ejaculated deep within her.**

**Lifting up, Shadow Hunter needing to know who the woman was that looked exactly like his wife and still deep inside the lady under him; a spear appeared out of nowhere. Hunter unable to move stared in shock as it sped towards them.**

**The woman hearing a shriek of command in her head flipped them over. Instantly, the spear pierced her heart.**

**Once the woman yanked the Cree/Oriental under her, his head hit the edge of the rock dais. Hunter saw blood trickling across the rocky platform; promptly, he lost consciousness.**

**Stunned, the Cree/Oriental Shaman watched the lady drop dead on top of him...**

Feeling Shadow Hunter stiffen in shock, Fai wrapped her legs around him before drawing his head down.

Hunter quickly forgot everything as their lips met and passion replaced the astonishment. Once he relaxed against her, the

Cree/Oriental Shaman unable to help himself thrust hard into his wife as she rose up to meet him.

White Buffalo gasped slightly when a momentary pain shuddered through her at the feel of her membrane breaking; it confirmed to the man above her that the woman under him was a virgin and not Alexandrina... again!

Unfortunately, Shadow Hunter could do nothing to stop it now as it tore open at the ungentle thrust. Hunter stiffened, but she refused to allow him to retreat.

Fai groaned in pleasure next when the pain disappeared, allowing ecstasy to take its place.

Unable to stop now, Shadow Hunter cried out in passion as he felt the woman orgasm beneath him; they erupted together.

As the Cree/Oriental Shaman's seed entered White Buffalo, all three totems appeared above the Shaman then merged before entering the High Priestess of Mother Earth and the three were now complete.

*****

Nighthawk watched Dao disappear back into the Seeker's vaulted room to get his sister. He turned and looked around in awe... the lost Eden; he could hardly believe it. Walking ahead curiously, the Ojibwa/Cheyenne warrior heeded a call that he was dreading. Resolutely he kept going then suddenly a white buffalo stepped out of the trees and regarded him fixedly.

Starring back just as intently, Nighthawk finally nodded then broke the spear he carried so only three quarters of the length was left; he threw the broken piece down then followed when the buffalo turned to lead the way. Seconds later the youngest twin heard a cry of pleasure before the animal he was following disappeared as if it had never been.

Dropping to the ground, Nighthawk crept forward slowly as he cautiously entered a clearing; the two making love were oblivious to his presence and carefully he slithered closer trying to keep in the shadows as his cloak shimmered keeping him hidden. The

Ojibwa/Cheyenne warrior gripped the small spear tighter in his hand then waited. The Mother insisted, but could he... was the unrelenting question still in his mind as he hesitated.

When Shadow Hunter reared up in ecstasy, Nighthawk rose behind him; he put his arm around his mentor to grasp him around the shoulders before pulling him backwards. At the same time, the younger twin thrust the spear deep into the middle of the Cree/Oriental Shaman's back dead center.

Needing to make sure he had gotten it right; the warrior rose up on his knees and watched in satisfaction as the poison tipped arrow pierced the dragon before exiting the front of Hunter's chest.

Screaming in shocked pain, Shadow Hunter felt himself ejaculate a second time. The dragon on his chest opened both its claws, releasing its treasures before vanishing from the Cree/Oriental Shaman's chest. All that remained now was the three rings of eternity and they were glowing blood red.

Pulling out the spear, Nighthawk with tears of remorse trickling down his cheeks threw it into the water; the Ojibwa/Cheyenne warrior was heartbroken at what he had been force to do.

**"SHADOW HUNTER!"**

Screaming out her husband's name in stunned disbelief, Fai gathered him close as he shuddered on top of her then died in her arms. Sobbing, White Buffalo rolled them over and got to her knees.

The High Priestess of Mother Earth, seeing her sword lying inconspicuously in the sand grabbed it. Turning in a fit of rage, she jumped to her feet and thrust her sword into Nighthawk; just as a scream of warning pierced the air... time seemed to stop.

*****

Dao with the older twin walked through the gateway and Red Owl inhaled in disbelief at the beauty that surrounded them. kneeling instantly, she put both hands palm down before closing her eyes; she savoured the purity of nature untouched by the sinful hands of humanity.

Giving the Ojibwa/Cheyenne Medicine Woman a few more minutes, Dao finally beckoned urgently. "Come, time is precious now."

Nodding reluctantly, Red Owl got up and followed the Oriental Guardian obediently.

Hearing Shadow Hunter scream, Red Owl broke away from her guide before racing into the clearing calling her brother's name in warning. She was too late as the woman jumped up to tower over Blackhawk and the sword pierced his flesh; bringing the vision, she had in the Seeker's chambers to life.

Sobbing, Fai stood over Shadow Hunter protectively daring anyone to come close.

Racing over, Red Owl dropped down beside her dying brother then looked over at Shadow Hunter before turning back to Nighthawk with a heartrending sob. "I am so sorry!"

Nighthawk reached up and caressed his sister cheek then he smiled in acceptance before his hand dropped to his chest; within minutes he was dead.

Turning away with another reluctant cry, Red Owl ignored the sword that was pointed at her then crawled to Shadow Hunter. Chanting she brought her power to the surface then beseeched the Great Spirit for permission to heal the man she loved; even though, Hunter had chosen another.

Rushing over to Fai, Dao tenderly took the sword away from her before gathering her close as she crumbled into his arms in remorse. "I did not mean too...!"

Nodding knowingly, Dao stroked her hair soothingly. "I understand... go be with your husband."

Dao pulled a handkerchief from his pocket then walked to the creek and wetted it before going to the younger twin; he draped it over the boys wound. It was too bad, the boy had shown great promise, but the wound had been fatal.

Pulling her robe closed, Fai turned away then knelt across from the Medicine Woman. White Buffalo watched the girl pull power desperately from her core trying to do the unthinkable... needing to bring back the dead.

Feeling compelled, Fai reached out and grabbed the healers arm. "Stop... you will kill yourself! Already your nose is bleeding, you cannot bring back the dead yourself. Only the Great Spirit, the Holy Spirit, or Mother Earth can do so."

Frowning, Red Owl reached up and wiped her nose with the back of her hand then looked down at the blood with a repulsive shudder. Looking up pleadingly, her voice quivered in desperation. "Please... help me!"

Nodding in agreement, Fai took the girls hand. She put it back on Shadow Hunter's chest. "To do minor cuts, broken bones, and other small injuries in a hurry; using the magic in your core would be enough, but you will feel weak afterwards since it will steal some of your life force... sleep will be needed to regain it back. You must learn to pull magic from Mother Earth. The Great Spirit allows a trickle to enter Earth knowing a small amount is needed to keep this world revolving; if you know how to find it one can accomplish small magic tricks and other oddities like changing forms. Eden here is pure magic and was hidden from humans in the Lords fit of rage over Adam and Eve's betrayal. Now it is a gateway to one of the heavens."

Taking Red Owls other hand, the High Priestess put it flat on the ground then laid hers on top. "Feel the magic pulsing under your hand. Once you do, pull it into your core which will be situated just below your rib cage, also called the solar plexus where some believe their Chi resides... here!"

Reaching over, Fai put her hand under Red Owls breast and pushed for emphasis then kept it there. "Inhale slowly pulling the magic in, you will feel it infusing your body with power; once you take in all you can, bring it into your right hand and allow it to surround Shadow Hunter."

Shivering, Red Owl felt a vast power vibrating through her palm; she opened all her senses to her surroundings, now she could feel magic even in the air. Instantly, the Medicine Woman could feel the difference between her own magic and the pure magic around her... she began pulling it into herself.

She could feel a vibration in the pit of her stomach, as her nerves below her breast bone tingled; it sent flutters all over her skin then into every part of her body. Almost as if, the magic filling her was trying to escape through her pores.

The High Priestess, keeping her left hand over Red Owls on Shadow Hunter's chest and her right one pressed against the healers chest bone; Fai watched in satisfaction as the girls eyes glowed red as she drew in every spec of magic available to her. White Buffalo knew that as time passed she would become faster at finding what she needed. The final triplet now at full power and use to drawing in magic from others taught the new found healer through their joined hands how to pull in what was available around her.

Once trained, Red Owl would be responsible for finding others like her then help them to learn... much more in depth training of course and much slower.

Feeling, Red Owl at full capacity Fai nodded in approval. "Okay, begin humming slowly; as you do bring the magic down into your right hand to form a barrier around Shadow Hunter. Once it is in place, it will keep the magic solely around him and it will be time for you to release all your healing powers including your own magic into him. Do not stop even for a second because once you hesitate, the magic can turn on you then tear you to pieces. Pure magic is dangerous so it must be handled with confidence and authority or death is possible. The key is need. You must want him to live, even if it means dying in his place! Very few people can wield this much power, usually it's only allowed once in a lifetime. To do this again in your life span will kill you instantly. Do you understand... are you sure it is Shadow Hunter you wish to save, not your brother?"

Looking over at her brother, Red Owl frowned grimly; she

searched for any signs of life, but there was none. Her gaze lowered to Shadow Hunter. He had saved her life twice then clothed and sheltered them without ever asking for a thing in return. Her love for the Cree/Oriental Shaman would stay her secret knowing now that they were never meant to be.

Nodding determinedly with no hesitation, Red Owl let the woman who had just killed her brother guide her through her first real healing. Slowly she formed the shield around Shadow Hunter; it seemed to take her forever to get it completely sealed.

Finally, the woman helping her nodded in approval before the Ojibwa/Cheyenne Medicine Woman sent every spec of magic inside herself, hurtling through her palm. She watched in satisfaction as a misty film filled the magic barrier. Feeling weak suddenly but chanting steadfastly, the healer begged the Great Spirit and Mother Earth to help her heal the man she loved.

Chanting, Fai lent her strength to the healer; suddenly, the ground beneath them heaved then blackness crept through the trees as the magic keeping Eden hidden unravelled.

Grabbing his torso, Shadow Hunter bolted upwards with a gasp of shock. Looking down at his chest, the Cree/Oriental Shaman was relieved to see the dragon gone.

Rushing over, Dao beckoned urgently as the ground heaved again before trees began toppling. "Come we must leave now or we will be trapped here!"

Dao helped Shadow Hunter up then grabbed Fai and put her arm around the Cree/Oriental Shaman. "Help your husband, I will help the healer."

Nodding, husband and wife stumbled forward then disappeared.

Gathering a weak Red Owl, Dao helped her stand then tried keeping his body between brother and sister so she would not see him lying there.

Red Owl pushed away from Dao with a resolute expression then sat beside her brother. "Go... I wish to stay with my twin."

Knowing there was no use arguing with her, Dao turned then

raced after his charge. He caught up to them quickly; putting his arm around Shadow Hunter, they hurried to the flickering shadow ahead.

Thankfully, they stepped through before jumping off the dais just as the ground in the Seeker's chambers rumbled; it quivered angrily beneath their feet.

Turning, the three stared in shock as the platform cracked then a billow of dust rose high; everyone covered their eyes protectively. It was several long minutes before the dust settled and out of the rubble the twins emerged choking and coughing but thankfully, both were alive.

Fai smiled in approval then reached out and took Red Owls hand to help her negotiate the rubble. "Sometimes when a great sacrifice is given; one will be returned tenfold:"

Red Owl smiled then took her brother's hand to help him. "A white dove landed on Nighthawk and his wound disappeared before the gate we needed to step through materialized in front of us. As we staggered through, blackness was all that was left behind."

Dao rushed past them, digging through the rubble he tried to find his carpet and the three hides that were underneath it... they were gone.

The Tianming Monk turned to Fai in trepidation. "The carpet of the Guardians and the White Buffalo hide has disappeared."

Nodding knowingly, Fai reached down and lovingly stroked her belly. "The White Buffalo is no more... the rise of the Ryuu Dynasty will now begin!"

# CHAPTER FIFTEEN

Fai looked around in awe; Ireland was one of the most beautiful islands in Europe, with its emerald green grass and misty forests that reeked of magic and fairy-tale creatures.

Over the last decade, tourism and vandalism had overrun the Stonehenge's and Monoliths… destroying the beautiful relics. The forests too had all but disappeared, thankfully reforestation had brought back a few of the wooded areas.

They were here looking for the Stonehenge that Dao saw in the Mother's caverns. It had been his first stop with the carpet of the Guardians, while looking for the Garden of Eden. Unfortunately, with the carpet destroyed they needed to come here physically to try finding the stone circle he had seen.

This was the last prison they needed to find, but it was a daunting task since Ireland seemed to have Stonehenge's or Monolithic ruins everywhere; the Druids had also used them in their rituals at one time, changing some of them drastically.

Four months of searching had paid off though; now, three Seekers at each of the other prisons would keep tabs on the black pillar for them and give warning of any changes.

Today they were on a tour with thirty other tourists. Once nearing the Standing Stones of Beltany, which was just south of the town Raphoe in County Donegal, Ireland.

The three travelers listened distractedly to the tour guide as they stood just before the circle waiting to go in. "This stone circle, which is said to date from circa 2100 to 700 BC. Is evidence that it may also have been a sacred site of Neolithic monuments, possibly with early passage tombs! It overlooks the now destroyed passage tomb complex at Kilmonaster. Beltany is dominated by Croghan Hill to the east on the summit of which there sits a Neolithic mound also most likely a passage tomb; although, it was never excavated. Today Beltany has sixty-four stones of varying height and width enclosing an earthen platform. The centre is greatly disturbed and most likely was the result of digging by locals in the 1700s, looking for available loose stones to build farmsteads and field boundaries. This evidence was given orally to the Ordnance Survey field officers in 1830s, which is written into the records. It states that locals recalled the removal of vast heaps of stone and sepulchral type graves with bones..."

Shadow Hunter took hold of Fai's hand to help his pregnant wife over the rough terrain when the guide began leading them to the stones; came to a grinding halt suddenly when she stopped dead. Everyone else continued walking into the stone circle not paying the two any mind as they walked around them, even her Guardian not noticing anything amiss kept going.

Hunter leaned towards his wife curiously when Fai refused to move. "Is something wrong, love?"

Fai reached down then stroked her belly soothingly, with a frown of uncertainty as the twins now four months started kicking at her insistently. This was the first movement she had felt from them since entering her second trimester and it was anything but gentle. Shrugging perplexed White Buffalo took another step then halted once more. "I don't know the babies don't like it here!"

Dao noticing the two missing went back to the entrance of the stone circle in excitement then beckoned Fai and Shadow Hunter insistently. Even though there were gaps that people could wander through and many were; it just seemed more fitting to walk through what seemed to be the doorway. "Come you two, this is the right place and the pillar is still standing strong."

Shaking off her trepidation, Fai allowed Shadow Hunter to eagerly pull her towards the stone archway that led into the circle. She felt a shiver course through her as she stepped through then heard a triumphant deep mechanical laugh reverberated off the stones before she disappeared.

Shadow Hunter fell to his knees in shock when the hand he was holding onto vanished and his wife with it. A loud crack of thunder shook the ground under them and a fissure opened as an earthquake hit, causing panic among the tourists as they ran for their lives.

Stumbling to Shadow Hunter, Dao clutched at his chest before dropping to his knees beside the Cree/Oriental Shaman; the burning was so intense, he could hardly stand it.

Chanting, the Guardian brought his ability to see beyond to the surface and saw Fai kneeling beside him now trapped between worlds as the black pillar exploded. Out of the broken ground, black winged Nephilim's flew up, now free... what had they done!

The pillars all around the prison that were exactly like the ones in Snowdonia that could only be seen by someone who has the ability to see beyond; broke apart too then disappeared into the fissure.

The beam of light Dao had seen before rising into the sky was now gone as a rip in the heavens showed a black nothingness. It vanished after a few minutes, but a black dot now replaced the light.

Shadow Hunter looked at Dao resignedly then smiled in acceptance as the ground beneath them opened and swallowed them both whole.

Fai watched the two most important men in her life vanish. Lifted her hand beseechingly, she jumped to her feet then wailed in denial. Causing even the Mother to shudder in fear as a violent shaking seized the Earth, and tilted it on its axis just a smidgen. It allowed all the prisons to open and release their terror upon the world.

Holding her head in agony, Fai wandered the world between for what seemed like forever; she was caught in a never-ending scream of rage. She wandered aimlessly at first but then feeling a need. She turned before allowing a soothing call to direct her.

Unexpectedly, Fai stood at the Seeker's chambers in Mother Earth's vaulted cavern before a red owl materialized in front of her. Instantly, the Medicine Woman of Mother Earth took its place.

Red Owl cringed in pain as the scream that was echoing eerily throughout the world in-between rang through her skull; she reached out determinedly then put both hands one on each side of Fai's head. Chanting, the Medicine Woman took the youngest triplets memories away then healed her.

Sighing in relief as the wailing diminished then stop Red Owl brought the Priestess of Mother Earth out of the wold in-between and back to the Seeker's chamber. She had been gone from the Earth for twenty years and in that time the world had imploded on itself and war was raging.

The Mother Earth had enlisted the aid of Red Owl to bring her Priestess home. Po had shown the Medicine Woman why the fetus's had to go through a thousand years before being born. Only in-between worlds did time travel fast enough for that to occur.

Twenty years had passed since Fai, Shadow Hunter, and Dao had disappeared in the big earthquake that started on the Island of Ireland then traveled throughout the world and changed it forever. Knowing the birth was getting closer; Po could not allow it to happen, in-between.

Looking around in wonder, Fai turned in a circle taking in the Mother Earth's caverns. Hundreds of robed men and women lined the walls humming soothingly. She knelt in the center of the three rings of eternity and put her hand down feeling renewed as a shiver of warmth coursed down her spin.

The center of the entwining rings had a black sooty look to it; for some reason she had a feeling, a great tragedy had marred the floor here. Why, she would even think so baffled her.

She felt disoriented then a kick in her stomach had her reaching down lovingly as she stroked her swollen belly soothingly. It was all that had kept her sane in the dark world she had been in for so long.

Unexpectedly, a contraction hit... groaning in shock she felt the world spin and she dropped to the ground out cold.

## Toronto... December 31, 2061

The woman lying on the hospital bed groaned as her belly rippled slightly when a contraction hit without warning. Opening her dark green eyes the young woman looked around her frantically. Where was she?

The whimper was not really because of the pain... she just knew. She felt a slight pop and a gush of liquid; just as a tall red headed nurse walked in.

The nurse tsked in sympathy then checked her watch... it was 11:45pm; she rushed over and saw a thick cream coloured amniotic sac with a tiny fetus still inside lying on the bed. A vaginal En Caul or veiled birth was a rare occurrence, usually magical.

In the thirty-five years of working as a nurse it was her first time seeing one. She just wished it were under better circumstances. Unfortunately, the baby was way too small to be alive and there was no movement.

The head nurse grabbed a scalpel sitting on a tray at the foot of the bed. Hiding the razor sharp instrument in the towel not wanting the woman to know yet, she fibbed just a bit. "Your water just broke; I will clean you up some."

Gently, the nurse put the fetus in the towel after severing the cord before cleaning up the woman quickly; avoiding looking directly at her, the red haired RN turned away. "There you go. I will get the doctor for you."

Cradling the towel carefully not wanting the sac to rupture and have embryotic fluid everywhere, the nurse hurried out then made a quick stop at the nurse's station. "You better send the doctor into two-eleven, the woman just lost her baby; I will take it down to the morgue."

The younger nurse nodded sadly at the news of the death then frowned in confusion, usually a practical nurse did those types of jobs; shrugging, she turned away before picking up the phone to page the doctor on call.

The six foot two head nurse with flaming red hair left and went to the elevators; reluctantly she walked in once the door swished open then turned and pushed the button that would take her into the basement.

The nurse absolutely detested going to the bottom floor... it was so eerie and deathly quiet. Not a soul was in sight as the door slowly slid shut which was highly unusual at this time of day, in such a busy hospital.

The woman's eyes watched in dread as each light going down lit up brighter than the last, as the old elevator creaked and groaned going down slowly. By the time she reached the final lower basement, the woman's eyes were huge pools of fear as the light flared brightly almost blinding the nurse.

All of a sudden, the woman staggered a bit as the elevator stopped abruptly with a sickening lurch. It felt like her stomach had just entered her throat; it was not a pleasant feeling at all.

There was a huge groan of denial from the elevator doors as they tried to open, finally with a loud squeal of reluctance they slowly obeyed. Protesting loudly, they squeaked open making the woman cringe as she thought of fingernails running across the chalkboard; she shuddered in response before stepping out into the dingy lit eerie lower basement.

The nurse swore she heard the scurrying of mice feet going down the hallway ahead of her. Shaking off her fanciful thoughts she knew it was only her imagination running rampant, there was no way there would be mice in this pristine hospital... even way down here.

Clutching the small bundle carefully even though it was dead, the nurse couldn't help feeling comforted slightly. She walked towards the doors at the end of the hallway; dragging her feet, reluctantly.

It seemed to take the red headed nurse forever to reach the morgue doors. Unable to put it off any longer she reached out in trepidation then turned the door handle slowly, wishing she were anywhere but here. Hesitating once more for a brief second, the nurse stiffened her back resolutely then slipped through the door into the front reception room. Looking around uneasily, she finally found the little Oriental man they all called Weasel.

The man was only four feet two inches and ugly as sin with his huge eyes that had big black bags under them. A squashed nose gave him a nasally squeaky voice. He had scraggly thin grey hair on his head plus a few grey whiskers on his chin. His eyebrows were a solid straight line and so thick they almost covered his eyelids. He hardly ever left his dungeon, they all hated to deal with him... he had a nasty temperament.

The nurse always felt like a giant when dealing with the Weasel since he was so small and slight; quickly she tried to hand him the blood soaked towel. "We have a stillborn, poor little thing isn't even out of its sac!"

The little man nodded impatiently then looked up before caulking his left eyebrow inquisitively. "What's the name of the father and mother?"

Shrugging, the nurse gestured unknowingly. "A Jane Doe, a couple dropped her off said they didn't know who she was. It seems the two found her lying on the side of the road lifeless, barefoot with no coat or identification. There is no sign of head trauma or a struggle; except for being dehydrated, we have no idea why she has been unconscious since they brought her in. She only came too when the little one was delivering so we have not had a chance to ask her anything. She looks Native American or Oriental, but nobody seems to know her. We do not know who the father is either."

The mortician frowned grimly, he hated Jane Doe cases they required a lot of extra paper work. He finally took the bundle from the nurse then shoed her out with a negligent wave of his hand. "I will see to it!"

The nurse gladly scurried from the room and never looked back.

The Oriental opened the bundle and put his hand on the little fetus to take the skin surrounding it off; he frowned in confusion, it was still warm then he felt a little twitch. He quickly tore open the sack and a tiny feeble cry escaped from the baby boy... he was still alive!

The mortician frowned angrily; what was he supposed to do with a live baby that nobody seemed to want.

Grinning nastily, Weasel thought of his nagging wife; she was always hounding him about his inability to have children. Maybe this would shut her up for a while. He bundled the baby up in a clean towel then went out the backway.

*****

The woman lying in the birthing chamber half sat up as she cried out in agony, the doctor frowned grimly. "Come on now push, the baby's crowning... harder!"

Doctor Kris looked up as the tall red headed nurse walked into the room; he mumbled at her irritably. "I thought you said she lost the baby!"

Frowning in surprise, the nurse nodded then she shrugged in confusion. "Must be twins... we did not have time for an ultrasound."

Inclining his head distractedly, the doctor put his hands around the baby's head... he could only tell by the feel since it was an En Caul or veiled birth; the embryo sack was quite thick so he could not see the baby.

Most embryo sacs were so thin you could see right through them but not this one. Dr. Kris had never seen the like before; he pulled gently until the little bundle fell into his hands.

Looking down in awe at the off white colour of the sac, he couldn't help being reminded of an egg shell. Shaking off his fanciful thoughts, the doctor quickly punctured the sack and pulled it away from the baby inside.

In relief Dr. Kris heard the baby cry before handing the infant to the nurse to hold while he tied off the umbilical cord and checked the time, it was12:05am then looked over at the woman on the bed with a congratulations smile. "You have a beautiful little girl... she's a New Year's baby too!"

Taking her daughter, the black haired woman with one white strip of hair over her left eye and one red strip on the right with a red/white entwined colour in the center then looked at the doctor matter of factually. "And the other one was...?"

The nurse looked at the doctor in consternation; she had not thought the woman knew of the other baby. She sighed sadly and shook her head as she looked back at the dark skinned woman in sympathy. "No, I am sorry the other one didn't make it and I did not check its sex."

Staring at the nurse grimly, the woman lying in the bed unexpectedly smiled knowingly. "He is not dead!"

Doctor Kris looked at the head nurse in surprise.

Shrugging grimly, the nurse mumbled faintly not wanting the new mother to hear her. "Denial, the other one was also an En Caul birth; I did not break the sack to check its sex!"

The doctor frowned thoughtfully; he got up then beckoned the nurse over. "So you do not know for sure it was dead, a baby can live in the sac for at least ten minutes?"

The red headed nurse shrugged dismissively. "There was no movement at all, it was dead! The woman just doesn't want to believe it."

Doctor Kris finally nodded sadly; some woman just could not accept the loss of a baby. At least she was not having hysterics and demanding to see the infant. He wasn't sure why the nurse had taken it upon herself to take it to the morgue before it could be examined. He would have to discuss this with the Chief Nursing Officer.

Turning towards the door, the doctor paused and whispered low. "Clean them both up then put them in a room. I think we should keep her an extra day; you better hope she doesn't demand to see the other one. Once the shock wears off she just might, we will know more tomorrow."

Smiling serenely, the woman lying on the bed ignored the two others as she stared down at her beautiful daughter. The events leading up to the birth was still a bit hazy, but the death of her husband and Guardian were now starting to the surface.

Fai wiped the blood away from the babies left shoulder then bent her head to put her lips just below her infant's collarbone and just above her heart before kissing her lovingly there.

A tiny reddish mark was left then the black haired woman blew on the skin gently before lifting her head away... the mark disappeared.

Not liking that at all, the baby gave a hesitant cry of pain. Quickly, her mother put her to her breast and the infant instantly latched on hungrily.

The woman's face glowed slightly for a moment in supreme pleasure as her daughter took her first drink of nourishing breast milk. The infant would need to drain both breasts in order to get every drop of colostrum from her milk; it contained special antibodies that would protect the little one from diseases and infections that people in this age seemed susceptible too.

Her baby's immune system would need the extra boost too and there was an added enzyme in her milk, which was imperative to the little ones power. Her daughter's bones had to have extra calcium as well, for someday her magic would peek. "Shh, my little dragon it is only a momentary pain."

Looking up with a frown at the nurse when she came for the baby, the woman shook her head decisively. "Just bring me water and a cloth, I will clean her myself!"

Frowning perturbed, the nurse nodded at the intense stare of the strange black haired woman with two white and red strips in her hair then nodded and did as she was told.

While the dark haired woman cleaned then wrapped her baby in the hospital blanket, the nurse washed the older woman up. Afterwards, she brought over a wheel chair before helping mother and baby into it for the trip to the room assigned to her.

The nurse helped the black haired woman into a hospital bed before trying to take the baby again, so she could be taken to the nursery. She was rebuffed rudely.

Nodding resignedly, the head nurse put some papers and a pen on the little table then wheeled it over. "That's fine dear, here are the papers you need to fill in for the birth of your infant; I hope you have chosen a suitable name for your new baby? I will be back shortly to pick them up."

Giving the woman a good hour to fill in the paperwork, the tall red haired nurse walked back into the room. A curious smile was on her face, it lit up her weary brown eyes; she always loved this part. Thankfully, it made her long work days, worth it. "What did you name...?"

The question was never finished as the RN looked around with a frown; both mother and baby were gone. All that remained was the registration form for the baby's name. She picked it up and scanned it curiously.

Mothers name: Fai Alexandrina Magdalene Ryuu...High Priestess of Mother Earth!

Father's name: Shadow Hunter, a Cree/Oriental Shaman.

Baby's name: Vulcan Thomas Apollo Ryuu... first born at 11:45pm December 31st, 2060 twin to second born; Kenna Gaia Tanwen Ryuu... born at 12:05am January 1st, 2061

All the staff at the hospital looked for the woman and baby for over an hour, but the two had just disappeared as if they had never been.

**********

A shadow followed the little man down the alleyway; he waited and hoped. Suddenly, he felt it as the baby gave a cry of pain and the shadow grabbed his own left shoulder just below the collarbone and above his heart as the dragon tattoo that was there flared angrily.

The last Tianming Monk stepped out of the shadows and intercepted the little Oriental man.

The mortician stopped short in shock; he bowed deeply when he caught sight of the Samurai sword and sash proclaiming the man before him a monk. He whispered in awe, seldom was a Samurai ever seen around these parts. "Master!"

The Tianming Monk held out his arms in demand. "Give me the baby!"

Instantly, the Oriental did as he was told without one word of protest; not once did he look at the man in front of him.

Taking the tiny baby, the Tianming Monk opened the blanket as he checked the little ones left shoulder; he nodded in satisfaction at the telltale red mark as it glowed for an instant then vanished. He bundled the baby back up then turned away. Without any thought for the Oriental still bent over... the two simply disappeared without a trace.

The little Chinaman sighed forlornly then went back to his dungeon; he never spoke a word to anyone of the encounter or the baby boy either.

# EPILOGUE

The first of the Guardians, stood as still as a statue... unmoving. The slanted eyes and dusky skin gave away his Oriental background; they called him Lord Kaldair now.

Kaldair had been the first Guardian before the carpet had been weaved. It was at the same time Jesus was crucified then rose from the dead. His help in making the carpet was needed to seal the Guardians inside, until the appointed day that the hidden Eden was uncovered.

Once the carpet was destroyed, the souls trapped inside rose up to the realm in-between where some were reborn; others were snatched up by one of the Lords, Jesus, or the Great Spirit to become angels.

The lucky ones, like Kaldair became Guardians of the humans; if sent to other realms, like magic they became Paladins for good against the evil that was now taking control there. If the merge did not happen soon it would be too late.

Lord Kaldair stood in the shadows and stared fixedly at the little girl. She was watching television and couldn't see him of course; nobody could... unless he allowed it.

Kaldair sighed sadly, soon it would be time, he was dreaded it in one-way and wished time would hurry so he could get this over with in another. He knew time was running out though, soon the holocaust would begin but he hoped to talk the Almighty into changing the outcome.

The Lord of the Guardians had spent more time than anyone could imagine nurturing the descendants of this little girl in the hope of producing her. Lord Kaldair frowned as he watched his spirit Talia guarding his precious child.

There was one thing that troubled Kaldair though, the mother. The triplets had come out of nowhere and married the Shaman before two had died making a whole.

The Mother Earth had managed to hide that from him; he was sure, she was instrumental in that surprising turn of events. Why she interfered, he could not say... this wasn't the first time either.

After producing Kenna, the surviving triplet had disappeared but every once in a while she would show up again before vanishing once more. He had tried to find out who she was but was unable to, only the fact that she is from the White Buffalo line was known.

Even more shocking to Kaldair, which he did not know until recently was that the woman had remarried. How he had missed the final triplet reappearing after the big earthquake that started in Ireland, he could not say. He definitely would not have let her wed this sorry excuse of a man to raise her baby; why she picked him... he had no clue.

Suddenly, Talia disappeared before every colour imaginable flashed in Kaldair's eyes; a voice nobody but him could hear whispered in his mind. **"It is time Kaldair, the holocaust must begin now! The people have managed to unleash the Nephilim that were imprisoned."**

Lord Kaldair frowned troubled as he looked up imploringly. "Almighty please, allow me to try one more time! The good basically overrides the bad."

There was a momentary pause as the colours continued to flash in his mind before one word angrily thundered through his skull. **"WHY!"**

Kaldair cringed painfully as the angry question echoed through his head then he sighed in relief; at least the Almighty was willing to listen to him. "I think it was our fault the humans turned out the way they did. Everything seemed to go terribly wrong when we let magic and our presence disappear. It allowed the evil of technology to take our place. I know the Watchers went too far last time, but they are being punished for it. Your Lords have learned a valuable lesson from it. We will not allow ourselves to make the same mistake. Let me bring the magic back and try one more time before we give up on them completely!"

The pause was shorter this time; Kaldair grimaced in embarrassment as the Almighty reminded him of all their failures of the past. **"How many times have you tried Kaldair, first there was a flood and only one family survived except for the chosen ones that were hidden away. We sent a messenger down with a message and a bible was produced but only half of it was right, the humans managed to mess it up. I allowed my son to be born, with another message it got him crucified. There are so many more incidences that I could name, but the list is too long to state them all. Why should we try one more time, are you willing to assume responsibility again for the humans!"**

Lord Kaldair nodded emphatically. "Yes, I will vouch for them Great Spirit... willingly!"

Again, there was a pause but longer this time then the first; Kaldair fidgeted uneasily as he waited anxiously. Finally, the answer he had been hoping for came to him. **"Alright Kaldair one more chance, but if you fail this time... YOU and the people will know my wrath!"**

Kaldair bowed his head quickly in acceptance of the ultimatum, before the Great Spirit could change his mind. "Gladly, will I accept punishment if I fail this time. I'll contact the others and we will gather the ones we wish to save."

The colours dimmed in front of Kaldair's eyes, but he heard one more question whisper in his mind. **"How will you begin it this time?"**

Kaldair bowed low without giving a complete answer. "Fire will be used, Great Spirit."

**"Very good Kaldair, I'll leave it up to you but one more chance is all you have!"** With that ultimatum ringing through his skull, the colours flaring in front of his eyes disappeared suddenly.

Lord Kaldair turned; he looked sadly at the little girl then sighed resignedly as he mouthed three words before disappearing to gather the humans he wished to save. "Sorry, little one!"

Then he was gone.

Kenna raced across the front room, her show finally over. She looked over her shoulder thinking she heard a whisper then turned back when she didn't see anyone.

Suddenly, the little girl squeaked in shocked surprise as she barred into something and fell backwards. As she staggered, she hit the side table causing the lamp to rock for a horrifying second then it crashed to the floor before shattering. A second loud bang happened at the same instant and she cringed in fear.

Kenna righted herself quickly before looking up in surprise at her glowering father. She gasped in fear and raced around her dad as he reached for her, but she was too quick for him; the little girl ran into her bedroom.

Diving under her covers on her bed, Kenna quaked in fear as she heard her father's heavy uneven footsteps marching purposely towards her bedroom. She had smelt the alcohol when the liquid splashed on top of her head before the glass fell.

Kenna knew this time she was in big trouble; not only for running in the house, which she wasn't allowed to do. The breaking of the lamp, and her father's glass with his precious alcohol in it would make the punishment even worse.

The man stormed into his daughter's bedroom, he stood over her bed as he stared down angrily at the quaking blankets. He hadn't wanted this stupid child or the woman who had produced her; over the years, he had come to hate both of them.

He still could not figure out how she had trapped him in this marriage; as the years passed his dreams of beating his wife and her daughter to death before going back to his tribe to marry the woman he was supposed to have wed, haunted him. Something always stopped him, though. That and he wasn't really a violent man... until recently that is.

At first, he had fought his dreams; always it was the same nightmare repeated again, and again. In the last three years, as his drinking worsened he had quit fighting the violent dream as much. Especially, since his father had died and couldn't protect his granddaughter anymore.

He hated his wife especially, since he hadn't wanted to marry her in the first place. At one time, he had been betrothed to the Medicine Man's daughter; it was a tradition that had been in his family since the beginning of time. It was always a woman from a different tribe.

For instance, his father had married the Medicine Man's daughter from the Comanche tribe and became the Medicine Man of the Comanche. He had been betrothed to the Medicine Man's daughter from the Cheyenne tribe. If he would have married her as he should have; he would have become the Shaman of the Cheyenne.

His expression turned pensive as he thought back, but the more he remembered the angrier he got. A black light appeared on his shoulder suddenly, it fed his anger further. The woman appeared in his dreams first, always standing in the background staring fixedly at him; before she disappeared she would say something, but he could never hear what she said.

A month before he was to marry his betrothed, the woman showed up out of nowhere. Not even one person knew who she was or what tribe she came from.

The next thing he knew he was standing in front of a preacher in a chapel in Las Vegas marrying the woman. He couldn't remember how he had gotten to Las Vegas or even his honeymoon.

The child wasn't his, he was almost positive. It wasn't till the woman disappeared, which she did periodically, that his senses seemed to come back to him. Every time she appeared, he'd be right back in a daze. Neither, would he be able to remember anything until she disappeared once more.

He had started drinking just after her first disappearance, and hadn't stopped since. Now he was just a shell of a man living in this God forsaken city; instead of the distinguished respected

Shaman that he should have been, living in the desert in Montana with his Indian ancestors.

He finally shook off his pensive mood angrier now than he had ever been; he reached down and pulled the blankets away from his terrified daughter as the black light on his shoulder egged him on.

**********

Lord Naphual the Lord of Warriors watched closely as a young red-haired boy walked slowly down the street heading home from his training in the martial arts. He had been watching the boy for some time; he was sure this was the one Lord Kaldair had told him to find.

Aidyn Brando Kai Feng was his full name, according to the Lord of the Guardians. Naphual found that quite interesting. Aidyn meant fire in the Gaelic language, which is the founding language of Scotland but thought to have originated from Ireland. Brando meant firebrand sword it was Italian in origins. Kai meant fire or flames it was Scottish. His last name was Feng; it meant Phoenix in the Chinese language.

Despite the fact, that Aidyn's hair was a fiery red; his Asian ancestry was glaringly apparent. His eyes were black and tilted sharply downward with the typical dark baggy pouches under his eyes. The boy's skin was lighter than his Oriental ancestry though, closer to a light olive colour.

Aidyn was about nine years old; he had been training since he was three. Lord Kaldair made sure, that every few years the boys masters would go out of business before a new one with different fighting skills could set up shop, wanting the boy to have a new teacher. But now he had learned everything the humans could teach him, it was time for more intensive training that only he could give. Still knowing it was the right boy, Lord Naphual stayed hidden watched him a bit longer.

The boy walked home slowly feeling every ache and pain his workout had caused him. For some reason, his master had worked him especially hard tonight... more so than on any other night. As if, it was his last. It probably was, every time a master worked him like this a new one would show up soon afterwards. He wondered who his next teacher would be.

Sighing forlornly, Aidyn kicked a pebble out of his way; he stopped in surprise when the stone stopped short before a shadow fell over him. The boy looked up at the three men blocking his way.

The largest of the three smirked nastily down at him. "Where are you going, Red?"

The boy eyed the three men warily. He knew they were looking for trouble. He assessed the men again, as they started surrounding him. He quickly decided that the largest man, who had first spoken was the most dangerous of the three... probably the leader.

The second man on the right was the tallest of them all but he was reed thin and bonny; he looked like a walking scarecrow.

The third man was short, quiet stocky; he had small mean beady eyes, reminding the boy of a grizzly.

Aidyn sighed in resignation, knowing he wouldn't be able to talk his way out of this one but knew he had to at least try. "Look you guys, I'm not looking for any trouble just let me pass and we can forget about this meeting!"

The three laughed before looking at each other playfully, but it was the bigger man who turned back to the boy and spoke for them all. "Listen to the Chink boys, he doesn't want any trouble. Well you are in trouble Red, since this is our territory; we don't allow Chainman in our territory."

Aidyn tried hard to hold onto his temper, but knew he couldn't hold out for long as the three roared in laughter. The boy's masters had always grumbled about their inability to teach him how to keep his anger under control.

Aidyn's instructors would be proud of him this time as he made a violent effort to control his anger then tried again. "Look guys, I really don't want to hurt any of you so please step aside and let me pass."

The three men looked at each other incredulously then laughed harder in derision. The leader snorted in disbelief before turning back to the boy when he quit chuckling with his buddies at the arrogance of the kid. "Look, you dirty yellow skinned bastard child!"

That was about as far as the man got, as the boy dropped to one knee and brought his fist up; connecting solidly in-between the man's legs. The leader dropped with a high squeal of pain.

Before the other two bullies could even take a step to help their friend, the boy was spinning around. He brought stiffened fingers up then extended his arm to connect with the smaller man's chest in-between his ribs. The man dropped like a stone as his chest bone snapped at the contact.

Whirling again, Aidyn brought his hand up now curled so his palm was prominent before jumping forward so his palm could connect under the tallest man's chin.

The man's jaw snapped shut; the power of the blow caused him to bite a piece of his tongue off, he fell backwards with a scream of pain.

*****

Lord Naphual smiled in satisfaction. He had to admit he was impressed, Aidyn was quick... he could sure move. His short temper needed seeing too, though. He finally stepped out and let himself become visible to the boy.

Aidyn was still spinning around but stopped short; he crouched in fear and confusion when a strange man that he had never seen before materialized right in front of him. "What evil is this?"

Lord Naphual chuckled in delight at being considered evil. "I'm not evil; I'm your new teacher. My name is Lord Naphual. I am the Lord of all Warriors."

The boy stood up slowly, he eyed the Lord curiously. "Buddha, are you? How do I know if this is true?"

Naphual shrugged indifferently. "I was known by that name at one time, but not anymore."

Lord Naphual gestured enticingly for the boy to come closer. "Look into my eyes... if you dare; it will show you the truth."

Aidyn approached hesitantly not being able to refuse a dare, but stayed ready just in case it was a trick then gazed into the Lords eyes. The boy gasped in shock as he watched his life right from birth flicker from one moment to another in quick succession.

Finally, when it was over; Aidyn stumbled backwards in awe then bowed deeply with hands pressed together in front of him in a show of respect. "Master, why have you chosen me?"

Lord Naphual smiled in approval then gestured around him when Aidyn stood back up straight. "The world, as you've known it is doomed. A new world will be made from the ashes of the old; it will need warriors to fight for good, you will be such a warrior. We have been arranging your lessons since you were three, now it is time for you to finish your training with me."

Lord Naphual put out his hand, palm up in invitation. "Come, it is time to go."

Aidyn hesitated; he stood for a moment longer staring at the hand. He knew if he took it, his life would change forever. But what life did he really have to look forward to now. He had no family that he knew of... his foster parents hated him. He looked into his new master's eyes once more assessingly before reaching out and clasped his hand.

The big man on the ground holding onto his private parts, watched in puzzlement as the kid talked to thin air; he blinked in utter amazement when the boy reached out his hand then disappeared.

The sky turned black at that moment; people looked up in fear as angry looking storm clouds raced across the sky faster than anyone could imagine they would be able to go. The clouds were so black not even a hint of the sun, moon, or even a star could be seen once they completely blanketed the sky.

Lightning flared and thunder rumbled, shaking even the Mother Earth. The wind howled fiercely, it raged at unprecedented levels never seen before... even a hurricane paled in comparison. Rain, sleet, and hail thundered to the ground; nothing was safe as windows broke everywhere from the punishing downpours and wind.

All over the world, T.V. reports were flaring warnings to stay indoors and keep all animals inside. People stared in horror as they watched reports of the dead and dying rising steadily higher; even the Covid nineteen pandemic seemed mild now.

Then reports started filtering in suddenly of people disappearing. In a church in Manhattan, two families disappeared right before the preachers eyes. In a crowded restaurant in Northern Alberta, five boys and three girls disappeared while having a night out with their mother. More and more reports flooded the telephone lines as 911 calls all over the world for help overwhelmed the operators; it was mostly the young taken.

Then animals started disappearing next. Pandemonium broke out in the streets as people ran out of their houses, braving the unprecedented storms sweeping people away. They lifted hands to the sky screaming and begging to be taken as well. A few had their wishes granted before disappearing, but most cried out in vein.

**********

The man grabbed his stepdaughter in a blind rage; he shook her violently as he lifted her up. "You were told never to run in the house, now look what you've done!"

The little girl sobbed in fear as her father dropped her back on her bed. She looked up imploringly at her father, but knew it was useless as she watched him unbuckle his belt.

Even though Kenna was only six years old, she had always known her father hated her... why she didn't know. How she knew, she wouldn't be able to tell you; it was instinctive, a feeling deep down since he had never actually told her he hated her.

Kenna had always tried to stay away from him as much as possible, except for when her grandfather was around; he had a calming effect on his son. The two would play chess late into the night, which was the only time she would or could sit on her father's knee. Unfortunately, her grandfather had died last year and her father's drinking had worsened since then.

The girl watched her father in horror as he wrapped the belt around his hand. This time, he left the thick belt buckle hanging loose. She screamed in fearful denial and turned on her bed to flee, but her father was too fast for her; he grabbed her foot before pulling her back towards him. "Oh no you don't, you have defied me for the last time!"

Kenna screamed in terror and pain as the belt buckle hit her repeatedly, it seemed the agony would never stop.

Kaldair appeared in the bedroom; he flinched as the belt fell again and again. He stared at Kenna in horror, as her father continued to beat her. He watched for the change but so far, nothing was happening. "Come on little one... please!"

Lord Kaldair balled his fists by his side to keep from stopping what was happening. He kept mumbling almost in a chant, the same phrase repeatedly. "I must not stop the beating... I must not stop the beating!"

Unfortunately, the girl was fighting the change; even half dead as she was... she still fought it. Kaldair couldn't make her transform, as much as he wanted to stop the flogging; it had to be done with free will, she had to begin it on her own.

Suddenly, the buckle hit the girl in the face and left a deep gouge in her cheek. Kenna screamed a cry that was impossible before her eyes a dark green, turned to red in a heartbeat.

Kaldair sighed in relief as Kenna began to glow; he shone as well as he helped the girl to change.

The man stopped suddenly with the belt raised to hit his daughter again; he stared in shock as he saw his daughters eyes turn from green to red unexpectedly.

The black light by his shoulder that had egged him on disappeared abruptly, its job done.

The man heard a loud 'snap' echo around the room; he stumbled back in fear until his back hit a corner, now he had nowhere left to go. He watched horrified, when his stepdaughter stood up on the bed before an eerie grey glow surrounded her from head to toe. He flinched and gasped in terror as he heard more bones cracking one by one. Yet, she stayed standing straight upwards not moving at all except to twitch in pain when a bone broke as she screamed in rage and pain.

As Kenna's bones split apart one by one, the pain intensified until she could barely stand it. She threw her head back in terror, a blood-curdling scream of uncertainty and fear spewed forth. It was so loud it could be heard across the world; causing the Mother Earth to trembled in fear and anticipation.

Lord Kaldair glowed as he tried to help mend the girl as fast as he could. Every time a bone would break, he would reach out to Kenna's mind then show her body how to repair each break with gristle and sinew. This way when she changed in the future there would be no pain, only minor discomfort.

It was just about finished when suddenly Kenna let out another scream that should have been impossible; Kaldair covered his ears in shock. He stumbled suddenly as the Earth beneath them shook in reaction... quickly he righted himself. Ignoring his own pain, he finished helping the girl.

Thankfully, Kenna quit screaming as the pain receded. Finally, everything was as it should be. Lord Kaldair reached into her mind once more then showed her how to change her shape.

The girl's stepfather cowering in the corner uncovered his ears when the screaming finally stopped, but the sound still echoed through his scull like a bell. He looked up then sighed in relief when the reverberation finally died away. Thankfully, now he couldn't hear his daughter's bones snapping anymore either; he inhaled in shock seconds later as she started growing.

Watching in amazement, he saw her face start to change. Kenna's chin disappeared before her mouth expanded then got longer and longer until it looked like a snout. Fangs appeared where her eyeteeth had been.

Kenna's forehead broadened then rose higher. Her skin turned leathery and rough looking before her hair started falling out; slowly the black tresses settled on the bed surrounding her. In the blink of an eye, she was completely bald.

The young girls, eyes glossed over suddenly then got larger and wider. Three small bumps started growing on top of her baldhead, which resembled horns.

She dropped down onto the bed on all fours before her arms started expanding, bulging muscles quickly replaced soft skin; her fingers became clawed similar to an owls but much larger, although they were more flexible than a birds.

Kenna's stepfather watched in shock as she squatted slightly, her feet grew longer before also becoming clawed. The girls legs grew longer, her three hamstring muscles thickened with power.

The girl's body arched back suddenly, allowing her chest to deepen and become muscular. Behind her front legs where her shoulders connected appeared a large bone that extended up, a bend appeared before another bone extending it even further. Sinew and muscles fanned out below her spine and ribs, it grew along the ridge till it got close to her back leg forming a skeleton of a wing; once the leathery skin covered it, they grew thicker.

As she was transforming, she was also growing in height and breath. She had just about reached the ceiling when the bed couldn't take the strain any longer, breaking beneath her.

Her stepfather watched in amazement as something started growing out of her lower back just above her tailbone. It got longer and bigger around then spikes started emerging. He gasped in disbelief, as he finally realized it was the biggest tail he had ever seen. He looked up and saw that what use to be her shoulders were now pressed against the ceiling.

Kenna quit growing in body, but her neck was getting longer and sinuous with spikes forming; they continued going down along her back until they met up with the spikes forming on her tail.

She finally heaved upwards, allowing the roof to give way around her so she could stand at her full height. Although, she was still a baby and would grow larger as she aged. At present, she now stood ten feet tall from the bottom of her feet to the top of her shoulders. With her head and neck added to that, her total height was fourteen feet tall.

Kenna's transformation now complete threw her head back in shock then screamed in rage and fear. As she did so, smoke billowed out of her nostrils; leaving an acidic acrid taste on her tongue.

Opening her jaws, Kenna tried to spit out the awful taste. It allowed more smoke to escape causing her to cough vigorously. Suddenly, a spec of flame escaped.

The dragon felt a burning coming from the base of her neck when chemicals stored in separate chambers rose up. They entered a chamber in the back of her throat where her Adams apple would normally be. There they mixed with a catalytic enzyme to go through a powerful exothermic reaction, allowing a boiling puff of acrid gas and vapour to be released.

Experimentally, Kenna tried again to breathe fire... this time she succeeded. The little girl wouldn't learn until much later that it was hydroquinone and hydrogen peroxide giving her the foul taste in her mouth.

Putting her head back inside the house, Kenna blew fire at the opposite wall then lashed her tail out. She knocked the roof down so she could move around better, not wanting to be blocked in any longer.

The girl turned her head so it was further inside, looking for her father. It wasn't long before she found him in the corner cowering in disbelief and terror. She brought her head down closer to him to glare furiously into his eyes for a long moment, considering what to do with him.

The man flinched when he realized her eyes had completely changed too; they were now red with black specks shooting across them, her pupil were gold. They were round and glassy looking, as clear as glass. He could even see himself in there depths.

Kenna's stepfather cringed in fear and pleaded urgently. "Please, forgive me!"

When Kenna screamed in rage at her father, smoke billowed out of her nostrils enveloping him in an acidic haze. "Look at what you have done to me, you have betrayed me!"

The man gave a final scream of fear as the baby Dragon lashed her tail out; Kenna knocked down the rest of the house right on top of her father. The young Dragon lifted her head out of the house, leaving her father to his fate.

Kenna spread her wings now that she had more room, her wingspan was enormous, measuring from tip to tip ten feet at present. She tried lifting herself up then dropped back down unexpectedly. She tried again in frustration, this time she managed to get above the ruined house.

All Kenna could think of was finding her mother as she hovered there for a moment; unsure which way to go. She finally decided on a direction before flapping her wings furiously. All that accomplished was to cause the dragon to go higher than tilt awkwardly to her left.

Kenna quit moving her wings so much, which allowed her to drop back down slightly; righting herself, she tried only flapped her wings twice… it lifted her up a bit.

It took the dragon a few more minutes to figure out how to go forward, because her wingspan was a bit small for her body size and weight. After a few frustrating minutes, Kenna took to the night sky when a voice in her head taught her a spell that lightened her body mass noticeably.

Screaming in rage, the she Dragon destroyed everything around her with fire; what she couldn't burn a soft voice in her head was teaching her spells that she could use to destroy everything that fire could not.

People ran screaming and crying for mercy through the streets, but found none; if there was forgiveness in the little Dragon's rage, it could not be allowed free rein.

Lord Kaldair followed Kenna and watched over her, even helping her when needed. When he saw the fighter jets coming, he sent out his thoughts again and showed her how to erect a protective shield around herself that would stop any missile from touching her. For a year, he followed the dragon around; watching as she completely destroyed the Earth.

Fires, earthquakes, and volcanic eruptions also helped to completely change the face of the Earth. Most of the landmass disappeared, what was left became desert, waste, or mountainous with not a living thing to be seen.

Lord Kaldair knew that some humans and animals had escaped by going underground; if they survived, they would be changed forever. He also knew there were other islands far away from here, not much lived in or around them now. Someday that might change but he doubted that.

Finally, Kenna's rage played out; the little Dragon dropped down onto an island in front of some mountains, there she transformed back into a little girl.

Lord Kaldair showed himself to her at last.

Kenna instantly crouched in fear ready to run.

Kaldair smiled at her gently before holding out both hands so she could see they were empty and he posed no threat to her. "Do not be afraid, Kenna, I will not hurt you. My name is Lord Kaldair and I am the Lord of the Guardians."

The girl stood up slowly as she frowned thoughtfully; how did he know her? Kenna had never seen him before.

After a few minutes of listening to him give reassurances, Kenna recognized his voice; she smiled up at him shyly before asking her question curiously. "I do not know you, how is it that you know my name? I could hear your voice in my head teaching me things, right from the beginning?"

Kaldair's smile widened in agreement, he nodded pleased that she recognized his voice. "Yes. Several Lords of the Great Spirit will be teaching you now. Come here now so I can touch you to dispel some of your suffering, since I feel some responsibility I would like to help you."

Kenna frowned grimly at that before approaching hesitantly; she was still not completely sure about him, but did not want to be left alone out here. "Okay."

Getting close enough for Kaldair to touch her, most of the horror Kenna had endured slipped away. Unfortunately, he could not take it all since it was necessary for her to remember why she became the Dragon in the first place.

A woman materialized beside Kaldair suddenly before waiting patiently for him to finish and introduce her.

Lord Kaldair turned away from the little girl, he gestured to the woman in introduction. "This is Lady Crystalia; she is the keeper of the souls yet to be born. Since this is the place, you came to rest on first this will be your new home. Crystalia will teach you all about magic; she will show you how to build a castle with it. Learn well my little Dragon, for the fate of the new world lies on your slim shoulders."

The girl nodded in agreement, although she didn't really understand what he meant; Kenna was just glad to have others here with her. She turned to the woman expectantly when Lord Kaldair disappeared.

Lady Crystalia held out her hand in invitation; she smiled gently. "Come child, it is time for you to learn."

Kenna trustingly took the woman's hand, eagerly listened as her first lesson began.

Here ends, The Seeker & the Shadow Hunter
This also completes my second trilogy series
The Curse of the Dragon Medallion

# Out of the ashes of the old
# A new world will unfold!

## Watch for my next trilogy
# The Rise of the Ryuu Dynasty
### Book #1
### Shayla and Lashein's Quest

# A BRIEF NOTE TO MY READERS

Here is a list of some of the research material that I found quite interesting and used off the internet. I use Wikipedia the most, since it also gives highlighted references to click on for more research information.

- ➤ https://en.wikipedia.org/wiki/Cree
- ➤ https://en.wikipedia.org/wiki/Ojibwe
- ➤ https://en.wikipedia.org/wiki/Mi%EA%9E%8Ckmaq
- ➤ https://www.healthline.com/health/pregnancy/en-caul-birth
- ➤ https://www.reproductivefacts.org/news-and-publications/patient-fact-sheets-and-booklets/documents/fact-sheets-and-info-booklets/multiple-pregnancy-and-birth-twins-triplets-and-high-order-multiples-booklet/
- ➤ https://www.verywellfamily.com/identical-triplets-2447414
- ➤ https://www.verywellfamily.com/how-many-placentas-are-there-in-a-twin-pregnancy-2447486
- ➤ https://en.wikipedia.org/wiki/Wicca
- ➤ https://astronomy.com/news/2020/12/as-heavenly-bodies-converge-many-ask-is-the-star-of-bethlehem-making-a-comeback
- ➤ https://en.wikipedia.org/wiki/Japanese_sword
- ➤ https://en.wikipedia.org/wiki/Masamune
- ➤ https://en.wikipedia.org/wiki/Kris
- ➤ https://www.britannica.com/topic/Braille-writing-system
- ➤ https://en.wikipedia.org/wiki/Archery
- ➤ https://en.wikipedia.org/wiki/Enoch
- ➤ https://en.wikipedia.org/wiki/Seven_Heavens
- ➤ https://www.sciencefocus.com/nature/could-any-creature-evolve-to-breathe-fire-like-a-dragon/

# BIOGRAPHY

I was born in Dalhousie, NB, but I have lived most of my life in Alberta. Presently, I am living in Falher; it is a town in Northern Alberta, known as the honey capital of Canada plus the home of the largest bee.

I married a wonderful loving man, Michel Pelletier; I have two daughters, a stepdaughter, and two stepsons. So far, I have four grandsons, several step-grandsons, and step-granddaughters. I now have 1 great granddaughter.

I love to fish, dance, and golf... above all is to write. Writing has been a passion for me since I was in my early twenties. It quickly became an addiction, I find hard to stay away from for any length of time.

I was published in 2010 by a company in the US. It did not work out well for me so I recently became self-published. Thankfully, with the help of PageMasters publications based out of Edmonton.

I have 3 series planned with at least three books in each set. If all goes as planned, I am hoping to have a full trilogy saga in the near future. Possibly, with more on the way, if the writing bug continues to bite me.

The first set of books begins the journey that will tie my three series together; they start from early to the mid 1800's in the USA as a western romance.

The second series is my transition from romance to fantasy, it will become a western fantasy; it's set in the late 1800's and continues into the late 2000's, which starts in England then bring you into Canada, where I will stay until the end!

My third series will be full fantasy. It will be the beginning of a new world and reappearance of magic in its full glory; including forgotten creatures, evil villains, different cultures, and unlikely people. With several surprises that even, I am unaware of yet!

www.ingramcontent.com/pod-product-compliance
Lightning Source LLC
Chambersburg PA
CBHW072054020726
47501CB00003B/587